THOSE WERE
THE DAYS,
TOVARISH

THOSE WERE THE DAYS, TOVARISH

George Oscar Lee

To order additional copies of this book, contact:
Xlibris Corporation
1-888-795-4274
www.Xlibris.com
Orders@Xlibris.com
21965

QUOTES

We in the Soviet Union have everything, even milk for the
sick.

Lavrenti Beria, NKVD National Commissar

Can you still play the old songs? Play, darling. They waft
through my woe.

Rainer Maria Rilke.

It was here in Leningrad that they learned about Russian sacrifices in defense of the city during the 900 days of siege. To Leslie, a former soldier himself, those losses seemed incomprehensible. Another day of sight seeing and the group flew home to New York via Stockholm.

Being tourists in Russia wasn't too bad, but the Schiffs were glad to be back home. They couldn't predict how their lives would be changed by that trip. And now just a few years later, Leslie was invited to the Bidnyis for a birthday of their son, Vladimir, in Brighton Beach. He glanced once more at the invitation. It read December 7th at 7 PM, which gave Leslie another few hours of rest, enough time to call for car service, and a nice nap.

"December 7th, December 7th, wasn't that Pearl Harbor Day?" He wondered aloud. Leslie put on the TV set and for a few minutes watched a football game. Soon he fell asleep with the TV playing and as if in a dream, he heard in the far distance playing taps . . .

CHAPTER II

At 6:30 an LCVP (Landing Craft Vehicle Personnel) carried a group of infantrymen on June 6th, 1944 towards its landing point. They were destined for a very unpleasant day and a reception on Omaha Beach—Normandy.

Among those soldiers was a very scared 19 year old corporal Leslie Schiff of the United States 1st infantry Division. The bad weather on the prior day improved slightly but the Channel's waters were still very rough. Leslie, never a good sailor to begin with, vomited over board several times, completely oblivious of the exploding ordnance around him. By the time they hit the beach itself, Leslie was seasick

The beaches were bombed over and over again but it was recognized that neither the bombers nor naval guns could produce a pinpoint accuracy in destroying German guns emplaced in concrete and steel.

Once disembarked. Leslie hardly managed to run 200 yards on his wobbly legs, when he was wounded in his thigh by a piece of shrapnel. At first it felt as if someone had kicked him very hard. The blood running down his leg soaked his pants and he soon lost consciousness.

He was very lucky indeed because medics soon spotted him and brought him to a safe place where doctors patched Leslie up to the point where he was transferred on a stretcher back to the hospital in Salisbury, England. There he found out that his buddy John Hogger from the boot camp in Kilmer, N.J. lost a leg and part of his jaw.

In the Military Hospital # 203 in Salisbury he spent 3 months recuperating while being pampered by nurses both American and

British. However the doctors couldn't do much for John Hogger who died of extensive wounds just as Leslie was getting better.

Leslie insisted on being present at John's military funeral. There were many other burials on the same day. He never knew the words of the "Taps" until some one handed him a sheet of paper with the following words:

Day is done
Gone the sun
From the lakes from the hills from the sky.
All is well safely rest
God is neigh.
Fading light
Dims the sight,
And a star gems the sky, gleaming bright
From a far,
Drawing nigh.
Falls the night.
Thanks and praise.
For our days.
Neath the sun, Neath the stars. Neath the sky,
As we go this we know, God is nigh.

The music gave him a lump in his throat. Only years later did he came across the origin of "Taps".

After being discharged from the hospital, he was cleared for further duty and posted to the Army's A.P.O. near Leeds. There he was promoted to the exalted rank of sergeant and awarded Bronze Star and Purple Heart He spent the rest of war years in utter comfort and after V.E.Day was one of the first G.I. 's to be honorably discharged and shipped home via troop carrier "S.S.Gen.Caldwell".

The ship docked at the Navy Yard, where Leslie was given a hero's welcome by the entire population of Brooklyn. Among the greeters he spotted his own mother, a small woman barely 5 feet tall, wearing a large hat.

Leslie smiled. His mother had been working for years at Gimbels Department Store in the millinery department, first as a hat maker and later as a sales lady and hats were her specialty. She always looked very elegant and well groomed in those hats and this time she didn't disappoint Leslie either.

He ran up to his mother taking her into his arms and held her as tight as only he could.

"It's OK son. I'm so happy to see you back from the war. Let's go home. The subway is just a few blocks away."

No mother, today we are taking a taxi, I'm rich. I got my pay and it is my treat." He didn't want to tell her that he won almost $ 300 in an all night crap game aboard the ship. He put his duffle bag over his shoulder and at the same time stopping a yellow taxi in the middle of the road.

"Where to, Sarge?"

"Take us to 41-30 46th St. in Long Island City."

"OK Sarge, just hop in, I'll put your bag into the trunk."

In less than half an hour the cab pulled in front a gray 6 story high building in a predominately lower middle class street in a mixed Jewish-Irish neighborhood.

The cab driver accepted the fare but wouldn't take the offered tip. "Good luck, Sarge".

"Welcome home son, it is good to have you back.

"Mom, it is good to be back."

Leslie was thinking about his father but he never talked with his mother about it. The subject was carefully avoided. Really, there was nothing to talk about. Leslie hardly remembered him, because he was four years old when his father Jack died of acute tuberculosis, acquired in New York's garment sweat shops.

His mother never remarried and as far as Leslie's memory served him she never was in company of another man that he could recall. All she had as family was her brother Sam, who owned a Pharmacy on Austin Street in Forest Hills.

Sam was the rich guy of the family and whatever Sam said nobody dared question. Leslie started to work for his uncle while still in High School first as an errand boy and later as a soda jerk.

It was a fun job, allowing Leslie to earn a few dollars while having a chance to meet all the pretty girls of the neighborhood.

It was here at Sam's Drug Store's soda counter that Leslie was smitten by Alice Rabinowitz a very pretty brunette. No question about it. It was love at first sight. In time they both graduated from their High Schools and enrolled in two different colleges for different reasons. She went to Queens College and he to City College that was much cheaper.

And than came the sneak attack by the Japanese of Pearl Harbor. Everybody was volunteering for the Service. Nobody wanted to stay at home and be seen as a 4F by the girls of the neighborhood. Leslie jokingly informed all his customers that he was changing from Uncle Sam Pharmacy to Uncle Sam's Army.

From the induction Center in Queens he was shipped with many other young men to Camp Kilmer in New Jersey. The boot camp so dreaded by the raw recruits, somehow didn't scare Leslie. He enjoyed the easy camaraderie among men and the very rare furlough to see Alice and his mother.

At the time of his induction into the Service, Leslie completed few semesters of College, as a result he was picked for possible duty in an intelligence unit that was being formed in Georgia. However upon his arrival in Atlanta, The Army had different plans for him and sent him to the nearby town of Newnan for training in hand to hand combat, sharp shooting and the use of explosives.

There was nothing memorable of that period to Leslie with the exception of the fact that he lost his virginity in a town called Carrolltown to a black prostitute. The entire affair lasted hardly five minutes and left him poorer by three dollars.

It was also in Newnan, Ga. where P.F.C.Leslie Schiff became Corporal Leslie Schiff and was shipped overseas via Port of Charleston, South Carolina.

It wasn't the length of the ocean that made Leslie seasick it was the motion from the moment of his embarkation. His facial expression resembled squeezed lime.

Once in England he learned to live with the confusion of orders and counter-orders and what was meant by the "right way, the wrong way and the Army way", which had to be obeyed, even when it meant doing the same thing over and over again.

Time flew and on June 6th 1944 came the Operation Overlord and Leslie was in it lock, stock, and barrel as the saying went.

"If John Wayne can do it, so can I" said Leslie to his friend John Hogger whom he met in Camp Kilmer. "Let's go get the Krauts!"

CHAPTER III

Yefim was one of many children called bezprizornyie, homeless who ran the post-war streets of Moscow, making their living by stealing or begging. He never knew his father and wasn't even sure of his last name.

He only remembered his mother with whom he lived on Oktiabrska Ulitsa # 47 apartment # 801. It was "'obshchezytie" where one kitchen and one bathroom served several families at the same time.

Yefim's life, as he knew it, ended the day his mother was called for sabatovka, to work on her day off, to clear some mines left over from the war. She never came home. Some neighbors said that a mine exploded and that there were many casualties. Yefim cried and cried for his mother, refusing any food given to him by the kind-hearted neighbors. With food being scarce, less and less was offered to the 12 year old orphan.

He was hungry and there was no choice but to sell what hadn't been stolen till now—a few meager articles of clothing. Even here he was cheated because he didn't know the street value of it. Soon all her things were gone. The only thing of value that he knew was his mother's gold chain with a small star of David attached to it. He knew his mother would be very angry if he sold it. He wanted to keep it for the day that she would come back to him. He put that chain into a small piece of bread and hid it in the lining of his *foofaika* along with a photograph of his mother wearing a Red Army uniform.

Yefim met other boys in the same predicament, some of whom were older and some even younger but all equally hungry. To stay alive they had to steal and seeing what the older boys did, Yefim soon formed his own gang with his own plan of operation and his was masterpiece of simplicity. They used as decoy the neat appearance of one of the gang member Vasily, nicknamed "prilichnyj", who with his alter boy personality, would approach the soon to be victim, usually a babushka selling her wares on the open bazaar, pretending that he wanted to buy whatever the poor woman was selling, only to tell her that he didn't have enough money to purchase the given item.

Sometimes the babushka would take pity upon the boy and hand him few potatoes or a piece of bread. In such a case the gang would leave her alone and look for another victim. Such a person would soon be approached by 4 or 5 boys coming from different directions at once, grabbing the desired items and running in different directions to a pre-selected place. Yefirm's gang used an abandoned storage room of Moscow's Metro Station. They became so efficient that they ate well, dressed well and even started to smoke "machorka" and drink vodka occasionally. Yefirm's wolf pack never traveled as a pack in order not to bring the attention of authorities to themselves.

Once caught by the city "miltoshka" Yefirm resorted to tears: "Oh comrade militionier. I'm lost, my mother is here someplace and I must find her. Please don't hold me." Usually it worked because he looked too decent to be one of those "bezprizornys."

Sometimes Yefim had to bribe his way out with a three rubble note. The Militia was so corrupt that they would take money from anybody. In addition to Vasily there was Dimitri called "ryzhyi" because of his red hair and a boy full of pimples Eduard called Edik.

They were more afraid of other gangs than of the Militia, because sometimes they had to share their "catch" with them, since they were older and usually much rougher. Yefim's gang existed for several months, however their luck ran out, because they were followed by an undercover Militiaman, whose job it was to combat juvenile delinquency and clear the Moscow's streets of the undesired elements.

The detective, Lt. Ivan Lebiedev was a young Army veteran, who realized that those kids were mostly orphans and the best solution for them and the Soviet State was to take them to an orphanage, which he knew, resembled more a boot camp than an orphanage. Still it provided food, medical care and technical training. Surely it was better than the mean streets of a big city. As the Moscow's orphanages went, the one on Lysenko's Bulvar was the best. It was there where Lt. Lebiedev was bringing the very young human flotsam for their and State's salvation. "Boys, instead of a jail I'll bring you to an orphanage where you'll have a chance to become good Soviet citizens. This is your only chance and if you aren't going to take it, it will be the Siberian gulags for you. And don't think that you can run away from this hiding place. My men surrounded the place. What you don't believe me? Have a look yourself!"

"Dima! Have a look outside, see if they are there!" said Yefim. Dima went and came right back. He didn't have to say anything. His facial expression said it for him. Yefim became the spokesman for the group. He figured out that the orphanage was better than jail and would be easier to run away from there than from the jail up north, besides the bitter winter was coming. "Spasibo-Thank you Comrade Lieutenant, we all agree to come with you."

"Chorasho, good, I'm glad that you have listened to reason. Take with you what ever you need, hopefully not stolen goods that people are looking for and let's go. By the way, should any one of you try to run away from the truck, the rest of you will go straight to jail, poniatno? The lieutenant smiled reading their minds. "It is not bad there at all. Believe me. One of these days you all will thank me. The place is run by a good friend if mine. Lubov Moiseevna is a very decent and just woman."

Hearing that, Yefim didn't hesitate any more. His own mother was called Nina Moiseevna, maybe a relative? Seeing Yefim's readiness the rest of the gang went along with Lieutenant's "suggestion", there was really no other alternative.

In less than an hour Lt. Lebiedev delivered the four rehabilitation candidates to Lysenko's Orphanage. He wasn't afraid that anybody is going to jump off the truck because an armed soldier rode with them in the open truck.

Well boys here is your new home for the next few years. Make a good use of it. From time to time I'll stop by to check on you to see how you are doing. I have a hunch that you won't disappoint me. Good luck to you."

"Good afternoon Lieutenant. Whom have you brought us this time?" These words were spoken by a large a bit heavy gray haired woman wearing a white laboratory coat.

"Boys, this is Comrade Lubov Moiseevna, the director of this institution. Don't you ever, and I mean ever, try to fool her. She knows every trick there is. Trust me, I know, before I went to the Army I was one of her pupils."

Now everything was clear to Yefim. He understood the lieutenant.

"And who are these fine young fellows, Lieutenant?"

"Please introduce yourselves" he instructed the boys.

Each of the boys stated his name, patrinomic and last name. When it came to Yefim he just blurted out "Yefim—I don't know my father's name, but my mother was Nina Moiseevna."

"You poor boy, what shall we call you than?"

"You just called me poor. In Russian it is Bidnyi, so I'll be Yefim Bidnyi, if you don't mind."

"Not at all Yefim Bidnyi"

CHAPTER IV

A few hundred kilometers north-west of Yefim's orphanage in the majestic city of Leningrad there lived another boy by the name of Maksim Ziemtsov, just 5 years older, for whom life couldn't be sweeter or more promising.

Just by being a son of a Hero of Soviet Union who lost his life as the Great Patriotic War was coming to it's end, Maksim or Max for short, had every advantage bestowed upon him by the grateful nation, starting with a two bedroom apartment on Gogola Street not far from Dzerzhinski Street and Nevsky Prospect, which he shared with his mother Dr. Natalia Isaakovna Ziemtsow, a pediatrician at the nearby Children Hospital # 18.

Max graduated from the 10th grade and every higher institution of learning wanted him including Frunze Military Academy his father's Alma Mater. The Superintendent of the Academy himself— Col. Rudolf Shubin came to Leningrad to enlist Max into Frunze. Max knew of course the appalling losses, suffered by the population of Leningrad, during those terrible 900 days, when over 150,000 German artillery shells rained on the city and over 100,000 explosive and incendiary bombs were dropped.

Max very politely declined the honor saying that he would like to become a painter or a poet and Leningrad was the right place to be at.

"Remember, my boy, any time you change your mind, I'll have a place for you at Frunze's".

"Thank you Comrade Colonel, I thank you in Maksim's name and in my own" said Natalia Isaakovna. "More tea Colonel ?'

"No, thank you Comrade Doctor, I have to rush, my driver is downstairs waiting for me. It was good seeing you both. Do svidania" They shook hands and the colonel left the apartment. Both mother and son exchanged smiles. Military career wasn't for Max and definitely not for his mother who lost her husband in the war and wasn't about to risk loosing her only son.

Natalia Feldstein, the 22 year old daughter of Isaak Feldstein, a grain merchant from the city of Vilno, Poland, had met Max's father, Michail Ziemtsov, a sub-lieutenant of the Red Army in September of 1939 when the Eastern part of Poland was occupied by the Soviets. After a brief appearance of the German Wehrmacht and the Lithuanian thugs, The Red Army seemed like liberators.

Due to severe shortage of housing, the Feldsteins were forced to give up one of their bedroom of their apartment on Mickiewicza Street. That bedroom became Lt. Ziemtsov's quarters.

Isaak Feldstein was aware of the mutual attraction that existed from the first time his daughter and the lieutenant met. However, he an Orthodox Jew couldn't condone any kind of romance under his roof. Natalia who was taking medical courses didn't have any plans to marry Michail whom she called Misha. On the other hand Misha was ready to marry Natalia whom he called Natasha from the minute that he laid his eyes upon her.

On June 22nd 1941 everything was suddenly changed. Germany attacked Russia and some Jews started to run away. It was Isaak's idea that Natalia should run away with Michail to Russia but not before they were married.

The same day a "Chuppah" was arranged and a Rabbi quickly pronounced them man and wife according to the laws of Moses and Israel. That was the last time that Natalia saw her parents.

Misha turned out to be a very decent and gentle fellow. He obtained for Natalia papers identifying her as a wife of an officer of the Red Army, thus she was sent to safety, deep into the bowels of Russia with many other wives and biezhentsys.

While Natalia knew that Russia was a big country not until she started to see it did the sheer vastness of the land, really hit her. Just to imagine 130 nationalities. Forty religions. One sixth of world's land. One seventh of its population and 12 time zones.

Changing trains several times, she reached the town of Nizhnyj Novgorod, where Natalia after much confusion was able to continue her study of medicine. The Red Army seemed to "swallow" every available doctor and a new cadre of doctors was needed.

It was there in Nizhnyj Novgorod, that Misha on his last furlough, managed to leave Natalia pregnant. During that period, his career seemed to take off. Rapidly advancing through the ranks, he reached the level of a full colonel. It was also his daring during very intense fighting for the city of Koenigsberg in Prussia, that Misha received a title of Hero of Soviet Union from hands of Marshal Rokossovsky the Commander of the White-Russian Front.

However the glory was short lived, because few months later, just as his unit was entering Berlin in the last days of April 1945 a sniper bullet ended his life. Natalia was unaware of it, because on the orders of the Government, she made her way to the newly liberated city of Leningrad, where an acute shortage of doctors existed.

The official letter announcing Misha's death arrived together with a whole bunch of Misha's own love letters and poems, written prior to his demise. During that time, Natalia, five months pregnant, was working in a Children's Hospital.

A baby boy was born and Natalia named the boy Maksim after Misha's father, thus his full name was Maksim Michailovitch Ziemtsow. As his nationality she entered: "Russian", even though she knew that according to the Jewish tradition, he was considered a Jew. She wrote letters to her family in Vilno and a friend of hers did visit the town of Vilno. Letters came all back marked "addressee unknown" and the friend confirmed the bad news. Nobody from her family survived the war.

Her son Max became her entire universe, she would sing to him Jewish songs and lullabies over and over again, and as Max grew he knew each song as well as Natalia did. She also told him every detail of her family life in pre-war Vilno at the same time being very practical in life she realized that schooling was very important and to succeed in the Soviet Union, Max would have to join the Komsomol Communist youth League. Being a son of a war hero, every door was open for him.

With Komsomol as a stepping stone, the next move would be joining the Party itself. Only after having the party "biliet" he could be considered a part of "Homo Sovieticus" elite. Maksim or Max as he liked to be called, loved arts and contemporary Leningrad was boundless and multi-faced. While no longer the former St. Petersburg, a city of predominately classical architecture, a city of porticos and colonnades, displayed a panorama that was unique and unforgettable, arousing in him strange emotions, especially during the White Nights, when the sun sunk behind the horizon for few hours.

All he had to do was take a stroll down the Nevsky Prospect to see sights illuminated by golden radiance, as if by magic.

He could recite poetry of Pushkin or prose of Gogol or Dostoyevsky. He never tired of visiting the Hermitage, the Winter Palace, the Stroganoff or Vorontsoff palaces.

One fine Sunday crossing the Fontanka, Krukiov and Griboyedov canals, Max decided to study art and to become an artist. He informed his mother about that decision. Seeing him so determined, she said "if that what you want to do with your life, go ahead but become a really good one. Good luck to you. You surely will need it."

For a hero's son a place was found at the most prestigious School of Art—the Chudozhestviennyj Institut". The school was accepting only the very best and most dedicated students. There was a question whether Max was the best, but his dedication was beyond doubt.

CHAPTER V

Coming back to civilian life was tougher than Leslie imagined. The war had left impact on him that was hard to shake off. And yet he had to forge ahead. He wanted to do something worthwhile with his life, and his mother wanted the same for him. He would have to please her and himself. After graduating from City College of New York, he was accepted by N.Y.U. Dental School in downtown Manhattan.

Wearing his G.I. khakis, Bronze Star and Purple Star, he had an appointment with the Dean of Admissions, who said something that stayed with Leslie for the rest of his life. "The medals got you into the school but won't help you to study. In order to stay in school you'll have to work, and work hard. If there is any consolation, just remember, that I held a rank of lieutenant colonel in Army Intelligence. Is that clear sergeant?" "Yes Sir Colonel! Quite clear. I'll hold up my end, Sir."

There were no ifs or buts, he had to do it there wasn't any way to get around it. The first year was mostly academic, didactic studies, sciences, histology, identifying body tissues under microscope. He found Bio-Chemistry a boring course, having taken it in college, and microbiology was his toughest course, the reason being that his professor, Dr. Ranion, took an instant dislike to Leslie and vice-versa.

Gross anatomy took another year. He became laboratory assistant dissecting cadavers, learning also about dental materials, their physical and molecular properties. Days changed into weeks, weeks into months and months into years. He never reached the top 10% but by the same token he wasn't on the bottom of the scale either. He held his own somewhere in the middle.

He got through the Dental Anatomy course, the size and shape of teeth, morphology—all that was finally behind him. The third year was the hardest for him. Pharmacology, the interaction of drugs, required an awful lot of work, just memorizing the names of thousands of chemicals. By comparison the restoration, radiology, periodontal studies were much easier on him.

Slowly but surely he was becoming more and more at home with general dentistry: inlays, crowns and root canals, which he actually hated.

In his favor was that Leslie had an aura of competence about him that patients liked and trusted. His friendly and easy manner and sense of humor was very much appreciated, especially with younger patients. Also his diagnostic skills improved with practice. It took him 4 years of full medical training to get his degree. Meanwhile, his girlfriend Alice Rabinowitz graduated from Queens College with a Masters Degree in Social Studies. Two months later they were married.

It wasn't too long before Leslie was tipped off by his uncle Sam, who as a pharmacist knew every doctor and dentist in Forrest Hills, about a sudden death of Julius Rosen, D.D.S. His modern office was located in the newly constructed Kennedy House on Queens Boulevard.

The grief stricken widow sold her late husband's office to Leslie for a very reasonable sum of money. The widow wanted to get away from Forest Hills in a hurry for a very good reason. Her husband, Julius, actually died of a heart attack while having sex right in his office with a female patient.

Leslie had very little money of his own. His uncle Sam put down the initial payment and the balance the widow accepted in promissory notes at 10%.

Luck was with Leslie because about the same time a two bedroom apartment became vacant and the building's superintendent was glad to have another doctor as a tenant, thus adding to the prestige of the house and never mind that Dr. Schiff would take care of his teeth gratis.

The late Dr. Rosen's patients became Leslie's patients. Leslie's various diplomas along with his army pictures as well as his Bronze Star and Purple Heart were displayed under lock and key in the waiting room. Quickly his fame as a caring dentist with a nice disposition spread throughout the neighborhood bringing him more and more patients. Soon two hygienists and a full time receptionist were part of his staff.

A year later a son was born to Dr. and Mrs. Schiff, whom they named Geoffrey. The two bedroom apartment became a bit tight. The superintendent Carl Slater promised Leslie a larger apartment as soon as one became available, at the same time hinting at a bonus for the favor.

"No problem Carl, but from now on you'll have to pay me for all your dental work and especially for those braces that your daughter will need this summer."

Within 2 weeks, if by magic, Leslie had a sunny, new 3-bedroom, 3 bathroom, formal dining room apartment facing Queens Blvd. The apartment was freshly decorated and it was the very best in the building, the envy of every other tenant.

The superintendent surpassed himself by assigning an extra parking spot in the basement of the building for Dr. Schiff, even though they had only one car.

The third bedroom Leslie wanted to give to his mother but interestingly enough both his wife Alice and his mother were against the idea for different reasons.

Alice didn't want to have another woman under the same roof and his mother didn't want to mix into their private lives and was only too glad to be invited every other Friday for dinner and to have the opportunity to play with her only grandchild.

As it happened his mother retired from her job at Gimbels Department store just ahead of their going out of business after 135 years. Her retirement was very timely because she started to show the beginnings of Parkinson's disease.

Leslie always a very good son, arranged an admission to the very best assisted living hotel in Long Beach, Long Island, for her.

where she was in company of many other individuals in similar circumstances.

Years later, after Geoffrey's 13th birthday and Bar-Mitzvah ceremony, Leslie's mother died peacefully while asleep. The physician who treated Leslie's mother also attended her funeral and being a close friend of Leslie mentioned to him that Parkinson's might be hereditary disease. Leslie just dismissed that notion altogether.

In the early years of his practice, Leslie was indeed a very caring doctor, who would many times open his office for an emergency in the middle of the night or during the Holidays. Soon he noticed that a number of his patients were taking an unfair advantage of him and consequently he had to stop that policy. Although he heard many jokes about the dentists in dental school, he was quite taken back, when one fine afternoon a rather pretty female patient in a low cut dress suggested to him that she would perform oral sex on him in an exchange for two crowns.

"I'm sorry miss I don't accept a barter arrangement and I can't be your doctor any more. Ask the receptionist for your files and X-rays and find yourself another dentist." The embarrassed, red faced woman got up from the chair and said to him: "You son of a bitch. You don't think I'm good enough for you?" "I have been called worse. My bill for this visit will be in the mail." He never did mail her the bill but by the same token, he also didn't hear from her either. Starting with that episode, he always insisted that one of his assistants be present while he performed dental procedures.

Another excitement in his life was caused by wife Alice, who announced her second pregnancy, after so many years of trying. They wanted desperately another child but nature didn't cooperate. Three months into that pregnancy Alice started to have great pains. In a trip to her obstetrician they discovered an abnormal pregnancy that had to be terminated at once. With that operation went Alice's last chance of having another child. "At least we have Geoffrey, thank God." Said Leslie to cheer up his wife. In the meantime Geoffrey was growing up rather fast or so thought his father.

Like so many boys his age, Geoffrey went through the Woodstock period. Beattles, occasional pot, but overall he did well in High School, graduating with honors. While accepted by several different Colleges he chose Boston University which was far and at the same time close enough to home. His absence from home was good for him and for his parents. They both needed a bit space. Four years later, the proud parents flew to Boston for Geoffrey's graduation. They didn't have to ask him about his future plans. It was understood from the very beginning that Geoffrey would follow in his father's foot steps.

Once Geoffrey started courses in Leslie's Alma Matter the N.Y.U. Dental School, Leslie hired another dentist on part time basis in their office, thus Leslie and Alice started to travel more often and for longer periods. They managed to see England where Leslie showed Alice places that he had seen in the service, France, Holland, and Scandinavian countries. They also went to Puerto Rico, Mexico, Guatemala and the Caribbean.

And so when the N.Y. Dental Association informed Dr. Schiff about a guided tour of Russia's Moscow, Leningrad and the Asian parts of the Soviet Union a trip totally tax deductible, they were one of the first to sign up for the trip. They were not about to miss such a bargain. After all they were true New Yorkers. "Russia, here we come!" said Leslie and Alice in unison.

CHAPTER VI

As the orphanages in Russia go, the "Lysenko Street Orphanage" known simply as Lysenko's wasn't any different than hundreds similar institutions throughout Russia. If anything, maybe a shade better than the rest, thanks to the caring attitude of its "zavieduyushchaya"—manager Liubov Moiseevna.

Yefim's trio consisted of "Dima"-Dimitri, Edik "Ryzhyj" and himself. Upon their admission to the orphanage they went through delousing procedure, in which their clothing that was subjected to the boiling temperatures of the oven. Their hair was cut and washed with a combination of gray soap and kerosene.

Try as they may, the authorities never won the war against the omnipotent lice. At best their numbers were reduced to an acceptable level. Some of the boys clothing was in such bad shape that it had to be replaced with used but freshly cleaned and repaired hand-me-downs. On very rare occasions brand new clothing was issued, the envy of the entire institution.

Before submitting his clothing to the delousing station, the boys were advised to remove from their pockets anything of value. To those "treasures" belonged items such pocket knives, combs, some money, photos and old letters. Dima had a wrist watch not in working condition but a watch nevertheless, a source of pride of the entire trio.

Yefim had some money which he removed from his jacket along with the piece of bread, where his mother's gold chain was hidden.

After the delousing procedure, the boys underwent a medical and dental examination provided by a team of three women physicians clad in white laboratory coats.

Whether they were real doctors or 'felchers"-doctor's assistants, Yefim couldn't care less. Yefim was basically in good physical shape albeit a bit undernourished. Dima had skin irritation between his fingers, which doctors didn't like and treated right on the spot with some red paint.

After completion of the medical check up, the boys were directed to supper, where they were each given a bowl of cabbage soup with potatoes and real meat. The meal was followed by an unlimited amount of kipiatok coming out of a large samovar. Pieces of black bread were the evening's desert.

Having finished their meal they were shown to their komnata, a medium sized room where two bunk beds and a large table took up most of the room. One of the beds was already occupied by a boy with Asian features.

While Yefim was wondering what to do, Dima and Edik grabbed one bunk bed for themselves, leaving Yefim with no choice but to share the remaining bunk bed with the other boy. Yefim didn't fancy climbing the four-prong ladder to get to the upper bunk bed, so he turned to the boy and said:

"What are you? A Kalmyk or a Tartar?"

"No. I'm from Bashkiria and my name is Magomet".

"I don't care if you are from Vladivostok, what the hell are you doing in my bed?" screamed Yefim.

"Who said it is your bed? I slept there three nights already. I'm going to complain to the diezhurnaya."

"You do that and we'll hang you by the toes at night, you stoolie! I'm counting to 10. Take your stuff and up you go Mogamet, you'll will be closer to God at the same time."

Nobody was more surprised than Yefim, when Mogamet without another word collected his things and went up the ladder. Thus with tacit approval of Dima and Edik, Yefim became the boss of the komnata.

Satisfied, Yefim quickly made his bed, popped up his pillow and was asleep within minutes.

Sometime in the middle of the night, he heard Mogamet softly crying:

"Ya chochu mamu,ya chochu mamu-I want my mother, I want my mother."

So do I, you silly bastard, so do I. These words didn't come out of Yefim's mouth but tears were flowing until he fell into a deep sleep.

CHAPTER VII

Maksim Ziemtsov's school in Leningrad was considered a W.U.Z.(Vyshoie Uchobnoie Zaviedienie), or school of higher learning. Once accepted, Maksim felt that he made the right choice by enrolling in it. What he didn't know was how much work the teachers, instructors and professors would pile on him.

Some subjects like History of Art required a lot of study and memorizing. Other subjects had problems of their own caused by permanent shortage of writing paper and sketching supplies. Very often Maksim had to wait until a given charcoal pencil was made available for him to use it. Waiting wasn't exactly his virtue.

Trying to rush his schoolmates he would get an answer in the form of a less than polite poem:

Pomior Maksim da i chren s nim.

Polozhili yevo v grob Da mat yevo yob.

Maksim croaked "and to hell with him. They put him into a grave and screwed his mother."

Shortages seemed to be universal throughout the school but he made progress nevertheless, especially in French, the language of Russia's aristocracy. The study of objects, perspectives, and anatomy were of great help to Maksim as was the attention paid to him by Prof. Mikhail Mikhailovich Skriabin (there was a rumor that Skriabin was related to Comrade Molotov) who had the patience of an angel in dealing with students despite hobbling on one leg with a help of a crutch. The other leg was left at Stalingrad.

Skriabin had a favorite saying that he repeated over and over again to all students, "Look and see"—"Look how the light hits the object and see where the light is coming from." It was no wonder that the students nicknamed him "Look n' see".

Within the first year of study several young men and women were heading for stardom. That much was obvious from their sheer talent. Unfortunately Maksim wasn't among them. Not that he didn't try hard, indeed he tried, working late into the nights but the only promise he showed was in copying other people's work. He displayed no real talent of his own.

As "Look n'See" would say: "Maksim, you're not too bad but Glazunov or Shilov you won't be." Challenged Maksim worked even harder and his work at best was as passable just like his grades.

His mother liked the watercolor landscapes which Maksim would bring home. His oil paintings seemed never to dry. Whatever paintings Maksim could spare, his mother took to her office to proudly decorate the barren walls.

"Mother, I must tell you the truth. I do like to paint but I don't have any real talent like some other guys in my class. At my very best I could only become a 'me too' artist." "Don't worry my son. It is not the talent that counts in life but what you do with it! Did it ever occur to you to obtain a position such as curator of a museum?"

"Isn't that more of a political appointment, mother?" asked Maksim.

"Surely it is, but you have to have a background in Art in addition to political savvy. You are already a member of Komsomol, see where this affiliation could bring you."

The idea of becoming a museum curator, implanted in his head by his mother started to grow. That was a goal worth pursuing.

The principle of W.U.Z. was another war invalid with a left arm entirely missing. Pawel Kostenko a former artillery major was known to Maksim due to his membership in Komsomol's unit attached to the University and by sheer coincidence Pawel Kostenko was in charge of that department, thus Kostenko's and Maksim's paths crossed many times during the school year.

"Kandidad Nauk" Dr. Kostenko was a very likable and full humored individual despite his disabilities. The second of which was a hearing impairment, a typical complaint of former artillery men. He would remark to Maksim: "The Fritzes took just my left arm thank God, because even a communist must say from time to time "Spasibo Bogu". At least I can write, eat and wipe my own ass. Don't forget I'm right handed."

Occasionally, Maksim would find Dr. Kostenko in his office totally drunk. At such a time, Maksim would excuse himself and quietly leave the office. The secretaries were used to Kostenko's binges. Whatever daytime nightmares Kostenko had, Maksim knew the cause of it: The Great Patriotic War.

Kostenko was an ethnic Russian born in Kharkov in the Ukraine. Kostenko's family were Soviet partisans and during the war they were caught and hanged by the Germans. It has been told that their bodies, including that of Katia his wife, were hanging for a week before Fritzes allowed them to be brought down. That much was public knowledge.

Kostenko as the Komsomol's Secretary had Maksim's file and knew everything about him and his family, being a son of a war hero accounted for many privileges.

During one of his frequent visits to Kostenko's office, Maksim found him just slightly intoxicated. Either Kostenko didn't have a chance to get drunk or simply he was sobering out.

Maksim was about to excuse himself and leave the office with his standard:

"Excuse me Comrade Kostenko, I see that you are busy, I'll see you another time." But Kostenko said in firm but polite tone: "Zachodi, Maksim, zachodi"—Come in Maksim and do sit down.

"Thank you Comrade Kostenko." said Maksim, sitting down on a comfortable chair near Kostenko's desk.

"It's all right Maksim, I've been watching you for sometime already. If I would had a son, I would like him to be like you, so well brought up and well mannered. By the way how is your mother Dr. Natalia Isaakovna? It must be hard for a war widow to bring up a young man these days. But she has done a splendid job. Unfortunately there are many women in the Soviet Union in similar predicament. To some "eto voina a drugim krova doyena." To some it was a war to others a milking cow. Yes my boy that how it was and still is. I'm going to tell you few things, maybe I shouldn't but I need to get them off my chest. And you if you as so much as you peep one word about our conversation it is going to be the end of you. Poniatno? Is that understood?"

"Yes Comrade. I understand you completely.

"Well then, Maksim. You live in the heroic city of Leningrad, the Art capital of the Soviet Union but did you know that Bolsheviks were the first to loot the churches? They sold the Imperial family's crowns, necklaces, tiaras, Faberge eggs. If that wasn't enough they helped themselves to the Old Masters hanging in the Hermitage Museum. Those items were bought originally for Catherine the Great, Tsar Alexander I and other nobles, yes, paintings by Boticelli, Rembrandt, Cezanne, Van Gogh, Degas, Poussin, holy icons of XV and XVI century among others.

"Yes Maksim there is more. The stolen booty was dumped in 1920-1930s at ridiculous low prices to buy tractors and so on. Those idiots I should actually call them criminals, had the gold icons melted down and picked clean of their jewels, when these items would have fetched much more money had they been undamaged. Even now shady characters like Gulbenkian and Armand Hammer are stealing our national treasures. So what do you think my boy can be done to prevent this outrage? No wonder that I'm driven to drink!

Maksim thought about saying that Comrade Kostenko had many other just as valid reasons to hit the bottle, but he kept that thought to himself. Seeing that Kostenko was dozing off he tip-toed out of the room quite shaken by what he heard from Kostenko. On the way out he told the secretaries that Comrade Kostenko didn't wish to be disturbed for the rest of the day. Maksim was tempted to put up a sign: L'abus d'alcohol est dangereux pour la sante.

CHAPTER VIII

Coming back from vacation is always a bit tiresome as the Schiff's found out. Ignoring the jetlag Leslie became very busy from the first day of his homecoming from Russia. A number of his patients awaited his return, rather than avail themselves to the care of a younger but less experienced dentist, Dr. Geoffrey Schiff.

It became abundantly clear to Leslie that it would take a number of years for Geoffrey to be fully accepted by Leslie's patients, who were with him since he started his practice.

On his first free moment Leslie instructed his lawyer to send Affidavit of Support to Bidnyj family in Moscow. With his connections in dental field, Leslie was confident that he could arrange a dental technician's job for Yefim Bidnyj. Finding living quarters for them, represented even lesser problem, since one of his longtime patients was an owner of several apartment buildings in Brighton Beach a section of Brooklyn, N.Y.

"Well, I have kept my word given to Bidnyjs, everything else is up to Russian and American Governments. Don't you agree with me Alice?"

About six months later, Leslie noticed that his fingers started to shake uncontrollably, just as he was removing an infected molar from patient's mouth. Luckily, Geoffrey was in the office to continue with the procedure.

This phenomenon lasted but a few minutes and disappeared only to reappear few weeks later in the form of a tremor. At the same time his legs became weak and numb with limited walking power. That too would last only for a short while. Somehow Leslie learned to live with these so far rare occurrences but still he promised himself to consult a physician next time.

"Alice, there is nothing to worry about. I think that I'm bit overworked. You know, a middle aged man and his problems." "Leslie, you must see a doctor in any case you are due for your yearly physical." "Yes darling, I'll take care of it."

As much as he was free of any tremors for several months, he dismissed the whole episode as a temporary nuisance.

Unfortunately it was more than that because Leslie developed an neurological problem of double-vision and that caused an immediate reaction because Leslie couldn't function as a dentist anymore.

Alice phoned her family physician who recommended a specialist in this case. A taxi took them to the office of Dr. Kleinert located on Park Avenue and 76th street in Manhattan. They hardly had spent five minutes in the elegantly appointed spacious waiting room when a Phillipino looking nurse showed them into Dr. Kleinert's cabinet.

An impressive looking gallery of diplomas was visible behind Dr. Kleinert's desk. A collection of photographs of rich and famous people complemented the other wall. After a brief introduction, Dr. Kleinert took Leslie's medical history paying special attention to the fact that Leslie's mother died of Parkinson's disease. Dr. Kleinert proceeded with his examination with Teutonic thoroughness.

The telephone rang and the voice on the speaker said : "Dr. Kleinert, I have Professor Holland of Mount Sinai on the line for you, Sir."

"Please tell him that I shall return his call in few minutes."

Dr. Kleinert confirmed Leslie's worst fears. He inherited his mother's disease for which he knew there was no known cure.

"Dr. Schiff, I hate to be the bearer of bad news but the news isn't entirely bad. You have Parkinson's in a relatively mild form as yet. And that is the key—'as yet'. Hopefully it will never come to the tendency to wobble and fall which would make your job as a dentist totally out of the question. In the meantime I'll give you a prescription for Sinemet. It is a gold standard medication that virtually everybody takes. Its two main ingredients, Carbidopa and

Levodopa, came from the wilds of the tropics but they show some promise. In the meantime, Dr. Schiff, enjoy your life. Carpe diem."

Alice and Leslie left Dr. Kleinert's office in total silence. There was nothing really to say. Leslie still didn't believe Dr. Kleinert's diagnosis or rather he didn't want to accept it but deep down his guts he knew that Dr. Kleinert was right. Another doctor's opinion was in his mind superfluous. Carpe diem to you too, bastard.

Upon their return to Queens, Leslie had his prescription filled at his old Sam's Pharmacy and curiously Parkinson's manifestation subsided for a while. A short while . . . .

CHAPTER IX

A few weeks after being admitted to the Lysenko Orphanage, Yefim, Dima and Edik, along with the rest of the boys were issued new outfits, closely resembling the uniforms of military cadets.

Whether it was the new uniforms or the fact that winter hit hard and early a marked disciplinary improvement in the behavior of "Lysenko's" inmates took place. Also surprisingly enough, the orphanage was well supplied with coal and wood despite prevailing shortages of heating material throughout Moscow. Various chores that were shunned up to this moment were welcomed and even fought for.

The "enemies" were the countless white and innocent looking snowflakes, that kept falling and falling from the gray skies. The snow removal from the premises was an everyday occurrence. A day that only half of a meter of snow had to be removed was considered an easy day, since that had to be done before the boys marched to the nearby school.

Fights between the "Lysenko's" boys and the rest of school's pupils were harshly punished. The worst part of that punishment was a collective one. It didn't matter if Ivan—threw a single snowball the rest were punished just the same. As a result everyone was watching everyone else not to cause any trouble.

Yefim liked the school even though he was just an average student. If anything he was good with his hands. He scored very high in an aptitude test, his teachers were amazed by his mechanical ability. From that time on, he was directed towards trade subjects of the school. Yefim enjoyed working in school's work shop at the same time he was captivated by the sheer beauty of Russian literature. Classics written by Pushkin. Tolstoi, Lermontov or Nekrasev stirred his imagination. Every free moment he spent in the library where the enchanting world would magically appear before his eyes.

The librarians knew and trusted Yefim and from time to time they would suggest another book which Yefim would simply devour. To the street smart kid that was the real education hidden in those marvelous and sometimes mysterious books. The ugly part of life was already known to Yefim and books offered an escape from it. He could also see the different side to human sexuality and not the one offered by Edik who would often masturbate any place and any time he pleased.

Yefim had reached an age that made him ready to try any version of that forbidden fruit. The problem was that in the all-male orphanage there were no girls. The exceptions were of course the employees in the main office—young women—who looked upon Lysenko's boys as so much dirt, and the old babushka type of women, short and fat, who worked in the communal kitchen and didn't even come under the definition of women. There were also a few unapproachable nurses, called either med sisters or "felchers" who didn't fit into any boy's category. However it must be noted here that Edik bragged about fucking the head nurse who was an easy two meters tall. Of course nobody believed him, but that didn't stop him from bragging about that trophy. By no stretch of the imagination could any boy include some of the female teachers since most of them were sour old maids or had the distinct personality of a prison warden.

The only woman treated with utmost respect and not called a blad, was the director of the institution, Lubov Moiseevna. She was looked upon like an icon or a mother.

Sometimes being in the right place and in the right time can change one's life and that was the case with Yefim.

According to the calendar the winter was supposed to yield to spring for some time now, but that particular year the winter didn't want to be replaced even though it was late April. A considerable snow fall blanketed Moscow including the Lysenko's Orphanage. Here again the boys removed the bulk of the snow, leaving behind here and there a small patch of snow which the noon sun changed into a small puddles. A couple of hours later, the winter made its appearance freezing those puddles into slippery ice.

Yefim noticed that condition as he was navigating in the courtyard trying to reach the library from his dormitory. At the same time walking from the opposite direction was Lubov Moiseevna carrying a large bundle of office files. Instead wearing her regular warm and comfortable felt boots "valenkis", she wore a brand new pair of leather boots.

Most likely the paper files obscured her view because she slipped on an ice patch and fell backwards, hitting her head against a protruding cement wall. The scattered sheets of papers from the files covered half of the courtyard.

Yefim noticed the whole thing but was unable to catch her in time. He ran towards her as she lay on the ground and blood was gushing from a cut in her head.

He heard her saying "call the nurses, call the nurses quickly!" Yefim yelled for help and quickly took his jacket off to put under her head. He then ripped off a part of his own shirt and used it to stop the flow of blood.

Without realizing he acted out a scene from a recently seen war movie. Within minutes the nurses showed up taking over Yefim's job.

"You have done well, young man, what is your name?"

"My name is Yefim Bidnyj. Please don't let her die.'

"Don't worry Yefim, she will be all right thanks to your quick thinking. You can go to your room and wash up, you are a mess."

The nurses and the two male orderlies who came in the meantime put Lubov Moiseevna on a stretcher and brought her to the dispensary. A dispatched city ambulance also made its appearance. The woman doctor applied eight stitches to Lubov's head and announced: "There is no need to take her to the hospital now, besides, we have no room or empty beds."

The very next day Yefim was called to the main office of Lubov Moiseevna. She looked pale sitting behind her large desk clattered with papers. Half of her head was heavily bandaged.

"Come closer Yefim want to give you a kiss and thank you for saving my life. That was very nice of you. Here is something for you."

She gave him a package wrapped in Moscow's newspaper "Pravda". Go ahead and open, it won't bite you." Yefim did as he was told. Inside there was a brand new uniform a bit larger than his old one, two new shirts and a box of "Red Star" chocolates the likes of which Yefim had not seen in years.

"From now on I want you to help around my office. It is better than shoveling the snow or working in the laundry room or even in the kitchen. You'll get here that extra bowl of soup."

It seemed to Yefim that Lubov Moiseevna knew everything, including that extra bowl of soup that the cook would give to the boys working in the kitchen.

"Spasibo—thank you very much Lubov Moiseevna, I'm glad that you are fine." A genuine relief was heard in his voice, which Lubov took a notice of.

Yefim came to his room to share the chocolates with his friends even Mogamet got some. From that moment on Yefim became a bona fine hero who saved Lubov Moiseevna's life, even his teachers treated him with respect.

The life of the new office boy was quite acceptable to Yefim and when two weeks later Lubov said to him: "Next Saturday afternoon I want you to come with me to visit my half sister. She has two daughters about your age. Do I have to tell you to be neatly dressed? I guess not." somehow he wasn't surprised but very glad about it.

That night he couldn't sleep. Finally, he'll meet some nice girls, and who knows, maybe he'll be lucky.

CHAPTER X

Was it fate that brought Maksim on a bright Sunday afternoon to Lomonosov Square right next to Alexandrinsky Theatre? Most likely, because there on the bench in front of the white Tuscan columns sat a girl whom Maksim had noticed during some courses he was taking. All that he knew about her was her name Galina but somehow he never spoke with her and now she was sitting with a sketching pad on her knees, totally absorbed in her work. She reminded Maksim of Greta Garbo, perhaps because of the way she parted her jet black hair.

He quietly approached the young woman and from over the shoulder glanced at her pad, just as the late-afternoon sun caught a portrait painted with sympathy and care by an artist whose understanding of her subject seemed far deeper than the contours of the old Russian muzhik's face.

"It is really an excellent piece of work" said Maksim.

As if woken from a dream, Galina turned her head towards Maksim: "you startled me" said she. "I was kilometers from here. Don't I know you? Aren't we taking the same classes?" "Yes, indeed. My name is Maksim Ziemtsov." "And I am Galina Shtern."

"Pleased to meet you."—They shook hands but Maksim held her hand a bit longer than was the custom.

"I'm sorry Galina. Please forgive me for being so forward. I think that for a moment I got lost in your eyes."

"It was a very sweet thing to say Maksim, please sit down next to me." Not knowing what to say, Galina continued on another subject:

"Did you know that all these buildings are harmonious with Architect Rossi Street which leads to the Theatre and is the only one in the world built entirely from the designs of the same architect? Its only rivals are Uffizi street in Florence and Rue de Rivoli in Paris."

"No Galina, I didn't know about that however I'll be glad to take you there some day, I promise."

"Don't forget that Maksim. I'll hold you to it."

"It's a deal but in the meantime may I treat you to some ice cream?"

"Yes Maksim, I thank you."

From the street vendor Maksim purchased two Eskimo sticks of vanilla ice cream, the only flavor in the wagon.

They ate their ice cream chatting away about school, the instructors and their future plans as artists. They talked a bit about their own families. Galina had a younger sister living with her mother in Moscow. Maksim confessed to being an only son.

They also discovered certain familiarity because both of their fathers were killed while serving in the Red Army during the war and now their families were headed by mothers. He told Galina that his mother was a pediatrician working long hours, sometimes in daytime and sometimes at night, be it during the week or weekend. Because of her profession they had a telephone at home.' Our number is 11-76-05.'

"That is nice, I don't have a telephone where I live but I'll be glad to call you from time to time. My mother also works long hours, she lives as I told you in Moscow and she holds a very important position. She is a prokuror, a District Attorney."

"In that case I better behave myself."

"Yes, you should always do that Maksim but I must also tell you that I really enjoyed our impromptu meeting and now I must leave."

"Galina, if you permit me I would like to take you home. Where do you live?"

"It's a bit far from here, in the new residential complex on Lenin Prospect, where I share a room with my aunt Fedora."

"No problem Galina, it will be my pleasure."

Changing buses and trolleys while chatting at the same time, they reached the eight story building where Galina resided.

"Galina, I would very much like to see you soon again."

"Yes Maksim, I had a very nice time with you and feel like I have known you for years and I want to see you too. Do you remember the words of this old song: "Tolko noch korotka ras tavatsa nuzhno"—"the night is short and we must part."

"Yes, I do know that song but now it has a new meaning for me."

She quickly kissed him on the lips and without another word ran into the open door of the lobby. Maksim stood there for another minute or two hoping that she would come out again. Realizing that she went home he decided to do that too.

That night he came home very late. The door to his apartment was opened just as he found the keys.

His mother seeing his tired but smiling face said:

"Don't tell me you have met the girl of your dreams?"

His face confirmed her diagnosis.

CHAPTER XI

Being diagnosed with a Parkinson's disease even in its mildest form by a renown specialist in the field didn't appease Leslie at all.

He fully realized that his days as a dentist were over. There was no way to compensate for the double-vision problem and occasional tremor of his hands. Old habits don't die quickly, because everyday Leslie would show up at his office, joking with his patients being taken care of by his son Geoffrey. His experience and the personal knowledge of each patient attributed to the fact that every one of his former patients, stayed with his office and went along with the change. The thing bothered Leslie most was his inability to read for a prolonged period of time. Reading was his passion, starting with his daily N. Y. Times and several professional periodicals and magazines not to mention a wide variety of books.

At best, he could only glance through the papers that he once lingered on while having breakfast.

Another passion of his was playing bridge. At least in this respect he was able to find a solution in the form of a plastic card holder and playing cards with larger numbers and figures. Prior to his own discovery of Parkinson's, Leslie and Alice would play bridge on the average of once a month with their close friends Sammy and Julia Ross. It was Alice's idea to increase the frequency of games to weekly sessions. The ladies took alternate turns to cook dinners and after that they would sit down to play cards. Coffee or tea and pastries would follow later. Any monies won or lost went to a mutual piggy bank out of which tickets to Broadway shows were purchased. After a while, instead of cooking themselves they decided to frequent the neighborhood's restaurants. To make the game more interesting, Leslie teamed up with Julia and Alice with Sammy. Both couples were looking forward to that evening of fine food and a game of bridge.

Mr. and Mrs. Ross lived nearby on 108-38 69th drive in Forest Hills, hardly one stop from Schiff's on the subway. By car it was just minutes away, but parking was always the problem and it took longer to find a parking spot than the drive itself. Discouraged from driving, Leslie started to use a local car service, which became an integral part of his daily routine.

Gradually he became less and less involved with running the dental office thanks to a fine job performed by Geoffrey. Leslie and Alice started to look even more towards their weekly bridge sessions with Julia and Sammy.

One could describe Julia Ross as a sweet but basically shy person, but that characteristic added an extra dose of charm to her personality. Her husband Sammy was just opposite, bright, outgoing, sports minded, self made man, he projected native intelligence combined with self assurance.

Their friendship started years ago when Leslie opened his office and Julia became one of his first patients. Sammy became another patient some time later.

It was Sammy who invited the Schiffs for drinks and dinner. Soon they discovered a mutual fondness for bridge and thus their friendship bloomed and brought them closer. Several times upon returning from a bridge game at the Ross' house Alice would mention how witty and charming Sammy was at the game.

"Be careful Alice. You may yet fall in love with him."

"Don't worry Leslie I simply like the guy, he is fun to be with." In this respect they both agreed too. Sammy was quite a guy.

At the same time, Sammy whose office supply company was located in the nearby town of Douglaston, was most helpful and soon became irreplaceable. Often he would take care of problems or errands which Leslie couldn't or wouldn't handle himself for various reasons. The standard joke among them became "Let Sammy do it" instead of "Let George do it".

One early afternoon when Alice went shopping, Leslie received an upsetting call from Julia Ross who without any preamble, almost screaming while sobbing said "Your Alice and Sammy are having an affair."

"Julia, you must be kidding, aren't you? How do you know?"

"A wife always does, besides a friend just told me that Sammy and Alice were seen having lunch at Alexander's".

"Oh, you are reading too much into this. Having a lunch together doesn't prove anything, Julia."

"Leslie, you are so naïve!" and she hung up the phone.

Somehow her hysterical voice and her accusation didn't quite register with Leslie. He figured that Julia must have been under some inner pressure or she read too many cheap novels. After all Sammy was his good friend whom he trusted. Having a lunch in public place? The whole thing was ridiculous and not worth even mentioning. Besides he trusted Alice, his wife and the mother of his child.

A couple of hours later, Alice came home from shopping trip laden with several packages.

"Honey, how was your day? Did you spend a lot of my hard earned money?" "Not really Leslie, I bought you a pair of silk pajamas and a matching silk bathrobe and few things for home. I also bumped into Sammy at Alexander's. It was lunch time so he invited me for a bite. Their hot pastrami is really the best. We chatted for a while but I told him that I had to rush home and cook dinner for you. Well, excuse me. I'm off to the kitchen. Be an angel and try out those sexy pajamas."-With these words she left the room.

A couple of months later Alice had to go away for a couple of days to visit her sick mother in Philadelphia. There were a couple of messages on his answering machine, but otherwise he didn't hear from Alice herself.

Instead he received a registered letter with return signature requested, from a lawyer in Reno, Nevada representing Alice, in which he informed Leslie that Alice was asking for an amicable divorce. Reason given: "insoluble differences".

Leslie read and re-read the letter several times over. All of a sudden he felt feint and fell to the floor, hitting his head on the way down, against the edge of his own desk. Everything went blank . . .

CHAPTER XII

Yefim could hardly wait for that promised Saturday. Since early morning, he was getting ready to accompany Lubov Moiseevna to visit her sister. He spent an unordinary amount of time in front of a mirror, trying different ways to comb his unruly hair, which— finally with the help of Vaseline and spit was brought to some semblance of neatness.

He was told by Lubov Moiseevna to be by her office at 9:30 in the morning. Not owning a watch, he was there at 9 o'clock, judging by a large kitchen wall clock. He had to wait a full hour, because Lubov was only able to leave at 10 O'clock carrying with her a large parcel in a fishnet bag.

"Yefim, please take this bag from me. We need to take a bus or a trolley to the Metro. I think that trolley # 36 might be most convenient for us."

"Excuse me Lubov Moiseevna, where does your sister live?"

"Oh, they live on First Brestkaya #33 apartment 47 in the building # 2."

"Isn't that parallel to Gorki Street?" asked Yefim.

"Yes, you're quite right. How do you know that?"

"Lubov Moiseevna, I used to live in the Metro, don't you remember?"

"Of course, how silly of me. My mind isn't as good as it used to be."

"You have nothing to worry about. Should we then take the Metro at Kievskava Station?"

"You are right again my boy, that's where we're going."

"In that case we'll have to make stops at Krasnopresnenskaya, Belorusskava. Novoslobodskaya and finally Rizhskaya and from there shouldn't be too far."

"Yefim, I'm impressed with your knowledge of the city, let's go. I must also tell you that you look very nice today."

"Thank you very much Lubov Moiseevna."

Luck was with them on that day because they didn't have to wait too long for the trolley, which was crowded but room for two more was found. A ten minute ride brought them to the entrance of the Metro.

As many times as Lubov was in it, she couldn't help but to admire the beauty and cleanliness of the stations. The floors and the ceilings were kept spotless. Each station had a different architectural scheme. There were statues, murals as well as chandeliers, mosaics, graceful columns, stained glass panels and extremely long escalators. After all, she remembered when the Metro was built in 1935.

Yefim announced each forthcoming station ahead of the conductor.

"I wish I knew all the stations from Moscow to Vladivostok as well as I know this Metro, Lubov Moiseevna."

"If you want to know those towns all you have to do is to take the Red Arrow Express on the Trans-Siberian Railroad from Moscow and the main towns will be: Novosibirsk, Krasnoyarsk, Irkutsk, Khabarovsk and finally Vladivostok."

"Maybe one day Lubov Moiseevna. We are getting off at the next station."

"Talking to you Yefim I didn't realize how fast the time flew."

At the station an elderly babushka was selling small bunches of Lillies of the Valley. Yefim bought two bunches, spending all of his own money plus money that he borrowed from his friends.

"Yefim, why did you buy two bunches?"

"One is for your sister and the second is for you Lubov Moiseevna." My Goodness, what do we have here? A real gentleman, how refreshing! You are a sweet boy! Come here, let me give you a kiss. Don't worry nobody is looking."—She embraced him and kissed him warmly on his cheek.

Yefim turned his head slightly as not to show his tears. Only his mother kissed him like that and that was very, very long ago.

From the station it was just a short walk to Lubov's sister apartment which was located in a standard six story building.

A small, squeaky elevator brought them to the fourth floor. The apartment itself was at the end of a long corridor full of cooking smells emanating from different apartments.

A small piece of paper was attached to the door marked Liudmila Moiseevna Shtern—informing that the door bell was out of order and would they please knock at the door. The door was opened even before Lubov had a chance to knock at it.

A middle aged woman resembling Lubov but much trimmer stood in the door way: "Welcome, welcome to our house. You finally made it, Lubov and who is the young man with you?"

"That is Yefim, the boy I told you about and Yefim this is my sister Liudmila Moiseevna Shtern."

"Pleased to meet you Yefim and thanks for saving my sister. Wait let me call my daughter Elena."

"These flowers are for you Liudmila Moiseevna."

"Thank you, that was very nice of you. I love flowers."

"Elena, Elena. Come out from your room. Our guests have arrived! From an adjacent room a teenage girl made her appearance. Seeing Lubov she gave a shriek of delight:

"Auntie Luba, how good to see you. I have missed you something terribly." Oh, you naughty girl, you should have come to see me."

"What? Come to the orphanage and being eaten up alive by your inmates? No thank you auntie."

"Come here Elena and I'll introduce you to a young cannibal who just saved my life. Wouldn't be for him you wouldn't even have an aunt anymore."

"Yefim, meet my favorite niece Elena. Elena this is Yefim I told you about." Pleased to meet you Yefim, thank you very much for saving my aunt."

He just struck forward his hand, unable to utter a single word. His face turned crimson red from embarrassment. Both of them didn't know how to proceed further. Liudmila came to the rescue. "Elena will you please prepare our Tulskiy Samovar. Our guests would like tea I'm sure. Luba and Yefim please come to the table and let's have something to eat, you both must be starving after such a long trip."

They barely sat down to a meal when the phone rang in the kitchen. Elena quickly ran to answer it.

"Mama, it is Galina calling from Leningrad. She says she has met a boy and fell in love with him. Do you want to talk to her?"

"Not now. Tell her that we have guests. I'll call her later on her hall phone, maybe by that time she will fall out of love.

"She sends her love to Auntie Luba."

Even though Liudmila Shtern was a prokuror, she was also an excellent cook. Her cabbage soup with boiled potatoes was praised by all and the meat stuffed "pielmeni" were superb. Yefim said that he never have eaten anything better. In this respect he was more than truthful, something that Lubov Moiseevna could attest to.

Hot, dark Georgian tea with strawberry jam and homemade cheesecake completed the meal.

"Elena, please take our young friend Yefim to your room and play some music, nothing too loud. I need to talk to my sister. We'll do the dishes a bit later."

"Chorosho-very well mother. Yefim please come with me."

He followed her to the other room watching her graceful moves. Elena's light brown braids seemed to be synchronized with each of her steps.

Yefim had never seen the inside of a girl's room before. To him it was sheer paradise. The presence of two beds were quickly explained by Elena:

"That one, by the window belongs to my sister Galina who is attending school in Leningrad. One day she will be a famous artist."

In one corner of the room stood a large piano. At the opposite side there were several bookcases filled with books from ceiling to floor. On the adjacent wall hung a few nicely framed oil paintings bearing Galina's signatures and several photos of the entire family taken some years ago at Sochi on the Black Sea. There was also a picture of a captain in the Red Army whom Galina identified as her father who died in the war, right next to the pictures of Generalissmo Stalin with his gold star medals of Hero of Soviet Union, a rare picture of a bald Lenin taken in 1920 on his 50th birthday and a smiling picture of Karl Marx. He looked like he just swallowed a dozen of sausages.

"Elena, my father died in Stalingrad and my mother was killed while removing an unexploded bomb or mine shortly after the war, right here in Moscow."

"I'm so sorry for you Yefim, really I'm. We have to heal the wounds of that terrible war, plant new trees and shrubs and breathe a new life into our country. Come and let me play something nice for you."

They walked forward to the piano, she sat down on a stool pointing to an empty chair for Yefim. "How long have you been playing, Elena?"

"It seems to me that I've been playing the piano all my life. I have attended a Conservatory for the last six years, practice for hours every day and occasionally give concerts. I'll get you a ticket for my next performance. So, what can I play for you?"

"How about 'Swan Lake'?"

"Say no more, just close your eyes."

Elena moved her stool a bit closer to the piano. She seemed to be totally transformed and so was Yefim who was hoping from Elena's first cord that she would play forever, and only for him.

CHAPTER XIII

Galina ran up the stairs leading to her apartment on the 3rd floor in a jiffy. Quietly she opened the door as not to wake up her aunt Fedora.

Although her aunt maintained always, that she was a light sleeper, the truth of the matter was that thieves could have come at night and carried everything out and Fedora would keep on snoring just like she was doing right now.

She undressed near the bed, putting parts of her attire on an adjacent chair. Fedora's snoring didn't bother her since she was used to it by now, still, sometimes she wished, that Fedora would snore in a different key.

Considering the acute housing shortages in Leningrad, Galina considered herself very lucky to have an aunt who was willing to share her only bedroom with her.

Galina became very fond of her unmarried aunt Fedora, a sister of her late father. During the Great Patriotic War, Fedora was mobilized for the defense of Leningrad. She lived through the German blockade, hunger, deprivation and frostbites. After the war, as a participant in the defense of the city and full time combatant, she was awarded several medals, a pension and a small one-bedroom apartment. Actually the presence of her niece was a blessing.

At the same time, aunt Fedora was also minding her own business, rarely inquiring into Galina's private life, always requesting the same from Galina, especially on those days or rather evenings, when she was entertaining her invalid friend.

On those rare occasions, Galina would have to leave the apartment for the night to assure them privacy. Spending a night with any of her classmates wasn't a great problem. The girls were very understanding and much more mature in this respect than Galina herself.

Coming back home on such days, Galina would find her aunt and her friend Evgeny sleeping sometimes together but mostly separate. Fedora sleeping on the floor and Evgeny in Fedora's bed. Galina's bed was never disturbed.

An empty bottle of vodka, a leftover jar of pickled mushrooms, a spilled pot of cabbage soup a la Provencale-Fedora's specialty, cigarette butts in and out of an ashtray, spoke volumes of a desperately lonely and unhappy people. The scene seldom varied and Galina would clean up the room without a word, wash the dishes and by the time Fedora and her friend Evgeny would wake up she had some strong, hot tea prepared for them.

As soon as Evgeny had his tea, sometimes served in bed, he would get dressed, attach his wooden leg, kiss Fedora's hand and ask Galina's forgiveness for making a mess out of the room. After lighting a cigarette he would slowly and quietly leave the apartment, the only noise made was by the two rows of medals pinned to his old military tunic.

Neither Fedora or Galina would bring up the subject of Evgeny, yet many times she heard her aunt crying: "He is such a lonely man, he lost his entire family."

This time there was no Evgeny and Galina slept peacefully, as only the young and innocent people can sleep. In the excitement of the evening, Galina forgot to set the alarm. Luckily for Galina, Fedora woke up earlier this morning and seeing Galina still sleeping despite the late hour, woke her up, pointing to the clock and saying: "Get dressed, I'll prepare breakfast for you."

"Spasibo"—thank you auntie, sorry I overslept. Yesterday I met a young man, a fellow student, who made an enormous impression on me. Something tells me that I would like to see him again and the sooner the better. How much time do I still have? 5-10 minutes? Let me give him a fast call."

She ran to the public phone located in the hallway, deposited a 2-kopek coin and waited what seemed liked an eternity for the dial tone. To the operator she said" Gor-do"—"an outline line" and dialed 11-76-05. "Please God, let him answer fast."

Her prayers were heard, because Maksim himself answered promptly since his mother was on night duty: "Da-Yes?"

"Maksim? This is Galina. Forgive me for being so forward but I would like to see you again."

"I'm so glad Galina that you called, I also would like to see you. Is this evening early enough?"

"Yes indeed, if we won't see each other at school, let's meet in front of Gorki Bolshoi Drama Theatre on Naberezhnaya Fontanki number #65."

"I know the place well, would 4 o'clock be convenient for you?"

"Yes, yes, yes, it's perfect—see you there, I've got to run I'm late for my classes."

The operator was asking for more money but Galina was already gone.

"Aunt Fedora, that was Maksim. I just spoke to him; I'm going to see him this afternoon,

I'm so happy!"

"Silly cow, have at least some tea. Even people in love have to eat too."

"I'm different, I won't eat because I have no time to eat and still am in love. Bye, bye,

Auntie."

Fedora was glad for Galina. The young people have it much better than her generation. Fedora's best years were lost during the war. Hopefully, her sacrifices were not in vain.

CHAPTER XIV

Somebody was trying to reach him, it sounded like Jeoffrey's voice but he couldn't be sure. All that he was hearing in his mind was a haunting melody of "Taps." Was it for him or for his army buddy Jon Hogger? Surely it all begun during the Normandy invasion after the landing.

Only a narrow strip of land separated Leslie's unit from the Germans. At night Leslie heard the moans of a soldier who lay mortally wounded on the field. Not knowing who that was, Leslie decided to risk his life and bring the stricken man back for medical attention.

Crawling on his stomach, Leslie reached the wounded soldier and began pulling towards his own lines to safety. When Leslie finally reached his unit he discovered a dead Canadian soldier.

He used his flashlight on the face of the dead soldier and suddenly went numb with shock. In the dim light he recognized the face: it was his own son Jeoffrey!

Did he enlist in the Canadian Army without telling him? What now? Was he supposed to ask the Army band to play a formal dirge for his son?

No, no, no, a thousand times no! Jeoffrey was alive and well and the "Taps" were being played for him and Alice. Who is calling me now?

"Dad, dad, please wake up! You had a nasty fall and hit your head against the desk. I have to take you to the hospital, you might have a possible concussion."

Leslie was trying to gather his thoughts. Thank God it wasn't Jeoffrey who was dead and the melody of "Taps" was only a sad and distant memory.

He now clearly remembered the letter sent to him by Alice's attorney. It would be foolish to fight the divorce. For all the practical reasons the marriage was over. He felt so betrayed, especially now when he contracted Parkinson's disease.

The entrance of two burly Emergency Medical Service technicians called in by Jeoffrey, further interrupted his thoughts.

One of them quickly checked Leslie out and said:

"This man has to be moved to the hospital for X-rays and a complete examination."

"I'll come along, I'm his son, Dr. Jeoffrey Schiff."

"Are you a medical doctor?"

"No, I'm a DDS."

"Good enough, come along."

Leslie began to protest but his tongue and body felt like it was encased in cement.

He was brought by ambulance with screeching sirens to a local hospital on the Van Wyck Expressway.

After a thorough examination and X-ray, the attending Emergency Room physicians declared Leslie fit, albeit having a very minor concussion. They recommended a 48-hour stay in the hospital for further observation. A Jamaican nurse with pearly white teeth gave Leslie a mild sedative and by the time they reached the 5th floor on the way to a patient's room, Leslie was sound asleep.

Jeoffrey accompanied him to the room. There wasn't anyone else there since it was a private room, which Jeoffrey requested. He remained there for the rest of the day watching his father sleep.

In a hushed voice he made several calls to his office and cancelled all his patients for the next two days.

Easy going and fun-loving Jeff was faced with a difficult situation. His mother's sudden disappearance or abandonment, so out of character for her, and his father being in a hospital with a concussion added to his own doubts and confusion.

There was nothing he could possibly do to change his mother's mind, but from now on he would have to pay close attention to his father. He believed that the miracles of modern medicine would surely add years to his father's life. Jeoffrey's duty will be to add life to those years. Two days later Jeoffrey picked up his father from the hospital and brought him home.

"Pops, now that mom is gone, let me move in with you, just for a few days." "The answer is no, Jeff, I do appreciate your offer but it isn't necessary. I'll have to get used to living alone. I only hope that mom will be happy with Sammy. Personally, I doubt it very much. I'll give them a year or two at the most and she'll be back."

"Will you take her back Pops?"

"No, never! I never realized that she wasn't happy with me. I was under the impression that we were an ideal couple. Don't forget, we were high school sweethearts and I have been true to her during my entire life. Believe me, I had plenty of offers but for me there was only one woman, your mother."

"Pops, I'm really sorry for you and also for mom because she lost of man of your stature.

Please Pops, let me stay with you just this night, ok? I'll just go home and grab a few things and be right back. In the meantime I'll order some Chinese food—you always liked Chinks. How about some wan-ton soup, egg rolls, Mongolian beef and fried rice?"

"It sounds delicious, don't forget the fortune cookies" jokingly suggested Leslie.

Jeff went to the kitchen and placed the dinner order with the "China Sea" restaurant.

"Make sure that the food is nice and hot." And he hung up the phone.

"Pops, I'll be right back. If the food arrives before I return you can start on the soup."

"Will do."

After Jeff left the room Leslie was overtaken by self-pity. He was sick with an incurable disease and to add to his woes, his wife of so many years left him for another man. There was no reason to continue living, so why not end it before he becomes a burden to his son?

He went to his desk and sat down on his comfortable leather chair. He looked around at the familiar sights. On the right side of his desk there was the two-line telephone and to the left were assorted photographs, some in black and white and some in color. Pictures of Jeff as a child, Jeff's High School and College graduations, his favorite picture given to him by Alice on her 18th birthday wearing a Veronica Lake hairdo. Across the picture in bold, red letters was written "forever yours," What a laugh!

That "forever" didn't last too long seemingly. There was one more 8x10 picture that he put up recently. It was a photo of the two of them on their trip to Russia in front of the Kremlin, near Spasskaia Gate. Let's put an end to it all, it was nice while it lasted. Enough is enough. He reached for his pistol kept in the bottom drawer of his desk, right underneath a couple of files. It was a .22 caliber pistol, a gift from a patient by the name of Tony Scalamandre.

He lifted all the files but the pistol was gone. He had it there for years. Nobody knew about it, with the exception of his family. The maid that would clean his study would only dust off the top of the desk. She had been with them for too many years and was completely trustworthy. Nothing was ever missing or stolen. But there was something there that didn't belong on the desk. It was a Chinese fortune cookie. In frustration, Leslie opened the cookie and took out the small piece of paper, which read: "NO MONKEY BUSINESS!!!"

CHAPTER XV

Every mother knows her child and Dr. Natalia Isaakovna was no exception. Seeing the agitated and at the same time happy face of her son Maksim, she guessed the reason—a new girl in his life.

"While I prepare tea for the two of us, please tell me about her."

"Mother, there is so much to tell you that my heart is bursting from excitement. She is stunningly beautiful and wonderful. I'm sure that you will like her."

"What is her name?"

"Galina, Galina Shtern. She is a Moscowite."

"When did you meet her?"

"She attends some of my classes and I understand she is very talented."

"Shtern? The name sounds Jewish."

"Does that please you? After all, you are Jewish yourself."

"That is true enough, but most important is the human being behind the nationality or religion. That is why I married your father, even though he was Russian. My parents weren't exactly happy about it. It was during the war."

"You told me that you were very much in love with him."

"That is also true. Your father was the most gentle and caring individual that I ever came across. One in a million. I miss him so much that it hurts."

"Tomorrow after classes I am meeting Galina, and the first chance I have I'll bring her home to meet you. Nothing would please me more than if the two of you would become friends. Mom, I'm very tired and want to go to bed. Good night, see you in the morning."

With these words Maksim went to his room and was asleep as soon as his head hit the pillows.

It was a bright, sunny morning that greeted Maksim. He quickly got dressed into his Sunday best woolen, gray jacket and well ironed pair of slacks. Instead of a shirt he wore a black turtleneck sweater.

On the kitchen table there was prepared for him, by his mother, a buttered roll and a glass of milk, his standard breakfast. Dr. Natalia had the early shift at the hospital that morning, but regardless of her schedule, would always get up and prepare his breakfast.

This time, however, he was eating the roll on the way to the bus stop. Maksim was fairly sure that Galina and he did not have any classes together that day.

During the big noon break Kostenko's secretary informed Maksim that Dr. Kostenko wanted to see him at once. There was some element of urgency in her voice.

"I'm on my way," said Maksim.

Dr. Kostenko's receptionist just motioned him in. He knocked on the door and hearing "come in," entered the room. Dr. Kostenko was on the phone but he pointed to the chair for Maksim to sit.

Maksim couldn't help but listen to the conversation, pretending to brush off non-existing dust from his pants or gazing at pictures on the wall.

"We can't let the Moscow Yids rule the Ostankino Museum. They need a lesson in culture from us, the Leningraders. I have a young man in mind that will be ready for that position. I'll give you all the details later. Bye!" "You sent for me Dr. Kostenko?" "Yes I did, Maksim. How are you? Fine, I hope. I'm sorry if you heard a part of my conversation but I know that I can rely on you to keep your tongue behind your teeth if you know what I mean." "Honestly, I didn't pay any attention, my mind was on something else entirely." "You are one smart fellow, Maksim. You'll go places. It is sometimes more important to be quiet than to talk, but that is not the reason why I called for you today. You"ll be graduating in a few months and at the same time going to move up from

Komsomol to becoming a member of the Party. Remember what I told you, "Komsomol doesn't abandon its own," that is why I will personally endorse and support your candidacy. I've been watching you for some time now. You are a good student, a hard-working student, I might say, but a student that really lacks the talent to become a great artist. Your talent lies elsewhere—in my opinion, in your organizational capabilities.

Maksim wanted to know what all this had to do with Yids of Moscow, but he knew better than to interrupt Dr. Kostenko's monologue.

"Take for instance The Winter Palace, or Hermitage as it is called, with its 322 exhibition halls and more than two million exhibits. We need to have "our people", if you know what I mean by "our people" run such an institution. Here in Leningrad we have no problem, but Moscow's museums seem to be taken over by Yids and the biggest "bardak" whorehouse is the Ostankino Museum. It is no secret that Moscowites aren't exactly in love with Leningraders, but who cares, "fuck their mothers."

Maksim still did not know where this conversation was leading, but the answer was coming:

"I'll suggest to the right people that they send you upon your graduation to Moscow to become Deputy Chief to the chief curator of the Ostankino. As a graduate of our school you are required to work for three years wherever the Party decides to send you. On the other hand, the Party may send you lets say to the city of Krasnoufimsk in Sverdlov Oblast. Personally, I think that Ostankino is the right move for you and if you work out, you can eventually become the chief curator. Naturally, with that position go perks such as an apartment in the right neighborhood, a Zyguli car, entrance to special stores and all the privileges that a member of the Party is entitled to. So what do you say to that, young man? "What can I say? It sounds wonderful. I'm much obliged to you Pawel Ivanovich." "Keep your thanks and not a peep to anybody. Nobody at all! Got it? Now run along, I have to make another call. Bye!"

Maksim left Dr. Kostenko's office, his head spinning from that meeting. He would have to discuss this situation with his mother although he was clearly warned not to. He wasn't quite ready for the big time and didn't have a better or smarter friend in the world than his mother, and she would never betray him—of that he was sure.

Maksim hardly understood a single word spoken by his instructors during the remaining classes. His mind was on Kostenko's offer and his reference to Moscow's Jews. Didn't he know that Maksim was half Jewish and according to his mother, he was considered Jewish? In addition, Galina was also on his mind since the time of their rendezvous was coming closer.

As soon as the bell rang, Maksim was on his way to Bolshoi Drama Theatre on Naberezhnaia Fontanki, arriving hardly two minutes ahead of 4 o'clock. He didn't have to wait long. From the side street emerged the figure of Galina. She wore a maroon, two-piece outfit that complemented her figure as well as her face. Her smile upon seeing him told him what he longed to know. They were both deeply in love with each other.

CHAPTER XVI

In addition to Tachaikovski's Swan Lake, Elena played several other pieces by Chopin and Glinka. To Yefim she appeared to be an extension of the piano and the piano an extension of Elena. Yefim was completely mesmerized by her music.

When she finished playing, she turned toward him and asked:

"Did you like my playing maestro?"

"Very much, I never heard anyone play better."

"Thank you Yefim. Now let me show you some of our books. Did you know that an average Russian reads three times as many books as an American?"

"Maybe Americans don't have time to read books, being busy driving those big cars? Elena, you seem to have so many books. Where did you get them?"

"Most of them belong to my parents and my older sister Galina. I do have an extra copy of Jack London's "Call of the Wild." You will enjoy reading it. It is a present from me to you."

"Thank you very much, I do appreciate it. May I also write to you?"

"Of course, you can also call me on the telephone."

"We don't have access to a telephone at the orphanage, sorry Elena."

The last part of their conversation was overhead by Elena's mother and Lubov Moiseevna, who just walked into the room.

"Yefim, I'll let you use my phone once a week and for a short time only."

"Thank you" was said in unison by Elena and Yefim.

"Yefim, we have to get back. Where in the world did you leave my package? I need the fishnet bag, everything else stays here."

"I left it in the kitchen behind the door. I'll go and fetch it."

"Small wonder that we couldn't find it."

Yefim brought the package and put it down on the coffee table in the middle of the living room. Lubov took a beautiful hand embroidered blouse out of the package for Elena and a pair of warm gloves for Liudmila.

"Everything else in the package belongs in the kitchen. I was able to get some canned goods made in America. Now Yefim, say good-bye because we really have to leave."

"Aunt Lubov, thank you very much for the blouse, I love it."

"You are a sweet kid, Elena."

"Auntie, I am no longer a kid. Next year I will be 18, remember?"

After a few kisses and hugs Lubov and Yefim were on their way, basically reversing their steps. Lubov paid 4 kopecks for Yefim for the trolley and 5 kopecks for the Metro, simply because Yefim did not have any money of his own after spending it on the flowers.

"Yefim, you'll have to buy me some more flowers because the one you gave me I left at Liudmila's house, she said jokingly."

"I certainly will, Lubov Moiseevna, you can count on that."

The homebound trip seemed much shorter time wise.

Upon reaching Lysenko's Orphanage, Yefim thanked Lubov Moiseevna for a very lovely afternoon and went back to his room only to discover that one of his roommates had run away. It was his close friend Edik.

"What has happened?" asked Yefim.

"Edik said that he had enough of Lysenko, he felt like he was in jail. What's more, I'm going to do the same. To hell with Lysenko!" said Dima.

"Are you crazy too? Where can you go? The winter is hardly over and it is still pretty cold at night. What? Do you have it so bad here? Aren't you getting 3 square meals a day, room, schooling? Do you want to be a thief for the rest of your life?"

"It's none of your fucking business. It is good for you to say, after all, you're brown-nosing Lubov Moiseevena . . .

Yefim hit Dima right across the face: "Take it back you son of a bitch!" Fists started to fly.

Magomet who was lying in the top bunk jumped on both of them:

"You are both crazy. Do you want them to kick us all out from Lysenko's? Stop, you idiots! Dima, you forgot that Yefim shares every extra piece of bread that he gets with us.

Magomet was an unusual peacemaker. It was more the quality and sincerity of his voice that made them stop fighting.

"Govno-shit, Yefim do forgive me. I was out of line, I'm sorry."

Forget it, Dima. The problem is Edik's disappearance. That may complicate our lives.

Oh, well, I'm so tired all I want is to go to sleep. What a day!!"

He washed up and went to bed. His thoughts went to Elena, the time spent with her and the book she gave him. He reached for the book and looked at the cover, intrigued by the title and the name of the American author. He flipped through a few pages and started to read.

Sometime later, Magomet noticing Yefim sound sleep, came down from his upper bunk, closed the book on Yefim's bed and shut the light on the nightstand.

The next day was Monday and everything went back to the old routine. Yefim as well as his roommates were questioned as to the reasons for Edik's disappearance. Everybody denied having any knowledge or reasons that prompted Edik to go over the walls.

"Is it your sense of loyalty that keeps you from telling us Edik's whereabouts?"

"No, Lubov Moiseevena, we really don't know. I would never lie to you."

"Comrades, I do believe Yefim. We'll let the authorities look into it."

The following day Yefim wrote a long letter to Elena and posted it in the nearest mailbox.

Friday morning of that week, Yefim was called to the office of Lubov Moiseevna. She had a guest whom Yefim recognized immediately. It was Lieutenant Ivan Lebiedev, the same Police Officer who originally brought Yefim and his friends to Lysenko's Orphanage.

"How are you, young man? Do you remember me?"

"I certainly do Lieutenant, and how are you?"

"Yefim, this is not a social call. Lieutenant told me that the Moscow Police found a body of a young man dressed in Lysenko's uniform. We need someone to identify the body and since Edward was your friend and roommate I've selected you for that unpleasant task. You will go with lieutenant to his Precinct and he will bring you back. Right Lieutenant?"

"Of course Lubov Moiseevna. Either I or my driver, but he'll be brought home."

"Maybe that body belongs to someone else dressed in Lysenko's uniform?" meekly asked Yefim.

"Well, that is why we are taking you with us to tell us for sure. Lets go young man, we have no time to waste, our car is waiting for us downstairs."

There was a police car waiting right in front of the main gate of the orphanage. The driver kept the engine running to keep himself warm. Seeing the Lieutenant approach, the driver quickly threw way his burning cigarette and jumped out to open the door for him.

"Back to the Precinct, on the double" barked the Lieutenant.

"Tak tochno-as ordered, Comrade Lieutenant."

The ride that took them to the Precinct was both fast and bumpy. Yefim tried to engage the Lieutenant in light conversation but the Lieutenant was in a bad mood and as a result, Yefim kept to himself.

Upon reaching the Precinct, the Lieutenant spoke briefly with the sergeant on duty. He signed his own name to the roster list and asked Yefim for his last name and patronymic.

"It's Bidnyi, Lieutenant. Sorry, but I'm not quite sure as to my father's name."

"Never mind Yefim, never mind, let's just go."

They walked through a long, dark corridor. On the way to the morgue another policeman on guard duty stopped them. The Lieutenant showed him his badge and pointed to Yefim stating "he is with me."

Not bothering to return the policeman's salute, they walked into a makeshift morgue. The air, full of formaldehyde smelled awful. Even the Lieutenant kept a handkerchief in front of his nose. There were several corpses covered with dirty, blood spotted covers.

"Never mind the smell Yefim, a man gets used to everything. Come closer." He uncovered the corpse laying the in the furthest corner of the room.

"Come on in, nobody is going to bite you—who do you think it is?"

As Yefim tiptoed closer to the corpse, he was ready to vomit. The face of the body was totally crushed, most likely by a brick, judging by the pieces of brick still imbedded in what used to be a human face. But there was no mistake as to the corpse's hair. It was red and that was why Edik was called "ryzhi." To his horror, Yefim recognized his friend Edward.

"Yes, Lieutenant, it's him."

"Are you sure? One hundred percent sure?"

"I'm sure, Edik had red hair, and it's him I tell you. Let's get out of here, please!"

The Lieutenant must have moved Edik's hand because the entire arm fell toward the floor. The wristwatch, recently fixed, was gone.

"I need some fresh air, Lieutenant, let's go. I can't stand this place."

"Yes, we all need some fresh air." The Lieutenant cursed heavily and Yefim had to admit to himself that the Russian language in this respect was one of the richest.

"Just one more second." The Lieutenant took out a pen from his tunic and wrote something on the tag attached to the big toe of Edik's right foot.

The Lieutenant upon seeing Yefim's white, or rather green face, took pity on him. He brought him to his car and instructed the driver to take Yefim back to the Lysenko orphanage.

"Yefim, you be very careful in your life not to wind up like your former friend Edward. I would be very disappointed, remember that, young man."

Yefim had a problem speaking because of the bile rapidly coming up in his throat, and he puked at the side of the road.

It was at this very moment that Yefim made a decision to make something of himself, get an education and a profession.

"No, Lieutenant, don't worry, I do not want to become another Edik."

By the time they reached Lysenko's, Yefim realized that the orphanage was going to be his stepping-stone to a better future, or so he hoped.

CHAPTER XVII

The ringing of the phone brought Leslie back to reality. He picked up the receiver with an annoyed "Yes?"

"Dr. Schiff, this is Jose, the doorman. There is a delivery for you from a Chinese restaurant."

"Thank you Jose, just send him upstairs."

A few minutes later, Leslie heard the front door being opened. It was his son Jeoffrey carrying two large brown bags marked "China Sea."

"I met the delivery boy in the lobby, paid him and brought the stuff with me."

"Okay, let's eat while the food is still hot. I hate cold Chinese food."

Nobody had to repeat that twice to Leslie, because he quickly set the table for two and boiled water for tea. The soup was good but not hot enough.

"Let me put the soup into the microwave oven for a few seconds."

Clearly, the warmed up soup tasted even better. During the rest of the meal a light conversation took place. Jeoffrey was quite proficient in using chopsticks but Leslie, due to the occasional tremor of his hands, had to use a fork and knife.

"Pops, I enjoyed this meal tremendously, how about you?"

"It was real good. I'm about to have another cup of green tea, will you join me?"

"I'll join you but let me first read what's written in the fortune cookies."

At this point Leslie was tempted to ask Jeff what had happened to his gun but decided not to bring up the issue at this time. Poor Jeff, he didn't realize how close he came to losing his father.

"Okay, Jeff, open the fortune cookies."

"It's funny Pops, the Chinese restaurateurs open their businesses in the Jewish neighborhoods and use Japanese Haiku in their messages. Here is the first cookie:

"Since no poets are writing on Jewish themes in Haiku style, we decided to correct the situation:

> "We left the door open
> for the Prophet Elijah
> now our cat is gone."

Here is another:

> "Is one Nobel Prize
> so much to ask from a child
> after all I've done?"

"It is pretty funny Pops. I just made one up for you. Don't forget that to write in Haiku style you have to use three unrhymed lines of five, seven and five syllables respectively, so here it is:

> Hava nagila
> Hava nagila, hava
> Enough already

"Got it? I'm going to make a few calls and hit the sack. I'll sleep on the couch."

"You don't have to sleep on the couch, Jeff. Use the other bedroom."

"It's okay, I do prefer the couch this time."

"As you wish, I'll watch the TV for a while and also go to bed early. I could use a good night's sleep."

Leslie was watching his favorite program on TV—"National Geographic," when Jeoffrey knocked on the door.

"I might see you in the morning, Pops, sleep well."

"Good night to you Jeff, and thank you for spending the evening with me. I might get up a bit earlier and take a walk. I'll try not to make any noise."

The large double bed seemed to be so empty without Alice. He'll miss saying good night to her, those warm kisses and simply the touch of her silky skin. All of that was gone, only the bed remained the same. She left him for someone else, how was that possible? Was he that blind that he didn't see that she was having an affair? And what's more, with his best friend? Ironic, but he always thought that Alice and he made a very happy couple. "Happy couple, my ass" he said aloud to the four walls. He was becoming more agitated and couldn't fall asleep. He watched the news on Channel 2 and only after the weather report that promised the next day to be pleasant, if a bit sunny and cool, did he shut the lights and go to sleep.

Next morning, he got up fully refreshed and in a surprisingly good mood. He peeked into the living room where Jeoffrey was still sleeping on the couch. Funny, Jeff slept like he slept as a child, on his stomach and with a pillow piled on his head.

Instead of waiting for Jeoffrey to get up, Leslie decided to get dressed and go for a walk.

In the building's lobby Jose the doorman greeted him.

"Good morning Dr. Schiff. May I remind you that you didn't pick up your mail in several days. I also signed for a special delivery letter for you, which I think, came from Russia."

"Thank you, Jose. I'm going for a walk now and on the way back I will pick up my mail."

"As you wish, Dr. Schiff. The mail will be here when you return from your walk."

Leslie liked the morning walks, especially on sunny, cool days—early in the day before the world had a chance to put in its two cents worth.

He walked slowly and carefully all the way down to his favorite "Georgia" diner on Queens Boulevard in Rego Park. The owner, Greek-American Chris Gringas, greeted him warmly, after all, he was a long time patient of Leslie.

"How are you Doc? Are you having the usual?"

"Thank you Chris, the usual will do me just fine."

"Maria! Maria! For my friend the doctor: a glass of orange juice, two eggs over-hard, raisin bagel not toasted, cup of hot, and I said "hot" decaf coffee—and don't forget plenty of water with lemon. Got it?"

"Yes boss, I got it."

For years Chris insisted that Leslie's breakfast would be on the house and Leslie always refused.

"You see, Chris, you can afford to treat me to breakfast but I can't do that in my office. I'll pay you and you will pay me and we will stay friends forever."

Leslie enjoyed his unhurried breakfast. Invariably Chris would bring to his table the morning papers with his second cup of coffee.

Walking back to his apartment Leslie noticed that more and more shopkeepers were the new immigrants. The Koreans had most of the groceries, flower shops, and cleaning stores. Indians or Pakistanis ran the stationary, candy stores and newsstands. Leslie could never tell them apart. There were also a few shops run by Russians like shoe repair shops and beauty parlors.

No question about it, his old neighborhoods of Rego Park and Forest Hills were changing and changing rapidly.

Upon reaching his building Leslie went to his mailbox to retrieve the accumulated mail. There was, of course, the usual junk mail, bills, and a few dividend checks, but there was also a letter from Moscow.

Leslie had a smile on his face. He knew the senders. He will help them come to the United States of America to start a new life. He had a project that would make his life worth living again.

CHAPTER XVIII

"Am I late Maksim?" Galina asked and at the same time shook his outstretched hand.

"No, Galina, you're exactly on time. The Moscow's Raykom could set the Kremlin's clocks by your punctuality. It is good to see you, Galina."

Sometimes Maksim would become tongue-tied in the presence of attractive women, but this time he could hardly curtail his exuberance. He was a bit afraid of coming on too strong on a first date and yet . . .

"Galina, I must confess something to you. I couldn't sleep last night just thinking about you. May I call you Gala?"

"I'm also ashamed to admit that I had trouble sleeping thinking about us and yes, you can call me Gala, providing that I can call you Max. Is that a deal?"

Both were amazed how easy it was for the two of them to communicate and how many things they had in common. They walked the length of the Nevsky Prospect without having a definite goal.

At one point, while crossing a street, Max took her arm in sort of a protective way to help her avoid a large pothole. As long as Galina didn't object to it, he kept holding her arm.

She was telling him about herself, about aunt Fedora with whom she was living, and her mother and sister residing in Moscow. Max was listening with great interest to every word that Gala would utter. They talked about their school, courses and future plans since both of them were due to graduate in a few months.

Gala mentioned that she would like to teach art in schools but she anticipated some problems in job placement because there was a rumor that the authorities were holding back hiring Jews because most of them were Zionists and as such considered to be enemies of the State.

"That is a lot of bunk. Whoever came up with that kind of nonsense?"

"It's easy for you to say because you are ethnic Russian and son of a Hero of the Soviet Union."

"That might be true, but my mother is Jewish and somehow I feel Jewish too. As I said, it is a lot of bunk. Didn't our Comrade Lenin say that religion is the opiate of the people?"

The conversation was becoming a bit too heated for Max and noticing the "Kavkazsky" restaurant right on the Nevsky Prospect #25 he suggested they go inside for a bite.

Unfortunately, the restaurant was closed and no explanation given. Walking further down they reached the "Moskva" restaurant. This time the restaurant was open but the waiting period to be seated was over an hour. Max approached the manager who seemed to read Max's mind:

"Young man, save your money. There is absolutely nothing I can do for you this evening. Try the "Aurora Café" down a few blocks on the left side of the street. That is your best bet. I got to run."

Max was glad he took his advice because there was room for them at the "Aurora." As soon as they were seated they heard thunder, lightening crossed the darkened skies and it started to rain.

Max began to recite a poem he thought was quite apropos: "Liublu grozu v nachale maya," "I love a storm in the beginning of May" when Gala interrupted with:

"We are still in April and thank God we have a roof over our heads, so let's order some tea, Max."

A waitress with a bored expression made her appearance. "Most of the dishes listed on today's menu are gone. The only things left are cabbage soup with meat and fried sturgeon with potatoes and tea. Do you have your coupons?"

Max didn't have any coupons with him nor did Gala. Instead, he gave the waitress a 3-ruble note, which she promptly put into her pocket without changing her facial expression.

"Do you want "Kvass" our most popular apple juice drink?"

"No thank you, we would prefer some hot tea instead.

The waitress shook her head and left the table.

"Max, you didn't tell me what you would like to do after graduation?"

"What I would like to do is one thing but what the Komsomol or the Party may have in store for me is another thing. One thing for sure is that I would like a Moscow assignment. That is the place where the action is."

"That would be great. You would also meet my mother and sister."

"I was planning on it anyway, rest assured."

"Look, our food is coming finally."

She was right. The waitress brought both courses at the same time. There were also two portions of Cheburaki—meat patties in baked dough coverings. Seeing their surprised faces the waitress commented "you are students and in love, aren't you?" It was more a statement of fact than a question and by the time they managed to say "thank you" she was already gone.

They ate the food with gusto as only young people can. The conversation flowed freely and they seemed to be on the same wavelength all the time.

"Gala, I'm like a wanderer in the Sahara who can't get enough water, just as I cannot get enough of you. When can I see you again?"

"I want to see you, too, Max, but I have papers to write and have to get ready for finals."

"So do I, Gala, so do I, but I want to see you."

"The very earliest would be on Sunday and then only for a brief moment."

"But that is in three full days", Max said, in horror.

"Parting is such sweet sorrow. Who said that? Pushkin or Shakespeare?"

"Who cares, but three days? How will I last?"

"Oh, you poor fellow—I'll call you or maybe will see you in class. Look, Max, it stopped raining. It's getting late, we better get going!"

In high spirits they left the restaurant just as a taxi was discharging some French-speaking tourists. Max quickly approached the driver and spoke with him briefly.

"Gala, it is all arranged, he will take us home. First you, than me. It is on the way to his own home. Come, get in."

Gallantly, he opened the door for her and sat next to her. "Gala, this is better than waiting for busses. Who knows, with our Baltic climate it may rain again."

The rain stopped entirely and the clear, if a bit salty air, permeated the area. Sitting next to Gala was intoxicating in itself. The driver expertly pulled in front of Gala's building and witnessed their warm embrace and long kiss.

"I'll call you Max, and thanks for a lovely evening. I had a great time."

"The pleasure was all mine, and I can hardly wait to hear from you."

Max was going over in his mind about every word spoken during the evening. Only when the driver stopped in front of his house did he come to himself and paid the driver the agreed upon sum.

"Thank you comrade, it is time for me to go home already, it has been a long day and I need another drink."

From under his seat he took out a bottle of vodka and offered it to Max. "Have a drink."

"Thank you comrade but I have school exams tomorrow, and I better have a clear head. Maybe another time."

"Very well then—"Za Rodinu"—"To the Fatherland.""

"To the Fatherland" said Max, entering his building.

CHAPTER XIX

The violent death of Edik shook Yefim to the core. He, Yefim, did not want to end up the same way. Surely, there wasn't much future in being a petty thief and if Elena ever found out that he belonged to that category of people, she wouldn't have given him the right time of day. There had to be a solution to his dilemma and unexpectedly, such a solution presented itself.

Several weeks passed since his visit to Elena Shtern. During those weeks he called her a couple of times, always keeping his conversations brief as requested by Lubov Moiseevna. While his calls were short, his letters to her were long, polite, and respectful, yet full of admiration and wit.

On the other hand, Elena's letters were friendly but non-committal in nature. One afternoon as he was about to ask Lubov for permission to use the phone, she said:

"Wait, Yefim, before you call her. Sit down, I need to talk to you." She took out an official looking letter from an envelope.

"In two days, according to our papers, you will be eighteen years old. Personally, I suspect that you are at least nineteen. We kept you in the orphanage as long as we could. Also, in less than a month you will be graduating from the 10th class-system and you will be released from Lysenko's Orphanage. We have many orphans to bring in from the streets of the city of Moscow. What I have in my hands is a draft notice from the Selection Board of the Red Army. You have to appear in two days for the medical examination prior to your induction at Mayakovski Street #98, 3rd floor, room #304. If you pass the medical you will be inducted into the Army. And you will serve between 2-3 years depending upon the branch of services. Most likely you will be conscripted, as you seem to me to be in very good shape. If they reject you, which I doubt very much, it will be due to "political" reasons, basically in your past, and not a fault of yours. Still, you didn't belong to the Pioneer or Komsomol movements. If and when this should happen, we'll offer you a position on our staff. However, you'll be working only half a day. The other half will be spent attending a school for dental technicians. It is a very good profession in the Soviet Union and the course takes about 6-12 months to complete. We have only three openings for the entire orphanage and I am offering you one, providing, of course, that the Red Army won't claim you first. Here is the notice that you must show the officials at the Induction Center. And now, if you wish to call Elena, go ahead and keep it short. I'll be back in three minutes."

She stuck the letter into Yefim's hand and walked out of the room.

Yefim quickly glanced at the letter. Lubov was right, the Red Army wanted him but he did not want to become another Chapayev, Budionnyj or even Zhukov. He would have to answer that question in a couple of days but in the meantime, he would call Elena.

Unfortunately Elena wasn't home and Yefim spoke to her mother.

"Please tell Elena that I called and in two days I have to go for a medical examination prior to my induction into the Red Army."

"Well, Yefim, I'll tell her, and good luck to you."

Just as he hung up the phone, Liubov came back into the room.

"Is everything alright Yefim?"

"Not quite, Elena wasn't home."

"Sorry to hear it, but I have to get back to work. Remember, Yefim, even if you are inducted they will postpone the swearing in ceremony until you graduate from the school."

"Thank you very much Lubov Moiseevna for all your help and advice. I don't know what I would have done without you. I only hope that one day I will be able to repay your kindness."

"Don't worry about it Yefim, besides you already did. Aren't you the young man who saved my life? Go to your room and get ready."

He had plenty of time to get ready, almost two full days.

Yefim reached the Red Army's Induction Center on Mayakovski Street ahead of the scheduled time. Hundreds of young men were milling about. Most of them were smoking, joking and even sharing the ever-present bottle of vodka.

Yefim turned in his draft notice to the sergeant on duty and was given a metal tag with the number #117 engraved on it.

"Your number will be called within an hour. It may, however, be earlier or later, it is hard to say. You are not allowed to leave this building, is that clear Bidnyj?"

"It is, comrade sergeant."

"You are learning fast."

Most of the future recruits came from the part of Moscow where Yefim's orphanage was located. Yefim was mistakenly taken for an officer's candidate because of his school uniform; still, he waited almost three hours until he heard:

"All those holding numbers from 110 to 120 go to room 1-A.

Ten young men, including Yefim walked into a large hall subdivided into 10 rooms each attended by a Red Army doctor and one or two nurses.

Yefim was directed to a cubicle marked #7 attended by a doctor wearing the insignia of Senior Lieutenant and one buxom female sergeant.

"Get undressed Bidnyj, stay only in your underwear, hang your clothing on provided hooks, and get moving. We don't have a whole day Bidnyj."

Yefim undressed quickly and faced the doctor who checked his eyesight and asked him to read the chart attached to the opposite wall. The doctor also looked into his throat, listened to his heartbeat, took his blood pressure and asked him to do some sit ups, each time saying to the sergeant, "fine, fine, fine."

"Well, young man, you seem to be in good shape. Any complaints?"

"Yes, comrade Senior Lieutenant. From time to time I have pains in my lower abdomen."

"Well, let's see, that is why I am here. Lie down on this cot."

The doctor expertly started to move his hands across Yefim's stomach.

"It is right there, doctor."

"Yes, I can feel it now, but stand up for me please, turn your head to the right and cough."

Yefim coughed as ordered.

"Do it again and again." And Yefim coughed several times.

"It's enough already. You have a small hernia, which may grow into a large one.

For the time being you will be released from your obligation to serve in the Red Army.

However, you will have to be seen by comrade Major to approve my decision. Sergeant,

Take this man to see Major Shuster."

"At your service comrade Senior Lieutenant. And you, turning to Yefim, just take your clothing with you, it isn't far, follow me."

The doctor gave the sergeant a file containing Yefim's papers. Yefim followed the sergeant through a long and drafty corridor to another office containing modern medical equipment.

"What do we have here sergeant?" pleasantly asked a silver—gray haired major wearing a white laboratory coat.

"A small hernia, comrade Major."

"Well, let's see it," and the major repeated the same test previously administered.

"Sorry, young man, the Red Army can't use your services, you must be disappointed.

You may go as soon as I sign all these papers. In the meantime, get dressed."

Yefim wasn't disappointed at all—to the contrary, he was very glad about it and almost ran all the way back to the orphanage.

The first thing he did upon his return to Lysenko was to see Lubov Moiseevna. He told her what had happened at the Induction Center. She smiled and said:

"Now we'll be able to send you, upon your graduation, to the Technical Dental School.

Here, call Elena and tell her about it. Today I'm giving you a full five minutes." And she walked out of the room so as not to disturb his privacy.

CHAPTER XX

"Mom, I'm home," said Elena, putting down her books on the kitchen table. "I'm starved, but what are you doing home so early?"

Liudmila Moiseevna Shtern was sitting quietly on a chair facing the outside window. It was clear from her face that she was crying.

"Mom, what has happened? Are you alright?"

Liudmila didn't respond but gave a big sigh. In her hand she held a large piece of paper that Elena removed, and upon seeing what was written, started to read aloud, as if doubting the words.

"Comrade Editor:
My household consists of one horse, four sheep and five "dessyatins" of land for a family of eight people. My question is, must I enter the kolhoz? I think not. I'm sure if you would come and take a vote maybe 10% would be in favor of the Kolhoz. Do not force people to join the kolhoz; there is no sense to it. It's better to hang myself than to join the kolhoz and it's better not to be born than to join the kolhoz.
Signed: Ilya Bogdanov-Bierozka Rayon"

"Mom, I don't understand. What has that note got to do with you? Obviously it was written years and years ago before the collectivization."

"Someone has found this note in one of my old books that I very rarely use. I was questioned as to why I didn't bring that note to the attention of the proper authorities. Also, I am being accused of being a Zionist."

"Is that some kind of a sick joke?"

"No, it isn't a joke at all, I wish it were a joke. In the meantime they suspended me from my job until further notice."

"This cannot be, mom. You are a faithful member of the Party and papa died defending the Fatherland."

"All of that has nothing to do with the issue. You see my child, Karl Marx expected that the Frenchman would begin the social revolution, the German to continue it, the Englishman to finish and, as far as the Russian is concerned, Marx left him way in the back.

The Russian was, is, and always will be an anti-Semite. The same old gendarme in a new uniform. There is a fundamental difference between the communist program and Soviet reality. The State grows more and more despotic and bureaucratic to support a privileged minority; we, my child, were part of that group.

Now the more privileged, the "sine qua none" started to blame the Jews, the professional scapegoats, for all the mistakes and shortcomings of the regime. It is the fault of the Jews or it is the Zionist clique, but never, never, their own. The Authorities also reviewed some of my cases dealing with "refuseniks." "Aha" they said. "You're Jewish and that is why you helped them!" Never mind that I acted within the law. They don't see it, all they see are cases where a Jew was helping a Jew. And maybe that is how it should be. Elena, I don't know what is going to happen but as of now I'm no longer the "*prokuror*," the local D.A."

"Don't worry mom, it must be some kind of mix-up, after all, you are not related to Leon Trotsky, Kamenev or Zinoviev."

"Believe me, my daughter, if they need to connect me with those individuals they can do it very fast, even find eyewitnesses to that fact. Remember the Russian proverb:

"If you want to hit a dog you'll always find a stick." If I'll be able to escape their bloody paws, I'll consider it a pure miracle. It might be a good idea to consider the possibility of migrating to Canada, the USA, Australia or Israel, even though the hot climate and language will be tough to absorb."

"You're not serious, mom, or are you?"

"I don't know myself dear child, but please NOT a word to anyone, not a single word."

"I understand it fully, but what will I do in those countries?"

"You're a brilliant pianist, young and pretty. Don't you worry, you'll do all right."

Now let's get something to eat. You did say before that you were starving. Do your homework and I'll put something together for dinner."

It was true; Elena upon her return home from the Conservatory felt that she was famished. But had a loss of appetite after hearing what her mother had to say. The shrill sound of the telephone interrupted her thoughts further.

"If it is my office tell them that I am not at home and will return the call a bit later."

"Allo, allo." No mom, this call is for me. It is Yefim."

Yefim kept her on the phone for what seemed a long time. He told her about the visit to the Induction Center and being rejected from the Red Army and the offer of part-time work and part-time courses at the Dental Technician's School. Elena was pleased with what she heard because that gave her an idea. Perhaps Yefim would also like to leave Russia and start a new life. After all, there was nothing to keep him here. The only thing that Elena could think of would be her, so the next time she would see him she will approach him lightly, very lightly to succeed.

CHAPTER XXI

It is funny and at the same time interesting how life resembles a pot of water waiting to boil. For a while nothing happens, an occasional air bubble may surface to the top, and in a while it starts to boil furiously.

And that is how it was with Max since he met Galina. Not only did they begin dating as often as their schedules allowed, but they also worked hard until their graduations.

The eternal question facing all students upon graduation applied to them as well. "What do we do next?" What are we going to do with out diplomas?" But whatever the future will bring, let's celebrate the present.

Max's mother, Dr. Natalia Isaakovna had wanted for a long time to meet Galina. Now she had a perfect excuse—a dinner to celebrate their graduations to which she also invited Fedora, Galina's aunt.

In preparation, Dr. Natalia took off a few days from work in order to straighten out the apartment and cook the meal. Max offered to help but Natalia refused, saying:

"If you want to help just stay out of the kitchen, there is no room for the two of us."

"Besides, I'll manage it by myself very well, trust me, my son."

Max wasn't offended by it simply because he didn't have any free time.

Dr. Kostenko, who took such an interest in his life, recommended Max to the party. Finally, with much fanfare, he was admitted. While the party offered many privileges it also expected an unbounded loyalty. Thus, when the Party Secretary hand delivered the "billet," the official membership card, Max had a feeling that he sold his soul to the devil.

This time the devil was personified in Dr. Kostenko who kissed him on both cheeks and the Secretary who just shook his hand and said:

"The Party decided to send you to Moscow's Ostankino Museum to be an assistant to Curator Professor Kiryl Vasiliev. Comrade Kostenko has enormous confidence in your abilities. I'm sure that you'll do everything to justify his faith in you. I'm also sure that a Son of a Hero of the Soviet Union won't bring shame to the Party of Lenin and Stalin.

"Comrades, of that you can be sure."

"You'll be going to Moscow in 2-3 months. In the meantime learn all you can about Ostankino Museum, every little bit of it, is that clear?"

"Yes, comrade Secretary, I do understand the importance of it."

"Before you go to Moscow you'll be briefed as to your assignment. It also would be helpful if you marry a Moscowite. It will make it easier to deal with their bureaucracy in placing one of our own into their midst. Again, congratulations and much success."

"Spasibo—thank you very much comrades."

The meeting was over and Max returned home, just a few minutes ahead of the invited guests. The apartment looked absolutely charming.

"Mom, you are a magician." "Where did all these things come from?"

He was referring to the new tablecloth and napkins in the dining room, and the blankets and rugs on the couches and floors.

We always had them. I kept them in the closets for years. Somehow I never had the occasion or desire to display them. I don't know why but I feel that this dinner might be important to us all. To change the subject, how did your meeting go?"

Max didn't have chance to reply because there was a knock at the door announcing the arrival of their guests.

After making the introductions Max took their coats and hung them up in the closet. He couldn't help noticing the look of interest in his mother's eyes when she met Galina.

Natalia was well prepared for her company. A separate table served as a well stocked bar. An ice bucket held a bottle of champagne and two kinds of vodka, a plain and "Piertsovka," the kind that Fedora only drunk, plus bottles of red wine and a rare 5-star Ararat cognac.

"Let's have a drink in honor of our new graduates" suggested Natalia.

The mood was becoming more upbeat with each drink. Natalia and Fedora smiled at each other, fully understanding, without saying, "these young people are hopelessly in love." Max and Galina also didn't have to say it because they were in it.

"Please come to the table". That announcement was very welcomed.

Course after delicious course was consumed with gusto. Max couldn't remember a finer meal ever. Just before the dessert and tea, Natalia asked Galina:

"Could you come with me to the other room, I would like to chat with you?"

"Of course, with pleasure, Natalia Isaakovna, please excuse us."

Max and Fedora remained in the dining room feeling a bit uneasy. Fedora broke the silence with "let's have another drink." They both had a drink and than another, during which Max tried to make light conversation which wasn't entertaining at all. He was wondering what his mother was talking to Galina about.

Finally the door opened and the two women came out smiling and holding hands. There was something new about Galina because she was wearing a beautiful amber necklace that belonged to his mother.

"Max, we had a nice chat and I can tell you that she is a lovely young lady whom I would not mind having for my daughter-in-law."

Wow! That Max didn't expect. He thought that his mother would throw a tantrum.

"Mom, I'm so glad that you like her too."

"I've a question for Galina. Now that you have graduated what would you like to do?"

"I would like to teach art, either here in Leningrad or in Moscow where I'll have to return to because there are some problems at home. My mother lost her job, accused of being a Zionist. My younger sister Elena is a concert pianist and very busy with her professional life. My mother may need me till that anti-semitic nonsense stops."

"We started to have the same problem at the hospital where I work. The management complains that they have too many Jewish doctors and not enough Russians. Being a war widow of a "Hero of the Soviet Union I'm not afraid of being fired, but still it is very unpleasant to say the least. What about you, Max?"

"The Party wants to send me to Moscow to become an assistant Curator of the Ostankino Museum in about 2-3 months. My problem is different. I can't see my life without Galina being there with me. She fully knows how I feel about her, therefore, in the presence of her aunt Fedora and my own mother, I am asking for her hand in marriage."

Galina, will you have me?"

For a while it was very quiet. Galina got up slowly from her chair and walked over to Max.

"My dear Maksim! I do love you with all my heart and the answer is a resounding YES." She embraced him and kissed him for what seemed an eternity. The first to reach the young couple was Natalia. She kissed both of them and said: "You have my blessings" followed closely by Fedora who started to cry.

"May I use your phone?" "I would like to call my mother."

On the third ring Liudmila Shtern answered the call. Galina told her about the marriage proposal.

"She seemed to be very pleased the way things turned out and can hardly wait for us to come to Moscow. Now she wants to speak with Natalia Isaakovna."

The two women spoke at length, getting to know each other. At one point Liudmila asked Natalia if she was familiar with a poem by Boris Pasternak titled "Wedding," and she began to recite:

Guests came until dawn
To the bride's house for the celebration,
Cutting right across the yard
Bringing their own music . . .

And Natalie finished:

Only wedding noises
Soaring in through a window
Only a song, only a dream
Only a gray pigeon.

"I have one more question to ask of you." "What will you do if we decide to go to America?"

"What is the problem? We will go with you, after all, we are a family."

CHAPTER XXII

This time upon returning to his building, Leslie checked his mailbox, which seemed to be more stuffed than usual. In addition to the regular regular "junk" mail, which Leslie promptly threw into a large trash basket, there were also Edison and telephone bills, some "thank you" notes from affairs attended by Leslie and Alice during those good days, advertisements of the opening of a new Thai restaurant, a cleaning store offering a 10% discount if prepaid, the latest copy of Time magazine, a Readers Digest whose "Humor in Uniform" jokes he always enjoyed, and a solicitation for a donation to four different Jewish organizations. On the bottom of the pile was a letter from Russia.

Colorful large stamps depicting Soviet astronauts were all over the envelope. Leslie opened the letter, which mercifully was written in surprisingly good English.

Just the first sentence brought a smile to his face because it read "Dear Sir and highly respected Dr. Schiff." Half of the letter was devoted to questioning the status of his health and the other half explained that they applied for exit visas, a process that could take from 6 months to 3 years. The paper was lined and written in violet ink or some kind of indelible pencil.

Well, he thought, I did send them papers. I've kept my part of the bargain; the rest is up to them. Hopefully, I'll still be around by the time they will get to the United States.

In the elevator going up he met Clara Goldstein, an old patient of his and the worst he ever had. A few years ago she had dentures put in and since that time she stopped bothering him altogether. She lived one floor beneath him and he was pleased to greet her:

"Nice seeing Mrs. Goldstein, have a nice day"

He took his keys from his pocket in order to open the door to his apartment, only to find that the door was already open. He was sure that he left the door closed. In this respect he was very careful.

Sometimes Jeff would come and leave the door open. The young people these days seemed to be always in a rush and forgetful.

Leslie walked in and shouted: "Jeff, is that you?"

"Yes, Pops, I'm home. We have company."

Leslie walked into the living room and on the couch sitting next to Jeff was his wife, Alice.

She looked pale and distraught. It was obvious that she had cried a lot. The two-piece suit she was wearing was familiar to Leslie but it seemed to be two sizes too big. She must have lost a lot of weight.

An awkward silence prevailed. Neither Leslie nor Alice knew what to say.

"Pops, I have patients waiting for me, I must leave. Please be civil to each other. I do love you both very much."

A couple more minutes passed by and Alice started to cry.

"Alice, you look very tired. Can I make a cup of tea for you?"

"Thank you Les, I'll make one for you." She got up and went to the kitchen leaving Leslie in shock.

She returned in a few minutes carrying a tray with tea, lemon, cookies sweet n' low and even napkins, which she habitually forgot to bring. This time, nothing was missing—after all, she had years of practice.

They drank their tea in silence, and finally Alice spoke. Leslie could see that the words did not come easy to her:

"Leslie, I made a very big mistake. I'm very, very sorry."

"Let me tell you something too. The word "sorry" is the most abused word in the English dictionary. Just by saying "sorry" do you think you can eradicate the pain you have caused me?" You and my so-called best friend? Have I been a bad husband to you? Don't you know that you were the only woman in my life? Besides you I never needed anyone else in the entire world! I had plenty of chances—women were flocking to me, I am not that bad looking either. But not me! Because you, Alice, were my whole world and now that world is shattered (like in Humpty-Dumpty, "all the king's horses and the king's men can't put Humpty Dumpty together again). Yes, Alice, I do know that I've become like an old shoe. Comfortable, predictable, and no longer exciting or elegant. And then came Sammy who swept you off your feet. Alice, do you know the difference between rape and intercourse? No? It is salesmanship! And Sammy was a good salesman who sold you a bill of goods. I suppose that screwing around in motels, back seats of cars or doorways might be considered romantic these days. But not in my book, Alice! I couldn't care less how many women Sammy slept with because my trust was in you. And you, my dear, betrayed that trust! So tell me Alice, why did you come back? You felt sorry for your sick husband or did Sammy kick you out? Or maybe you caught him with another woman? What do you want Alice! Money? Take whatever you want or need, what else do you want from me? And to think that only a couple of days ago I wanted to blow my brains out because of you! What an idiot I've become. If it weren't for Jeff who hid my gun you would have been a widow instead of a divorcee. God, what a laugh!"

All throughout his harangue Alice was crying bitter tears and her body shook uncontrollably. She kept repeating over and over: "I'm sorry, I'm so sorry, please forgive me. I've made a mistake. Can't you find it in your heart to forgive me?"

"I really don't know what to tell you Alice. You can't just waltz in and out of my life any time you wish. I have to think about it. You did hurt me deeply and now look at yourself, you are one big mess. Stay here, but in the guest room. If you see the door to my bedroom closed, do not come in. I will tell you tomorrow about my decision. I'm going out, I need to clear my head, Alice."

"Thank you Leslie, may God bless you."

He didn't hear the rest because he went to the bedroom to change. He then walked out of the apartment without looking in her direction.

He walked aimlessly for a while and went to the neighborhood cinema, seeing three different films. His head was spinning. After leaving the theater he stopped at a kosher delicatessen for a quick sandwich and diet coke. He reached his house in a few minutes.

There was Alice with her shy smile sitting at the kitchen table, set for two.

"Les, I prepared some food, would you like to have a bite?"

"Thank you Alice, I already ate. I'm very tired and going to hit the sack, good night."

Without waiting for her reply he went to his bedroom, closing the door behind him. He got undressed but couldn't find his pajamas. As he took out a pair of fresh pajamas he just remembered where he put the old pair. It was in the cloth hamper with the rest of unwashed linen that had been lying there for weeks.

From the medicine chest in his bathroom he took a sleeping pill, which he washed down with a glass of water. He knew full well that this night he couldn't possibly fall asleep without the pill. In a few minutes he fell asleep.

He woke up at his usual time finding Alice, fully dressed, at the foot of his bed.

CHAPTER XXIII

Some people believe that every human being has a guardian angel. Yefim Bidnyj belonged to that category of believers. He was fully convinced that Liubov Isaakovna was his angel. She was the one that spread her protective wings over him, since the day he arrived at the Orphanage. Once the threat of induction into the Red Army was removed, she arranged for his part-time job at the Orphanage and enrolled him in the Vocational School of Dental Technology.

Learning the new craft was a multi-step process, starting with the theoretic background at school to practical application at the laboratory, where the knowledge of plaster and wax casting was essential beginners' indoctrination, followed by porcelain to metal attachment. A difficult process at best, it started with non-precious metals to semi-precious such as silver and palladium with 2% of gold, and in time, high noble 52%-88% gold. The final product was aesthetically finished and polished to perfection.

He soon grasped the essence of being a good dental technician. It was transformation of a patient's wax impression into a working model, be it acrylic, porcelain or gold.

Very often Yefim was asked to bring the finished items such as crowns, partials, bridges or dentures to the dentists' offices. In time, from a deliveryman he started to assist in taking impressions. Those impressions taken by Yefim were the most hermetical and had the best fit. Word got around about Yefim's unique talent and dentists or other dentists in difficult cases recommended him.

Almost from the beginning of the course Yefim started to make his own limited workshop in his room. Needed tools he made in the Orphanage machine shop and sometimes improved upon existing ones.

He demonstrated the usefulness of his designed instruments to some dentists who were so impressed they requested duplicate copies.

Patients who requested gold teeth had to bring items made out of gold, such as coins, rings, and watches or sometimes old gold teeth. Invariably, some scrap would remain and Yefim started to accumulate them even though it was against the law. His preoccupation with Vocational School and the laboratory did not leave much time to discharge his part-time duties at the Orphanage. The combination of his age and lack of performance at the Orphanage forced Liubov to discharge Yefim from Lysenkos. At the same time he was told to vacate his room as soon as he could find another one. Liubov had to take that step because of the pressure from other members of the board. Besides, it was high time for Yefim to be on his own.

Finding a room was a problem unto itself in crowded Moscow. Hearing about Yefim's predicament, Lysenko's old custodian Stepan Ivanovich Stepanov, who lived with his wife in a nearby housing complex, offered him one of the rooms in his two-bedroom apartment, registering Yefim as his own grand nephew.

Now that Yefim was able to earn some additional money on the side, paying rent wasn't a problem. Noticing the sad state of Stepanov's teeth, Yefim promptly replaced them with new gold ones, earning his eternal gratitude.

At this time, Anna Stepanov started to cook and mend Yefim's clothing. In his favor, whether at school, at work or at home, was his disposition, carefully developed. Always respectful, keeping a chipper attitude and avoiding arguments at all cost.

As he progressed in his future plans he didn't neglect Elena, who was part of it. The extra money he was now earning allowed him to dress much better and from time to time he was able to present Elena with a gift of gold jewelry, sometimes even made by him.

Upon graduating from the School of Dental Technology he was recommended to the most prestigious dental laboratory of Moscow "Profsoyuz#15." Yefim clearly understood the need for additional experience and his present job offered him that possibility.

It was also clear to Yefim that since his new job, there was a remarkable improvement in the relationship between him, Elena, and Elena's mother, especially after she lost her job. It seemed to Yefim that he had shed his image as an orphan boy and that he was genuinely welcomed in their home.

Another piece of news coming from Elena was that her sister Galina would be coming home from Leningrad in a few months for good, bringing along her fiancée whom she wanted to marry in Moscow shortly after her arrival.

As Yefim remembered, the conversation went along these lines:

"Where will the young couple live? With you?"

"In the beginning with us, until they get settled. It shouldn't be too long because the Party promised Max, Galina's future husband, an apartment of his own. We'll be squeezed for a while, but what can you do?"

"Congratulations are due your family, Elena. I must confess I haven't been to a real wedding."

"Wait and see, you will be invited."

"Would a double wedding be more expensive?"

"What do you have in mind, Yefim?" "For myself, I would like my wedding to be separate, a day all for myself, a day that I will remember for the rest of my life."

"Exactly my sentiments, Elena."

CHAPTER XXIV

Few people were as keenly aware of the complications and dangers resulting from applying for an exit visit from Russia as Liudmila Moiseevna Shtern was.

Just by applying to OVIR, the Agency responsible for issuing those visas, one could lose his or her job, be forced to give up the apartment they lived in, and be asked in less than polite language to pay for the education received in the Soviet Union. Usually an amount that one could not possibly raise, even if one should sell all of his worldly possessions. Needless to say, no works of art, icons, samovars, personal jewelry or books printed before 1961 were permitted to be taken along.

In addition, all household items had to be packed in special wooden cases manufactured by one factory only, resulting in long delays unless one was willing to pay off the corrupt officials.

All these obstacles paled in comparison to the treatment of Jews during Stalin's bottomless pit of iniquity. During the Great Patriotic War a Jewish Anti-Fascist Committee was created with Stalin's blessings for the purpose of winning the support of the West for Soviet's war effort.

The Anti-Fascist Committee publicized Jewish suffering and spoke of Jewish aspirations. This approved activity, after the war, came to be viewed as bourgeois nationalism and deemed treason to the Soviet Union.

Thus, many Jewish writers, scientists and doctors were killed at Lubianka prison. Only one person was given a prison sentence and that person was a biochemist by the name of Lina Shtern, Liudmila's husband's older sister. The trials and executions of those people, which included a famous Yiddish poet, Peretz Markish and Lozovsky, deputy foreign minister, were secret. Lina Shtern found out about it, still believing that in the new Soviet Union Yiddish life would flourish as it never had before, and held the unshakable conviction that the Soviet regime emancipated her people.

Liudmila got her job as a Public Prosecutor while unmarried and using her maiden name. Had she been married at that time to Iosif Shtern she would have never gotten that position, of that she was more than sure. Iosif died defending the Soviet Union and she lost her job because of sheer anti-Semitism. So much for the emancipation of her people, of which Lina Shtern spoke.

One of these days she would have to take a trip to visit the dreadful OVIR, which was located near the G.U.M., the largest department store in Russia, with its daily 300,000 customers.

On the east side of Red Square there are two large buildings between Kuybishev and Razin streets. One building is the home of G.U.M. and the other impressive building houses the offices of OVIR. That was the building that Liudmila knew sooner or later she would have to visit. In the meantime, she postponed it like she would a visit to the dentist. She would have to face unbearable pain before acting upon it.

This time, however, would only be a trip to G.U.M. where, according to the rumors flying around Moscow, there would be a sale on imported, French nightgowns at a very low price.

The lure of an imported product at a low price was irresistible. A lure that many of Moscow's ladies were fascinated by and rushed to take advantage of this rare opportunity.

The lines were long but moving rather well, since only one garment to a customer was allowed. In front of Liudmila stood a woman wearing a uniform of a captain in the M.V.D. (Ministiertvo Vnutrenich Diel) Ministry of Internal Affairs.

There was something vaguely familiar about that person and not until the woman turned back to face Liudmila and started a conversation did she realize who that person was.

"How are you Comrade Shtern?"

"Forgive me Comrade Captain but I can't place you. I have a feeling that we met someplace or somehow."

"I'm Ella Kozakova. Let me refresh your memory. A couple of

years ago you gave my youngest brother Sieroza a big break. You saved him from a long prison sentence."

"Oh, yes! I do remember it now but I don't think you were a captain then."

"You're right, I was just a sub-lieutenant who came from the far eastern city of Vladiwostok just in time to see my kid brother set loose with a stern warning and not even a probate."

"I recall that case now. I had a gut feeling about your brother. He seemed to be a good boy who had wrong friends, so I took a chance because there was no sense in sending him to an overcrowded jail. He would only come back as a hardened criminal.

By the way, was my hunch about him correct?"

"Yes, Comrade Shtern, very much so. He graduated from the 10th grade school and is now a student at the Moscow Institute for Foreign Languages, getting straight A's. We are very proud of him and we have you to thank for it."

"I'm really pleased Comrade Captain."

"Please call me Ella."

"I'll do that providing you call me Liudmila."

By this time the line had already reached the cashier. They had to pre-pay for the merchandise and only with a receipt in hand; they went to pick it up.

"What size?" Barked the saleslady.

"Large please, do you have it in blue?" answered Ella.

"Be grateful that we have it only in red, do you want it nor not?"

"I'll have it in red, thank you."

"And you" pointing to Liudmila.

"I'll take a size medium."

"Next" . . . and two packages in cellophane wrapper were dropped in front of them.

"Real bitch, she could have been more polite," said Ella.

"Well, what are you going to do?" "Teach Moscowites good manners? I'm afraid it is too late for them. Let's open our packages and check out our bargains."

They both opened their packages. The nightgowns, although red in color, were made of luxurious, silky, textured rayon and had authentic labels of "Jacques" of 22 Rue de Paradis-Paris-France Marque ET Modeles Desposes (registered styles and trademarks).

"My gown seems to be too large," said Liudmila.

"And mine too small. Someone marked these boxes wrong, let's swap them."

"Good idea, Ella." "Let's do it and if you have a few minutes to spare, let me treat you to a glass of tea." "I was about to suggest the same and surely I can spare a few minutes."

On the 4th floor of G.U.M. next to the ladies apparel department was a small teashop, with standing room only. As a captain in M.V.D. Ella was served immediately upon asking for two teas.

"One of these years I would like to visit Paris, it must be a very romantic city."

"So would I," replied Liudmila. "But you can do it. Many people of your nationality are applying for exit visas, mainly to their historic homeland, Israel, or Canada, or even to the USA. I know all about it because after all, I'm the "natchalnick," the manager of OVIR's department that issues those visas."

"Maybe I should apply if I ever want to see Paris," said Liudmila.

"You, Comrade Shtern, you of all people?" Ella seemed very surprised.

"Yes, Ella, me too. I lost my job because someone denounced me as a Zionist.

I don't have much choice. Life for us Jews is becoming constantly more difficult.

I won't be able to help some innocent boys like your brother anymore."

Ella looked around and lowered her voice considerably, saying:

"You helped my family and I'll help yours. Come anytime and I will give you all the proper papers. You fill them out and I shall personally process them for you without any fuss and without our famous Soviet red tape. Remember not a single word to anyone, not a word, do you hear me?" Is there anyone else in your family who wants to go with you?"

"I don't know exactly, Ella, maybe my two daughters and their future husbands."

"Is there anyone among them currently serving in the Red Army?"

"No, no one."

"That makes it a bit easier. I'll make sure that at my end everything goes smoothly. The rest is up to the country you want to go to."

"Maybe you will visit us someday?"

"That is an interesting idea, however, "vlasti" the Soviet Government, will never let a captain of the M.V.D. leave the country."

"Here is my phone number and the number of my office. If you decide to come, ask for me only and nobody else. Should anyone ask you, just tell him or her that Captain Kozakova is handling your case. Good luck in whatever you may decide."

"Thank you very much Ella. I will let you know. What a nice day we had. Too bad that G.U.M. didn't have blue nightgowns.

CHAPTER XXV

As the day of her graduation from Moscow's Conservatory was approaching, Elena Shtern was becoming progressively more nervous and worried. In addition, she had trouble sleeping.

Her task given by the Conservatory was to play Modeste Mussorgsky /Rimsky-Korsakov's "A Night on Bald Mountain," a difficult piece at best, and Mikhail Glinka's Waltz-Fantasy" in B minor.

She spent every free moment practicing these two pieces over and over again to the point that each single note seemed imbedded in her head.

"Mother, I can't practice anymore. If I do it one more time I will hate the piano forever."

"Then leave it for a day or two. Take time to relax a bit. See that poor fellow Yefim who has already called you several times. There are also letters from him in the kitchen."

Elena was so preoccupied with her test that she completely ignored Yefim's repeated attempts to get in touch with her. She was contemplating the best way to get in touch with him when the phone rang. Elena picked up the receiver. It was Yefim by the magic of telepathy.

"I'm really worried Yefim, I wasn't trying to avoid you. I simply had to get ready for finals at the Conservatory. I do hope you understand and forgive me, it is my future. Don't forget that I have to compete against some of the most capable and talented young people and it won't be easy. Be patient for another couple of days. If I pass, you and I will be celebrating."

"Elena, I just called to wish you luck. I'm sure you will do just fine. But no matter what,

I want you to know that I love you like I never loved before."

"Well, thank you Yefim for the good wishes. As soon as I get the results of the test I will let you know. By the way, I also think that I'm in love with you." With these words she hung up the phone.

Moscowites are conceited people. They think that their kilogram is heavier and the meter longer but the hours were always taking the same amount of time.

She showed up for her test well ahead of the appointed time, dressed in a pleated navy skirt and white silk blouse and wearing her mother's single strand of pearls. Her hair was combed and held with a navy ribbon, which gave her a more mature look.

Exactly at 9:00 A.M. she was called to a large room, welcomed by her teacher and mentor Vera Ryzhkova, who whispered "Don't worry, you'll do fine." There were six other people in the room, all members of the faculty.

Elena took her place behind a big royal piano, and made sure that the piano stool was comfortable and at the proper distance from the piano. She also made sure that her notes were clearly visible. When asked if she was ready she shook her head affirmatively. The same cold voice said, "Please proceed."

This was it! All the years of hard work were being put to the test. She knew that her life and future depended on her performance. It was now or never.

She began to play with all her concentration. The piano became an extension of her own soul. Under her fast fingers each key produced the tone that she wanted. Elena glided with ease through several difficult passages in the middle and towards the end of her performance, drawing bravos from the faculty.

Someone came into the room but Elena kept on playing fully concentrating on her task, giving a sigh of relief after the last note.

This time the bravos were louder and longer, the loudest coming from her coach, Comrade Ryzhkova and another man standing next to her. This probably was the man who came in during her performance thought Elena. He looked vaguely familiar.

"Elena, that was very good indeed. Would you mind playing it once more for Comrade Simonov?"

It was more than a request, it was a direct order. Holy Moses! Elena just realized who the man was. It was no other than the legendary Boris Simonov, the conductor of the Moscow Philharmonic. He was the first Russian to win the Santa Cecila Conducting Competition in Rome, Italy. He was also the man who toured with his orchestra to Hungary, Yugoslavia, England, France, and the highly publicized successful seven-week tour of the United States. And now this demi-God asked Elena if she would please play for him once more.

"I'll be honored, Comrade Simonov."

Someone brought her a glass of cold water for which she was very grateful. She stretched her hands and fingers a bit and started to play those so well practiced pieces.

She felt so at home with the theme and rhythm of distinctly Russian pieces, that she gave the performance all her heart and soul and it was recognized at the end of her performance by enthusiastic bravos.

Elena was shaking like a leaf in autumn's wind, overtaken by her own emotions.

"Congratulations young lady. It was a brilliant performance indeed. I was given to understand that you are about to graduate. Please see my personal secretary Aida Stepanova. I want you on my staff if you are agreeable," said Simonov.

God Almighty! Was she willing? She would be willing to swim the Volga in the wintertime for a chance to play for him and now he just offered her a job with the most prestigious philharmonic orchestra in the world.

"I'll be there and thank you very much for the opportunity to play under your baton, Maestro."

"That is perfectly alright with me, just a couple of questions if you don't mind. Judging from your name, you are Jewish aren't you? If so, do you intend to migrate to the United States where some of my best talents are heading? And the second question is, are you related to Isaac Stern the American violinist?"

"No Comrade Simonov. We do not intend to leave our Motherland and go to a Capitalistic society, and as far as I know, we don't have any relatives in America by the name of Stern."

"I'm glad to hear it because I don't want to waste my time and energy coaching a promising artist only to lose him or her to some impresario like Sol Hurok in the West."

"I assure you, Comrade Simonov, you won't have any problems with me."

CHAPTER XXVI

Graduation time was also approaching rapidly for Galina and Max. The written tests that Galina was so deathly afraid of were a cinch for Max. However, when it came time to submit their own original work in both oil and watercolors, the roles were reversed.

Galina was the true artist fully recognized by her teachers. The subjects of her paintings seem to jump out from the canvasses and even the colors she used had a life all their own.

The best thing that could be said about Max's work was "not bad." There was something mechanical and flat in appearance in his work. It was obvious to the faculty that Max was no artist himself but that he knew art and artists extremely well. This was one of the reasons why Dr. Kostenko with the blessings of the Leningrad's Communist Party, decided to place Max as an assistant curator of Moscow's Ostankino Museum.

It was a political move as well on the part of the Leningrad C.P. to place as many Leningraders into the Moscow Districts.

They both graduated with honors. Galina who truly deserved it and Max, who actually worked hard, got it on the coattails of his father's title of the "Hero of the Soviet Union."

The only person who came to their graduation was Galina's aunt Fedora. Max's mother had several emergencies in her hospital and wasn't able to find a replacement. Liudmila Shtern, Galina's mother, couldn't come either but she didn't give a reason.

The faculty and the student body were in a festive mood at the Graduation Ceremony. The speeches seemed to be endless. Every speaker thanked the Community Party and their leaders for their "enlightened foresight and progressive thinking." The school band played patriotic music and marches to everyone's contentment.

Max, whose last name started with the letter "Z" was one of the last to receive his diploma from the hands of Dr. Kostenko.

"Congratulations Ziemtsov. I want to see you in two days about 10:00 A.M. in the morning. I'll let you rest for a couple of days."

"Thank you very much Comrade Kostenko. I'll be there on time."

Aunt Fedora came up to Galina and Max, hugging and kissing them and wishing them much luck. To Galina she winked her eye in a conspiratorial way, whispering into her ear that she won't be sleeping in her apartment that night.

"You young people should go someplace where there is hot, gypsy music and cold vodka. I'll leave the two of you alone; you certainly don't need an old woman like me hanging around you. Have fun, do svidania."

She left before they had a chance to meekly protest her departure.

"Max, why don't we drop of our diplomas and bags at my house since it is much closer and then go to some cozy place. By the way, Aunt Fedora won't be home this evening."

"Don't laugh Galina, but my mother is also not at home. She is on duty at the hospital. We have two places to choose from but since you live closer, let's go to yours."

"Very well, let's go and not waste time."

They reached Galina's apartment in a relatively short time. She opened the door and walked in first. They dropped their diplomas and books on the nearest chair.

""Max, I feel like having a drink, what about you?"

"I thought you would never ask. Do you have vodka at home?"

"Have you ever seen a Russian home without vodka?" That is like asking a priest if he has a cross."

She brought down a ¾ filled bottle of vodka and two glasses from the kitchen's cupboard.

"Max, please pour me a drink. "naley I nie zhaley"—"pour and don't skimp."

Max didn't have to be asked twice, he poured two generous drinks.

"Galina, let me make a toast. This is to us and only to us. I believe this is the beginning of a good life. Your health—"Na zdorovie."

Max drank his share in one long gulp. Galina emptied better than half of the drink. A wonderful feeling of warmth and well being spread throughout their bodies. She turned on the radio just as some romantic dance music came from Kiev's station.

Max put down his drink and slowly approached Galina. He embraced her; his hands went underneath her turtleneck sweater, feeling her silky skin. His fingers found and released the catch of her brassiere, holding her breasts in both of his hands. Her nipples hardened under his touch. He looked at her face and could only see her full, ruby lips.

At first, he kissed her gently and sensually and suddenly began to kiss her with urgency. Galina responded to each of his kisses with a passion she never knew she had.

She felt his strong muscular body lifting her off her feet and carrying her to the bedroom. They helped each other undress until both of them were stark naked. They liked what they saw.

"Galina, my Galina, I love you!"

"I know that Max, be gentle and don't rush. Don't worry, it is the right time of the month."

Max was aroused to the point of explosion. Galina's kisses had the effect of hot coals upon his body. He had difficulty penetrating her. Her long legs were holding him closer and closer. Several more movements and they mutually reached climaxes.

A sweet wetness engulfed them and the tension disappeared, replaced by a state of sublime happiness. At that point they fell asleep in each other's arms. That was how Aunt Fedora found them the following morning.

Instead of waking them up Fedora left the apartment without making a sound. She was happy for her niece. How different was her own youth spend during the blockade of Leningrad. She slept with many men, sometimes not knowing even their first names.

She also remembered digging the anti tank ditches, the freezing cold, the constant German bombardments, the response of Russian

artillery, the whining of the 203 mm howitzers, the screeching of
the multi-rocket "katiushas," the hunger, the death of many, the
wounded crying for their mamas, and the blessed glass of vodka.
The ever-forgiving vodka that helped her to forget the horrors of
the war.

The touch of a man, any man, made her feel human again, so
thank God for vodka and the occasional cigarette.

Much later in the day Fedora came back to apartment and
found Galina and Max gone. The apartment itself was never cleaner.
In the bathroom hung a freshly washed bed sheet with faint traces
of blood in the middle.

CHAPTER XXVII

There was no fooling around with Dr. Kostenko. Ten o'clock was ten o'clock, not a minute earlier or later and Max knew the routine well. Therefore, he made doubly sure to be there on time. He checked in with Dr.Kostenko's secretary, Larissa Ivanovna.

"Yes, Maksim, Dr. Kostenko is expecting you." And she announced his arrival.

Whatever his reasons that day, Dr. Kostenko wore his bi-medaled uniform. His facial expression was all business. Max stood in front of his desk, almost at attention, following his hunch that Kostenko wasn't about to ask him to sit down. His hunch was fully justified.

"Well, Maksim, you finally made it. It's time for you to move on. Moscow's Ostankino has been notified about your appointment to the staff of the Museum. You are expected there two weeks from today. That should give you ample time to get ready. As I said to you before, you will have to work with the curator, Professor Kiryl Vasiliev, from whom you can learn a lot. Be smart and play close attention to him. Remember that wisdom has two parts" a) having a lot to say and b) not saying it. Any questions Maksim?"

"I have a few Comrade Dr. Kostenko, and the first one is of a practical nature. Where would I live?"

"I anticipated that question. Since you are a bachelor you'll be living with other bachelors in their quarters on Yakimanka Street near the Church of Ivan the Warrier. Too bad that you are not married because we could put you up in a nice apartment for Party members on First Brestkaya."

"Did you say First Brestkaya, Comrade Kostenko?"

"Yes I did, why do you ask?"

"I have a girlfriend whose family lives on that street, they are all Moscowites."

"Is there anything serious between you and your girlfriend?"

"Yes Comrade Kostenko. Very serious. I'm hoping to marry her next year. Maybe she'll have me sooner."

"That is entirely up to you both but don't marry just for the sake of an apartment."

"No, Comrade Kostenko, I genuinely love that girl."

"Anybody I might know?"

"Yes, Comrade Kostenko, she is Galina Shtern, a fellow student."

"I do recall who she is. She is a fine artist; I've seen some of her work that might help you in your job. Well, you have two weeks ahead of you. Either way, single or married, you have to do your job and do it right. The Party is counting on you."

"I'll have the answer for you regarding my living accommodations within a couple of days."

"Very well Maksim, here are your papers."

He started to look for them on his crowded desk, lifting his daily "Izviesta" newspaper, to no avail. Since he couldn't place the papers he yelled for his secretary:

"Larissa, where the hell are Ziemtsov's papers?"

"They are still on my desk. I'll bring them to you right away, Comrade Kostenko."

"Here are your papers, everything is in it with the exception of your Residence Permits.

As soon as you tell us whether you want to remain a bachelor or get married, we will complete your arrangements. Now you may go, Maksim."

"Thank you very much for everything Comrade Dr. Kostenko."

Outside his office Max checked the contents of the big gray envelope. The first paper was the most important one; it was his transfer document with many stamps and signatures:

"KOMANDIROVOCHNOIE PREDPISANIE #224
Maksim Michailovich Ziemtsov s polucheniem sievo
predlagayou vam
Otpravitsa v Moskwu

"Upon receipt of the enclosed we suggest that you, Maksim Michailovich Ziemstsov travel to Moscow . . ." These were his marching orders. Max smiled at the word "suggest". They might s well have written, "we order you," the results were the same.

He knew better than to ignore the Party's "suggestions."

He came home, meeting his mother in the vestibule of the house. She was carrying a big bag of groceries and a smaller bag of mandarin oranges. Max relieved her of the heavy bag containing mostly potatoes. His mother kept the oranges.

"I stood in line for these over an hour, but I got them almost as the supply ended. I stopped at the store after finishing my shift at the hospital. How did your meeting with Kostenko go?"

"Well enough. I have something to show you mother."

"Fine, let's go upstairs and unpack our groceries. I'll make us a cup of tea and then we'll talk about your meeting. Does what you have to show me have anything to do with that meeting?"

"Yes, mama, quite a bit."

"It must be really important, I can tell by your face. You could never hide anything from me even when you were a small boy."

"You are so right." They opened the apartment door and put away the groceries.

His mother put on water for the tea using an electric samovar.

"It will take but a minute. Now tell me what transpired in Kostenko's office."

Max told her about the meeting in greatest detail and showed her the papers he received from Kostenko.

"This looks very impressive but where are you going to live in Moscow?"

"That brings me to the next point I want to discuss with you. As a bachelor they will put me up with other single men. If I was married, I could get an apartment."

"Max, what would you like to do? Sooner or later you will have to make decisions on your own. Marrying someone just for the sake of an apartment doesn't make much sense or does it?"

"Mama, I would like to marry Galina, I am deeply in love with her. Although I am young and probably could wait a bit, I am sure she is the woman for me."

"Did you ask her to marry you yet? She is indeed a fine girl and good human being. Personally, I like her a lot, but it is not I who wants to get married. So, what are you going to do?"

"I'm going to ask her to marry me as soon as possible. I have two weeks to do it in."

"Time is running fast. Why don't you give her a call or even better, go to see her?"

"I can arrange a nice dinner at Vostochny on Nevsky Prospect or Severny on Sadovaia Street. Both managers were my patients at one time or another. Go, call already, you got me all excited."

On the third try, Max was able to "catch" Galina.

"Dushenka"—"my little soul" I would like to talk to you about something very serious. When can we meet?"

"Oh, dear God, that really sounds very serious. Tell me what is on your mind darling?"

"I would like to tell you that in person."

"Good news I hope."

"The very best."

"Let me guess. You want to marry me, right? If that is the question, the answer is YES. I am ready whenever you are."

"How about this week? Today is Monday, so what about Friday? Does that suit you?"

"It does. It will give me time to notify my mother and sister."

"Tell her that we'll be living on First Brestkaya Street."

"Oh really? Max, you will love my mother."

"I'll pick you up in a taxi and we'll drive to the nearest office of Z.A.G.S. to get married."

"Max, my heart is bursting into a million pieces from happiness."

"I'll catch every little piece and put it back together because I need it to function for many years to come."

CHAPTER XXVIII

Several weeks passed by and the relationship between Leslie and Alice remained in the same state of suspended animation.

Leslie was polite to Alice but at the same time was as cold as a Siberian taiga in wintertime. Many times seeing her pale face or hearing her cry at night in the other bedroom, he wanted to put his arms around her, but the idea that she left him for another man reminded him of a traitor to one's country.

Alice was losing weight; hardly touching food and the food that she prepared for Leslie went uneaten. When asked why he wasn't eating, he replied that he was not hungry, but at the same time he would go out of the house and eat in any of the restaurants or diners in the immediate neighborhood.

With Alice's birthday soon approaching his son Jeffrey urged him to take Alice out to a well-known steak house. Leslie softened his attitude and asked Alice to join him.

"Oh, thank you, thank you, Leslie. I'm so grateful to you." She said and embraced him.

Leslie felt embarrassed and guilty seeing tears forming in the corners of her eyes.

"Don't worry Alice, we'll make it yet, just give me more time."

"Take all the time in the world as long as you come back to me. Believe me, I have learned my lesson the hard way. You were, are and always will be by only true love."

Old habits are tough to break. Since her birthday fell on Saturday, they both got dressed befitting the occasion.

Even though it was a bit windy they both decided to walk those 8 or 9 blocks to the restaurant. They walked reminiscing about the good old times. Leslie was warm and witty describing their relatives or friends at various social functions. Alice was a good listener, laughing and sounding more and more like Alice during her High School years.

They reached the street where Manero's Steak House was located. All they needed now was to cross the very busy Queens Boulevard and two service roads to reach their destination. With the green light in their favor they managed to cross one service road and the boulevard itself, but the light changed and the impatient New York drivers kept on going, leaving the Schiffs trapped on a small island awaiting the next change of lights.

Concentrating on the traffic they didn't notice, until it was too late, a "Daily Mirror" truck delivering newspapers, jumping the curb and hitting Alice, standing to the right of Leslie, with its left front fender.

She fell backwards hitting her head against the pavement, bloodying the area. The truck driver whose name was Joe Santini as Leslie found out later, jumped out of the cabin screaming, "I'm sorry, I'm sorry."

Who said that you couldn't get a cop when you need one? This time, a passing police cruiser stopped immediately. While one police officer called for an ambulance, two other men rendered first aid to Alice, and the fourth officer interviewed the driver. From afar Leslie heard the driver say, "I just had a couple of beers, officer."

Within seconds curiosity seekers surrounded them. The New York cops wanted none of this. Assistance came from "Bob's Barber Shop" when one of the barbers brought out a bed sheet and a woolen blanket.

For once Leslie was thankful for the cops and their experience. Just as Leslie was giving all the personal data to the sergeant in charge, a local ambulance pulled up.

The emergency personnel expertly lifted Alice from the ground onto a stretcher, and straight into the ambulance. What cops left undone the Emergency Medical Service men quickly attended to, at the same time talking to Leslie.

"I'm not a doctor but this woman will require hospitalization and maybe an operation."

"At the moment she is stabilized."

"Where are you taking her?" asked Leslie.

"To the nearest hospital on the Van Wyck Expressway."

"Can you take her to St. Francis Hospital in Port Washington on the North Shore? I have a friend there, Dr. James Rubin, the Chief of Staff."

"It's highly irregular."

"Would this change your mind?" And Leslie put three crisp $100 dollar bills into his hand.

"Consider it already done, Dr. Schiff," and said to the driver "Mike, St. Francis Hospital, and step on it."

"Yes, sir, boss, St. Francis it is."

Very few sounds are more horrifying than the wailing of an ambulance siren. Leslie cursed some of the motorists blocking the ambulance's right of way. People are so uncaring and involved in their own little worlds. The city had so many red lights and they all seemed to be against them.

Leslie asked for permission to call his son Jeff to meet them at the emergency entrance of the hospital.

The driver of the ambulance was making excellent time but to Leslie it seemed like an eternity. He held her cold hands and was hoping that the sedation was causing her not to feel any pain.

The driver pulled into the circular driveway in front of the fluorescent sign EMERGENCY ONLY, behind which was the multi storied gray building, housing he hospital.

Jeff was already there as the emergency room attendants wheeled her right in.

Leslie and Jeff were held back.

The resident physician who looked like a Yeshiva High School graduate with his tiny yarmulka held by a bobby pin said:

"I'm Doctor Winston Goldstein. We'll let you know as soon as we can determine the status of the patient. Have you signed all the forms?"

"Yes I did. I would like to see Dr. James Rubin, he is a close friend of mine."

"Sorry, Dr. Rubin is currently vacationing in Aruba. Don't worry; we'll take good care of your wife. I have to run, but you are welcome to coffee and buns in the waiting room."

There was nothing else to do but wait. Jeff wanted to know how this accident occurred. Leslie described it as best he could. "It was an accident. We were in the wrong place at the wrong time. A simple, stupid accident."

"Anything else you can tell me, dad?"

"No, Jeff, it was an accident that simply happened."

Jeff kept on talking and Leslie remained silent, as there was not much to add. He just did not feel like talking. The accident had left him spent and shaken.

"Do you need me in this conversation?"

"Forgive me, Jeff, I am just so tired and upset. Let me rest a bit. I'm no longer a young man, the years have finally caught up with me."

Some four hours later Dr. Winston Goldstein came out:

"Where is Dr. Schiff?"

Both of them answered at the same. "I'm here."

"Are you father and son?"

"Yes we are. Tell us, how is Mrs. Schiff?"

"She is a very lucky person indeed. Her hip operation took some time but the results are even better than we hoped for. She will have to be hospitalized for two, maybe three weeks followed by rehabilitation of six to nine months. She is heavily sedated and you will have to wait several hours until she will be able to talk with you. I suggest you get some sleep. There is nothing you can do for her at the moment. Go home and rest. Any questions."

"Conventional wisdom has proven that when a doctor says six months it is usually twelve. Which is it as far as her rehabilitation is concerned?"

"No, in her case I am almost 100% sure that it will take only six months for her to come back to herself. She has good bones and appears to be in fairly good health.

Here is my card, call me if you need me day or night. If you will excuse me, I am also very tired. I've been on my feet for the last eighteen hours. So long."

"Jeff, why don't you go home? I'll stay here until she comes out of the Recovery Room."

"I never realized how much you always loved mom."

"I hope you never have any doubts Jeff."

CHAPTER XXIX

Thanks to Comrade Simonow, the conductor of Moscow's Philharmonic Orchestra, Elena Shtern obtained a position with Rosia Concert Hall, where the world's famous musicians and artists, both Soviet and foreign performed.

Her job was very prestigious and at the same time presented an opportunity for advancement, provided that one had the talent and the political clout to back it up. The best musical talents were concentrated in that theatre, talents that were "sine qua none."

Elena loved the place, which was located near the gigantic Hotel Rosia and Cinema-City "Zaradie" and was within a 5-minute walk to the Red Square and its spectacular view.

She became an understudy to Svetlana Chapayova, a well-known piano virtuoso. There is a saying in show business "break a leg" and Svetlana broke her leg in a freak accident near her dacha. Elena was called on to replace her during an upcoming concert in honor of the Italian Communist Labor Leader, Togliatti.

It wasn't a festive occasion such as May 1st or the Anniversary of the Great October Revolution, but big enough to print the program in Italian.

Elena was given two tickets gratis, which she gave to her mother and Yefim. The concert itself was a total sellout and the ticket scalpers were selling those tickets at a premium price.

The Russian public traditionally dresses as best they can for concerts. Red Army officers and war veterans wore their medals and battle ribbons.

The seats given to Elena were on the 2nd mezzanine a bit to the side but offering fantastic acoustics. Yefim looked at the program and recognized the name of Elena Shtern:

CONCERTO LIRICO
14 Settembre 1987
SOLISTI:
VALERIA MAYAKOVSKAYA
SOPRAN0
TARAS BACHEVSKIY
TENORE
PETER KIRILOV
BARITONO
AL PIANOFORTE IL MAESTRA
ELENA SHTERN

P R O G R A M M A—PRIMA PARTE

P. Mascagni	CAVALLERIA RUSTICANA	Pianoforte solo
	Intermezzo	
Buzzi Peccia	LOLITA	Baritono
	Romanza	
G. Meyerbeer	L'AFRICANA	Tenore
	O Paradiso	
G. Verdi IL	CORSARIO	Soprano
G. Bizet	CARMEN	Tenore
	II Fiore	
G. Debussy	ROMANCE	Soprano
P. Mascagni	SERENATA	Baritono
G. Puccini	LA BOHEME (duetto)	Soprano e Tenore

SECONDA PARTE

G. Puccini	MANON LESCAUT	Pianoforte solo
W.A. Mozart	DON GIOVANNI (duetto)	Soprane e Baritono
	La'ci darem la mano	
R. Leoncavallo	MATTINATA	Tenore
W.A. Mozart	COSI FAN TUTTE	Soprano
	Come scoglio	

G. Rossini	GUGLIELMO TELL	Baritono
	Resta immobile	
F. Lehar	LA VEDOVA ALLEGRA (duetto) Soprano e Tenore	
	Tace il labbro	
	CANZONE NAPOLETANA	Baritono
G. Verdi	LA TRAVIATA (duetto)	Soprana e Tenore
	Brindisi	

Yefim's thoughts were interrupted by the announcement of the presence of the Secretary of the Italian Communist Party, Giacomo Zecchini, the Labor Leader of Italy, Franco Massaro, and well-known Italian film critic, Mario Mainardi.

Elena was the first artist to open the program. Yefim sat throughout the entire performance mesmerized. If the long applauses were any indicator of Elena's artistry at the piano, she must have been excellent. Liudmila told him that she never heard Elena play better.

Elena was planning to see her mother during intermission but there was such a commotion backstage with the change of costumes and scenery that she couldn't come out at all. They would have to be patient and wait until the end of the concert and the official dismissal. There was also the possibility of attending a cocktail party for foreign guests.

There were eight curtain calls. The audience did not want the artists to leave the stage. Finally, the dimming lights forced the public to leave the Concert Hall.

Liudmila and Yefim waited for over an hour until Elena came out from the side door carrying 3 bouquets of flowers given to her by the adoring public. They both congratulated Elena, and Yefim gave her flowers that seemed to be a poor cousin to those she held in her hands.

The crowded but efficient Metro brought them home. Liudmila served a light supper along with "Shampanskoie."

They hardly finished eating when the phone rang. It was Galina calling from Leningrad.

Liudmila's face turned white and then red. All that Elena and Yefim could hear was: "Oh, really?" and "I don't know if I can make it on time. Hello, hello, hello," and the phone went dead. Liudmila tried to call them back but to no avail.

"What is all about, mother?" asked a worried Elena.

"Your sister is getting married next week to that fellow, Maksim Ziemtsow and they are both coming to live and work in Moscow. She said it is already all arranged."

"So what is the problem, mother?"

"I don't know if we can get to Leningrad in time for the wedding and I don't know the first thing about her fiancée."

"How much did your parents know about papa?"

"You don't understand, those were different times altogether."

"But I understand perfectly. It still boils down to a man and a woman. They want to get married. I trust my sister, she is a very level headed person. Don't worry, everything will be alright."

Yefim felt superfluous during the exchange between mother and daughter, and using the late hour as an excuse, he left for home.

The Metro was empty of people by that time and the trains seemed to be waiting for him. There were a few drunks, full of vodka, sleeping off their bouts.

He opened the door to his flat. Instead of his neighbor Stepanova who usually would wait up for him, this time there were two men wearing leather coats. His long experience living as "bezprizornyi" on Moscow's streets prior to his acceptance to the Orphanage, told him that he was again dealing with "Miltoshkas."

"Yefim Bidnyi, you are under arrest" said the shorter and a bit stockier policeman.

"On what charges "grazhdanie" citizens?" asked Yefim in his best not guilty voice.

"Not that we need a reason, but since you have asked us so politely, we will tell you that it's for stealing 300 grams of gold from your dental laboratory."

"That is a lie! I did not steal anything."

"Tell it to the judge, let's go."

"Can I say goodbye to "babushka" Stepanova?

"I see no harm in it" said the other policeman.

Stepanova must have listed to the entire conversation because she came out from the other room.

"I'm not guilty, remember me to Lubov Moiseevna and Elena."

Stepanova did not say a word she just shook her head. She understood everything. After all, most of her family was arrested at one time or another. Despite Stalin's words that "life was easier and happier," life was not a picnic.

CHAPTER XXX

Something was happening with the Soviet Union—that much was as clear to Max as to everyone else. One couldn't put his finger on it but changes were in the air since the time that Chernenko died and Gorbachov became the General Secretary. His anti-alcoholism program, the so-called, "dry law" was anything but popular with the Russian masses. The same could have been said for "Perestroika" the economic reforms.

A disaster such as Chernobyl on April 26, 1986 could not be covered up. The highly controlled press still had to release unpleasant news, usually buried on the last pages of the newspaper, thus the public did find out that Andrei Sakharow, the father of the Soviet Union's atomic bomb was freed from 7 years of exile in Gorky and that Joseph Brodsky a Jewish "refusenik" living abroad, was awarded the Nobel Prize for literature.

Other news was even more puzzling to the average Ivan. Gorbachov was awarded "Man of the Year" by the American "TIME" magazine. The Soviet Air Force was rattled by a 19 year old German named Mathias Rust, who managed to land his Cessna #172 smack in the middle of Red Square in Moscow, totally undetected. The Air-defense Commander Koldunov was removed from his post. He was lucky because Stalin would never have dealt kindly with him.

The only news that Max's mother found of personal interest was the announcement that Soviet diplomats went to Israel for a first official visit since 1967 and a book by Boris Pasternak titled "Doctor Zhivago that was published in Russia even though "samizdat" copies had been circulating for some time.

While all those changes were affecting the Soviet Union, Max was also anticipating a major change in his life; a marriage to Galina and a possible career in Moscow. Friday, the day of his marriage was upon him.

Max originally planned to pick Galina up in a taxi and they would go together to the offices of Z.A.G.S., but Galina insisted that they meet there at 10:00 A.M.

"You are not supposed to see me until the marriage ceremony" she told him.

"What kind of old wives' tale is that?"

"That is an old Jewish custom, my mother told me so."

"I have never heard of it. Who is coming with you?"

"Only my aunt Fedora. My mother called, she can't come but she will have a reception for us in Moscow."

"Too bad. My mother and my best friend Oleg Kuriatin will come with me."

"Very well then, see you tomorrow at ten o'clock." Galina then hung up the phone.

Oleg Kuriatin's father was a "bolshaia shishka" a big shot in the building industry. He had a car "Zhiguli" which Oleg used most of the time. It was Oleg who suggested that he would drive Max and his mother to the offices of Z.A.G.S. on Lomonosov Street. Max agreed to this and Oleg brought them on Friday about 10 minutes ahead of the appointed hour.

Waiting for Galina, Max registered his and Galina's names and was told that he had about an hour wait until they would be called in. The office of the Civil Registrar seemed to be busy that morning.

Max waited impatiently for Galina's arrival.

"Don't worry Maksim, she will be here. Girls don't like to miss their own weddings," said Max's mother, and she was right. Galina came together with her aunt Fedora some 20 minutes late. Max had never seen Galina looking more radiant or pretty. She wore a two-piece gray suit with a matching hat and she carried a bouquet of flowers. Her smile said it all: "I'm yours, Max!" Natalia Isaakovna greeted Fedora like an old member of the family. They took an instant liking to each other. They soon discovered that they had a lot in common.

The waiting room was full of young and a few not so young people, all smiling and laughing. Max and Galina filled out some additional forms, often joking about some questions.

Max brought the completed forms to the clerk on duty and paid for the marriage license. It was a sum that seemed to be ridiculously low and he said so to the clerk. His response was:

"Getting married is cheap, getting divorced is very expensive, young man."

"In that case, I'll stay married."

Finally they were called into the room where the marriage ceremony was to be performed. Mendelsohn's Wedding March was heard in the background. A middle-aged woman introduced herself as Judge Lena Rumyantsova and addressed the young couple in the best of the Party line. Max and Galina hardly paid attention to those words; they heard them so many times over. She concluded with the words that the Soviet homeland expects much from these well educated people and her tone softened a bit when she added: "I wish you much luck, health, happiness, and a long productive life." Departing further from the official Party line, she said, "I wish above you a peaceful and cloudless sky and to always be surrounded by well wishing friends. And now you may kiss the bride."

Max didn't have to be asked again. He kissed Galina with an extra long kiss drawing laughs from everybody in the room, while Fedora threw confetti at them, much to the disapproval of the judge.

They all left the judge's chambers, only to hug and kiss each other in the waiting room.

"From here we are all going to Vostochny Restaurant on Nevsky Prospect, where I have arranged for a separate banquet room. I have taken the liberty of inviting a few of our friends. They will join us in the restaurant."

"So, let's go and not waste any more time. I'm starving and I bet you that my newly wedded wife is also hungry."

"I don't know if we can squeeze ourselves into my car," said Oleg. "Maybe Galina can sit on Max's lap."

"It will be my pleasure," said Galina. "It's only too bad that the restaurant is so close."

Laughing and joking they reached the Vostochny Restaurant. To Max's total surprise was the presence of Dr. Kostenko and his wife Maria, whom he hardly knew. Natalia Isaakovna also invited two of her colleagues from the hospital, a husband and wife team, both doctors. A few of Max's and Galina's school friends were also invited making it a total of 14 people, all very eager to celebrate the young couple's wedding.

Max and Galina sat at the head of the table and Natalia and Fedora on both sides next to the newlyweds.

The table was set artistically and all kinds of *"zakuski"* awaited the invited guests. Several people made toasts in honor of the young couple and a drink of vodka alternating with champagne and 5 star cognacs "Ararat" followed each toast.

Dr. Kostenko made the longest and the funniest toast. Luckily the waiters started to bring hot food courses, which ended the toast "contest."

From time to time, someone would yell *"gorko"*—"bitter" which was a signal for Max to kiss his bride to make it "sweet" and when one of the invited guests, a friend of Galina by the name of Yaroslav, took out an accordion, the party started in full swing.

The Russian spirit and an accordion are definitely soul mates. Dr. Kostenko, quite tipsy by this time, insisted that each guest had to sing a song. Surprisingly the biggest bravos went to Fedora for her "chastooshki" a medley of peasant ditties.

Towards the end of the feast the manager of the restaurant personally brought in a very large wedding cake, from which Galina and Max took the first slice.

No Russian wedding is a success unless all the guests are drunk, and in this case they nearly succeeded.

Fedora told Galina that she was going away with her friend to some "dacha" emphasizing that it would be for 3 solid days and nights. Natalia made a similar offer but Max decided on Fedora's option, stating that he was more familiar with Galina's bedroom.

On a separate table near the bar there were several gaily-wrapped gifts, which Oleg collected and put into the trunk of his car.

After much hugging and kissing only Galina and Max got into Oleg's car. The rest of the guests and the members of the family made their own arrangements to go back.

Oleg, a faithful friend, brought them home along with the gifts, commenting on a large and very heavy package, raising the curiosity of the newlyweds. Although tired, they decided to open just this one box.

It was Dr. Kostenko's gift, a very large, multi-colored crystal vase made in Czechoslovakia, inside which they found an envelope containing another priceless gift, a Moscow's Residence Permit, made out to Maksim and Galina Ziemtsov.

Their most pressing problem of housing was now magically solved. Upon hearing this, Oleg gave them a bear hug and left the apartment.

Too tired to do anything else, they got undressed and fell asleep in each other's arms as soon as they hit the pillow. They woke up some hours later and made love. This time it was unhurried, befitting the husband and wife they now were.

CHAPTER XXXI

Two detectives expertly whisked Yefim out of his apartment into an unmarked police car waiting downstairs. Behind the steering wheel with the motor running, sat another detective smoking a "Bielomorski" cigarette.

The arresting officers put Yefim between themselves in the back of the car. Yefim tried to engage them in conversation but the police officers weren't in the least bit interested. So much so that one of them said to him:

"Keep your trap shut!" The second one hit Yefim right between his ribs, saying "is that understood?"

The message was clear enough. The mean streets of Moscow taught Yefim to keep away from such men. They could beat him up within an inch of his life without ever leaving a mark on his body.

They brought him to the local Militia Precinct and turned him over to the sergeant on duty, who told him to empty all his pockets, remove his belt, tie and shoelaces, and to put them into a brown, well-used envelope with a string around it.

"Don't worry comrades, I am not about to commit suicide," said Yefim. The same officers who hit Yefim in the car hit him again, but this time much harder.

"Before I leave, let me tell you that we don't like wise guys here and we are not your comrades, you got it?" Or do you want me to remind you once more?"

"It is not necessary, citizen," replied Yefim.

He was brought to a general pen filled with about 20 men of various ages and appearances, a great of majority of whom were obviously under the influence of alcohol. There was no room to sit anywhere. Two fellows whose hands, arms and faces were heavily tattooed occupied the only bench. These men someone told him were "blatnyie," veterans of the Soviet Penal System. Nobody in the room had the courage to wake them up.

Yefim sat on the floor, resting his back against the wall. He hated to get up because his pants were falling off without the belt. Out of boredom he struck up a conversation with a young conscript of the Red Army who was on a drunken binge and freely admitted he was AWOL from his army unit.

"There is nothing to worry about, the MP's will get me today or tomorrow, put me in a brig for 6 months and then discharge me from the Army. That is what I want, my friend. What about you?"

Yefim told him that he was accused of theft, not mentioning that gold was involved. That would have been too dangerous.

"What is the big deal, everybody steals something."

Yefim decided to end this conversation, one never knew who he was talking to, it could be an informer.

While pretending to fall asleep he actually did, despite the noise and screeching of the door leading to the cell.

Some hours later Yefim judged to be well past midnight, he was awakened and led to another room at the end of the building for interrogation. Every time someone approached Yefim was told to stop and turn to face the wall until the other person passed by.

Sitting behind a large desk was a heavily built man about 40 years old, busy reading some files, totally ignoring Yefim's presence. Yefim stood in that uncomfortable position for at least 10 or 15 minutes before the man spoke to him, who first bent the goose-neck table lamp in such a fashion that the strong light fell directly onto Yefim's face, blinding him for a while.

"I'm lieutenant Yakovlev, you'll surely remember my name as long as you live. It says here that you were a "bezprizornyi" and later admitted to Lysenko's Orphanage. Is that correct, Yefim?"

"That is correct Lieutenant."

"Now Yefim, let's cut the bullshit, where did you hide the gold?"

"Lieutenant, I didn't steal that gold, I am innocent of the charges."

"Svoloch"—scoundrel! Are you saying that we in the Soviet Union arrest innocent people? "He got up and hit Yefim across the face with the back of his hand.

"All I said Lieutenant is that I didn't take that gold and I didn't say anything against the Soviet Union."

"Yefim, Yefim, do you think that I was born yesterday?" He sounded almost friendly now.

"Just tell me where that gold is and I will go easy on you, I promise. So what do you say, Yefim?"

"I really would like to oblige you Lieutenant, but I have no idea where that gold is or who might have taken it."

"Well, Yefim, I tried to be nice to you and help you, but perhaps you need a couple of days in the cooler to think about it. Some people suffer from a temporary loss of memory and you might be one of those people."

As he called someone on the intercom his head cast a weird shadow on the wall right next to portraits of Lenin, Dzherzinsky and Andropov. An armed guard entered the room.

"Take this piece of shit to the barber for a haircut, our specialty, and after that take him back to the general pen until he gets his memory back. Out of my sight!"

The guard took him to a room where six barbers were busy at their craft. The floor was full of all kinds of hair. After a while Yefim's hair was there too.

Yefim never knew how cold it got once your hair is gone. He spent 3 days in the general pen before they moved him to a cell where he was the only prisoner. The only benefit was that he had his own bed. He couldn't get much sleep because in the daytime the guards made it impossible. The regulations did not permit it, but at night, at all kinds of hours, he was brought to Lieutenant Yakovlew for interrogation.

Yefim always stuck to the same story no matter how tired or sleepy he was. There was nothing else he could have told him. It was the truth. It was getting harder and harder to resist Yakovlew.

Yefim reached a point that while sleeping at night he could tell by the steps of the guards which one was coming to fetch him.

About 3 weeks after his arrest he received a food parcel from Elena. The bread and sausage was cut up into the smallest pieces possible. The small note attached which the "censura" didn't confiscate, said, among other things: "we're working to help you."

That help came about one month later. A visitor came to see him. It was Major Lebiedev, no longer a lieutenant. The same Lebiedev who brought him to Lysenko originally.

"Lieutenant, no I mean Major, what a surprise. I don't believe my own eyes. What are you doing here?"

"I was about to ask you the same question, Yefim. It was your god-mother, Liubov Moiseevna who asked me to look into your affair and I've done a little investigating on my own. After questioning some of the members of your cooperative, I found that the missing gold was actually misplaced or even better, miscounted. The manager thought that you as a former "bezprizornyi" stole it and falsely accused you of theft. He apologized and withdrew the complaint. As a result, you are free to go. The best I am keeping for last. The members of the cooperative decided to fire the manager and appoint you as their manager, just to make up for the injustice done to you. So let's pick up your stuff."

Yefim did not have to be asked twice. Thanks to the presence of Major Lebiedev the famous Russian bureaucracy was reduced to an hour and Yefim left the building breathing fresh air.

Major Lebiedev dropped Yefim right in front of his building. "Major" said Yefim, I will never forget your kindness. Someday I'll repay it, God willing."

"Never mind Yefim, just take care of yourself. If you keep mentioning God's name you may make a believer out of me. The Party would not like that."

Before Yefim entered the house he swore that he would do anything to leave the Soviet Union and start a life somewhere else.

"Babushka" Stepanova crossed herself several times when she opened the door and saw Yefim.

"*Gospodi Bozhe,*" my God, it is you, Yefim!" She kissed and hugged him. All his personal items were meticulously washed and ironed. She again had someone to look after.

Yefim took a long, hot bath to get rid of the accumulated filth and lice. He changed into fresh clothing and checked his winter jacket. The gold star squeezed into a piece of bread was still there. He told Stepanova that he was going to visit Elena and her mother.

The way they received him left no doubt that Elena loved him. He was sure that her mother looked upon him like he was her own son. If he weren't yet he would be in the very near future. That is how everyone felt.

CHAPTER XXXII

It must have been a combination of menopause and depression caused by losing her job, synonymous with a loss of prestige that caused Liudmila Shtern to wallow in self-pity.

A war widow for some time now, she dedicated her life to the upbringing of her daughters and to her job. The first task she accomplished with excellent results.

Elena and Galina received the very best education available in the Soviet Union and now they were on the verge of getting married to what seemed to be very nice fellows.

The lack of a job, plus the anticipation of the empty nest syndrome was something that Liudmila wasn't looking forward to. At age 50 she was still a fairly attractive woman, but in post war Moscow a single man was a rarity. Men her age had the pick of the crop of women half her age. The very few available elderly men filled her with disgust. Most of them were veterans, some so partially wounded or disabled that they surely were not for her. She was not about to become anyone's nurse.

Through the grapevine she found out that more and more of Moscow's Jews were applying for exit visas. It didn't matter where as long as it was out of the "Worker's Paradise."

Liudmila felt completely Russofied, brought up in a Russian milieu; she didn't know any Yiddish, had never entered a synagogue or felt a personal connection to the Jewish people or its history. Instead she cultivated a profound devotion to the Russian language and literature, memorizing entire contents of books by Chechov, Gogol, Dostoyevsky, Pushkin and most revolutionary writers such as Mayakovsky, Anna Akhmatova, and Mikhail Zoschenko. Would it not be for the fact that her internal country passport defined her nationality as *"Yevrei,"* Jewish, she would have gladly remained Russian.

And where could she go with her profession? What country needed a former Soviet prosecutor who spoke mainly Russian? Israel, where many Soviet Jews went was not for her. She did not like Middle Eastern climates, she didn't know the language, and how could she possibly live without snow in the winter? Was the United States a possibility? She read quite a bit about the country and its people from legal and not so legal sources. No, she wasn't crazy about Americans. They were so conceited, so "uncultured" and so "materialistic." Someone had offered her the definition of an educated American as one who knew what P.C.B. stood for, knew who Vermeer was and read at least two Shakespearean plays, one of which was "Romeo" and the other "Juliet." The States were not for her; too crowded, too pushy, too loud, too many blacks.

On the other hand, Canada might be much closer to her heart; even the climate was closer to that of Mother Russia. The country itself was more European and the French language was commonly used and could come in handy since she spoke some French that she had learned in school.

One of these days she would have to stop at OVIR's office to see Ella Kozakova to get additional information and pick up application forms.

The telephone rang, interrupting her thoughts further. It was her sister Liubov:

"Liudmila, I just got a call from Stepanova, Yefim's landlady. She told me that Yefim was arrested today for stealing gold from the Dental Laboratory."

"It is hard to believe, he seems to be such a nice young man. Elena will be heartbroken."

"I don't believe it either, I watched him grow up. I feel that he is innocent. He didn't do it, someone else did and pinned in on him."

"So what are you going to do about it?"

"I have a friend in the Militia, a certain Major Lebiedev, he owes me a favor or two. I will have him look into it."

"I can also help. I know a few lawyers who could be of help when it comes to trial."

"Maybe it was a mistake, but you and I know that mistakes do not happen in the Soviet Union."

"Liubov, I forgot to tell you the big news. Galina is getting married this week and she and her husband Maxim are coming to Moscow, since the Party transferred him to be the assistant curator at the Ostankino Museum."

"Congratulations Liudmila! Are they going to live with you?"

"*Bozhe schrani*," no, God forbid. The Party arranged for an apartment not far from us."

"You are a lucky woman, you'll have your kids near you."

"You are so right, come to think of" it replied Liedmila.

"Stay in touch."

"Goodbye Liubov, I hear someone coming in. Its Elena most likely."

It was Elena with her smiling face so full of self-confidence.

"How was your day Elena?"

"The usual. Practice, practice and more practice. These people I work with are perfectionist, real slave drivers. Nothing escapes them, no wonder they are the best in the world."

"Can I make you a cup of tea? I need to talk to you, Elena."

"Mom, that sounds serious. Is everything alright?"

"Well, yes and no," said Liudmila setting up the tea kettle. "Aunt Liubov called this afternoon just before you came in with the news of Yefim's arrest. He is charged with theft for stealing gold from the Laboratory where he worked."

"Mom, I don't believe it, not Yefim!"

"Neither do I. Remember that here in the Soviet Union everyone is guilty until proven innocent."

"What are we going to do about it mom?"

"We won't be able to speak with him for the first few days or even weeks. Liubov knows someone at the Militia who will look into the case and I will contact a criminal lawyer that I have worked with previously."

"Mom when I hear about arrests I wish that we would all leave Russia."

"Be careful what you wish for, because your wish may be granted. I also have some very good news for you. Your sister is getting married and she and her future husband are coming to Moscow to live and work."

"Where will they live? With us? It would be very tight."

"Don't worry, Elena. Since the Party is moving them they have also arranged for an apartment not very far from us."

"That is great, and I will have my sister nearby. Are we going to the wedding?"

"Regretfully, no. They will be here within a week or 10 days. We'll prepare a nice reception party."

"Mom, what shall I get them as a present?"

"Wait and see. Once they get settled you will have a better picture of what they will need."

"You're right mom."

"Let me call the lawyer I told you about to see if he can see me tomorrow. Maybe I'll get to see Kozakova at the OVIR. Now if you will excuse me, I'll prepare dinner for the two of us."

"Mom, I brought home "samizdat" copies of "Iskhod" (Exodus) by Leon Uris and Edward Kuznietsov's "Prison Diaries," very interesting material."

"I'm sure it is, but it is also very dangerous. I strongly suggest you don't advertise it among your friends or co-workers, and be very careful with whom you speak on that subject. It is one thing is to leave Russia for the West, something else entirely is to be sent North or far East of Russia."

"I do know what you are talking about and promise to be careful."

"You better be Elena, and also remember to speak slow and think fast."

CHAPTER XXXIII

The nurse handed Dr. Natalia Isaacovna a list of names of sick children waiting at the General Admission room.

"Today we seem to have quite a few patients. What has happened? Are there any children that need immediate attention?"

"Yes. Comrade doctor, a few of them, but I think the worst is that 11-year-old girl, Yulia Kagan, who was treated by "feldsher" Pietrov, of dubious reputation. The girl has shortness of breath and is coughing and wheezing rather badly."

"Well, nurse, bring her right in."

"She is with her grandfather and is afraid to leave him even for a moment."

A few minutes later a skinny, scared girl with long blond braids and big eyes walked in holding on to the hands of her grandfather.

"Yulia, come here my child. Don't be afraid, I won't do you any harm. Your grandfather is here with you. I just want to listen to your heart and lungs. It won't hurt at all, I promise."

Using her stethoscope on Yulia's body, Natalia did not have any doubts that the poor girl had asthma and the wheezing sound was hard to listen to.

She asked the grandfather what medications the girl was taking.

"Just aspirins, comrade doctor, just aspirins," replied the grandfather who was a tall and burly man wearing thick eyeglasses.

Based upon her extensive experience working with children, Natalia was sure that she had in front of her a case of allergic asthma. She applied an anti-histamine spray and gave the grandfather Cortisone tablet to last for 5 days.

"Where are Yulia's parents?" Natalia asked the grandfather.

"They are both working. Since I'm a pensioner I brought Yulia here."

His Russian was good but had the intonation of "zapadnik," people of her home region. She was much too busy that day to get into a discussion with Yulia's grandfather.

"I want you to stop giving Yulia aspirins and use only the tablets I gave you, is that clear?" I would also like to see Yulia in 5 days. Either you or any one of her parents should come with her on that day."

"Most likely it will be me, comrade doctor."

"Suit yourself. Nurse! Next patient please."

It was a tough day for Natalia. She managed to examine some very neglected and abused children and there were a few cases of T.B. that required special handling.

On the appointed day, Yulia and her grandfather came to the clinic carrying a bouquet of flowers for Dr. Natalia. Amazingly enough the child looked much better. Her cough and wheezing subsided almost completely. Natalia's diagnosis was correct. Yulia's asthma was caused by her allergy to aspirins.

Dr.Natalia re-examined the child and was very pleased with the progress made in such a short time. Just to be sure, she prescribed the anti-histamine tablets for another 10 days.

"Yulia, in ten more days you will be just fine."

"Thank you very much comrade doctor for making me feel better," said Yulia.

"You are welcome my child and thank you for the lovely flowers."

"And I thank you for helping my granddaughter. Comrade, I believe that I know you.

Aren't you Natalia Feldstein from Vilno?"

"Yes I am, but who are you? I don't remember you at all."

"I'm Marcel Liebeskind. You were my classmate at Epstein-Speiser Gimnazium on Archangielska Street #11 between Wiwulski and Szeptycki Street He then proceeded to remove his thick eyeglasses. Natalia was in shock because she recognized the once handsomest boy at school with whom all the girls were in love, likening him to Tyrone Power, the famous movie star.

"This is me, so many years later. At first I attended the Tushiya School on Chopin Street #3 not far from the railroad station, and then transferred to your school. I must confess that I had a terrible crush on you, Natalia." Without realizing it, they had begun to speak in Yiddish and Polish, languages of their youth.

"No Marcel, I didn't know. I thought that you were so stuck up because all the girls were after you."

"Just the opposite, I was very shy as a young man."

"Do you remember any of our teachers?"

"Yes, I do. Maybe not all of them, but surely most of them. Let me see, Fassell taught us mathematics, Adler Latin, Meltzer German, Morgenstern Polish."

"It is amazing how well you remember them. Did you ever play "hooky" on the Lutheran Cemetery on Mala Pohulanka Street right next to Wielka Pohulanka?"

"No, never. I was too scared to do it."

"More important Marcel, what brought you to Leningrad?"

"It's a long story, do you have the time Natalia?"

"Today, we are not so busy, I can spare a few minutes."

"When the Germans invaded Vilno in 1941 I ran away to the forest and joined the partisans and fought in their ranks till the Russians liberated us. One of the Russian officers accused me of collaborating with the Germans. I was so upset that I struck him in the face. That cost me 10 years of my life. The NKVD sent me up north. In Kolyma I met my future wife Evgenia. We were released about the same time and decided to get married. We have one son Boris and Yulia is his only child."

"Where is your wife now?"

"Unfortunately she died about 4 years ago of T.B. which she contracted at the Gulag. What about you Natalia?"

"I got married to a Russian officer just as the war broke out and ran away deep into Russia. My husband was killed near Berlin in April of 1945. I do have a married son and as you see I am working as a doctor at this clinic. What about you, Marcel?"

"I worked as a mechanical engineer for a number years, finally retired and am living with my son. I am very lonely, spending most of my time at the libraries waiting for my papers to migrate to Israel. You might remember my older brother Chaim who went to Palestine in 1938. Somebody told me that he was killed while serving with the Jewish Brigade. Only years later I found out it was someone else by the same name. I also adopted my mother's last name, Kagan, and that caused some additional delay in the time it took to find each other. You know life is like an onion, many layers and you cry occasionally. My dream is to reach Eretz Israel, but it isn't that easy. I recall Yevtushenko's poem "The Heirs of Stalin:"

> To double
> To triple
> The Guard at this slab
> So that Stalin may not rise,
> And with Stalin
> The past . . . .
> We rooted him
> Out of the Mausoleum
> But how root Stalin
> Out of Stalin's heirs?

"Marcel, I would like to continue our conversation but I have patients to attend to. Why don't you come to my house tomorrow for dinner let's say around 6 o'clock? Here is my address and we can talk about old times. I still have a bunch of photographs from school. I think you are among them."

"You are so lucky, Natalia, I don't have a solitary picture of my family. Everything was taken away from me. I just have memories of better times. I'll be more than glad to come and thank you again for Yulia."

"Grandfather, I can say thank you myself. I'm a big girl. *Spasibo*, doctor and *Do Svidania*."

"*Do Svidania*," Yulia, you are a sweet girl.

CHAPTER XXXIV

"Are you Leslie Schiff?" This question combined with a shake of his arm woke Leslie up from a deep and uneasy sleep. For a second he couldn't recall how he ever got to this place, but the sight of a man in a white lab coat quickly brought him into reality.

"Yes I am. What is happening with my wife?" he asked.

"She was moved to an I.C.U., the Intensive Care Unit."

"I know what I.C.U. stands for," said Leslie, slightly irritated. "On whose orders and on what basis was she moved?" "I'm her husband, Dr. Schiff."

"Are you a physician?"

"No, I'm a D.D.S."

"Well, sir, it was on Dr. Goldstein's orders. He felt that your wife needed additional care. By the way, I'm Dr. Mohan Mehta."

It certainly wasn't Leslie's imagination but Dr. Mehta's tone of voice became more polite after Leslie mentioned his title. He didn't care much for the people from India or Pakistan, either as patients or as professionals with whom he came in contact. It seemed to Leslie that Hindus who came from the lower castes always tried to sound more important than those who achieved some position of power in the States. He found them impossible to deal with, but now, surely wasn't the right time to discuss this subject.

"Dr. Mehta, what was the real reason my wife was moved to the I.C.U?"

"Dr. Schiff, your wife developed pleural effusion and Dr. Goldstein felt that her needs would be better addressed in the I.C.U. Would you like to see her now?"

"Yes, Dr. Mehta, I would."

"Then follow me, please."

They walked to the end of the corridor and took the elevator to the 18th floor. The doors to the unit were closed. One could enter it by lifting the telephone receiver and ask to be admitted, or as Dr. Mehta did, swipe an I.D. card through the door slot.

Dr. Mehta stopped shortly at the nurses' station located in the middle of the unit and talked briefly to a very tall, blonde nurse.

"I just checked with the head nurse. On doctor's orders, your wife received a blood transfusion because as I understand it, she lost a lot of blood during the accident. She is in room #1818 on the other side of this station."

After taking a few more steps, they entered Alice's room. She was all alone in a big, sunny room looking very pale, but her smile upon seeing Leslie, was the same broad smile that caused Leslie to fall in love with her so many years ago.

Alice was connected to the main monitor by many different tubes that were checking her blood pressure and temperature. The telemetry's electrodes attached to her chest were giving instant information to the nurses at the station. The I.V. tubes were providing her needed nourishment, drip by drip. Alice looked wide-awake and coherent, even if a bit too pale.

"How are you sweetheart? It's so good to see you Alice."

"I'm very cold, but otherwise fine."

Leslie looked around and found another blanket and covered her up.

"Is this any better?" asked Leslie.

"Just a bit, I'm still cold."

Dr. Mehta, who listened to the conversation, stopped a passing Filipino nurse and asked her to bring another blanket. The air-conditioning was blowing directly at Alice's head. By moving her bed just another two feet out of its direct range, the situation improved immediately.

"How is it now, Alice?"

"It is much better. Leslie, you are my savior in more ways than one."

While this conversation was taking place Dr. Mehta was checking all the monitors.

"Dr. Schiff, your wife is doing very nicely. You can stay here as long as you like, but please don't tire her out, she needs her rest, and just by looking at you, I can see that you could use some rest as well."

"Doctor, we won't tire her unnecessarily. Thank you for your attention."

"Alice, do you realize that you are in a very lucky room. This room number is 1818. In Hebrew, #18 symbolizes "Chai"—life. #1818 is double life for you and me. I am taking it as a good omen."

"Since when have you become so superstitious?"

"I'm not, I believe in good signs only. I'm so sorry Alice that I have been acting like a jerk lately. Will you forgive me?"

"I think that we both acted like jerks. Life is too short; so let's make the most of it. You, Leslie are my entire life."

"Let's not forget our son Jeff."

"How can we. How is he taking it?"

"He should be here soon."

Dr. Mehta walked into the room again.

"There is a young fellow here by the name of Dr. Schiff. Is that your son?"

"Indeed he is, can he come in?"

"Yes, we'll let him in but please, not too long. We don't allow two visitors at the same time. You'll be getting me into hot water, as we have strict rules here with no exceptions. I'll bring him in myself."

"Thank you, Dr. Mehta, we understand."

Jeoffrey walked in carrying a very large bouquet of flowers. He kissed his mother and embraced Leslie.

"How are you, mom?"

"I'm fine Jeff, especially when your father is with me. I'll make it. We, as a family will make it."

"No question about it, Mrs. Schiff. As I've said before to your husband, you are looking good. Tomorrow I'll have you moved to a private room for a few days and after that you will be able to go home, and follow through with rehab. And please, no flowers in the I.C.U!"

Dr. Winston Goldstein, whose yarmulke on his head was even smaller this time than when they met the first time, spoke those words. The bobby pin holding it was covering half the yarmulke. As young as he looked, there was a certain authority about him, and one had the feeling that the man knew his craft. Leslie didn't have any doubts about Dr. Goldstein. That man was a dedicated physician with the quiet authority of a man who knew his skill.

CHAPTER XXXV

"Galina, are you all packed?" asked Maksim over the phone. Tomorrow morning my friend Andrey Moroz will be picking me and my luggage up at 8 o'clock and we should be at your place about an hour later. Will you be ready?"

"I should be. Basically I am all packed. I have my books, records, clothing, bedding and even some additional pots and pans that aunt Fedora gave me. But where are we going to put all our stuff?"

"Don't worry, Andrey has a truck."

"Very well then, see you in the morning, my darling." She hung up the phone.

"Maksim, it looks like you are finally leaving. I will miss you terribly. I knew that the time would come when another woman would take you away from me, Galina is that woman. I do hope that you will call and write often and if possible, will come back to Leningrad. It will be very lonely without you. I won't have a man in the house to fuss over."

"Don't worry, mother, I will be in touch with you and who knows, maybe you'll come and join us in Moscow."

"Everything is possible. I want to work for another few years before I retire. I'll sit in a park and feed the pigeons. Oh, Maksim, I forgot to tell you that a few days ago a man walked into my office with his sick granddaughter and can you imagine, we knew each other way back in Vilno? All the girls in the class, including your mother, were in love with him. His name is Marcel Liebeskind. That evening you spent with Galina, Marcel came over and we had supper and reminisced about the old carefree days in Vilno. It was very nostalgic and we both cried."

"Do you intend to see him again?"

"Of course, we were very good friends once upon a time." By the way, he is a widower."

"You should see him, by all means. You won't be so lonely."

"His brother is going to send him all the papers for migrating to Israel."

"Would you like to go there too, Mother?"

"I haven't thought about it. What would I do in Israel? No, I would rather stay here in Leningrad and wait for my grandchildren."

"Mother, you are impossible. Let me enjoy my life and hopefully, my career."

"I was just kidding. Is there anything else that you need?"

"No, thank you. I'm all set. See you in the morning. Good night, mother."

"Good night, Maksim, sweet dreams."

Good old Andriusha showed up in the morning with a truck that belonged to the cooperative where Andrey was employed as a chief Supply Officer.

"What do I see—books, and more books? What do you have in mind? To open another library in Moscow?"

"I have other things besides books. Be a good sport and help me carry everything down."

"Well, somebody must help the newlyweds. It might as well be me. So, let's go."

It took just a few minutes to load the truck with Maksim's worldly possessions.

"Andriusha, please stay with the truck, I want to go upstairs to say goodbye to my mother."

"All right, but don't be too long."

Saying goodbye to his mother was very difficult. She was sobbing quietly.

"Mom, everything will be fine, don't worry so much. We are only going to Moscow. I will be in touch all the time. I have always loved you and always will."

"Before you go, please sit down on the bed for a minute or two."

"Mom, that is an old superstition."

"So what, just do it for me."

He sat on the bed impatiently, wondering how his mother, a doctor of medicine, could be so superstitious. Maybe she knew something that he didn't know.

"Do svidania mama, I'll call you as soon as I arrive."

"Go and don't turn around."

Andrey was already honking his horn.

"Keep your shirt on, I'm coming."

A similar scene was being repeated at Galina's household but with fewer tears.

Once outside the city limits, Andrey was driving along highway #10. It was a road leading to Moscow via the city of Novgorod and Kalinin. The "ORUD" Safety Traffic Authority's Militia stopped them briefly.

Max showed the officer his papers. When questioned about the cargo of the truck, Andrey mentioned that the two passengers were newlyweds, which in turn drew a remark from the officer:

"It is a game about sex and the marriage is just a punishment."

It was a long and tiring trip. They made several pit stops for fuel for which Andrey insisted on paying.

"As long as the gas is 16 kopecks per liter and oil is 37 kopecks, I'll pay. It is my wedding present to you both."

"Andriusha, you are a good friend. Thank you."

They finally reached their destination on First Brestkaia Street in the vicinity of Tishinkiy Rynok, hardly 15 blocks from Galina's mother's residence Galina's and Max's future apartment was located in a lovely 6-story building. One of the better Stalin style houses.

The concierge, Viktoria Borovkina expected their arrival and took them to their apartment on the 4th floor. Whoever lived there before left the apartment in very good condition. The high ceilings had some design painted on them and there was plenty of closet space, which Galina noticed immediately. The apartment itself consisted of one bedroom, living room, bathroom and a large kitchen. The apartment's balcony faced the street.

"Why don't you young people bring up your stuff? Later on I will introduce you to your next-door neighbor. Down in the basement I have a table and four chairs which one of the tenants would like to sell. It's pretty new as a matter of fact and you can use it in the meantime. The price is very reasonable. I'll also throw in a mattress so you won't have to sleep on the floor."

"We'll take it comrade Borovkina. I'll have my wife look at it while we bring up our belongings."

To accomplish this, Maksim and Andrey made several trips to the parked truck. At the same time Galina, with the help of the concierge, brought up the table and chairs.

"Max, the mattress is too heavy for us, could you and Andrey bring it up?"

"No problem, Galina, that is what I am here for," said Andrey smiling.

The mattress was old but in satisfactory condition. They would use it temporarily until they could obtain a new one.

Someone knocked at the door and Galina went to open it.

It was an old, gray haired lady holding a tray on which a loaf of bread and saltshaker was visible. It was an ancient Russian custom to greet newcomers in such a manner.

"This is your next door neighbor whom I wanted to introduce you to," announced Viktoria Borovkina. "Her name is Lydia Ivanovna Charkovskaia."

"Pleased to meet you. We are Galina and Maksim Ziemtsov. Oh, my God, it's an honor indeed. Max, this lady is a living legend. She is the former prima ballerina of Marinski Imperator Theatre of Saint Petersburg. She actually danced for Tsar Nicholas II."

"My children, that was many years ago, now I am just an old lady."

"Lydia Ivanovna, we apologize for not inviting you to have tea with us, but our samovar is not unpacked yet."

"That is why I am here. I want to invite you to my place for tea. It will be nice to talk to young and cultured people."

"Thank you very much for your offer but we have a lot to do. We still have to unpack and get ready for bed. Maybe tomorrow, if the offer still stands."

"Yes it does. I wish you much luck, *do svidania.*"

"I'll also say, *do svidania.* I also have to leave. Stay well, lovers," said Andrey.

"Thank you for your help, Andriusha." Galina gave him a big kiss and Max shook his hand. "Have a good trip back."

They unpacked as much as they could. Galina found a bed sheet and a blanket, which she put on the newly acquired mattress.

Exhausted, they fell asleep in each other's arms, happy to be in Moscow and aware that the next day Max was due to report at Ostankino Museum and Galina would have a chance to visit her mother. Both were looking forward to the next day.

CHAPTER XXXVI

It was a close call for Yefim, much too close for comfort. He considered himself very lucky to be able to escape the clutches of the Militia in such a short time.

Growing up in a society whose motto was "*blat vyshe narkoma*" or "pull" is more important than a National Commissar, Yefim didn't have any doubts that it was Major Lebiedev who got him out of jail. One of these days Yefim would have to reciprocate one way or another. The most important thing was that he was free.

Free to see his Elena and free to work at the Dental Laboratory where he was now immensely pleased with his new position of "manager." He enjoyed the work and the responsibility that went with it. He developed a friendship with one of the new workers recently transferred from another major Laboratory, a fellow by the name of Ghenady Feldman, whose dental expertise was well known and appreciated.

As the time passed, Ghenady and Yefim became close friends. Yefim found out that Ghenady was the nephew of Alexander Feldman, the famous Jewish activist of Kiev who got himself in trouble with the Authorities on several occasions. From Ghenady, Yefim also found out about the tactics the Soviet regime used, trying to discourage Jews from applying for exit visas.

"Yes, Yefim, a growing number of Jews including many who are holding responsible positions in scientific fields are refused permission to emigrate. At the same time they are being denied employment in their professions. OVIR never gives you a real explanation for the refusal. Usually they will say the reason for the rejection is "state security," "army service some 10 or 15 years go," "departure inexpedient," or "your mother's or father's secret work" or even "not enough close relatives in Israel." My uncle spent 3.5

years in jail and finally in 1977 he reached Israel, and that is the place where I also want to go.

Yefim envied Ghenady who seemed to know what he wanted out of life.

The idea of leaving the USSR appealed to Yefim, but he didn't have a definite idea as to what country to emigrate to. Israel, the USA, Canada or Australia were the same to him, as long as Elena went along.

In the meantime, Elena was making steady progress in her professional life, getting more recognition as a musician. Her confidence in her own abilities grew and she wasn't about to discard her achievements and leave "Mother Russia" for some unknown land. Besides, she liked to quote the Marquis de Custine who visited Russia in 1839 and said: "The more I see Russia, the more I agree with the Emperor when he forbids Russians to travel and makes access to his own country difficult for foreigners."

On the other hand, she was truly happy when Yefim was released from jail and it was she who suggested to Yefim a few days later that they sleep together.

Caught by surprise Yefim agreed. As they started to enjoy each other more and more, Elena would spend her nights in Yefim's room.

In the beginning Elena's mother questioned the wisdom of the relationship requesting that Elena inform her on evenings that she would not be home and insisted that Elena be careful because an unwanted pregnancy would complicate their lives.

"Don't worry mother, Yefim will marry me anytime I say so."

Liudmila Moiseevna Shtern gave her a look which Elena recognized as "what do these young people know of life?"

"Elena, are you still in competition with your sister? Just because she got married doesn't mean that you have to get pregnant. You won't be the first girl whose boyfriend knocked her up and left her to get an abortion."

"No, mother, I don't mean to offend you either. I just want you to know that I'll be careful. However, there is another problem. Yefim has a friend at work who constantly pumps his head with ideas of emigrating. Personally, I am not too keen on it. What do you think, mother?"

"As long as you have brought up that subject, I must tell you that I'm toying with the same idea. I also want to do something with the rest of my life. It is no secret any longer that I was kicked out of my job for being Jewish. Maybe the time has come for the Jews to leave this country of "Black 100" and move to our ancient motherland or maybe to the New World. I don't foresee any problem for you young people. With your education and good professions you will get adjusted easily in any country and they will be glad to have you, but me? That is another case altogether. Do you think I can get a man at my age? Maybe I'll just become a nanny to my grandchildren, that is if you'll take me with you?"

"Mother, don't worry. You'll always have a home with us. I'm sure that I am speaking for my sister as well."

"Thank you my child for the offer. It is better than jumping off the Krimsky Bridge."

"Mother, let's not get too dramatic either. Sorry I have to rush off, I promised Yefim I would spend the evening with him. Don't wait for me; I just need to take a few items with me and off I go. I promise you, mother, everything will be fine. Do trust me, please!"

"What choice do I have? Of course I trust you, just be careful."

"I'll do that, mother, I love you."

"And I 'll listen to the radio, my favorite singer, Iosif Davidovich Kobzon is giving a concert. I love his voice. Did you know that he is Jewish?"

There was no answer. Elena had already left the room.

CHAPTER XXXVII

Today was to be a big day for Maksim, because today he was starting his new job at the Ostankino Museum.

He made sure to get up early enough to get dressed in his best suit, have breakfast with Galina and leave himself enough time for a trip on Moscow's Metro to reach the Museum by 8:30 A.M.

It took him a few minutes to get to the crowded "Bieloruska-Radialna" Station to catch a train minutes later. He watched the stops as the train sped ahead. There was the First Mayakovska, 2nd Gorkovskaia, Ploshchad Sverdlova, and at Novokuznitskaia he changed trains for the Kolezhnikovo-Ruzhskaia linia and got off at its next stop. He reached his destination with time to spare.

Although Max had seen the Museum years ago, he was still very much impressed by the former palace of the wealthy Count Pyotr Sheremetyev and the architecture of Pavel Argunov.

The Ostankino Museum would open to the public at 10:00 A.M. but the employees' entrance located on the side street was in full use. The guard at the door was informed to expect Maxsim Ziemtsow who was politely directed to the main office located on the 3rd floor.

The office manager, a woman in her forties introduced herself as Tamara Panfilov and greeted him warmly: "Good morning Comrade Ziemtsow, welcome to Ostankino. Professor Vasiliev is tied up in a conference that may last up to a couple of hours. I was told to make you comfortable, and if you wish to walk around you are welcome to do so. If you need any help, just get a hold of me."

Upon seeing his disappointed look, Tamara quickly added: "Would you like a cup of tea?"

"*Spasibo,* I just had breakfast. If you don't mind, I'll just walk around."

"Go right ahead, we'll see you later."

Located on the lower floor were the most elegant woodcarvings. The palace halls were filled with valuable paintings. He passed the hall that was used as a theatre and walked into a room where twelve paintings by Paul Gauguin were displayed. The paintings belonged to his Tahitian period, painted in the tropics and extolling a world untouched by civilization. The contours of the figures and objects in local colors lay on the canvasses sometimes fluid and sometimes smooth, but always exquisitely delicate.

Max walked over to another room and was stopped by a guard. Max told him: "I'll be working with Professor Vasiliev." "No problem, comrade" was the guard's reply.

While walking into the next room he felt the guard's eyes upon him. The room housed the works of Henri Matisse, mostly his 1900-1913 period. As one of the leading French artists his paintings were striking in their decorative quality and saturated colors. The radiant colorfulness of his canvases gave out a feeling of gaiety and happiness.

"How do you like Matisse?" That question came from a medium sized elderly man, dressed in a typical Russian peasant outfit, including high boots of soft leather.

"When I look at these old masters I am transported into another world altogether," answered Max.

"Don't we all. By the way, I am Vasiliev and you must be Ziemtsov."

Hearing that, Max turned to face him. It was totally unexpected that Professor Vasiliev himself came to see him.

"Forgive me Professor Vasiliev. I lost track of the time."

"No, Ziemtsov, it was I who got through early. Come, we'll walk over to my office for a chat."

"I am at your service Professor Vasiliev."

"I was watching you looking at the paintings. You had the same look on your face as the village women looking at the ancient church icons. I can tell that you like art. Oh, here is my office, do come in Maksim."

"After you, Professor Vasiliev."

"I see that you have good manners too. After all, you're a Leningrader and I do like Leningraders. Will you have some tea with me? I'll ask Tamara to bring us two glasses."

"Thank you kindly Professor." He rang up Tamara who brought in two glasses of strong tea and a miniature dish of strawberry jam.

"Maksim, you and I are going to have a very frank discussion. I don't care if you report the subject of our conversation to the Party. However, if you are smart, you'll keep it to yourself. You see my young friend; I love being a curator of this museum and do you know why? My father was the curator before me and do you know why the Party keeps me here? Simply because I am the best man for the job. I know and love every item in this place. I can tell the background and history of every one of its 100,000 items. I do want to preserve the quality of this Museum for centuries to come for the benefit of the noble Russian people. Can you understand that Maksim?"

"I think I can."

"I knew that sooner or later the party would send someone to spy on me but I'm not afraid of them at all. You see Maksim, I've recently been diagnosed with lung cancer and the doctors are giving me a year or two to live. When I was told that some young Turk by the name of Ziemtsov was coming to replace me, I did a little research of my own. Have a look at this photograph and tell me what you see."

"Two Red Army officer cadets."

"Have another look, a closer look. Use this magnifying glass as the photo is old but still visible and identifiable."

Max was shocked to recognize his own father and the other young man who very much resembled Professor Vasiliev.

"Yes, Maksim, your father and I were very close. It was I who later wrote poems to your mother in your father's name. So do you understand now where you and I stand?" I'll show you and teach you all there is to know on how to run a Museum, but you better love this job more than your own wife. Is that clear so far? We shall start with the Administration. I'll have Tamara introduce you to every member of our organization. The second lesson and very important one is about the security of this place. You must always keep in mind that we have paintings worth many millions of dollars or Swiss Francs—paintings that people would kill for. Do I make myself clear?"

"Yes, Comrade Professor Vasiliev. Perfectly clear."

"Please call me Professor. The word comrade irritates me to no end. Today the Museum will close at 5:00 P.M. only to reopen at 6:00 P.M. to welcome a delegation from the Swiss Embassy and their guests. There also will be a special security detail of M.V.D. agents acting as waiters or waitresses because we will be serving drinks and Caviar, among other things. Of course you are invited. I also understand that you got married recently. Congratulations are due. If you can get in touch with your wife, she is most welcome to come. I would like to meet her too."

"I'm sorry, but we don't have a phone installed as yet."

"Too bad, maybe next time. I have to run. We seem to have some problems with the Maintenance Department. Let me turn you over to Tamara, she will keep you busy all right."

And keep him busy she did. She introduced him to every department including the Department of Restoration.

"This department is extremely important because here we restore many old and neglected items that come our way. You'll have to spend a lot of time in here to learn the various ways and techniques used in restoration."

Tamara was an exciting woman who loved her job and was always full of enthusiasm. Maksim had a feeling that the two of them would work in harmony. The hours seemed to fly. In the late afternoon Maksim received a telephone call at the office from Galina:

"I'm calling to find out how your day is going?"

"Everything is fine, where are you now?"

"I'm calling from a public phone in your general area."

"Wait a minute." He turned to Professor Vasiliev who just walked into the office.

"Professor, I have my wife on the line. Could she come here this evening?"

"Absolutely, invite her to the party. I'll leave word with the guards to let her in."

"Galina, you have just been invited to a party at the Museum for foreign guests. Please come here before 6:00 o'clock. Can you make it?"

Of course, Max. I will be happy to. Let me fix myself up a bit and I will see you later."

She hung up as the coin dropped in the box.

Shortly after a team of M.V.D. agents dressed as waiters and waitresses arrived tp set up tables, that were soon laden with hors d'oeuvres, wines and vodka on ice. By 5:45 P.M. they were ready to receive guests, most of whom arrived shortly after 6:00 P.M. Galina was among them.

Professor Kiryl Vasiliev now dressed in an elegant double-breasted suit was there to welcome them.

The guests, as Max was told, were members of the Swiss Embassy and several businessmen of various nationalities currently visiting Moscow, plus the ever present representatives of major Swiss newspapers.

Leading that group was the Cultural Attaché of the Swiss Consulate, Dr. Conrad von Hoetzendorf, a tall man in his late twenties or early thirties. The conversation was held mainly in Schweitzerdeutsch and French.

Max became cognizant of the fact that Professor Vasiliev was fluent in French. A harpist located discreetly in the corner of the hall played a medley of classical arias. The waiters circulated among the guests offering drinks. It seemed that the ladies preferred wines and the gentlemen various flavored vodkas.

Max was introduced briefly as the new assistant curator. He gave everyone a shy smile and proceeded to the table to get some food he suddenly realizing that with the exception of the glass of tea that Tamara gave him that morning, he had not partaken of any food at all.

As he approached the decorated bowl containing appealing *pielmeni*, so did Dr. Conrad von Hoetzendorf, reaching for the same dish.

Dr. Conrad asked the waiter: *est-ce qu'il y a de la viande dedans?*—Is there any meat in it?" The waiter, without any hesitation, answered in excellent French: "Yes, a little, just enough to give it a special taste."

Seeing Maksim's surprised look, Dr. Conrad said to Maksim: "I suppose he is your average Russian waiter." What surprised Maksim even more was the quality of Dr. Conrad's Russian language.

Maksim could not possibly foresee how that chance encounter would forever change his and Galina's lives.

CHAPTER XXXVIII

There are stages in life's journey when people realize more through instinct than by reason, that suddenly great blessings are preordained by superior powers.

That is how Dr. Natalia Isaakovna felt on the evening she invited Marcel Liebeskind to her apartment for dinner. While she was preparing a simple, non-elaborate meal, Marcel looked at her as though she were the eighth wonder of the world.

They were no longer in Leningrad but magically transferred back to their pre-war town of Vilno, conversing in Yiddish. All that was needed to start a heated conversation was for one of them to say, "do you remember . . . ." and a lively discussion would follow.

Natalia had heated up the dinner twice because they were more interested in talking than in eating. She felt that Marcel no longer was seeing her as a middle-aged widow with a grown son, but as a young high school student wearing the obligatory white silk blouse with a navy bow and a matching pleated skirt. By the same token, she did see him when he took off his glasses as a skinny young man with dreamy eyes and wavy jet-black hair.

They moved aside the uneaten dishes to make room for Natalie's family album. There were pictures of her with members of her family, parents, grandparents and siblings, pictures of Natalia as a student at the Gymnasium, Natalia on skis in Zakopane, Natalia on a bicycle, Natalia walking with her friends and a large class picture where Marcel stood erect in the second row right behind her. Each photo was a relic not to be duplicated. Their cheeks were red with excitement. They were once again young and carefree.

"Natalia, I don't know what is happening to me. I would like to see you every day for the rest of my life and beyond."

"It is amazing because I have the exact same feeling. My son Maksim is leaving Leningrad for Moscow and I'll have more time to spend with you. We'll see where it will bring us. Is that fair enough?

"Thank you very much Natalia. You have made me very happy by saying this."

Natalia had prepared herself emotionally for the day when her only son would leave her either for the Army, a job in another city, or another woman. Whatever the reason, she would remain alone in her old age.

Since the day that Marcel came to her office with his granddaughter, Natalia had a strange feeling that her life was about to change and that feeling was totally justified.

After Maksim's marriage and departure, Marcel started to come around almost daily. He would be waiting for her outside the clinic come rain or shine, sometimes bringing flowers if he could get them, much to the envy of Natalia's co-workers. They would travel together to her apartment, jointly fixing dinner while listening to music on the radio. After the meal, they would recite poetry to each other. On other nights, weather permitting, they would walk in the nearby park or go to the cinema. While all that was very pleasurable, she still kept in touch with Maksim and Galina, who were making steady progress. Natalia promised to visit them as soon as they were all settled.

In the meantime the deep friendship of Natalia and Marcel was slowing evolving into a mature, adult love. On several occasions after coming back late from a show or concert, Marcel stayed overnight at Natalia's place, always insisting on sleeping in a separate bed in Maksim's former bedroom.

Natalia jokingly mentioned each time that her bed could accommodate two. Marcel would politely answer with: "Not until we get married." There was no question about it, Marcel was a gentleman in the purest meaning of the word, the likes of which Natalia had not seen in a very long time.

As a physician she worked different hours and shifts at the hospital, which frequently allowed her to enjoy free days in the middle of the week. On one of those free days they decided to obtain tickets for a popular concert at the Pushkin Theatre. To get there they walked along Sadovaia Ulitsa, where she noticed a sign on a tall gray building—ZAGS—where marriage ceremonies were performed for residents of Moscow. That gave her an idea.

"Marcel, how would you like to get married?"

"Nothing would please me more."

"Well, let's go inside and do it," said Natalia as if it were the simplest thing in the world.

They were in luck. There were just a few couples ahead of them. Two hours later they emerged as Mr. and Mrs. Marcel Kagan. Luck must have been with them because the cashier at the box office after hearing they had just gotten married sold them the last two tickets to the upper loge.

Upon their return to Natalia's apartment, she gave Marcel a bottle of champagne to open. Marcel's toast was simple and direct: "This is to us, may we live long and enjoy each other in health, L'Chaim."

The marriage was consummated right there to each other's mutual satisfaction. The next morning, Natalia, who hadn't missed a day in years, called her office at the clinic and informed them that she was not coming to work that day, giving them some kind of medical reason in Latin.

The fact was that the newlyweds did not want to get out of bed, even serving breakfast there. A few days later Natalia notified her son Maksim that she married her high school sweetheart. Max was very glad to hear this and said:

"Mother, I wish you and Marcel every happiness under the sun."

Marcel brought Natalia to meet his son and daughter in-law. Thanks to Natalia, their daughter Yulia was completely cured and the entire family was grateful and most happy to welcome Natalia to their midst and treated her like visiting royalty.

Marcel notified his Israeli brother about their marriage. That Natalia was a Feldstein from Vilno was more welcome news. All the necessary official papers and invitations to emigrate to Israel were mailed with utmost dispatch.

Six months later permission was granted for Mr. and Mrs. Marcel Kagan to leave the Soviet Union for the ancient Jewish homeland. Everyone wondered about the extraordinary speed with which their exist visas were obtained. Some attributed it to the fact that Natalia was a widow of a former hero of the U.S.S.R. Others thought it was because Marcel Kagan was actually related to the infamous Lazar Kaganovich of Kremlin.

Prior to their departure, they made a trip to Moscow to visit Maksim and Galina. After spending a few days with them and seeing that the young couple were making progress in their respective careers, they returned to Leningrad, hoping to see them again.

With their luggage packed according to regulations, they left Leningrad by train to the Port City of Odessa. There they boarded a ship due for Marseilles, France, where they changed ships for one that was bound for Port Haifa in Israel.

At Haifa, Marcel's entire family and a score of people from Vilno welcomed them. To add to Natalia's indescribable happiness there was also her cousin whose whereabouts were unknown to her until now.

Once their luggage was located they went through the emigration officials with a minimum of fuss. One of the Israeli officials said to them in Russian: "Welcome to Israel" to which both of them replied in pure Hebrew: "We are from Vilno and we do speak the language."

Their luggage was loaded into cars of the relatives and the entire caravan left for the city of Ramat-Gan. To Natalia's and Marcel's complete surprise and astonishment, they walked into a completely furnished apartment on Haroe Street #117. Everything was brand new, including the modern Swedish furniture.

Fresh flowers were in crystal vases and the refrigerator was filled to capacity. Nothing was missing. Natalia sat in a chair near the window and said through her tears: "I'm home, I'm finally home."

A telegram expressing these same emotions was sent from Ramat-Gan to Maksim in Moscow.

CHAPTER XXXIX

It's early morning in Forest Hills and the sky is beginning to show streaks of light over in the east behind the row of apartment buildings on Queens Boulevard.

Leslie was watching the rush hour traffic, the never-ending stream of cars, taxis, buses and trucks moving slowly towards Manhattan.

It was his long time habit to drink a cup of decaf coffee while watching the traffic. He claimed that this ritual helped him to think clearly.

Thank God, Alice was feeling much better and as a matter of fact, she was to be discharged from the hospital this afternoon and he was going to pick her up. Jeoffrey wanted to come along but Leslie insisted that Jeff should attend to this patients.

"I'm perfectly capable of doing it myself," he told him. "I'll just take a cab both ways."

"Have it your own way, but call me as soon as mom comes home, okay dad?"

"Don't worry, I'll do just that."

The apartment was spic and span thanks to Carmen, their longtime housekeeper who had just returned from the Dominican Republic where she had been staying with relatives over the past three months.

"Dr. Schiff, I went shopping and cooked Mrs. Schiff's favorite dishes. I'll be glad to have her back."

"How much did you spend Carmen?"

"No sir, I wouldn't take a nickel. It is a "regalo" from me. She is such a nice lady."

Those words spoken yesterday by Carmen were still ringing in his ears. "Nice lady" she called her and Leslie had to admit that

Carmen was right. He would have to swallow his injured masculine pride and eradicate her infidelity from his head. After all, everyone is entitled to one mistake in life.

The phone rang and it was the doorman notifying him that the ordered cab was in front of the building. Leslie was ready. He spilled the remainder of his cold coffee into the sink and left the apartment.

Leslie gave the cab driver the address and locale of the hospital. For once he was grateful to the driver for keeping silent and concentrating on driving, leaving him to his own thoughts.

Only when he pulled up in front of the hospital did the driver speak up: "Shall I wait for you, sir?"

"I don't know how long it will take to have my wife discharged. It may take as long as an hour. Do you still want to wait?"

"No problem, sir, I'll just get something to eat at the cafeteria and wait for you right here."

"Let me pay you at least for the trip from Forest Hills."

"It is not necessary, I know who you are. Some years ago you treated my wife."

"Is that so? Fine, I will see you later."

Leslie walked into Alice's hospital room where he found her all packed, dressed and ready to go. To Leslie she looked really great.

"Les, Dr. Goldstein wants to speak to you."

"Where is he?"

"I think he is making his rounds and should be on this floor."

"I'll take a walk or have the nurse at the station page him"

Leslie stopped at the nurses' station to inquire as to Dr. Goldstein's whereabouts.

"Please wait here a minute, I'll page Dr. Goldstein for you."

A few minutes later Dr. Goldstein made his appearance. After the customary exchange of greetings he said to Leslie:

"I discharged your wife. Physically she is just okay. However, I feel that emotionally she seems to be very vulnerable. She should be handled like fine Dresden china, very carefully indeed. Do you understand me?"

"I certainly do, doctor, I'll do my utmost. May I also thank you for your attention and care."

"You are welcome. As they say, it's all in the line of duty. Good luck to both of you,

I have to run, bye."

Leslie returned to Alice's room where he also found Dr. Mehta. "I'm glad to see you, sir."

"And I am glad to see you too, Dr. Schiff."

"We wish to thank you for all the courtesies extended to us, and we are much obliged to you, doctor."

"You're welcome, she was such a good patient."

"Alice, let's go honey, we have a cab waiting for us. Let me carry your bag."

"Once a gentleman always a gentleman, and that is why I love you Les."

Les kissed her gently on the mouth.

"We are on our way to a new beginning. Damn, the torpedoes, full speed ahead."

The cab brought them home safely. Jose, the doorman, helped Alice out of the cab."

"Welcome back Mrs. Schiff. It's good to have you back."

"It's good to be back, Jose, thank you very much."

Leslie opened the door to the apartment and said half jokingly: "Shall I carry you over the threshold?"

"That might not be a bad idea, but you did it in more ways than one, and that's why I do love you now more than ever."

"Alice, I forgot to tell you that Carmen prepared your favorite dishes. Would you like something to eat?"

"Great! I feel like eating something. Come, Leslie, I'll help you to set the table."

"Not today, maybe tomorrow."

Just as Leslie set the table for two, the doorbell rang. It was their son Jeoffrey.

"Hi, mom, you better add another setting for me, our family is together again."

"You bet your life it is," said Leslie, beaming.

CHAPTER XL

Liudmila Shtern wasn't able to get her family together for a family dinner in honor of Galina and Maksim's marriage, no matter how hard she tried.

The young couple was extremely busy adjusting to life in Moscow, their respective jobs, and getting settled in their new apartment.

Elena and Yefim were experiencing the same adjustments and were heavily occupied during the day and evenings as well. Yefim, who took over the managerial duties at the Dental Laboratory, had to work long hours six or seven days a week just to catch up with the workload.

Elena, whose musical career had taken off, was in great demand. She was coming home late in the evenings and finding Yefim usually asleep on the couch in the living room.

As a result, Liudmila lost her deposits at the *Vostochny* restaurant and the fashionable *Metropole*. Finally, she discovered a Saturday evening when everyone was free and no one wanted to miss an evening at *Yevropeiskaya*. She also invited her sister Liubow to join the family at the restaurant famous for its quality, variety of dishes and service.

After greasing the right palms, Liudmila obtained a very nice round table in the corner of the large dining hall. Upon studying the extensive menu, some opted for spring salad *Vesna* and fried pike perch with potatoes while others chose the traditional cabbage soup with meat, fried sturgeon or Caucasian *Shashlick* and *Chebureki* meat patties in baked dough coverings which were Maksim's favorites. More vodka was consumed than mineral water.

For dessert, the waiter brought in a large wedding cake along with tea and coffee. Several toasts were raised, the most touching from Yefim. He thanked Liubow for all the help and warmth she gave to an orphan and everyone else for their love, especially Elena's.

Max got up and announced surprising news:

"Next month, my boss and I, along with several high officials, will be invited to the Swiss Embassy for a cocktail party for the sole purpose of obtaining permission to exhibit Ostankino's paintings in Switzerland and other countries while permitting the Swiss to exhibit their collection of ancient and modern clocks and watches. Professor Vasiliev, my boss, has assured me that such permission will be granted as the Soviet Government wants to improve cultural exchanges between the U.S.S.R. and Europe.

However, there is a stipulation that the members of the Soviet delegation not be allowed to take along their spouses; security reasons they say."

"That is wonderful news Maksim. When do you think you'll be able to go?"

"I don't know exactly, Liudmila Moiseevna, it will take a year minimally, to put such a project together."

"I'm very disappointed, Max, that wives aren't allowed to join their husbands. I would very much like to visit Switzerland, I understand it is a beautiful country.

I've seen pictures of the Alps and they are just breathtaking."

"I guess the *Vlasti* are afraid that a couple may run away and seek asylum in the West, this way they can keep one member of the family as a hostage of sorts. Maybe they will make an exception for a Party member and the son of a Hero of the Soviet Union. Its worth a try."

At this point, Liubow entered into the conversation.

"Galina, if I were you, I wouldn't count on it, but still, this is all very exciting news."

Although Maxsim was a proud and patriotic Soviet citizen, the rest of the family did not know that simultaneously, Maksim was very self-conscious being in the company of foreigners such as Dr. Conrad von Hoetzendorf, a Swiss national, known to have a very high standard of living.

Maksim envied their self-assurance, fine clothing and the ease with which they approached other people. Soviets were able to develop Sputniks and the like, but when it came to international affairs they were simply clumsy, inefficient, and inexperienced. He, Maksim, would have a lot to learn, that much he knew for sure.

Liudmila got up and hit an empty glass with a fork.

"Attention! I finally was able to get everyone together to celebrate Galina and Maxim's marriage. We also heard exciting news which nobody can top."

"But I can, mother, said Elena. I am pregnant."

A dead silence overtook everyone at the table. Liudmila almost choked and nobody was more surprised than Yefim.

"Elena, you are joking, aren't you honey?"

"No, mother, I am not joking."

"How did that happen?"

"Don't be silly, Liudmila, it happened the same way it always happens with or without the benefit or blessings of a marriage ceremony, said Liubow."

"What are we going to do then asked Liudmila?"

"We, why we?" It is my decision and my body. Yes, I want to have that baby. It's Yefim's and mine. Next week Yefim and I will go to the offices of Z.A.G.S. and get married, so what is the problem?"

"It's music to my ears. Finally, I will have a family of my own. Elena, my love, you have made me very happy."

"I think that I need another vodka. I guess I am old enough to be a grandmother. Any more surprises?"

"Yes my dear Liudmila, just one more. I paid for the entire dinner so let's go home, enough excitement for one day," said Liubow reaching for her pocketbook.

"No more surprises, please. Let's go home. I'm a bit tired, I guess I am getting old."

"Don't worry, mother, you'll be the youngest grandmother on the block."

"Me, worry? What's gotten into your head? Come, kids, I want to go home."

"Yes, mom, we are all tired and ready for bed. Thank you mother and thank you aunt Liubow for the lovely evening."

"Good night everybody—*Spokoinoi nochi*!"

CHAPTER XLI

"Well Maksim, what do you think about this invitation? Should we accept it nor not?" asked Professor Vasiliev smiling as he handed the elegant envelope to Maksim.

Although addressed to Maksim, the envelope was already opened. He didn't even bother to ask who opened it. It didn't make any difference to him who did it. To ask too many questions wasn't very smart or "healthy" for that matter. The invitation was printed on very fine paper and had the Swiss Emblem and address of Pereulok Ogorodnaya Sloboda #2/3 in both the German and Russian languages. However, the text was in Russian.

"I'll do whatever the Party suggests, Professor Vasiliev."

"Don't be a *durak*. We'll attend the reception because it is in our national interest. There are, however, two different problems. We have to bring some kind of a gift and I think we can solve that problem easily enough. We do have in our Restoration Department many old icons. We shall take one of those icons; get a nice frame and gift-wrap it. That will take care of that problem. The second problem is our "baby sitter.""

"I don't understand what you mean by "baby sitter?""

"That is an expression I use to describe Lt. Taras Fioderenko of the NKVD. He usually comes along on any occasion where foreigners and Soviet people are involved. I simply hate his guts."

That was a very courageous statement on the part of Professor Vasiliev Maxsim thought.

"I never met the man."

"Avoid him like a poisonous snake."

"I'll be very careful, I assure you Professor Vasiliev."

"Let's go to the Restoration Department. There is one late XVIII century icon from Kazan that we can spare that might be an appropriate gift. You take care of the frame and gift wrap. I'll pick you up about an hour earlier with my car and that should get us there on time. We would hate to be too early or too late. They say that the Swiss live by the clock, so we shall see."

"Thank you Professor Vasiliev. May I be excused as I have a number of things to attend?"

Professor Vasiliev didn't bother to answer. He was already studying a pile of papers in front of him.

There were still a few weeks to go until the evening of the party at the Swiss Embassy and Maksim was busy at work and at home during that time.

It also took a couple of days to find the right frame. Satisfied with his choice he brought it to Vasiliev for his approval. Max asked Vasiliev's secretary if it was convenient for him to drop by.

"Yes, Maksim, they are waiting for you as a matter of fact."

"Did you say "they"? Who else is in his office?"

"I don't know, nobody tells me anything, but you go right ahead."

Maksim knocked at Vasiliev's door and upon a hearing a loud *zachodi,* walked in. Standing next to Vasiliev was another man.

"Come in Maksim, I want you to meet Lieutenant Taras Fioderenko. He is coming with us to the Swiss Embassy. And turning to Fioderenko he said: "Lieutenant Fioderenko, please meet my assistant curator, comrade Maksim Ziemtsow."

Shaking his hand, Maxim uttered politely:

"Pleased to meet you, Lieutenant."

"Same here, Ziemtsow."

Fioderenko was a tall, muscularly built man, prematurely bald with a pockmarked face and icy cold, pale blue eyes. He smelled as much like a policeman as he did of cheap eau de cologne. Maksim had the feeling that he was shaking hands with a reptile. Instinctively, he felt that he should beware of this man.

Maksim noticed that Professor Vasiliev was measuring each word spoken to that man, especially after Fioderenko took over the conversation. There was no doubt as to who was in charge.

"To begin with, I don't wish to be addressed as "Lieutenant" at the party as far as the *inostrantsy* are concerned but simply as

Comrade Fioderenko of the Culture Exchange Commission in charge of shipping those priceless paintings and their security while abroad on exhibition. Professor Vasiliev will be personally responsible for the success of this mission. He has done it several times before and we are sure he'll do it again to the glory of our motherland and the Communist Party. I will have with me a staff of 4 to 6 people designated as guards. All together we expect to be in Switzerland up to 3 months. Any questions?"

"Comrade Fioderenko, I do have a question. Can I bring my wife along?"

Both of them started to laugh so hard that they had tears in their eyes.

"Sorry, Maksim, not this time. And now, if you will excuse me, I have a lot to discuss with Comrade Fioderenko.

As Max left the room he heard the hushed voice of Vasiliev saying to Fioderenko: "Didn't I tell you that he is a *molokosos* still wet behind the ears?"

In a few more days the long awaited reception at the Swiss Embassy was about to take place. On the designated day Professor Vasiliev picked up Maksim who was standing in front of his building dressed in his best and only suit, carefully ironed by Galina.

"Hop in, Maksim. Fioderenko will meet us there at exactly 6:30 P.M. You Leningraders think that your city is the most beautiful city in the world. That may be so, but we in Moscow have nothing to be ashamed of. We'll take the New Arbat street and you'll see the Ministry of Defense, U.S. Embassy on Novinsky Bulvar, Christ the Saviour Cathedral, and the Gorky Museum, among other buildings."

They pulled up in front of what must have been a pre-revolution palace of some aristocrat or industrialist. The guard on duty carefully examined their invitations and papers.

"Please come out of the car. The valet will park it and bring it back when you are ready to leave. Here is your receipt for the car."

Inasmuch as Fioderenko's car was just behind them, they waited until he got through with the Embassy's guard and the three of them then walked into the vestibule of the building to be warmly greeted by the host himself, Dr. Conrad von Hoetzendorf:

"Welcome, welcome. Please do come in. It is a pleasure to see you all. We'll discuss business later but in the meantime, please enjoy yourselves. I will introduce you later to my wife, the staff and other guests as we go along."

Other guests were behind them so they moved ahead and were soon surrounded by several servants carrying a variety of drinks and *zakuski* beautifully arranged on porcelain platters.

Most of the foreign guests were dressed in tuxedos and their ladies wore long gowns with their backs exposed. The first "foreign" guest to approach them was the spokesman for the Polish Peoples' Republic, Pan Antoni Marchewka. Fioderenko spoke briefly with him and Pan Marchewka disappeared in the crowd not to be seen for the rest of the evening.

Professor Vasiliev mixed easily with the crowd, his knowledge of French and his old fashioned Russian charm seemed to be very helpful. Fioderenko surprised Maksim with his knowledge of German, which he spoke with a Volga-German accent.

Pleasant background music was coming from somewhere but Maksim couldn't locate the source. After a few drinks he could not have cared less about it, but he had to admire the host. Dr. Conrad seemed to be everywhere at the same time, smiling and talking with each guest. This time he came around with an attractive brunette in tow.

"Forgive me, I didn't have a chance to introduce you to my wife, Liselotte."

Seeing that Vasiliev and Fioderenko kissed her outstretched hand, Maksim did the same.

Frau von Hoetzendorf, upon noticing how shy and embarrassed Maksim was, took an instant liking to him and started a conversation ignoring everyone else for the moment.

"Conrad Ich moechte diesen Jungen sprechen." She spoke a limited Russian. Her knowledge of French and English wasn't of any help since Maksim didn't know English and his school French wasn't of any use. Somehow he was able to explain to her that he was the curator's assistant and that he was very much interested in art.

So was she, she told him.

"In that case, do come to our Ostankino Museum and I shall be your personal guide."

Further conversation was interrupted by the sound of silver bells, summoning everyone to the main dining room.

Fioderenko almost fainted when he read his place card and discovered that he wasn't sitting at the same table with Vasiliev and Ziemtsow.

In his brief, welcoming speech, Dr. Conrad mentioned that he wanted his guests to mix and meet other people.

There was nothing that Fioderenko could have done without creating a scene. Vasiliev found himself at a table of French speaking guests and with his continental manners, felt right at home.

Maksim, much to his consternation, was seated to the left of Liselotte, and on his right was a gentleman who introduced himself as Charles LeMay of Canada. He was wondering if this was sheer coincidence or had been done on purpose.

As self-conscious as he was among foreigners, he was also worried about what Vasiliev, and above all Fioderenko, would have to say about all this. In front of him was a menu written in French. He started to read it, but did not get too far.

SALADE DE SAISON
BALLOTINE DE POULET AUX CHAMPIGNONS
Ou
FILET DE SAUMON, SAUCE AU VERMOUTH ET A
LA CIBOULETTE
Ou
POMMES DE TERRE DARPHINETTE, ASPERGES,
EPINARDS ET CAROTTES
LEGUMES ASSORTIS
FROMAGE ET CRAQUELINS
CAFÉ SUPERIEUR
SELECTION GRATUITE DE VINS, SPIRITUEUX,
BIERES
DIGESTIFS ET EAUX MINERALES

"Don't worry, Maksim, I'll help you. Just order what I'm ordering or ask Charles to help you. He has been taught Russian by his *babushka* in San Francisco.

"Liselotte, don't forget to also mention my Master's Degree in Russian and Russian literature from Yale," said Charles Le May.

After a few more drinks Maksim stopped worrying about the food, which was certainly delicious. He seemed to be getting along famously with Liselotte. He even stopped calling her Frau von Hoetzendorf but simply Liselotte, which she did not mind at all.

After finishing the excellent dinner, the guests were served coffee and pastries. Dr. Conrad politely asked Professor Vasiliev, Fioderenko and Maksim to his study for cigars and cognac.

His office was the most elegant that Maksim had ever seen. There were leather sofas, bookcases, paintings on the wall and a rich carpet on the floor.

Dr. Conrad was brief and to the point:

"Here is a prepared contract between the Government of USSR and Switzerland regarding the loan of paintings from the Ostankino Museum for a period of 3 to 4 months. My government will pay all the expenses connected with packing and shipping and will insure it with Lloyds of London. Please take these papers and show them to your people. If it meets with your approval we shall start working on that project a month after it is approved. If we fail to hear from you within 30 days we shall cancel our offer.

By the same token, we shall also stop sending our exhibition of clocks and watches to your country, which would be a real pity as your Secretary General of the Communist Party, as we understand it, is a collector of old pocket watches. If this is all clear to you, let us join the rest of our guests. Regardless of the outcome of your decision to our proposal, it was our pleasure to have you at our Embassy this evening." With these words, Dr. Conrad handed a thick manila envelope to Fioderenko containing the proposal.

"Just one more thing, gentlemen. Thank you very much for your thoughtful gift of the lovely church icon. My wife Liselotte is an ardent collector of this kind of art. Not to be outdone, we also have gifts for you, products of our watch industry. I am sure that you will like our "Omegas."

"Chorosho, we'll bring your proposal to the proper people without delay. We also would like to thank you for inviting us. We had a marvelous time and thank you for the watches. They will remind us of Swiss punctuality. Good night, we bid you *Adieu.*"

"Forgive me for a minute, I promised Frau von Hoetzendorf to say good night before I left, I'll be right back" said Maksim. He rushed back to the dining room and found Liselotte engrossed in conversation with Charles LeMay.

"Begging your pardon, I just want to say *do svidania* and to thank you for all the courtesies extended to us. Do call us at the Ostankino so that we may reciprocate your hospitality. Of course our invitation to visit our Museum is also extended to Mr. LeMay."

"I may do that Maksim. Here is my card. You never know in life when it may come in handy.

Maksim glanced at the card. In addition to his name there was also his title of Chief of Visa Section of the Canadian Consulate at Starokonyushenny Pereulok #23 and his home telephone number.

As Charles said, one doesn't know the ripple effect of a single stone thrown into a lake. Without realizing it, Maksim had thrown that stone on that evening.

CHAPTER XLII

It was totally amazing how fast Natalia and Marcel adjusted themselves to the life in Israel. Very few immigrants had such a beginning. Marcel's family arranged a completely furnished apartment for the newlyweds, including dishes and all the modern appliances. Their knowledge of Hebrew contributed to their adjustment in great measure.

Only some archaic expressions like the use of "*madua*" for "why" rather than the popular "*lama*" betrayed them as "*Ole Chadash*," newcomers to the land.

A few months after their arrival in Israel Marcel fell into the habit of playing a card game called "kalooki" several times a week, which left Natalia bored. She was invited to play bridge with the ladies of their crowd but cards were definitely not for her. She had to find a way back to her professional life.

With so many Russian, Polish, South African and North American doctors arriving in Israel, Natalia realized that it was not going to be an easy task to get a job in her field, especially at her age.

Marcel's native friends suggested that she get in touch with Dr. Bertha Tepper, her former school friend from Vilno Gymnasium.

"If anybody can help you, Bertha can. She received her Doctorate from the University of Bologna in Italy and came to Israel just before the war in 1939. Rumor has it that she served in the Haganah during the war and later for the Mosad. As she spoke Italian like a native, she was attached to the Jewish Brigade and met her future husband, Zev, there. He is now Israel's foremost industrialist, and Bertha now represents Israel at the Geneva World Health Organization.

"That is an exciting career. I would like to get in touch with her. Does anyone have her telephone number?

"She is in the book, they live on Keren Kayemet Boulevard in Tel Aviv, a few doors away from Ben-Gurion's former home."

Without hesitation, Natalia dialed Bertha's number. After three rings someone picked up the receiver stating: "Tepper's residence."

"My name is Natalia Feldstein from Vilno, a school friend of Dr. Tepper. May I speak to her?"

"Just a minute, madam."

The next voice was Bertha's. She sounded as Natalia always remembered her, very self-assured.

"When did you arrive in Israel?"

Natalia told her briefly about her life since 1941.

"I absolutely must see you. We need to catch up on old times. How about lunch tomorrow at my place. Is 1:00 o'clock convenient for you, Natalia?"

"Yes, Bertha, it will be just perfect. I have your address and will see you tomorrow."

Everyone in the apartment heard the exchange between Natalia and Bertha that had just taken place.

"That is great, I have to be in that area around that time and will be glad to drop you off," volunteered Marcel's brother.

"Don't bother, I'll just take a "*sharoot*", taxi."

The next day, as Natalia found out, the vehicular traffic from Ramat-Gan to Tel-Aviv was extremely heavy and resulted in her arriving at Bertha's house approximately 20 minutes late.

The Teppers occupied the entire 6th floor penthouse apartment. Bertha herself opened the door and the two women fell into each other's arms, hugging and kissing like two sisters after a long absence.

"I was beginning to worry about you, Natalia."

"I'm sorry Bertha, I didn't realize what heavy traffic you have in Israel."

"Come, let's eat and after that we shall have our talk."

One look at the apartment and Natalia understood what a wealthy, well—traveled lady with good taste could accomplish in furnishing an apartment.

"You do have a lovely place, Bertha."

"Thank you very much."

A Polish maid whom Bertha introduced as Waleria served lunch on the patio. Bertha then added in Hebrew: "Her grandmother was my wet nurse in Vilno."

The two women ate and talked. It wasn't easy to compress the happenings of so many years into a couple of hours, but Natalia managed to tell Bertha that she would like to continue working as a doctor in Israel.

"It is very difficult for a person your age to compete with so many young people. The Government's policy is to let go of older professionals in order to create jobs for the younger ones. This applies to the army and the medical field as well. I know that you don't want to hear this, so let me call my good friend, Dr. Chaim Regev, the head of the Pediatric Department of Ichilov Hospital, and see what he has to say on the subject."

Bertha reached for the phone and dialed Dr. Regev's direct number.

"Regev here."

"Shalom, Chaim, this is Bertha. I need a big favor." She proceeded to tell him about Natalia's qualifications, including her experience, schooling, etc.

"How old is she?"

"She is over 60."

"Bertha, you know the rules, there is little I can do in this case."

"Chaim, she is a damn good doctor and very passionate about her work. I don't care what you can or can't do. Call it a *Chutzpah*. I need you to give her a job. As I recall, you owe me several favors, which are still due. Do I need to remind you of this, Chaim?"

"Okay, okay, Bertha, I'll see what I can do. Ask her to stop by my office tomorrow at 11:15 A.M. Shalom, Bertha, I have to run."

"Natalia, you heard the entire conversation, and you will go see him tomorrow. He is basically a good guy but too full of himself."

"I do know the type, I have worked with guys like that in Russia and I know how to handle them, trust me."

They talked some more about their families and their offspring.

"By the way, where is your husband Zev?"

"Right now he is in Svierdlovsk, Russia, buying timber for Israel."

"That is very interesting. Thank you for a delicious lunch and for your help. It's getting late and I have to get back home. Bertha, thank you again for everything."

"I'll have Zev's driver take you home. Let me know how you make out with Chaim Regev."

"You will be the first person I call. Shalom. Stay well."

"Shalom, and good luck to you Natalia. The driver is in the front of the house in a black Mercedes."

The return trip home seemed shorter to Natalia. She told her husband about her appointment the next day.

"If that is what you wish I do hope you'll get the position you want."

"Thank you, Marcel. I have to prepare all my diplomas, papers, letters of recommendation and so on." She also prepared clothing for the next day. In choosing her attire, she selected a more fashionable, "younger" look.

Recalling the heavy traffic of the previous day, she started her journey a bit earlier to make sure that she would be on time. She reached the office of Dr. Chaim Regev with minutes to spare.

She introduced herself to the secretary whose name, Ilana, was clearly visible on her nameplate.

"Yes, doctor, please take a seat. Dr. Regev will be here shortly."

There was nothing else to do but wait. And wait she did. She read all the available magazines and newspapers. She heard rushed steps and instinctively knew them to be those of Dr. Regev.

She was not mistaken.

"I'm terribly sorry, but we had problem after problem. I'm sure you have had days like that. Please come into my office." Turning to his secretary he said: "Please hold all my calls."

Dr. Regev's office was decorated with various diplomas, photos with famous people and many "thank you doctor" letters. On his desk was a large photo of his wife and children.

"May I see your credentials, doctor?"

"They are all in Russian."

"No problem, I can read them, as I have already seen quite a few. I see that you worked in Leningrad. As Soviet hospitals go, Leningrad has a good name. Tell me, doctor, why do you want to work in Israel? Haven't you worked enough? Unfortunately we do not have enough jobs for our young doctors freshly out of some of the world's best medical schools. What should we do with them, I ask you?"

"Doctor, I agree with you that there is a problem, but at the same time, I have years of experience which cannot be simply overlooked . . . ."

The telephone rang interrupting Natalia's speech.

"Ilana, I thought I told you, no calls."

"Sorry, doctor, but we have a cyanotic code blue."

"Can't they deal with it themselves?"

"This is your sister's grandchild. She swallowed a small toy that they can't dislodge on their own."

"Excuse me, doctor, I have an emergency!" and he rushed out of the room.

Natalia, who heard the entire conversation over the speaker said: "I'm coming with you."

Not waiting for the elevator, Dr. Regev ran down two flights with Natalia in pursuit. She took off her high-heeled shoes to keep up with him.

"What the hell has happened?" asked Dr. Regev.

"The child swallowed a small object, a toy, we were told, and we can't get it out. We will have to open the trachea."

"Let me try once more," said Natalia with such authority that everyone moved aside.

"You can't do it, you are not licensed in Israel," objected Dr. Regev.

"Never mind." Natalia quickly grasped the child, maneuvering its body in different positions and with one fast push against the baby's stomach, out of the child's mouth came a small, rubber locomotive, full of spit. Within minutes the baby's complexion turned from blue to its normal color. The personnel in the room all applauded Natalia.

Even Chaim Regev smiled. "Thank you doctor. You will start next Monday, three days a week only."

"Thank you doctor, thank you very much. It just so happens that my intentions were to work no more than three days a week. After all, I'm a lady over 60."

CHAPTER XLIII

"Yefim, take time to laugh, its music of the soul!"

"It's easy for you to say, Ghenady, but I have problems that you don't want to hear about, I can assure you."

"Try me, go ahead, I'm all ears."

"Elena just told me that she is pregnant."

"Congratulations, man. If you don't want the baby, tell her to get an abortion. If she wants to keep the child do the right thing and marry the woman."

"Abortion is out of the question and I am not about to abandon Elena either. I certainly wouldn't want to have my baby listed as a *bezimiennyi* or be *bezprizornyi* like I was until I was taken into an orphanage. I want my child to have both parents like any normal kid. We shall get married as soon as possible.

"Yefim, I have a great idea for you. Why don't you get married in Moscow's Central Synagogue. They have special chapels where marriages are performed in accordance with Jewish tradition. My father is very close with Rabbi Yehuda Leib Levin and we can get that chapel for you. What do you say?"

"I'll check with Elena. Personally, I don't care where as long as we do get married."

Central Synagogue does sound interesting. The question is, do the Vlasti allow such a procedure?"

"As a matter of fact they do, but they are really not too crazy about it. You should know that officially anti-Semitism is outlawed and was publicly condemned by Lenin.

Even Stalin compared it to cannibalism. All that changed, however, during the last years of his life when he developed a paranoid hatred of Jews in general and in 1948 ordered a mass arrest of all Jewish writers and intellectuals, killing many of them including doctors. He liquidated all the Jewish cultural institutions and prepared plans for mass deportations of Jews to Siberia. Luckily, he died before those plans could be implemented. Still, the situation of the Jews is not what it should be. There is discrimination against Jewish youth in the universities, inequality in treatment of Jewish religion, suppression of Jewish culture and prevention of reuniting Jewish families through emigration."

"Ghenady, you seem to be very well informed. I didn't know that much about Judaism.

All I know is that my mother left me a gold star of David, and that I am Jewish. Elena is also Jewish."

"Look, Yefim, your father died during the great Patriotic War and so did over 500,000 Soviet Jews who fought in the ranks of the Red Army. Out of them 160,772 were decorated for heroism and bravery, and that my friend puts the Jews fourth in the ranks of war heroes after the Russians, Ukrainians and Byalorussians— but all that is conveniently forgotten. However, my friends and I do not let the present Government forget it.

"Ghenady, I didn't know about that either. I'll talk to Elena and her family and we will see what can be done. One thing is certain; I do want to get married, be it at ZAGS office, Moscow's Synagogue, or the Russian Orthodox Church in Razan. Its all the same to me."

"I think that I am wasting my time by talking to you. You did not hear a word I said."

"On the contrary, Ghenady, I was just joking. The idea of a synagogue appeals to me very much."

"Do you know something, Yefim. You are a real *sukin syn*."

"I love you too, Ghenady, I want you to be my best man at the wedding."

"I'll give it some thought and let you know."

"Just don't think too long. Now I have to get in touch with Elena, *dosvidania*."

Yefim called Elena and repeated his conversation with Ghenady Feldman regarding the marriage ceremony at the Central Synagogue.

Elena listed carefully to every word he said. When he finished talking there was a moment of silence and Elena answered with:

"*Otchen interesno*, why not?" Let's get married there. Find out when it can take place, but remember, I need at least two weeks to organize everything including invitations to my friends and co-workers."

"As you wish, Elena. I'll go over with Ghenady to find out all the details."

"*Chorosho*—I'll speak to my mom. Bye for now."

While Yefim tried to reach Ghenady, Elena told her mother about the idea of getting married in the synagogue. She anticipated a cold reception to this proposal but did not expect a violent reaction:

"Are you totally crazy? Who gets married in a synagogue these days?" What do we have in common with those bearded old men? You must have lost all your senses to propose something like this. Tell Yefim to forget about it. You will get married like any other Soviet citizen."

"Mother, let me remind you that I am Jewish and so is Yefim. More and more of my Jewish musician friends are talking about migrating abroad, mainly to Israel. My Russian friends are getting married in a church that is the latest fashion, in case you were unaware of it. I'm going to get married in a synagogue whether you like it or not!"

Elena's mother started to cry bitterly. Upon seeing her tears, Elena went to her and said softly:

"I'm sorry, mother I didn't mean to hurt you."

"The world is changing too fast for my liking. After all, it is your wedding and you have the perfect right to choose the place for your wedding ceremony. If you want a synagogue, let it be a synagogue, as long as you will be happy."

"Thank you mom, I love you."

"I love you too, my child."

Yefim was only able to contact Ghenady the next day at work. He told him that Elena was willing to get married in a synagogue.

"I'll call the Rabbi and find out if he can see us today during our lunch hour. It isn't far from here anyway."

"Please do that for me, Ghenady."

Ghenady called the Rabbi from a public telephone and after speaking with him for a few minutes, he turned to Yefim and said:

"Yefim, you are one lucky son of a gun. The Rabbi will wait for us today at lunch time."

The few hours of work separating Yefim from lunch time seemed interminable. At lunch, Yefim told his co-workers that he had to pick up some supplies for the laboratory. This was nothing out of the ordinary and nobody questioned it, especially since Yefim was now the foreman/manager.

After a couple of stops by the fast-moving Metro subway train, Ghenady and Yefim approached the majestic looking synagogue, the second largest in the Soviet Union, after the synagogue in Leningrad.

"The Rabbi's office is around the corner, and by the way, Yefim, the Rabbi's real profession is mechanical engineering."

"You're kidding, of course, Ghenady."

"No, I am not kidding. He is an engineer."

Rabbi Levin was in his office. A middle-aged man with a neatly trimmed beard and friendly face, he reminded Yefim more of Tsar Nicholas II than of Moscow's Grand Rabbi.

Ghenady, whom the Rabbi obviously knew, introduced Yefim.

"Rabbi, this is my friend Yefim Bidnyi, the fellow I told you about."

"Shalom, Yefim. Ghenady Feldman gave me to understand that you want to get married.

Is your wife also Jewish?"

"Yes, Rabbi, she is."

"And both of you want to get married according to the traditions of our people?"

"Yes, Rabbi, although we both don't know too much about it."

"You see, Yefim, our beautiful Soviet constitution gives equal rights to all nationalities that make up our Union. Here, Yefim, I have a booklet for you which describes Jewish weddings and some forms to fill out. When would you like for the ceremony to take place?"

"In two weeks, if that is possible, Rabbi."

"Let me check my calendar. No, in two weeks it can't be done, we are all booked up.

Wait, I have a cancellation in 10 days, on a Thursday, which is considered a *mazel,a* lucky day for Jews to get married on. Would that day suit you?"

"Yes, Rabbi, we'll take it."

"Very well, Yefim, we shall see you on Thursday at 2:00 P.M., and please be on time."

"We'll do out best, Rabbi."

"I know you will my young friend."

Ghenady and Yefim returned to the Laboratory without anyone giving them a second thought. At the end of the working day Yefim was finally able to get in touch with Elena regarding the wedding day taking place within 10 days. Surprisingly, Elena accepted that day without a word of complaint.

"Yefim, we will have to hustle a bit more. I do have my pink dress and that will have to do."

The next nine days were very chaotic, but somehow on the tenth day they showed up on time at the Central Synagogue surrounded by family and friends, mainly comprised of their co-workers.

The Rabbi spoke briefly yet movingly about the roles of a bride and groom in a Jewish marriage. They were married under an ancient, embroidered Chupah according to the Laws of Moses and Israel.

Yefim crushed a 40 watt bulb wrapped in an old issue of *Pravda* with his foot, resulting in jubilant Mazel Tovs from the gathered guests. The loudest Mazel Tovs came from the non-Jewish crowd.

The wedding reception organized in the last minute, was held at the *Chaika* Restaurant located at the crossing of Gorky Street and Sadovoya Circle, near the Mayakovsky Square. The food and drinks were superb. Everyone was making toasts in honor of the young couple.

Yefim, nearly drunk, also made a toast to his wife and future son, Vladimir. Someone asked him how he knew that his first child would be a boy, and he answered: "It is a secret that only I know."

In less than 6 months a perfect baby boy, as predicted, was born to the Bidnyis. The proud parents name him Vladimir, Volodia by his father and Vova by his mother.

CHAPTER XLIV

A second honeymoon would have been the best description for the Schiffs, since the day Leslie brought Alice home from the hospital. He made sure that every few days they would go to see the best musical show on Broadway.

In quick succession they saw "Fiddler on the Roof," "Evita," "Man of La Mancha," "Oh Calcutta" and at the New York State Theatre, Kirow's Ballet. Regardless of price, Leslie insisted on fourth row center seats. Often they would combine dinner and a show on the same day. Thus stimulated, they would make love at least twice a week. That part of married life rejuvenated both of them.

Amazingly, Leslie's Parkinson's disease seemed to be on hold. Whether it was by design or mutual agreement, the subject of Alice's infidelity and her recent stay in the hospital was not brought up anymore.

Noticing a large advertisement in the New York evening papers about Atlantic City's hotels and casinos, Leslie booked a room for a few days.

On the 3-hour bus drive from Queens to Atlantic City, the Schiffs met several recently retired couples, some of whom were to stay in the same hotel as the Schiffs.

Some of these couples invited Alice and Leslie to join them at dinnertime but Alice politely declined that offer, preferring the company of her husband.

One can't visit Atlantic City without dropping into a casino. An evening of gambling sounded like a good idea. Consequently after having a dinner at the hotel's restaurant and seeing the "Paris Review" show, the Schiffs decided to try their luck at the casino.

"Les, we'll take $400.00 with us, $300 for you and $100.00 for me."

"That will be fine Alice, after all, it is not like we are going to gamble our rent money. I know that you do like to play the machines and I'll play Black Jack as long as my money will hold up. Do you agree?"

"That sounds reasonable, let's go in."

The peculiar noise of the jingle and clanging of coins greeted the Schiffs. Hundreds of one armed bandits, operated mainly by women of all ages, created bedlam reinforced by the sounds of machines paying off. The quarters were hitting the trays like hail on the roof of a car.

Alice changed $40.00 into quarters and looked for a "lucky" machine."

A woman got up from her chair and noticing Alice's interest in that machine said to her, "Honey, that machine is a real bitch, she took all my money, don't bother playing it" leaving the chair and several empty Coca-Coal containers.

Alice gave Leslie a smile saying: "Les, I found my "lucky" machine.

Out of sheer curiosity, Leslie watched Alice play for a few minutes. Her third quarter hit a minor jackpot. The flickering lights added to her childlike excitement.

"Here Les, take these two containers of quarters and they will bring you luck at Black Jack, I'll stay here for a while."

"Thank you Alice, I'll be over there, you can't miss me. See you later."

Leslie found a table where another person was needed and encouraged by a pretty dealer, he started to play. The proverbial beginner's luck changed slowly into a losing streak of bad luck. He lost his original $300.00 plus Alice's winnings.

Alice came over, bringing him additional money that she had won.

"Take it, maybe your luck will come back."

He tried, but to no avail, his cards refused to cooperate. In disgust he left the table. Towards the end of the evening Alice still had her original $300.00 but Leslie was the clear loser.

The few days spent in Atlantic City were pleasant enough; especially their morning walks on the boardwalk watching the Jersey shore and cloudless blue skies.

The trip back home was uneventful. A week later Leslie noticed a sudden change in Alice. She would stare at the walls for hours without saying a word.

"Alice, what is the matter with you? Aren't you feeling well?"

"It's all my fault, I ruined your life."

"Don't talk nonsense, snap out of it Alice, please."

It was obvious that Alice had fallen into a depression and needed medical attention. Leslie called a former college friend of his, a prominent Park Avenue psychiatrist, Dr. Robert Trachtenberg, and explained the reasons for his call.

"It sounds to me like a reactive depression, but by all means come to see me the first thing tomorrow morning. I'll tell my secretary to book you at 9:00 o'clock.

Don't worry, Les, we'll take good care of her."

The next morning after spending several hours with Alice, Dr. Trachtenberg prescribed Imipramine and other medications from a group of Triciclics.

"Let her use the prescription for 3-4 weeks. I am sure she will be fine and no electric shock treatment will be needed. A change of surroundings is recommended.

Why don't you and Alice fly to Florida for a few weeks? I have this lovely condominium on Williams Island and nobody is using it presently. I'm booked on a lecture tour till the spring of next year. I'll notify the Security people and my housekeeper Dolores about your coming. Stay there as long as you wish. The place is like a dream."

"What about your wife, Robert?"

"We are getting a friendly divorce. I kept my condo and Amanda my millions. Les, the place is magnificent, you'll love it. I'll have the keys and directions delivered to you by messenger. Enjoy, my friend!"

A few days later the Schiffs packed up their summer clothing and flew to Fort Lauderdale Airport where Leslie rented a car from

Hertz and drove south on Route #1 until 183rd Street, making a left turn to the Williams Island complex.

The Security Staff, alerted by Dr. Trachtenberg, awaited the Schiffs. They were polite and efficient. The luggage was brought by service elevator to the 26th floor where Dolores, the Cuban housekeeper, opened the doors for the Schiffs who were riding on a different elevator.

Dolores showed them the 3-bedroom, 3-bathroom luxurious condominium; its elegant living and dining rooms, very modern kitchen, well stocked bar, and above all, the glorious view from both balconies which faced the Biscayne Bay and the ocean. The view, that also included the sandy beach, was breathtaking.

"Dr. Trachtenberg told me to prepare a light supper for you. He thought that you might be too tired from the trip and wouldn't like to go out on your first day in Florida. I prepared talapia, rice and a tossed salad. There is a bottle of white wine in the refrigerator, if you so desire."

"Thank you very much Dolores. Dr. Trachtenberg was right, who would want to go to a restaurant? Could we possibly eat on the balcony?"

"No problemas Senora, it will take me just a few minutes. I'll be ready with supper by the time you both refresh yourselves."

The meal prepared by Dolores was just great and so was the bottle of Chardonnay, which they slowly emptied. In silence they admired the panorama of luxury boats and fishing vessels as the evening sun was drowning in the dark, emerald sea.

"Alice, I do like this place, it's absolutely charming."

"So do I Les, I'm glad that we came here."

They had a very restful night unaware of the noise made by an occasional seagull landing on their balcony.

On the following day after breakfast, they started to explore the area. Everything was at their disposal, starting with the Olympic size swimming pool, shady tennis courts, air conditioned exercise rooms stocked with the latest equipment, billiard and card rooms, bicycle and walking paths, and everywhere elegant, friendly, well-tanned people.

Excellent shopping malls were within a short auto or special mini-bus ride. They found a nearby Barnes & Noble bookstore, Loehmann's Department Store, and a Jewish Deli owned by an Egyptian called "Moe." A local pharmacy was within the confines of the Publix Supermarket.

After the initial impact of a new residence, Alice hardly paid attention to all those Floridian attractions. Her moments of silence were changing into hours of silence.

Leslie tried very hard to keep their conversation going but it was mainly a monologue on his part. One thing became obvious to him. Alice was not getting any better.

Towards their third week of stay in Williams Island, Alice ran short of her medication. Leslie called in the prescription and asked for delivery of the same. He was informed that the prescription would be filled in an hour but the pharmacy made no deliveries. He would have to pick it up.

An hour later, Leslie went down to the garage to take his car in order to drive it to the Publix Supermarket. The parking spaces at Publix were pretty much taken up but Leslie did find a spot for his car, just as another shopper vacated the place. The Pharmacy itself was located in the left corner of the Supermarket.

The pharmacist in charge told him that his prescription would be ready in a couple of minutes. "Is everything clear as far as the medication is concerned?" Leslie chatted with the pharmacist long enough to find out that he was Russian born and educated in Israel. He paid for the medication with a credit card and left the pharmacy.

He drove back to his building just as two Emergency Ambulances passed him by. A Fire Rescue truck and a large group of people milling around blocked the entrance to the garage of his building.

Leslie stepped out of the car and asked a nearby Haitian attendant:

"What has happened here?"

"Some white lady jumped from the 26th floor balcony."

CHAPTER XLV

Six weeks after the reception at the Swiss Embassy, Max got a telephone call at his office in Ostankino Museum from the secretary of Lt. Taras Fioderenko:

"Lieutenant Fioderenko wishes to speak with you tomorrow at his office at 2:00 P.M."

She also left the address of his office just two blocks away from Lubyanka Prison.

Professor Vasiliev who happened to be at the office at the time of Fioderenko's call, asked Max:

"What is that all about?"

"I really don't know what he wants."

"Max, I'm sure that he wants you to spy on me."

"Professor, you're not serious, or are you?"

"Trust me, I know what I'm saying. Be very careful and don't let him blackmail you on some small insignificant detail of your life. Keep in mind that he is coming with us to Switzerland whether we like it or not."

"I'll be very careful and thanks for warning me." For the rest of the day Max walked around like a chicken without a head.

Upon returning home, Max told Galina about Fioderenko's request.

"I don't have much experience in these cases but remember that you are a son of a Hero of the Soviet Union and a member of the Communist Party so don't let him push you around."

"That is the second piece of advise I got on how to deal with him. Let me take out some important papers which belonged to my parents and were signed by the highest members of the Presidium. This should keep him in line, I hope."

Max reached for a metal box lying on the top shelf in the main closet containing family papers and photos.

He selected just three documents. One was addressed to Senior Lieutenant Michail Z. Ziemtsov:

> *Dear Michail Semyonovich:*
>
> *Not having the possibility of personally presenting you with the ORDER OF KUTUZOV, second-class, which has been awarded to you by the Presidium of the Supreme Soviet of the USSR on 30th September, 1943, I am enclosing it in this letter.*
>
> *I congratulate you on receiving this meritorious award and wish you further success in military combat and your personal life.*
>
> *Mikhail Kalinin*
> *Chairman of the Presidium*
> *Supreme Soviet of the USSR*

The second document was addressed to Max's mother:

> *Esteemed Natalia Isaakovna!*
>
> *According to a communication from the Military Command, your husband, COL. MICHAIL SEMYONOVICH ZIEMTSOV, died a heroic death in the fight for our Motherland.*
>
> *For the courageous feat of your husband Col. Ziemtsov in the fight against the German occupation forces, the Presidium of the Supreme Soviet on March 24, 1945, awarded him its highest award, the title of HERO OF THE SOVIET UNION.*
>
> *I am sending you the official document of the Presidium of the Supreme Soviet of the USSR. Keep it in memory of your heroic husband whose feat will never be forgotten by our people.*
>
> *Mikhail Kalinin*
> *Chairman of the Presidium*
> *Supreme Soviet of the USSR*

A clipping from "Krasnoarmyanskaya Pravda:"

On July 28th, 1944, Major Michail S. Ziemtsov, commander of the 1366th Regiment, 319th Infantry Division attached to the 43rd Army, Second Baltic Front, received orders to break through the enemy defense near the Neshchedraya River in Vitebsk and to capture the village of Kovalevo.

After an exhausting March, Major Ziemtsov led his men in an assault on the German position. The Germans were so amazed at the boldness of Soviet Soldiers that they offered no resistance.

In an attempt to regain their position, the Germans threw 2 infantry battalions, 6 tanks and 5 self-propelled guns into the battle. They launched 12 attacks on the Soviet troops, but Major Ziemtsov, who had set up excellent defenses, skillfully commanded his soldiers and the attacks were repulsed. The Germans lost 700 soldiers and officers, 8 mounted machine guns, 4 tanks and 3 self-propelled Ferdinands.

For this operation Major Ziemstov was awarded the Order of the Red Banner and promoted to the rank of Lieutenant Colonel.

There was also a poem which Max wasn't sure was written by his father but he took it along anyway:

> Gallant Fritz went off to battle
> Armed from head to toe,
> Said he to the fairest Gretl
> Adieu, I've got to go.
> Fritz got all the way to Tikhun
> This pleased him no end.
> Then he met our *Katyusha*
> Who dispatched him round the bend.

Armed with these papers, the next day Max showed up at Fioderenko's office and to his surprise he was greeted like a long lost relative:

"Welcome, welcome, Maksim, please take a seat. How are you? Would you like a cup of tea?"

"Thank you very much Lieutenant, but I'm pressed for time. Can we get right down to business?"

Fioderenko's facial expression changed at once. No longer was he friendly.

"As you wish comrade Ziemtsov. Please look at this letter and tell me why Dr. Conrad von Hoetzendorf insisted on having you at the exhibition?"

"Forgive me, Lieutenant, I didn't read that letter and have no idea what you are talking about."

"Here, read it for yourself."

"Wait a minute, this letter is addressed to Professor Vasiliev, what do I have to do with it? Perhaps you should ask him first."

"We'll ask him in due time. In the meantime, we would like to hear from you on the subject."

"I don't know of a single reason why they would ask for me. Maybe they found me pleasant, well mannered and knowledgeable in the field of the arts."

"And nothing else comes to your mind?"

"Nothing that I can think of."

"Maybe Mrs. Hoetzendorf liked you just a bit too much?"

"You're mistaken, Lieutenant, she was just a perfect hostess, equally nice and attentive to each one of her invited guests."

"Maybe it had something to do with your wife?"

"You must be kidding. My wife? What in the world would she have to do with it?

She wasn't even there!"

"My good man, then you don't know that much about her family."

"I know all I need to know. I met Galina in Leningrad in school, fell in love and married her. What could be simpler?"

"Is her mother working?"

"Not at present as far as I know."

"Why not?"

"I guess they let her go because she is Jewish."

"Maksim, Maksim, are you going to tell me that we discriminate or we don't have freedom in the Soviet Union?"

"I didn't say that, Lieutenant, and don't put words into my mouth."

"Tell me please Maksim, in the Great Patriotic War, what were we fighting against?"

"Fascism."

"And what were we fighting for? Wasn't it freedom?"

"Yes, Lieutenant."

"Did we win?"

"Yes."

"Well, there you are, we have freedom."

"You are twisting words."

"Am I?" Then let me tell you about the Shtern family. Your mother-in-law had an aunt, a chemist by profession, whose education was paid by the Soviet Union, and how did she pay back for it? With Zionist activities and all she got was 10 years in the slammer.

Her brother, Dr. Michail Shtern, was arrested for the crime of soliciting bribes from his patients. Do I have to tell you that we have a free medical service in this country? Wait, that is not all. I kept the best for last. Take the case of her uncle, Grigori Shtern. From 1937 to 1938 Shtern was the Chief Military Advisor to the Spanish Republican Government. In 1939 he commanded the first Special Red Banner Far Eastern Army against the Japanese. During the Soviet-Finnish War in 1939-40 Shtern commanded the 8th army. He was even made a Hero of the Soviet Union and promoted to Colonel-General. In addition he was awarded 2 orders of Lenin, 3 orders of Red Banner, and was made a member of the Central Committee of the Communist Party. On October 28th of 1941 Stalin found out that Shtern was a traitor and had him shot."

"I don't know anything about it, but I believe that I've recently read in *Izviestia* that Shtern and many other faithful Soviet citizens were rehabilitated. Besides, what has all that got to do with me? You do know who I am, and if not, let me leave you copies of some important papers that belonged to my late father. Again, Lieutenant, I have no idea what you are driving at."

"If you knew anything about Professor Vasiliev that is anti-Soviet would you tell us?

That might advance your own career, Maksim."

"As far as I know, Professor Vasiliev is a hardworking, honest Soviet citizen, just as I am. We all have our jobs and responsibilities and catching crooks is not mine. By the way, Lieutenant, my mother-in-law is an old woman, all her relatives are long gone, so why not leave her in peace? And now we both have tasks that may need each other's cooperation. Remember the old Russian saying that one hand washes another?"

"That is why I didn't mention your own mother in Israel."

"Lieutenant! How low can you get?"

"All right Maksim"

"If you are finished, so am I. The interview is over I hope?"

"What interview? It never took place. *Do svidania.*"

CHAPTER XLVI

Elena just finished changing the diaper of her 6-month old Vova when the phone rang. To her astonishment it was the General Manager of the Moscow Philharmonic, comrade Alexander Matrosov.

"Comrade Shtern, let me come straight to the point. In the near future there will be a cultural exchange program between the United States and the USSR. Their musicians will be playing the music of Russian composers such as Tchaikovsky, Glinka or Rimsky-Korsakov, and our side will concentrate on George Gershwin's Rhapsody in Blue, which is virtually their national anthem. The problem we are facing is that our top soloists such as Yarmolova, Rayevsky or Davidoff are either sick or totally unavailable at the time that we need them.

"Comrade Matrosov, I have a small baby and I am still entitled to another six months of paid leave."

"Listen to me carefully comrade Shtern. Your former coach Vera Ryzhkova and the conductor Boris Simonov himself recommended you for the job. Keep in mind that the Vice-President of the United States will be attending the concert, and in America, vice- presidents sometimes become presidents. We intend to introduce you as a distant relative of Isaac Stern, the violinist."

"But he is not related to me!"

"Don't worry, I said a distant relative. Aren't all Jews related to each other? By the way, Ryzhkova mentioned several other possible candidates. Its up to you entirely."

"What am I going to do about the baby?"

"I was told that you have a mother, but if she can't help we will provide you with a woman to take care of your baby. You will be picked up and brought home at the end of the practice or recital."

"I do appreciate your help and the chance you are giving me."

"I expect you to be appreciative, very appreciative as a matter of fact."

"I need to speak with my husband regarding your offer."

"Fine, do that. You have till tomorrow to make up your mind. Call me by 3:00 P.M. the latest. If affirmative, be ready to start the following morning. Our staff car will pick you up at 10:00 A.M."

"Thank you comrade Matrosov, I will call your office without fail."

He hung up the phone without saying another word. It was an unbelievable offer. To play for the Vice-President of the United States and most likely all the bigwigs of the Soviet Union would surely kick off her career in the right direction.

Truthfully, the dynamism of American life, its huge cities, its skyscrapers, the Negro spirituals and distinctly American sound of jazz always fascinated Elena. She was sure that Yefim wouldn't object to Matrosov's offer. In Yefim's eyes, Elena couldn't do anything wrong. She was worried about Matrosov himself. He had acquired the nickname of Don Juan. She had seen him once or twice in the Philharmonic—a heavily built man of medium height with a dark receding hairline. Rumor had it that his father was Russian and mother Georgian, and that he had slept with every woman under his jurisdiction. Elena hoped that she wouldn't have to face that kind of situation.

Yefim came home from work at his usual time. His first step was to check on Vova, who this time was sleeping peacefully in his crib. By the time he washed up, Elena had his favorite meal of meat and potatoes prepared. She waited until he finished his supper and had his glass of tea before she told him about Matrosov's call and offer.

"This is a great opportunity for you Elena, take it without hesitation. Your mother isn't exactly very busy these days, she can help with the baby and so can I, in my free time. Go for it, Elena, and make us proud."

Elena found out that her mother, usually less than cooperative, this time volunteered to take care of the baby even before she was asked to do so.

The following morning Elena called Matrosov's office and informed him of her decision.

"I knew that you would take my offer. Be in front of your house tomorrow morning at 10:00 A.M., my driver will pick you up."

That evening Elena prepared everything she could think of that the baby might need and went over her routine with her mother.

"I know, I know. Who do you think brought you and your sister up?"

The next morning Elena went downstairs a few minutes ahead of time and found the Philharmonic's car and driver waiting for her.

"Good morning comrade Shtern. My name is Vania and I will be your driver.

Please get in." He then drove her directly to Matrosov's office.

Matrosov skipped the customary morning's greeting. He was all business.

"Comrade Shtern, here is your task. *The Rhapsody in Blue* will be planned in piano-orchestra version and the remaining pieces such as, *I Got Rhythm, Somebody Loves Me, Summertime, Fascinatin' Rhythm, Lady Be Good,* or *Liza,* will be played solo. Of course, changes are possible but at the moment that is our program. I'm sure that our American guests will feel right at home listening to Gershwin. You are expected at hall number 103-C.

She was asked at first to play in a lighthearted and jazzy style, reminiscent of the "roaring twenties" period. After a few weeks of playing in that style, the management decided on another approach, the more romantic style of the late nineteenth century.

Somewhere along the way, Elena created dazzling concert pieces imbued with charm, color, wit and imagination. That style had the immediate approval of the orchestra's conductor:

"I love it, we'll call it the Shtern style, because it has the clarity, purity and beauty of expression."

The next few weeks were even more grueling. Practice, practice, and more practice. Finally, the day of final dress rehearsal arrived, much to the relief of everyone concerned. Boris Simonov, the conductor, addressed the entire assembled crew:

"Tomorrow is a big day for all of us. The eyes of our Party and country will be upon us as well as the eyes and ears of the entire world. I expect you to do your very best.

And now, on a lighter note. As you very well know by now, our program is devoted to George Gershwin. It was said about him that whenever he met another famous composer, he would ask for free lessons. When in Paris he asked Ravel to give him some. The elegant Frenchman politely declined saying "why should you be a second- rate Ravel when you can be a first-rate Gershwin?" My friends, I am sure that tomorrow our comrade Shtern will deliver a first-rate Gershwin!"

Everyone applauded wildly for several minutes.

In a highly upbeat mood, Elena returned home to find her baby boy running a high temperature, which her mother, Liudmila and Yefim were trying to lower.

Elena did not get much sleep that night worrying about her baby, and the next day was supposed to be her biggest day ever. In the morning the baby still had temperature, albeit much lower. To calm her fears, Yefim promised to take the day off and stay at home and help Liudmila take care of the baby.

"I almost forgot, I have two tickets to the concert for you, please give them to Galina and Max. Bye, I have to run."

It was with a heavy heart that Elena left home for the Philharmonic. She couldn't stay home; too many people depended on her presence and performance.

The minute she arrived at the Philharmonic she was surrounded by people, some of whom simply wished her good luck or the traditional "break a leg." She went to her dressing room to change into an elegant, long black gown and to her surprise someone from the costume department brought her a diamond necklace and tiara to wear for which she had to sign her name. She did not have a clue as to whether or not these diamonds were real. Some important personalities including Matrosov came in to wish her success. She hardly paid attention to their words. A real stage fright overtook her.

It was her old coach Ryzhkova who recognized the symptoms and put her at ease:

"Elena, forget the whole world, just concentrate on playing and you will be fine.

Remember that music touches feelings that words cannot."

Her assurance came at the right moment because someone stuck his head into the open door and shouted: "Comrade Shtern, 3 minutes to go."

Elena just glanced into the mirror just one more time. An impressive, rather pale woman looked back at her. It was time to meet her audience.

She was greeted by a storm of applause. The audience liked the program and was looking forward to her performance. Strong Klieg lights shined into her eyes preventing Elena from seeing the crowded balconies and loges, full of dignitaries and bemedaled members of the Warsaw Pact countries. Whether the Vice-President of the United States was among the public, she couldn't tell. Perhaps after the concert at the cocktail party she would have an opportunity to meet him.

In the meantime, she kept bowing deeply and giving her audience her best smiles. The conductor came over and accompanied her to a magnificent white, royal concert piano.

She sat at the stool, adjusting the distance and the height a bit, and when prompted by the conductor she started to play *Rhapsody in Blue*, bringing to life the genius of Gershwin's music in a most unique, beguiling and novel way. Her exuberant musicality, keen interpretive insight and rare tonal beauty captured the entire audience.

When she finished playing there was just a brief moment of silence and then deafening applause and yells of bravos and bravisimos. There was such an outburst on the part of the public that Elena was asked to play the Rhapsody once more.

The entire concert was a smashing success. Dozens upon dozens of bouquets of flowers were thrown upon the stage.

Elena kept bowing, crying and smiling at the same time. Never had the walls of Moscow's Philharmonic heard such enthusiasm. A new star, "Shtern" was born.

CHAPTER XLVII

"Maksim, I'm glad you came into my office because I was just about to call you," said Professor Vasiliev. "I have some great news for you. The Party decided to send an exhibition of our paintings to Switzerland as a part of Cultural Exchange between our two countries. We have less than a month to get it ready for shipment and no effort or expense will be spared. This reminds me very much of the time when during the war, Stalin gave an order to Marshall Vatutin in 1943 to capture the city of Kiev by November 7th in time to celebrate the Anniversary of the Great Revolution and do you know what Vatutin said?"

"No, I don't know."

"He just said *"tak tochno"* comrade Stalin, it will be done. I know because I was Vatutin's Chief of Staff. The mere fact that over 200,000 Soviet soldiers lost their lives in that campaign was immaterial, as long as Stalin got his wish. And now the Party wants us to go ahead with the exhibition on the double. I already notified Dr. Conrad Von Hoetzendorf about our decision and he is coming tomorrow to select paintings with our approval only. It will be mostly the works of Gauguin, Matisse, El Greco, Picasso, Van Dyck, Rubens and Van Gogh. We could have also spared a few Rembrandts but for some strange reasons the Party decided against sending them outside the country. Still, we'll have about 120 paintings, enough to fill up 8 to 14 rooms depending on their size.

Don't forget Maksim, that each painting will have to be jointly insured with Lloyds of London and very carefully packed and handled. You know that my health isn't what it used to be and I have to rely upon you more and more as we go along. I'm sure you won't disappoint me."

"Professor Vasiliev, you can rely on me at all times."

"I know that. Dr. Conrad and some of his art experts will be here by 9:00 A.M. and I want you to be here much earlier, at the latest by 8:30—A.M. We will then go over the list of paintings suitable for the exhibition as well as for the shipment itself. It is a huge undertaking and the prestige of the Soviet Union rides on it. If we fail, heads will roll, of that I am sure."

"Professor, isn't there a remote chance that I can bring my wife along?"

"Don't bring that up again. The answer is no and the subject is no longer open for discussion. Is that clear enough Maksim?"

"It is, professor."

"Maksim, here is a preliminary list of paintings. I want you to have a closer look to determine if the paintings on this list are in condition to be transported all the way to Switzerland."

"This may take a couple of days. Perhaps we should do it together with the Swiss people. This may prevent future complications down the road."

"That is not a bad idea, but you start today and eliminate questionable paintings from the list. Tomorrow, in the presence of the Swiss, we shall make doubly sure that the paintings jointly chosen won't give us any problems. Your work is cut out for you, Maksim, you better start right away. Take as many people as you wish to help you and report to me at the end of the day. Any questions you may have we'll tackle at the same time."

"Professor, I'm on my way,"

Maksim fully realized that Ostankino's collection of classic paintings was one of the richest and most significant in the world. He would have to be extra careful with each painting. The experts on his staff would closely examine the quality of each canvass and frame.

As hard as he tried, he was only able to check out a couple of dozen during the entire day. After discussing the results of his work with Professor Vasiliev he went home, dog tired.

"You look beat, what happened to you?" asked Galina.

"We'll be going to Switzerland much earlier than was planned and we have to get the paintings ready for shipment."

"Can I come along?"

"Galina, don't start that again. I did ask the professor about that once more and he almost took my head off. Sorry, *golubka*, not this time. Let me have a bite and I'll be going to bed straight away."

He ate a bowl of soup which Galina prepared for him, drank some tea and as soon as he got undressed he went to bed where Galina found him sound asleep a few minutes later.

Fully rested, he got up early in the morning, got dressed, ate a rushed breakfast and left for work. While he was early, so were Lt. Fioderenko and his sour looking team.

Professor Vasiliev greeted Maksim with a brief "good morning" and told him to continue working on the list of paintings: "As soon as Dr. Conrad arrives I'll take him to my office to go over some papers. When we finish we will join you and check out paintings you have already chosen. I'll stay with you for a couple of hours and then you will take over. Today is not one of my best days. I woke up with a gigantic headache."

"Can I get you an aspirin or something?"

"Don't bother, it will go away in a while. It's probably the tension and the pressure from the Party. Enough about me. You go ahead with your work."

This time, in addition to his 3 men he also had two individuals from Fioderenko's office. One man, judging by his equipment, was a photographer and the other individual was a woman whom Fioderenko introduced as an interpreter by the name of Paulina.

Each painting was carefully checked, photographed in its original frame, given a number and entered into a special folder.

A couple of hours later, Dr. Conrad and his team caught up with Maksim. They started to review the paintings already seen by Maksim and his experts. This time they moved a bit faster. At best they could check out only 4-6 paintings per hour.

The broke for a quick lunch of sandwiches and coffee and continued working. Professor Vasiliev suggested they work one more day on this project but Dr. Conrad insisted on working until all the suitable paintings were checked out, regardless of the hour of the day.

After another break at 7:30 P.M. for a hot meal, Professor Vasiliev excused himself saying that he had to make several important telephone calls, but Maksim knew the real reason for his excuse. Professor Vasiliev had to lay down a while for a much needed rest.

"Maksim will continue working with you, Dr. Conrad. He knows almost as much as I do about art. I will see you soon."

They kept on working, this time checking out El Greco's "The Apostles Peter and Paul."

Dr. Conrad seemed to be totally fascinated with this particular work of art.

"Maksim, what else can you tell me about this painting by Domenikos Theotokopoulos better known as El Greco?"

"This magnificent work of art was painted between 1541-1614 and portrays two complex characters of two conflicting natures."

"By golly, you're right. I can see the expression on the face of Peter, the slightly bowed figure and hand sagging beneath the weight of the key to reveal a contemplative, passive nature inclined to meditation and doubt. Paul is represented as a powerful, resolute personage, he has the high brow of a thinker and the eyes of a fanatic, his hand rests authoritatively on the book."

"Dr. Conrad, you have captured it quite accurately. I can only add that the rich and glowing colors of the painting create an atmosphere so characteristic of El Greco."

"No question about, it's a beauty. Now, let us continue."

They kept on working and moving ahead. Here and there Dr. Conrad would make some observation but none of the paintings seemed to make the same impression upon him as did the work of El Greco.

Professor Vasiliev came down and kept them company until 3:00 o'clock in the morning. Finally, the job was done to everyone's relief as the men were falling off their feet from exhaustion.

Dr. Conrad was nice enough to offer Maksim a lift home. Paulina, the interpreter, mentioned that she lived near Maksim's building and asked for a ride to which Dr. Conrad agreed readily, suspecting that Fioderenko didn't want Maksim to get too close to Dr. Conrad.

Maksim, on the other hand, was so tired that he didn't care if Paulina rode with them or not. As it was, nobody spoke much in the car. Driving through the streets of Moscow they reached Maksim's building in a very short time. He was first to be dropped off. Paulina drove with Dr. Conrad another few blocks.

The next day Maksim came to work a bit late, only to be rebuked by Professor Vasiliev.

"We start work at 9:00 o'clock regardless of when we quit the night before.

Remember that we have just 10 more days to have everything packed and crated. The Party is sending us reinforcements of a dozen more professional carpenters and you, my boy, have to supervise them. Don't even think about taking a leak during the day.

Got it, Maksim?"

"Yes, Professor Vasiliev. I got the picture.

Professor Vasiliev's bark was worse than his bite. He was everywhere and his authority was never questioned. No wonder that the job was finished on the eighth day leaving two days to load those crates into two giant Swiss Air planes. The freight transport took most of the crates and some of Fioderenko's men. The remaining cargo was put into the luggage compartment of the second plane. Professor Vasiliev, Fioderenko, Maksim and a few other men from their staffs were comfortably seated in tourist class.

The huge Swiss Air plane flying between Moscow and Geneva picked itself up from the earth on Moscow's Sheremetino airfield and rose higher and higher into the clear blue sky.

The passengers, most of them foreigners, but some like Professor Vasiliev, Fioderenko or Maksim were Russians who seemingly had flown before on Tupolevs or Ilyushins inside the Soviet Union. But the feeling of comfort and relaxation on the Swiss plane was never felt on the Soviet planes.

The Swiss Air stewardess, well mannered and in an elegant uniform, seldom seen on Soviet planes, or even on international flights, appeared in the aisle with an armful of newspapers.

"What would you like to read?" she said in German, approaching Professor Vasiliev's seat: "London Times," Paris edition of "The Herald Tribune," Swiss paper, "Le Monde," Austrian or West German papers?"

"May I have "Le Monde and the Swiss paper?" asked Vasiliev and the stewardess handed him those papers to him with a charming smile.

"And you, Meine Herren?" addressing Fioderenko and Maksim.

Fioderenko opted for newspapers from Communist countries and to his surprise he was given some. Maksim declined the offer saying that he would glance at those papers after the other two men were through with theirs.

"As you wish, Mein Herr."

Professor Vasiliev knew only too well that reading international news in the Soviet press was like looking into a crooked mirror and he badly wanted the news from the civilized world.

Fioderenko gave Vasiliev a disapproving look which Vasiliev totally ignored.

Maksim, reading his own Russian novel sat quite contented in his new Spetz-magazine sports jacket and tailored slacks of East German origin.

The six-hour flight was uneventful and they landed at Geneva's Cointrin airport to be welcomed by their host Dr. Conrad von Hoetzendorf. It seemed that he took care of everything that had to do with "red tape" and their comfort because they were whisked through the passport control where Maksim had his Swiss visa stamped for the first time on his brand new Soviet passport.

"Our toll people are aware of your cargo and will be most cooperative. Have your security people help to load the crates onto our trucks guarded by the city Police and brought to The Art & History Museum on Rue Charles-Galland 2. Unfortunately, the last minute we had to change the location originally agreed upon at the Arian Museum on Avenue de la Paix #10 due to the bust of a main water pipe. That place would not have been safe enough for the exhibition. We deeply apologize for it since we didn't have the time to advise you earlier. For the people not directly involved with loading or unloading I suggest that I bring you over to the Hotel Richemonde, one of our better hotels, where The Government of Switzerland, acting as your host, has decided to put you up. You can check in, relax and then we shall all meet for dinner at the Restaurant Citadella at 8:00 P.M. if that is agreeable to you."

To Maksim it all made perfect sense, but Professor Vasiliev objected to it:

"Dr. Conrad, thank you so much for everything. We shall decline your kind offer for today. Maybe you can extend it until tomorrow. Today we must make sure that all of our paintings safely reached their destination. Although I am aware that Geneva has 30 museums, I am not familiar with the one that you have previously mentioned. Nevertheless I am sure it will be just fine as long as the Government of Switzerland is behind it.

"It certainly is, so let's put all of our energies into getting the job done."

The job was done efficiently and professionally, not one case was ever dropped. An uncooked egg had never had better care than those cases. Each painting, depending upon the artist, period or group, was put in a pre-planned room. Fioderenko's Security detachment joined by their Swiss counterparts, remained on guard overnight.

"Early tomorrow the task of unpacking and proper display will begin," remarked Vasiliev. "And on this happy note we all better go to the Hotel Richemond."

Dog tired, everyone welcomed that suggestion.

Never had Maksim seen a more luxurious room. His luggage was already in the room. A bowl of assorted fruits was delivered with the management's compliments. A brief note in Russian informed Maksim that the downstairs cafeteria was open 24 hours. That was also welcome news. He took a long, hot shower. Shampoo and other toilet articles were supplied. Maksim had one look around and decided that this kind of life was for him and Galina. How to get it was the big question, dreaming just wasn't enough. He would have to act upon it one way or another.

Just as he stepped out of the shower wrapped in a rich Turkish towel, the phone rang. It was Professor Vasiliev.

"Maksim, I'm still very tired but will join you for a cup of tea in the downstairs cafeteria in 15 minutes."

"That will be fine, see you soon."

He reached the cafeteria just ahead of Professor Vasiliev. The sheer selection and the variety of food was mind-boggling. He chose an open turkey sandwich with potato salad and Professor Vasiliev took rice pudding and tea with fresh lemon.

"Well, Maksim, how do you like it here so far?"

"I do like it very much, Professor."

"Don't let it get to you. Remember, you are a Soviet citizen! Don't you dare tell anyone what you have seen, *poniatno*?"

"I know what you are trying to tell me." He stopped just as Fioderenko with another man came to join them.

"Well, comrades, tomorrow we have a big day ahead of us. The Grand Opening is in 3 days, as advertised. We have much to do. I think I'll go to bed and get a good night of rest. See you all in the morning."

"I'll do the same, good night comrades."

The next day, thanks to Dr. Conrad and his people all the crates were opened and the paintings were properly displayed. A number of electricians saw to it that each work of art was adequately illuminated and the appropriate sign attached at the right height.

Once that was finished the maintenance crew thoroughly vacuumed the rooms, waxed the floors and polished them to a high brilliance. Fioderenko and his security team met with their Swiss partners to coordinate their duties and hours.

The Museum was ready for the Grand Opening and the onslaught of visitors anxious to see the much acclaimed treasures of old Russia. Just before the opening itself, Professor Vasiliev suffered a dizzy spell. Dr. Conrad Von Hoetzendorf immediately summoned a local physician who examined the professor, only to pronounce him to be in good shape, albeit a bit overtired. He suggested rest and some mild tranquilizing pills.

At the Grand Opening of the Exhibition, many dignitaries were present, both Swiss and Soviet, invited guests representing the world of art, industry, media, commerce and banking. Dr. Conrad von Hoetzendorf then made a speech about the growing Swiss-Soviet Cultural Exchange and cut the ribbon, officially proclaiming the opening of the Exhibition.

Professor Vasiliev led one group of guests from room to room, telling them in perfect French about the artists, their works and the history of the paintings. Maksim took over another group of dignitaries. Fioderenko's interpreter, Paulina, promptly translated his Russian into French or German. Mrs. Von Hoetzendorf who was among the guests came over to him and congratulated him on the fine work he was doing. Her encouraging smile was most appreciated.

The Exhibition itself was very well received by the public. Accolades were flowing like the river Volga. Professor Vasiliev was the unquestionable star. He simply dazzled his audience with his perfect French and knowledge of art combined with old-fashioned Russian charm.

An elegant cocktail party followed the closing of the Exhibition on that day. Mountains of Beluga caviar flown in especially for that occasion from Russia and the very best Swiss cheeses were artfully displayed on long banquet tables. Well-chilled vodkas and French liqueurs were at the easy reach of each guest.

Like all good things that party also came to an end. Tired but happy, the Russian contingent went to its hotel and the other guests to their respective homes.

About 4 o'clock in the morning a telephone call woke Maksim up. It was Fioderenko:

"Listen Ziemtsov, Vasiliev suffered a massive heart attack. He is being taken by ambulance to the nearest hospital on Promenade des Bastion. I'll go with him. You call Conrad and tell him what had happened, I need his help." And he hung up.

By this time Maksim was wide-awake. He called Dr. Conrad von Hoetzendorf on the emergency number given to him by Dr. Conrad just in case. He was soon patched up to him directly.

"Je suis vraiment desole: I'm very sorry Dr. von Hoetzendorf, and he continued in Russian, which Dr. Conrad spoke well. He told him what had happened to Vasiliev.

"Scheisse!" I'll pick you up in about 15-20 minutes. Wait for me in front of the hotel and we will drive to the hospital together."

Maksim quickly got dressed and rushed downstairs. He didn't have to wait long, as Dr. Conrad arrived in a couple of minutes. Maksim jumped into his car and Dr. Conrad took off even before Maksim had a chance to close the door of the car. He drove up to the emergency entrance of the Hospital and asked for the doctor on duty.

After a brief introduction, Dr. Conrad spoke with the physician in rapid Swiss-German, that Maksim didn't understand at all.

"Maksim, things are not good. Professor Vasiliev is in an Intensive Care Unit. He suffered a massive coronary stroke. While he has also been diagnosed with cancer, his immediate problem is his heart. His prognosis is not very encouraging. The doctors are doing their best to save his life. Nobody wants a political complication at this time. He probably worked too hard over the last few weeks. We can't see him now but I was told that Fioderenko is near him in the waiting room, so let's go there. Dr. Frisch will personally take us there."

The I.C.U. was located on the 5th floor. Dr. Frisch spoke briefly with the head nurse who brought Dr. Conrad and Maksim to a small room that served as a waiting room in this case.

There, on the leather sofa sat Fioderenko biting his nails. Ignoring Dr. Conrad at the moment, he spoke to Maksim:

"*Plocho*" it doesn't look good. I think he has just a couple more hours to live, at best.

I already spoke with Moscow and explained our situation to them. I was told to stay with Vasiliev and you, Ziemtsov will be at the Museum at the opening hours until further instructions.

Moscow may fly another man over but I told them that you will do fine in the meantime."

Turning to Dr. Conrad he said:

"I apologize for getting you out of bed so early in the morning but I couldn't help it. We have a big problem on our hands."

"Herr Fioderenko, be of good thoughts. Our doctors in Switzerland perform real miracles. Is there anything you need?"

"The nurse already brought me some coffee. I could use cigarettes badly."

"As a matter of fact I have an unopened pack of Pall Mall with me. Please keep it as well as the matches. I'll send you some more, and there is also a confectionary shop near the lobby."

"Much obliged Dr. Conrad. Can you also bring Maksim back to the Hotel? He has to change and get to the Museum."

"No problem, it shall be done. Just let me know if you need anything else. Good luck Herr Fioderenko, see you soon."

They left the Hospital. There was a moment of awkward silence, each one of them lost in his own thoughts. Finally Dr. Conrad said:

"Before I take you back to your hotel, I want to make a brief stop at my house. It is in the same canton. You will still have plenty of time to wash up, get dressed and get to the Museum"

"No problem, Dr. Conrad." Maksim wa actually curious to see how the rich lived.

A few minutes later they arrived at an elegant tree shaded villa on Rue de Vieux-Grenadiers. The servant opened the doors.

"Please bring 2 coffees into my study in about 10 minutes."

Not even in the American movies had Maksim seen such a house. The house itself was quiet; all the occupants were most likely asleep.

"Maksim, I brought you to my house because I want to show you something. It's in my study. Please follow me."

He opened the doors of his study and put the lights on. The first thing Maksim noticed overlooking a large desk was El Greco's painting, "The Apostles Peter and Paul," an exact copy of the original that was hanging in the Ostankino Museum of Moscow.

"What do you think you are seeing, Maksim?" An original or a fine forgery?"

Maksim took a closer look, even using a magnifying class from the desk. He was totally astonished. He couldn't tell the difference if his life depended upon it. Surely it was the very best forgery that he ever came across.

"This painting was done by a Russian master forger some 150 years ago and has been in my family for over 80 years. It is perfect in every sense of the word. I am willing to give you a million U.S. dollars for the original. I'll only have to change the frame. Dr. Frisch told me that Vasiliev would die within 1-2 hours; there is no cure for him. He and Fioderenko are responsible for the paintings. In the general confusion caused by Vasiliev's death, it shouldn't be too difficult to remove the guard from El Greco's room for 10-12 minutes maximum. The frames will be changed and nobody will be the wiser,and you, Maksim, will be a million dollars richer. I have with me prepared papers for a bank where I have deposited a million U.S. dollars. All you need is to fill in a number on any combination of letters and numbers known only to you and I will seal that envelope and have it delivered to the bank by special courier. The money will be yours to be picked up any time you wish. I'm sure that you heard about our legendary secrecy laws.

Nobody will ever be able to trace it to you. A million dollars is my offer. What is your answer?

Maksim was stunned by this unusual offer. It was true that Vasiliev and Fioderenko were responsible for the paintings and the exhibition. If he ever wanted to get out of Russia, this was his only chance to assure his future in the West. If Dr. Conrad wasn't afraid why should he be?

"Well, Maksim, what have you decided?"

"My answer is no. That is no to one million dollars. Make it a million and a quarter and the deal is yours. I want that $250,000 sent to my mother in Israel. Here is her address in Ramat Gan. I want her and her husband brought to Switzerland in a week or ten days for a month's stay in a nice "pensionat" where I can meet them. These are my conditions."

"Maksim, you have a deal."

Someone knocked at the door. It was Conrad's servant bringing coffee and some pastries.

"Thank you Johann, that will be all."

"Would you like some cognac with your coffee?"

"I wouldn't mind. This is to us and to future deals."

"Here, fill in any word or number. I will walk out of the room to give you privacy.

When I return I'll seal the envelope in your presence with red wax and put a stamp over it."

Maksim was thinking about what code to use when he recalled one of his mother's stories about their home address in Vilno. It was Mickiewicza Street #18. To his mind, this was an unbreakable code, and he wrote it down.

Dr. Conrad came back into the room. "Did you write down your code?"

"Yes, it's all done."

"Very well, let me seal it and I'll have my chauffer drop of the envelope at the bank in your presence and he will then take you back to your hotel. You have plenty of time because the Museum opens at 10:00 A.M. Personally I doubt very much if Vasiliev will last that long. If that is the case gather your security people by 9:45 A.M. and keep them for 10 minutes talking about Vasiliev and I will take care of the rest.

Maksim just shook his head. The time for action had arrived. It would be now or never. Within a few minutes Dr. Conrad's car driven by his chauffer stopped at the bank and the envelope given to the proper clerk. Another few minutes and Maksim was at his hotel.

He quickly shaved, showered and put on his dark "official" suit, the only one he had with him. As he was putting on the jacket he noticed a red light blinking on the telephone. There was a message for him from Fioderenko:

"Vasiliev died at 8:57 A.M. I'll be busy arranging the shipment of his body back to Russia. At best I'll be at the Museum by early afternoon."

As soon as Maksim arrived at the Museum he ordered all of Fioderenko's staff including the security detail to come to his office at 9:45 A.M. Some people objected to leaving their posts without a direct order from Fioderenko.

Maksim told them that he meeting would last just a couple of minutes and that Geneva was not Odessa.

At 9:45 A.M. the entire staff was assembled in his office and Max addressed the group:

"Comrades! It is my very sad duty to inform you that our beloved Professor Vasiliev died this morning due to a massive coronary attack. Everything that could have been done was done. Lt. Fioderenko will be busy this morning arranging the shipment of Professor Vasiliev's body back to Mother Russia for proper burial. Let's have a minute of silence in honor of an old Bolshevik. The Soviet Union is proud to have sons like him. Comrades, silence please!"

Everybody stood up. Paulina had tears in her eyes because she was very fond of the old gent as most of Fioderenko's men were.

"Are there any questions? Now is the time to ask." There were a few about Vasiliev's family, which Maksim answered as best as he could.

"If everybody is finished I want you to go back to your posts because visitors are about to come in to see our Exhibition. I'll stop at each room to double check if everything is in order. If there any changes, please let me know immediately."

Fioderenko's staff was shaken up a bit but went back to their duties. A few minutes later Maksim went to each room and asked each guard if he or she found everything in order.

"Yes, Comrade Ziemtsov. The Swiss are people one can depend upon."

"I thought so too, comrade."

On the way to the main hall he briefly met Dr. Conrad who paid him official condolences, adding quietly:

"Everything went fine. Your bank is Deutches Bank on Rue Jean Calvin #10. Herr Fischer is your personal banker and your parents will be here next week. Bye for now."

"*Spasibo*, Herr Doctor."

CHAPTER XLVIII

The hardest thing that Leslie Schiff ever did in his entire life was to call his son Jeff to give him the news about his mother's apparent suicide and being asked in turn: "Dad, how did it happen?"

The same question was put to him by Sgt. Nolan Long of the Aventura Police Department.

"I honestly don't know Sergeant. I called our Security to bring my car to the front of the building since I needed it to pick up medications from the Publix Pharmacy. That took maybe 5 to 10 minutes plus another few minutes to look for a parking spot at the supermarket. The prescriptions weren't quite ready and that took an additional few minutes. Getting back to the car and driving back to Williams Island again took a few minutes. I have, therefore, been absent from home 30 to 40 minutes during which time my wife, Alice, must have jumped to her death."

"Or maybe she was pushed."

"No, Sergeant, Alice was a gentle soul and didn't have an enemy in her life."

"Do we have your permission to check out those prescriptions?"

"Yes you may, Sergeant. I will give you the name of her physician and his telephone number."

"Do you think there is someone else who could have pushed her off the balcony?"

"No, Sergeant, I already told you that she didn't have an enemy in the world."

"Did you do it yourself Mister or rather, Doctor Schiff?"

"No, Sergeant, I didn't do it! I loved her much too much."

"Why are your hands shaking so much? Are you afraid of the Police? Do you have any reasons to be afraid?"

"Sergeant, I suffer from Parkinson's disease and what you see is one of the symptoms of it. I certainly am not afraid of you or the Police, simply because I haven't done anything wrong. It may be hard for you to believe but I loved my wife the old fashioned way. One more thing, Sergeant, whatever you say, do not patronize me. I am a World War II veteran who took part in the Invasion of Normandy and am a recipient of the Bronze Star and Purple Star. I'll answer all your questions truthfully and without any reservations. Why in the world would I kill my wife, especially now when I need her most?"

"I apologize, my own father was there too."

"Apology accepted. Is there anything else Sergeant, because I've got to make arrangements for burial services on Long Island."

"I'm very sorry sir, that will have to wait another 24 to 48 hours until our coroner has established the reasons for her suicide and has released the body. Please remain at your present residence. Maybe you can ask a member of your family to stay with you. I suggest that you get in touch with an attorney at law."

"Not a bad idea. I'll start by asking my son to join me."

"I'm sorry, Dr. Schiff if I was a bit rough with you. I'm just doing my job. Here is my card. If there is anything you may need, don't hesitate to give me a call."

Leslie glanced briefly at the card of Sergeant Nolan Long-Crime Prevention Specialist, Aventura Police Department at 20476 Biscayne Boulevard. The card included his phone, fax and pager number.

"Thank you Sergeant, let me bring you to the door."

After the Sergeant left Leslie called his son Jeff only to be told by his secretary that Dr. Jeff Schiff left for Florida from LaGuardia Airport.

There was nothing else to do but wait for Jeff's arrival. He was sure that Alice's body was brought to the nearby Aventura Medical Center and most likely was in the hands of the coroner by now.

A feeling of emptiness and self-pity overtook him. Should he also die the same way that Alice did? No, he could not do that to Jeff. He moved slowly to the bar and poured himself a full glass of Royal Salute Chivas Brothers whisky from Aberdeen, Scotland.

His thoughts brought him back to June of 1944. He was back in the war. Some drunk G.I. or maybe it was him, singing:

"Hey baba-reeba, hey baba reeba,
Mama in the kitchen, papa in jail,
Sister's on the corner, has pussy to sell.
Hey baba-reeba . . . .

Leslie fell to the floor and that was where his son found him.

CHAPTER XLVIX

With the applause still ringing in her ears Elena went back to her dressing room to change into street clothes. She barely had a chance to zip up her dress when Matrosov walked in through the door she thought was locked. He didn't bother to knock:

"Elena, you were really good this evening. Hurry up and come down to the Blue Room.

Many foreign reporters want to have a word with you and take some photographs. There will be tea and pastries served and Moscow's top "nomenklatura" will also be there. So please get a move on."

"Thank you Comrade Matrosov, just give me a minute to comb my hair and put lipstick on. Do you mind stepping outside?"

"Just hurry, we can't allow our guests to wait too long."

On the way to the Blue Hall many people greeted Elena, some even came over to give her a hug or a kiss. Matrosov was first to announce her presence:

"Ladies and gentlemen, here comes our new star, Elena Shtern."

Most of the people gathered applauded politely. She was immediately approached by several newspapermen, both foreign and domestic, all speaking at the same time in different tongues. It was Matrosov who again came to her rescue.

"Gentlemen, Miss Shtern will be glad to speak with each one of you but please, one at a time."

Elena hardly remembered the questions asked in languages that someone translated for her into Russian. She answered as best she could, giving most of the credit to the genius of Gershwin.

"Here is your tea, Elena, you must be very thirsty by this time. Try the delicious cakes.

He then asked those present to please excuse them."

The authoritative voice of Matrosov pulled her out of this crowd of newspapermen. She was grateful for the tea but some people still were coming up to her to get an autograph or to congratulate her. As the star of the evening, she stayed until most of the invited guests left the Blue Room.

"Elena, it has started to rain. Get your stuff and I'll drop you and my secretary, Faina, home on my way to my place. Meet me at my office, I need you to help me with some posters."

"I have everything with me, Comrade Matrosov."

"So much the better. Let's get Faina and those posters I spoke about."

His office was just a short walk from the Blue Hall. Matrosov opened the door to his office and pointed to a woman in her thirties or early forties, saying:

"This is Faina Salomonovna. She lives near First Brestkaya Street, where I believe you reside."

"Exactly right, Comrade Matrosov, I'm much obliged for the lift on a night like this."

"Never mind, just hold these posters, don't let them bend. My car is being brought up from the garage."

"Elena turned her head towards Faina and said: "Nice meeting you."

"Same here. I understand that you brought the walls down with your performance."

"Oh, you are too kind."

A small black car emerged from the garage for them.

"Elena, please sit in the back and hold these posters. Faina and I will be sitting up front."

A slight but steady rain was falling on Moscow. Street lights reflected an occasional puddle and the traffic was almost non-existent. A silence prevailed in the car. Perhaps it was the late hour or the weariness of the occupants. Some fifteen minutes later, Matrosov stopped in front of a gray drab four-story high building."

"This is where Faina lives, you're next Elena."

"*Spasibo, spokoinoi nochi.*"

Matrosov drove through an area that did not look too familiar
to Elena.

"Is that the road that leads to First Brestkaia Street?"

"Not really. I seemed to have made a wrong turn someplace.
We're actually much closer to my place. I might as well drop off
those posters and change my jacket. It will take but a minute. I
hope you don't mind, Elena?"

Actually, she did mind very much. It was very late into the
night and she was tired and worried about the baby, but what
could she say? Matrosov had been really helpful to her this evening
and what would another minute or so mean?"

"Not at all, Comrade Matrosov."

"Look, here we are. Please give me a hand with these posters. I
have other things to carry. It's only one flight up and we'll be on
our way."

His one bedroom apartment was pleasantly furnished, even
elegant by Moscow's standards.

"Elena, put those posters in that corner and please pour us
some vodka. It's a nasty night. I'll change my jacket for a
windbreaker and off we'll go."

She did as she was told. There was no harm in drinking a bit of
vodka on such an unfriendly night. She looked around at the wall
where several oil paintings depicting Georgian scenes of mountains
and wildflowers were hanging. There also a picture of Stalin in his
native outfit.

"Elena, do you like those Georgian scenes? What about this one?"

She turned around and to her dismay there stood Matrosov,
stark naked. His erected penis, long and skinny, looked more like
a pencil than a penis of a grown male.

"Elena, now is the time to show me how much you are obliged
to me and all the appreciation you talked about."

"You aren't serious Comrade Matrosov, or are you?" She started
to laugh. It was a nervous type of laugh, but a laugh nevertheless.

"You whore! What are you laughing at?"

She kept laughing even more pointing to his penis. He came
close to her and hit her across the face.

"Suck it, you whore!" Matrosov was becoming angrier by the minute.

"I'll do no such thing. Don't make a fool out of yourself. Get dressed and take me home and I'll forget this evening ever happened."

"You fuckin bitch!" and he hit her again, this time with his fist, knocking out her two front teeth. She started to bleed profusely.

In her fury she grabbed a large crystal bowl from the table and threw it at him. He sidestepped in time, but the bowl crashed on the floor into hundreds of sharp pieces. He made a move toward her but stepped on a jagged edge of one of those pieces yelling in pain. Elena used this moment to grab her pocketbook and run towards the door. She quickly opened the door while Matrosov screamed at the top of his voice: "I'll get you for this, you Jew bitch."

She ran down the flight of stairs like a hurricane and opened the doors leading to the street, falling into the arms of an elderly man who had been trying to open the doors from outside. He took one look at her battered and bleeding face and said:

"What happened to you, *baryshnia?*"

"Can you get me home to First Brestkaia? I'll give you 35 rubles. Please help me I have a sick child at home."

"Don't tell me you visited Matrosov?"

She started to cry.

"I understand it now. Come, my car is across the street at the Veteran's parking place. Here is a handkerchief, press it against your gums, it will stop the bleeding. He is one S.O.B. we would like to get rid of from this building, but he is a member of the Party and it isn't that easy to do. Let me help you."

He revved the motor several times until the engine responded.

"As soon as you get home put some ice on your face."

She shook her head and kept on crying. It was a 5-minute ride to her house. He dropped her off and refused the offer of 35 rubles.

"You may need it now more than I do, good luck"

"*Spasibo, spasibo, bolshoie.*"

Elena walked into her own apartment finding her husband and baby sound sleep. She washed the traces of blood from her face. She noticed in the mirror that the side of her face was swollen and black and blue from Matrosov's fist. There was an ugly hole where her two front teeth had been. She took a tray of ice out of the small refrigerator in the kitchen and started to apply it to her face.

The sound of falling ice cubes woke Yefim up.

"*Bozhe moy*, what has happened to you?"

Elena sat down on the stool and started to cry. Slowly and painfully she described the entire evening, starting with the concert itself and ending with Matrosov's rape attempt.

"We have to call the Militia," and he reached for the phone.

"Don't do it, I beg of you. Don't call. Nothing will ever happen to him. He can always say that I went up to his apartment of my own free will. Nobody forced me to go. I was so naïve. The Militia will believe him, a Party member. How is Volodia? she asked, trying to change the subject.

"He is just fine. I'm worried about you *moia golubka*. The swelling will go down and the teeth can be replaced as soon as we can, but I'll get that *sukin syn* one of these days, you can count on that. Nobody does that to my wife and gets away with it, mark my words."

He was white with fury. He squeezed his fists until his knuckles were just as white.

"Come, let's go to bed. You must be totally exhausted. Tomorrow we'll see what can be done."

"Please, Yefim, no Militia, promise me!"

"I promise, Elena."

The following day, Elena called Matrosov's secretary, Faina Salomovna, to tell her that she wouldn't be coming to the Conservatory because she was involved in a traffic accident and her hand was broken. The doctors told her it would be a long time before she would be able to play again.

"So sorry to hear that Elena. I got a call from Matrosov. He is also not coming in for a few days. He stepped on broken glass and can't walk. I'll keep you informed, and I wish you good luck with your recovery."

Faina kept her word because a couple of weeks later she mailed to Elena copies of foreign press reviews from her concert. Here is what Elena read with the help of her educated neighbors:

The Washington Post wrote: In her debut, "Miss Elena Shtern used a romantic effusion displaying an awesome technique and musicianship."

The New York Times praised her performance as: "Flawlessly poised with elegance and brilliance."

She received critical acclaim from Le Monde: "M-le Elena Shtern enchanted her audiences with an inspiring recital, she matched the sophistication, boldness and unequaled genius inherent in Gershwin's music."

Even *Pravda and Izviesta* had much praise for her. Elena put all those clippings in her desk, firmly believing that her musical career was over.

Yefim, as head of a Dental Laboratory, knew the best dentists in Moscow and consequently brought her to one doctor who also happened to listen to Elena's concert.

"I'll do it as fast and as best I can because I would like to see Elena perform again."

He was also the doctor who suggested that Elena play for foreign tourists at the "Hotel Kosmos," giving her the chance to earn extra money.

It was there that Elena met the American couple, Dr. and Mrs. Leslie Schiff.

It was a fortuitous meeting because the Schiff's sent her and the family the Affidavits of Support along with official invitations.

Elena, using her married name of Bidnyi, submitted those papers along with the copies of her concert reviews to the American Embassy.

Waiting for the Soviet permission to emigrate and for the American authorities to grant them permanent entry visas, took time.

Elena's mother decided to join them, which delayed their departure somewhat, but eventually, all the permissions were granted. Getting ready to leave the Soviet Union they started to liquidate some of their assets such as furniture, dishes, paintings and other items too difficult to transport to the United States.

In the middle of these preparations Yefim told Elena that he had an errand to attend to. He disappeared for a day and a half without an explanation. Elena didn't pursue it further but a couple of days later she got a call from Faina Salomonovna:

"I have interesting news which you won't find in the papers. Someone cut Matrosov's throat from ear to ear. He had many enemies, and many jealous husbands were after him."

"I couldn't care less about him. I wasn't too crazy about Matrosov to begin with, but that is water under the bridge by now. Goodbye Faina, and good luck to you with your new boss.

"Whoever it will be, will be better than Matrosov."

As soon as Elena hung up the phone she went to the bathroom where Yefim kept his two straight razors. One razor was missing and she wasn't about to ask Yefim its whereabouts.

Going to the United States now had a totally new meaning. Hopefully it was for a better life.

The Bidnyis said goodbye to Lubov Moiseevna, to Ziemtsov and all their friends and distant relatives.

"Come to see us." The responses were: "Maybe one day, who knows?"

A beautiful Pan American plane brought them to Rome, Italy where they stayed for a couple of days while some emigration snafu was solved. Another plane then took them to New York. There was nothing more beautiful than the sight of the New York skyline and the Statue of Liberty.

After getting through passport control and customs, they were met by Dr. Leslie Schiff. He was all by himself and his hands shook visibly.

"Welcome to the United States of America."

CHAPTER L

Dr. Natalia Isaakovna and her husband Marcel came home to Ramat-Gan from a long weekend with their friends in Savyon. This became almost a ritual, spending alternate Friday evenings playing bridge with Masha and Samuil Shneider.

Natalia was asked to cut her working week to two days only, thus giving a chance to work to the many young doctors newly arrived in Israel. While she objected to that arrangement in the beginning, she eventually became used to it and was spending more time with Marcel. He, in turn, was a man of many interests, always friendly and always in a romantic mood. In a way, Natalia was grateful to the heavens for having found a man with whom she could share her life. No longer was she a lonely widow looking at four walls.

While opening the door to the apartment, she asked Marcel:

"Would you please check our mailbox, we haven't done that in a few days."

"Not at all, you go ahead and I'll be right back."

Natalia switched on the lights and lowered the thermostat on the air-conditioner. After living so many years in Russia's Leningrad, she struggled with the oppressive heat of the Middle East.

Marcel came back with a bunch of envelopes and advertising material.

"Look, Natalia, there is another postcard from Maksim and a letter for you from a Bank in Switzerland."

First she read Maksim's card aloud: "Warmest regards from Geneva. Hope to see you soon."

The letter from the Swiss Bank was addressed to Frau Doctor Natalia Ziemtsov, nee Feldstein, and was written in German. It was an invitation to visit the Deutsche Bank in Switzerland to settle an account belonging to her father Isaac Feldstein of Vilno.

All expenses connected to that trip would be absorbed by the Bank. Would Frau Doctor be kind enough to contact the Commercial Attache of Switzerland in Israel for further details.

"The first thing tomorrow morning we'll have to go to Tel-Aviv. I'm curious to know what this is all about because I don't remember my father ever having any money in a Swiss bank. He was just glad to make a living in Vilno and scrape together enough money for my education. Marcel, what do you think?"

"We'll find out tomorrow. Any money you can get from the Germans is a "mitzvah.""

The next morning a "shirut" taxi brought them to the Swiss Embassy in a relatively short time despite the heavy vehicular traffic.

A heavily armed guard directed them to a receptionist, a young woman with striking red hair.

Natalia simply handed her the letter from the bank. The receptionist by the name of Anna-Marie lifted the phone and spoke with someone. All that Natalia could hear was "sofort, ja, ja." Anna-Marie hung up the phone and said to them:

"Maechten Sie Bitte warten paar Minuten," Pointing to the waiting room.

Natalia and Marcel made themselves comfortable glancing through a variety of newspapers. They were soon called by Anna-Marie: "Bitte gehen Sie nach Zimmer #307, Herr Dieter Feible erwarte Euch."

A small elevator brought them to the 3rd floor. Room #307 was just across the corridor. They knocked on the door and upon hearing a polite "Herrein," walked in.

Herr Feible greeted them politely in Hebrew and asked them to sit down. It became obvious from the start that Natalia's German was better than Herr Feible's Hebrew.

"Herr Feible could you enlighten us as to the letter itself?"

"In a minute. Could I see your Identity cards first?"

"Of course, here they are." And Natalia put her papers on his desk including a pre-war student card and recent Soviet and Israeli passports.

"That is all I need. I must also ask you if your father is alive?"

"Unfortunately, no. He was killed by the Nazis and their collaborators in 1942."

"I'm sorry, but I had to ask that question. You see there is a substantial amount of money waiting for you in Switzerland. You and your husband, if he wishes to go with you, will have to go there to claim it. I've been asked to facilitate your trip and to arrange your stay there, if you so desire. You and your husband will be flying Swiss Air, first class.

All you have to do is to call the Swiss Airline with the date of your departure and a ticket will be hand delivered to your home. In Switzerland you will be met at the airport by a bank official and brought to the Hotel Richmonde or straight to the bank itself. It's all up to you."

"I don't know what to say? Am I dreaming and have to pinch myself? Is this all true?"

"My dear Frau Doctor, we Swiss people are very pragmatic people. We mean what we say and say what we mean."

"We don't doubt that for a minute, Marcel jumped in. We can be ready in two days. Is that okay with you Natalia?"

"Yes, that will be just fine."

"In that case, I'll contact Swiss Air and they in turn will give you their flight schedule for that day. Is there anything else I might of help with?"

"Right now, we are overwhelmed. If there is anything else, may we call upon you, Herr Feible?"

"Absolutely, but first I need you to come with me to the Visa Section so that we can issue your visitor's visas. May I have your passports?"

They walked over to the Visa Section where Herr Feible handed over their passports to another clerk.

"Pleas sit down, your passports will be ready in a few minutes. Here is my card,and again, if there is anything you need do not hesitate to get in touch with me.

Forgive me but I have to run. As it is, I am late for my next meeting. Shalom and enjoy your stay in my country." He shook their hands and left.

A few minutes later their passports were returned. The Swiss visa was stamped in.

Rather than go home, they decided to visit the office of the Swiss Airline on Dizengoff Street and book their flight, not realizing what a busy office it was. It seemed to Natalia that half of Israel's population was going somewhere and the other half coming back from another place.

They were asked to take a number and wait their turn. Marcel estimated their waiting time to be more than an hour since there were 17 other individuals ahead of them and only four travel agents working.

Noting a large pot of coffee, they helped themselves to it and to some Swiss crackers. Marcel was right in his estimate because it took an hour and fifteen minutes until their number was called.

A middle-aged woman wearing bifocals introduced herself as Agnes Kadar. She spoke a fluent Hebrew albeit with a heavy Hungarian accent.

Natalia showed her the letter from the Swiss bank and Herr Feible's card. Miss Kadar read the letter and made two telephone calls. One in German and the other in French.

"Everything is in order. When would you like to leave?" she asked.

"Maybe it was Natalia's imagination, but Miss Kadar's voice was becoming increasingly more respectful, unlike the tone that Sabras or people who imitated Sabras usually took.

"We'll need about two days to get ready and would like to take an early non-stop flight so we could be in Switzerland by noontime the latest."

"Let me check our schedule for that day, just a moment. Yes, there is a morning flightat 7:35 A.M. which will put you in Switzerland by 12:13 P.M. the same day. Will that suit your needs?"

Natalia looked at Marcel and together they answered: "Yes, it would."

"In that case. Let me issue two first class tickets for that flight. Do you like to sit up front?"

"We have never flown first class. This is our maiden voyage."

"I'll assign two very good seats, #3A and 4A. You will be very comfortable. I'll have these tickets in no time."

They left the agency hardly believing what had been happening to them.

"Marcel, I need to clean a couple of dresses and dress slacks. What about you?"

How are your suit and jackets?"

"The suit needs pressing only but I could use a couple of white shirts and a decent tie or two. A haircut might not be a bad idea."

"Let's not waste any time. Some of the best men's stores in Tel-Aviv are around here.

I'm so excited; I will have a chance to see my son. Do you think that he had anything to do with our going to Switzerland?"

"Not in a million years. It is just a coincidence, nothing else, Natalia."

Full of high spirits they bought needed items for the trip including a new type of lightweight luggage on wheels. Acting on an impulse, Natalia walked into the elegant store, Beged-Orr and bought two leather jackets, made in Israel, for Maksim and Galina.

"Now, we are all set. Let's go home and pack."

To accommodate all their purchases they needed a large cab to take them home to Ramat-Gan.

Two days were barely enough to take care of the apartment and to pack. Their good friends from Savyon drove them to Ben Gurion Airport.

Despite the heavy security they were processed quickly and efficiently. The atmosphere in the Swiss Air waiting lounge was very relaxed, indicating what it would be like flying first class.

"Isn't it funny how fast a human being can get used to a better life?"

She was proven right as they were pampered and fussed over during their four-hour flight. Marcel quoted an old Jewish saying: "it pays to sell ones last shirt just to live like a millionaire."

The plane landed on time. The passport control and customs personnel were brief and polite, ending with a smile and "Wilkomen."

Near the "BAGGAGE" section stood a tall man dressed in a black suit, wearing a driver's cap and holding up a sign: "Dr. Natalia Feldstein."

It was their man from the Bank. He helped them retrieve their luggage, which he put into the trunk of the limousine parked outside the building. The driver introduced himself as Hans Zwiebel and asked them if they wished to go to the hotel or to the bank first?

Natalia asked him to drive them to the hotel first because she wanted to freshen up and put the luggage away.

"That is a wise choice because you don't have enough time to take care of your banking appointment since the banks close at 3:00 P.M. I can pick you up from the hotel tomorrow morning. We open at 9:00 A.M.

"10:00 A.M. will suffice and give us plenty of time to relax after our journey."

"As you wish, Madam. I will be in front of the hotel at 10:00 A.M."

"Thank you, Herr Zwiebel, that will be just fine."

"You are most welcome," said Herr Zwiebel pulling into the circular driveway of the Hotel Richmonde where the doorman opened the door of the car and took out their luggage.

Once registered they were brought to their suite on the 6th floor. The bellhop showed them all the latest gadgets in the suite. Marcel's generous tip was well received and rewarded with a hearty "Danke Schoen" repeated twice.

Just as they started to unpack their valise someone knocked on the door. Natalia who was closest to the door opened it with a scream: "Maksim, Bozhe moi, Maksim! How in the world did you find us?"

"Mama, it's a long story. Most important is that we are together again. How are you?

How do you feel? How was your trip?"

"Everything is just fine. You'll never believe what has happened to us," and she told him about the letter from a Swiss bank regarding her late father's account.

"That is fantastic mother, maybe you'll get lots of money and be able to have a comfortable old age. I mean you and Marcel, of course."

"Well, we'll be going to the bank tomorrow morning at 10:00 A.M. and we'll see what this is all about. That is tomorrow. Now, I want to know everything about you and Galina. How are the two of you? When are you due to go back to Moscow?" God, I almost forgot that we have presents for you both. Marcel, please help me find them."

"Mother, are you tired or hungry? We can order something to eat from the restaurant right in this hotel. If I remember correctly, you told me that you speak German fluently."

"That is true but Marcel speaks it even better and I'll let him order us a meal because I don't feel like going out on our first day in Switzerland."

While Marcel was on the phone ordering a meal for everyone, Maksim kept talking to his mother:

"I can't tell you how happy I am for this chance to see you today because tomorrow I have to fly back to Moscow. I've been replaced by Comrade Andreiev, a much older and more experienced man, who was a curator at the Tetriakov Gallery. You see, my boss Vasiliev died here in Switzerland just recently, and I was his temporary replacement.

I have a signed letter from Andreiev and Fioderenko who is in charge of our Security, that everything is in order as per our inventory. In a way I'm glad to go home because I miss my Galina terribly. Also, I want to tell you that I have an idea for emigrating to Canada. I met someone that might be of help in this case. Once we reach Canada it will be easy to visit you in Israel or maybe you'll come to us."

"I don't think that Marcel and I would like to move to Canada. We are too old to move again. We do know Hebrew and are quite comfortable there with so many friends from Russia. Still, we would very much like to see you and Galina and maybe grandchildren.

Are any of them on the way?"

"Mother, first you rushed us into marriage and now you are asking for grandchildren.

Don't worry, everything in its time, just be patient."

Someone knocked at the door. It was the hotel's waiter wheeling in a beautifully set table for three. There was a bottle of champagne on ice in the middle of the table.

"Good evening. The champagne is with the compliments of the management. May I serve you?"

"Thank you very much, but we'll handle it from now on," said Marcel and tipped the waiter. Would you be kind enough to bring us some hot tea in about an hour? Make sure it's hot and there is plenty of it. Also, bring some pastry if you don't mind."

"Of course sir. Thank you."

The sauerbraten Marcel ordered was the very best they ever ate. Even the potatoes, a staple in any Russian home, tasted different as did the vegetables. A few minutes after they finished their meal the waiter brought in the tea, an assortment of French pastries and a bowl of fresh fruit.

"Really, this is a meal fit for a king," remarked Marcel.

"Mother, I had to break up this lovely evening but I must get back to my room before my comrades start looking for me. I also have to pack because tomorrow morning I'm off to the airport. I'm sure that someone from Fioderenko's team will be with me to make sure that I board a Moscow bound plane. And so I must say good-bye right now."

He hugged and kissed his mother and embraced Marcel.

"Take good care of her."

"Don't worry young man, I love her too."

"Maksim, please, before you go, sit down on the bed for just a minute."

"Oh, mother, are you being superstitious all over again?"

"No, no, my son, it is the custom of our people."

A few minutes after Maksim left the room, Natalia took a long, hot bath and went to bed. She was tired and fell asleep without any difficulty. The excitement of the trip and seeing her own son had taken its toll.

In the morning they found a bouquet of flowers outside their door with a brief note in Russian *Proshchai-M*. Natalia recognized the handwriting as Maksim's.

After a substantial breakfast in the Hotel's cafeteria, they were ready to meet their driver at 10:00 A.M.

The ride from the hotel to the bank took twenty minutes giving them a chance to view a truly European city. According to a sign in front of the building, the bank was built in 1917. Everything within the bank was quite modern.

They were seen by one of the bank's Vice-Presidents, Herr Fischer. He politely asked them about their accommodations and their flight from Israel. Upon hearing their answers he said: "Shall we get down to business?"

"By all means, Herr Fischer, let's do it."

"Dear Dr. Feldstein, pursuant to the current policy of the Swiss Government regarding restitution claims, we discovered an old account belonging to your father, which as of this moment, is worth about $250,000 US dollars. You are at liberty to withdraw the entire amount or part of it. It is yours to do with whatever you please. However, I would strongly advise you to keep the bulk of it right here in Switzerland, the safest place on earth."

Both Natalia and Marcel were visibly shaken. A quarter of a million dollars! That was a fortune!

"Would you like to think about it? I will leave you alone for a while, and you can decide what you would like to do. He then left the room.

"Marcel, what do you think we should do with it?"

"This is your money, Natalia, do with it whatever your heart desires."

"No, Marcel, this is OUR money. We will use it to improve the quality of our lives and the lives of our children and grandchildren. Let's transfer $100,000 to our account in Bank-Leumi in Israel and keep the balance in here. Maybe we should also withdraw $5,000 and treat ourselves to a second honeymoon in Paris. We have never been to that city. Do you like my plan?"

"Yes, my dear, it sounds alright to me."

There was a polite knock on the door and Herr Fischer walked in. "What have you decided on?"

Natalia then informed him about their joint decision.

"I think that is a marvelous and clever idea. Remember that you can stay where you are for a week or two if you wish."

"Thank you very much, it is very generous of you but we'll stay another few days and then fly or take a train to Paris."

"If that is what you wish my secretary will help you make all the necessary arrangements. It was a pleasure and privilege to meet you."

"Herr Fischer, we don't know how to thank you Sir."

"Believe me, Frau doctor, I am being amply compensated for my service."

"Still, we thank you."

"You are most welcome. Enjoy yourselves. Wasn't it your fellow countryman Pushkin who said: "live while you can?" and rightly so. There are a number of papers you have to sign. My secretary will help you to withdraw $5,000. I suggest that part of the money should be converted to Swiss and French Francs in denominations that would be easier in your travels."

"How right you are. You seem to think of everything."

"It's the experience that counts, my dear Frau Doctor." He then rang for his secretary.

"Meet Frau Kugel, she will take good care of you. I have to bid you Adieu."

"Auf Wiedersehen Herr Fischer."

"Auf Wiedersehen Frau Doctor," and he gallantly kissed her hand.

Frau Kugel was a model of Swiss efficiency. She had prepared a file of various papers ready for Natalia's signature. The withdrawn money was exchanged into French and Swiss currencies in addition to US dollars. She also arranged for airline tickets since Natalia changed her mind about riding trains. As far as the hotel accommodations in Paris were concerned, Natalia insisted on the small hotel Atala on 10 Rue Chateaubriand near the Champs-Elysees and Arc de Triumphe, the same hotel that their friends from Savyon stayed in.

"Frau Kugel, this hotel will be just fine for us. Please make the reservation for one week."

Without another word she made the reservations in perfect French.

"Is there anything else that I can help you with?"

"I think that covers it all. May we call you if we encounter any problems?"

"I am always at your service, Madam Doctor. Our driver will take you back to the hotel.

May I suggest that you put your extra money into the hotel's vault for the duration of your stay."

"Good idea, thank you again, Frau Kugel."

They spent two delightful days in Switzerland. The snow-capped peak of the Alps reminded them of Ural Mountains, not as high, but surely as cold. The trip to Paris was short and uneventful. The taxi driver with whom they communicated in German brought them to the Hotel Atala, a small but comfortable place.

The next day they began visiting the city starting with the Louvre. They couldn't help but compare it to the Hermitage in Leningrad. Yet, only the Louvre had the famous painting of Mona Lisa. Notre Dame was compared to St. Isaac's Cathedral, the Seine River to Neva, the Palace of Justice to the Admiralty Building, Versailles to Petrodvorets and its Palace ground. The Eiffel Tower, which was criticized by Jean Cocteau as a "giraffe taking a leak", didn't have anything like it in the U.S.S.R. The view from the Eiffel Tower was truly spectacular; the town was practically in the palm of your hand. The D'orsay and Rodin Museums exhausted them completely.

The bistros, pastry shops and coffee houses re-energized them. The elegant women walking on Champs Elysees must have given Marcel additional pep because he made love to Natalia twice that week.

Like all good things, their visit to Paris that week came to an end. Natalia bought enough perfumes to open her own store in Ramat-Gan, along with assorted gifts for their friends. They were forced to buy another piece of luggage just to accommodate these gifts.

Still traveling first class on Swiss Air, they landed back on sun scorched Ben Gurion Airport.

Natalia paraphrased Herr Fischer of the Deutsche Bank, "live while living is good," and the living was good indeed!

CHAPTER LI

From J.F.K. Airport to the Brighton Beach section of Brooklyn via the Belt Parkway is hardly twelve miles. However, due to the heavy vehicular traffic, it took the two taxis hired by Leslie Schiff almost an hour to reach their destination.

Two taxis were needed to transport the Bidnyj family and their belongings. One of the taxis held Yefim, Elena and their son Volodia, Elena's mother Liudmila and Leslie. Yefim and all the family's luggage occupied the other taxi.

Surprisingly, Elena with her limited knowledge of English was able to communicate with Leslie. The rest of the family spoke no English at all.

She thanked him for picking them up at the airport and for finding them an apartment in Brooklyn. She asked about Mrs. Schiff.

"Unfortunately, she has passed away. I can't talk about it right now, please forgive me."

There was an awkward silence in the car. Elena looked out of the car's window, amazed at the sheer number of cars on the New York roads.

"You do have lots of cars in America," she remarked.

"Yes, we do," answered Leslie and the silence persisted until the taxi pulled in front of 3101 Brighton #2 building. The second taxi was right behind them.

Leslie rented a two-bedroom apartment from his lifetime patient, Mr. Freiman, the owner of the six—story building. He turned out to be most helpful in preparing that apartment for Leslie's sponsored Russian-Jewish family.

The apartment was freshly painted and a new refrigerator and oven were installed. Since the previous tenant had skipped town without paying the overdue 6-month's rent, all the furniture was left behind, thereby leaving the Bidnys a completely furnished apartment.

Mr. Freiman also asked the building's superintendent Stefan Przyczyna to find a crib for the new tenants. He found a crib, repainted it, and brought it up to the 5th floor along with two Princess phones and a 13" black and white television set. The superintendent's wife, Zosia, filled up the refrigerator with groceries paid for by Mr. Freiman.

As the luggage was put into the elevator, the Bidnyjs noticed that most of the tenants were Russian Jews like themselves. They felt right at home.

A number of women offered their help and promised to show the Bidnyjs around. The super and his wife were also on hand offering their help in bringing up the luggage. Liudmila opened the door to the refrigerator and upon seeing all the groceries, broke into tears. She said:

"Even a chicken they brought us!"

Leslie said, "Elena, I'm leaving now. I am sure that from here on you can manage on your own. Here is my telephone number, call if you need me. The rent is paid up for the next three months so you don't have to worry. Tomorrow or the next day a social worker from the New York Service for New Americans will stop by to see you. You will have to obtain Social Security cards for all of you. You will also have to take English lessons at the school nearby. I strongly suggest that you unpack your most important items and go to bed and get a good night's rest. Have all your belongings arrived?"

No, Mr. Schiff, we also shipped another container, consisting mostly of our books and music notes."

"Elena, I almost forgot to tell you that tomorrow I'll send you our piano. There is no one to play it in my house anymore."

"We don't know how to thank you Mr. Schiff." She bent down and reached his hand, bringing it to her lips.

"I have to rush. One of the taxis is waiting to take me home. Here is some money to help you get started. Consider it a gift from Alice, she always liked you and your music.

"*Do svidania*, Mr. Schiff.

Leslie's suggestion made sense but first she made tea for everyone and fed Volodia, who had slept peacefully most of the time, oblivious to the commotion around him.

By 3:00 A.M. everything had finally been put away. As she was falling asleep, Elena made mental notes of everything that was needed in the house.

It was Volodia's morning reveille that woke up the household. Shortly after that, the next-door neighbor, Evgenia offered to take them shopping.

"Let me come along," said Liudmila.

"Then I'll go too, and Elena can stay with Volodia," added Yefim.

Elena looked at the envelope that Leslie had given them, it contained $300.00. She gave each one $30.00 and said: "We could use more milk, potatoes, onions and fruit.

Liudmila was looking around for a bag to take along. Noticing this, Evgenia mentioned:

"Here in America they give you bags at the stores for nothing. All you have to do is buy their merchandise."

"Crazy country," said Liudmila, "but I am glad to be here."

Evgenia led them to Brighton Beach Avenue underneath the elevated trains. There were stores everywhere, bursting with all kinds of merchandise. The signs were in Russian and English and the language on the street was mainly Russian. Small wonder that the newcomers were calling the area a New Odessa.

Liudmila couldn't get over the variety of fruits and vegetables sold primarily by the Koreans.

"The Koreans have the best and the cheapest fruit shops; they stay open 24 hours, 7 days a week. Even our Russians can't compete with them, interjected Evgenia. "For everything else, we like the "International" store near Brighton #5. They have items that Moscowites would give their souls for. Above the store there is an excellent restaurant and nightclub, run by our boys. Would you like to see the store? They have at least 20 different kinds of kielbasa, herrings, breads like you never tasted in your life;

meats, fish, chocolates and candy imported from all over the world.

The store was crowded and doing a brisk business.

Liudmila's and Yefim's eyes were everywhere. No matter where they looked the shelves were filled with mouth watering merchandise.

"We could use some kielbasa, bread, pickles, cheese, yogurt and fish. We can always come back if we overlook anything."

There were long lines in front of each sales person. They stood in queue waiting their turn to be served. Finally there was just one man in front of them. He ordered just one item, a ½ lb. of caviar that he paid for with some currency that didn't look like dollars.

"What kind of money is that?" asked Liudmila.

"Those are food stamps," answered Egvenia."

"What's that?"

"I'll tell you later Evgenia responded, as they were next in line.

Liudmila asked the salesgirl for a stick of Moscow kielbasa.

"Wait a minute, aren't you Comrade Shtern?" asked the salesgirl.

"Yes, I am, but who are you?" asked a perplexed Liudmila. "I don't recognize you."

"How could you recognize me? I changed the color of my hair. I have an American haircut and makeup. I am Viktoria Finkelshtein. You saved me once from a 10 year sentence. Do you remember me now?

"Now, I do."

Some years before, Viktoria had been arraigned in front of her as a Moscow prosecutor, for "speculation," an offense that carried a 10—year sentence. Liudmila took pity on the young woman giving her a proverbial slap on the wrist.

"I never had a chance to thank you for what you did for me at that time. When did you arrive in the United States?"

"Only yesterday," answered Liudmila.

"Look, my family owns this store. Take any groceries you can carry home as my gift to you. I can also give you a job, either helping in the kitchen or here at the counter."

"But I can't speak English."

"It is not important, most of our customers are Russians, you'll learn as you go. I will pay you $7.00 an hour off the books, that's as good as $8.00 an hour.

"Thank you very much for your offer. I will talk to my daughter and stop by the store in the morning."

"I won't be in tomorrow, make it the day after at 3:00 P.M."

While talking to Liudmila she filled up bags with an assortment of products and canned goods. The bags were so heavy with merchandise that Yefim had difficulty lifting them.

Elena was dumbfounded when they returned carrying all those groceries.

"This is enough to feed an army. Where did you get it all?"

Liudmila told her about the strange encounter at the "International" store.

"Listen my kids. I am going to take that job because sure as hell nobody in the States needs a prosecutor who speaks Russian and knows Soviet law only. I'll earn money and bring home food. If you need me to stay at home with Volodia I'll do that too.

I have to do something with my life. I don't want to be a burden to you. Don't you agree with me?"

"Yes, mom, we all do." Elena turned to Evgenia and said:

"Thank you very much for taking my mother and Yefim shopping. Would you and your husband like to come for tea at 8 o'clock this evening?"

"We would be delighted," answered Evgenia and left the room.

"And now I have to find a job for myself too," stated Yefim.

"Don't worry, if God will give you a day He'll also provide you with food."

"That is a nice Russian saying, I hope that you are right."

A telephone ring interrupted further discussion. It was Leslie inquiring how things were and to tell Elena that the piano was scheduled to be delivered the next day.

"Thank you Dr. Schiff! Thank you very much indeed."

"Enjoy," he said and hung up.

Shortly after 8 o'clock Evgenia and her husband whom she introduced as Abrasha Razunski, walked in carrying a bouquet of fresh flowers with a note, "Good luck in your new apartment."

They were a charming couple. Yefim learned that Abrasha had been an architect back in Kiev but here he became a house painter, working on the restoration of old houses and apartments, where his skills as an architect came in quite handy.

"There is much money to be made in this business. Right now I am a sub-contractor and am learning the ropes. I hope to be on my own by next year and move my family to Long Island. There is room on my team for someone who is young and energetic, a quick learner and willing to work hard. What about you, Yefim?"

"Thank you for the offer. I am a dental technician. Let me look around for a while, and if nothing works out I will get back to you. Hopefully you will have still have room for me on the team.

"Fair enough. This calls for a drink."

"Elena, you heard what the man said. Do we have any vodka in the house?"

"Sorry, Yefim, we didn't have a chance to get any yet."

"No problem, Evgenia will get it, we are only next door. We'll drink to a better tomorrow."

"I'll cut up some kielbasa and herring in the meantime. Yefim brought a lot of it from the "International" shop."

"I heard about that from Evgenia."

Evgenia returned with a bottle of "Stolichnaia" vodka straight from their freezer.

"We have a 13 year old daughter Svetlana. If you ever need someone to baby-sit for Volodia she is available and quite responsible."

"That is very good to know."

During the remainder of the evening the Razunski's told them about life in New York and about food stamps.

"Tomorrow, I will be getting a piano. I don't know if Yefim mentioned to you that I was a concert pianist in Moscow. I think I would be happy teaching children to play the piano."

"Fantastic! We always wanted Svetlana to play. You see we can already barter. She will baby-sit for you in return for you teaching her to play the piano. We know many people in the building and in the area who would like their children to learn how to play.

In no time at all you will have a regular clientele."

"Oh, I'm excited about this idea. There is nothing better than teaching children that are eager to learn."

The Razunski's left everybody in high spirits. The future seemed to have taken care of itself. Only Yefim had his doubts.

"Let's see, said the blind man, let's see," he said to no one in particular.

CHAPTER LII

Maksim left Switzerland with mixed emotions. It took two of Fioderenko's men to accompany him to the airport even walking him to the bathroom just to make sure that he got on the plane bound for Moscow.

He just gave them an indulgent smile as if to say: "I know you're just doing your job."

He was not about to leave his Galina knowing full well that if he were not to return, she would be put in jail. No, he had to find a better way for them to leave the Soviet Union and to enjoy his secret bank account. If he had any doubts about his decision, those doubts dissipated at the passport control at Moscow's Airport when a uniformed clerk asked:

"What was the purpose of your trip to Switzerland?"

"None of your business. I you want to find out here is the telephone number of Party Headquarters. Call them and ask Colonel Kostenko. He will surely tell you.

"I am very sorry Comrade, it's just a habit. You can go." He quickly stamped Maksim's passport and handed it over. Even the customs officers waved him right through.

An airport taxi took him home but Galina wasn't there. He unpacked his valises and hung up his recently acquired Western clothing. He prominently displayed both his and his mother's gifts on the living room couch. He put on a kettle of water for tea.

Just as the kettle began to boil Galina walked in screaming:

"When did you arrive? Why didn't you tell me? I could have waited for you at the airport."

"I wanted to surprise you darling."

"You are forgiven. What did you bring me from Switzerland?"

"Just look at the couch. Whatever is on it is yours."

"*Oh Bozhe moi,* such luxuries! Thank you Max, very much."

"This leather coat is from my mother. I managed to see her there."

"How wonderful! You will have to tell me every minute detail of your trip, but first let me prepare dinner. You must be hungry."

"Galina, very little for me because I ate on the plane and those Swiss feed you rather well."

"Fine, then you can watch me eat," she said laughingly.

"While you are preparing dinner let me give a fast call to Ostankino to let them know that I'll be in the office tomorrow."

"Go right ahead."

He called the Museum's office. The regular office employees had already left for the day. The security guard answered the phone.

Maksim identified himself and the security guard whom Maksim knew as Yasha said:

"Welcome back, Comrade Ziemtsov. We have a new curator by the name of Nikolai Voronov running this place.'

"Thank you Yasha. Just tell them that I'm back and will be in the office tomorrow."

"What was that all about? asked Galina.

"It looks like Vasiliev was already replaced and I guess it was too early to put me in charge of Ostankino."

Maksim opened a bottle of cognac purchased at the duty free store at the airport.

"*Nalei-polniei*"—fill it to the brim" demanded Galina.

"As you wish, my *golubka.*"

The dinner was simple, almost Spartan, but the drinks and conversation went like Volga in the springtime—fast and furious. Galina wanted to know everything about his stay in Switzerland and he told her, withholding certain transactions for her own safety, which he intended to share with her once outside the Soviet Union.

"Well, Comrade Ziemtsov, that was very informative but now I want you to undress me and take me to bed. That is an order!"

"Galina, can't I take a bath first?"

"No, Max. I want you now as you are, sweat and all, *poniatno?*"

"As per your order Comrade General." He swept Galina off her feet and brought her to the bedroom. It was only after several climaxes that their pent up tensions and passion were exhausted. They fell asleep peacefully in each other's arms.

By the time Max woke up in the morning Galina was all dressed and ready to go to work.

"Thanks Max for a lovely night. It was even better than our honeymoon. Here, I've prepared breakfast for you. I've got to run, see you in the evening."

"Galina, before you go, just give me a kiss."

"Here is one, you have to wait until tonight for the rest."

Max got up and ate his breakfast like a hungry lion. He washed and dressed, and before leaving the apartment he remembered to take along a few bars of Swiss chocolate for the people in his office.

He was greeted warmly, especially by the office manager, Tamara Panfilov.

"Tell us how it was in Switzerland?" the office workers asked as Max distributed the chocolate to them.

"Well, it was nice . . . ."

"Tamara! What is that ruckus in the office all about?" a voice resounded over the intercom speaker.

"Comrade Voronov, it's Ziemstov. He just arrived."

"Send him to my office, right away."

"Yes, Comrade Voronov."

Maksim heard the entire exchange and said: "I'm on my way."

He knocked on the door of Vasiliev's former office and upon hearing *zachadit* he walked in.

"Good morning Comrade Voronov."

"It's Doctor Voronov."

"Sorry, I didn't know that Doctor Voronov."

"How is the exhibition?"

"It is being received very well by the public and tourists of Switzerland. The untimely death of Comrade Vasiliev complicated and changed everything. It is a good thing that the Party called me back because I am much too young and inexperienced to hold such a responsible position. In no way could I fill Vasiliev's shoes. Besides, he spoke French and knew his subject very well."

Maksim's words suited Voronov to a tee. Maksim wasn't a threat to him.

"For your information young man, I speak French, German and Italian."

"That is great, Dr. Voronov."

Maksim took an instant dislike to this short, conceited man in thick glasses but he played the role of a student in front of a schoolmaster.

"Well, Ziemtsov, continue with your duties until I have a chance to evaluate your performance and decide whether to keep you here or transfer you to another branch.

One more thing, Ziemtsov. I want you to contact the Zagorski Center of the Russian Orthodox Church. These people manufactured icons for the general public for years.

However, in their own *tserkiev* they found a few 17th or 18th century icons in need of restoration which they intend to donate to our museum. Speak to Father Filip Golikov, he is the one who contacted us. You may use Ostankino's car."

"Thank you Dr. Voronov. I will follow it up."

"Keep me posted. That is all Ziemtsov."

It became obvious to Maksim that he would have to be extremely careful in dealing with Dr. Voronov. As instructed, Maksim got in touch with the priest and made arrangements for a visit. Having a car at his disposal for this mission certainly made it easier for him to reach Zagorski Center. In the meantime, he kept a low profile.

Maksim was told that **batiushka Filip Golikov** was an old man, and that was not an understatement. Wearing a long gray beard he reminded Maksim of a picture of Count Leo Tolstoi at Yasnaia Poliana. There was a striking familiarity between the two. Father Golikov was at minimum 90 years old, hard of hearing and poor of sight, but he told Maksim: "I am old but not stupid." It was clear to Maksim that he was dealing with an intelligent person who had dignity along with a sense of humor.

"Yes, we do have a few old icons that need restoration. The Church would like for them to be displayed so that our Russian people would have the opportunity to view our saints. I 'll call in Father Rodion Kuznietsov and he will take you to them." He then rung a bell.

A few minutes later a young man dressed in a priestly cassock came into the room.

"You rang for me Father Filip?"

"Yes my son. I want you to show our guest from the Ostankino Museum, Maksim Ziemstov, our icons which we intend to donate."

"Please follow me Comrade Ziemstov. It isn't very far."

Father Rodion led Maksim through an orchard leading to a small building attached to an old *tserkiev*. One of the rooms served as a storage room although it was very neglected. Father Rodion moved aside a bookcase, revealing behind it a small niche full of dust and cobwebs. There, in a corner, were several old icons.

Maksim reached out with his left hand for the top icon, at the same time displaying his wristwatch.

"What a beautiful watch. Can I see it?"

Maksim was taken back a bit. This wasn't the time or place to show or talk about watches, and yet he could see that Father Rodion was mesmerized by it.

"Sure, father, here it is," and he took the watch off of his wrist.

Father Rodion put it on his hand and asked admiringly: "Where did you get it?"

"I was in Switzerland and bought it there."

"I can see that. It's a Tissot, Swiss made, and a good brand. Do you want to sell it?"

"I wasn't thinking about selling it, why do you ask?"

"I'm crazy about watches in general and this watch in particular. Look, I'm supposed to give you just two icons. I'll give you four instead, two for yourself. I know that you can sell them to foreigners for a lot of money. These are authentic 17th and 18th century icons. Look at this one, it is in almost perfect condition, as is the other one.

So what do you say, Comrade, do we have a deal?"

It was the second time in his life that Maksim was faced with an unusual opportunity.

"Yes Father, or shall I call you comrade?"

"Any way you please as long as the watch is mine."

"It's yours, but how will I take these icons?"

"Very simply. I'll wrap them in old issues of *Pravda* and put them in your car.

The icons for the Museum I will have to bring for Father Filip to see and to bless them before you take them to the Museum."

"Let's do it."

Father Rodion wrapped the two better ones in newspapers, tying them together with a string.

On the way back, Maksim dropped off his package into the trunk of his car while Father Rodion was waiting for him with the remaining icons on the way to Father Filip.

There in his office, Father Filip kissed and blessed those icons, while Maksim wrote him an official receipt for them.

"Fathers, we thank you in the name of Russian people for your donation."

"May the Almighty God bless you and keep you. Would you honor us and stay for tea?"

"Thank you very much but I have a long trip home. Maybe next time."

On the way home, Maksim was thinking how to best restore these icons. Of course he knew their great value but didn't know how to go about selling them. Suddenly he recalled that Liselotte, the wife of Konrad von Hoetzendorf, and Mr. Charles LeMay, the Chief of Visa section of the Canadian Consulate were ardent collectors of medieval Russian icons. Wasn't it Canada that Maksim was dreaming about?" Here might be the key. Maksim kept his card and had his home telephone number, but the question was how to contact him without raising suspicion. He was sure that the Canadian's phone was bugged. He, Maksim, would have to find a way and that would be that.

The next day Maksim returned the car to Ostankino's garage and reported to Dr. Voronov.

"Is that all you brought?"

"Yes, Dr. Voronov. That is all they gave me. The rest was totally beyond redemption but those that I brought are unique indeed."

"Yeah, they're not bad, come to think of it. You can go back to your duties, Ziemtsov."

"At your service, Dr. Voronov."

CHAPTER LIII

Never, but never in his life was Leslie Schiff more lonely than after the untimely death of Alice.

Total emptiness and self-pity overtook his being. He would sit on a chair near the window overlooking the traffic on Queens Boulevard for hours at a time, without actually seeing it.

Sometimes, if he was lucky, he would fall asleep in that chair, paying for that luxury at night when he couldn't fall asleep at all. On such occasions, he would take a book, any book that he could find and try to read. Instead of comprehending what he was reading he kept going back to the time when he had to ship Alice's body from Florida to the funeral home in New York, or to problems he had with the local authorities, coroners office, and the medical examiner. He had the worst problem with his own Rabbi who claimed that there is a religious law that forbids the victims of suicide to be buried along with the rest of the Jews at Pinelawn Cemetery on Long Island.

His thoughts would inevitably come back to the funeral itself. Jeoffrey's eulogy left an indelible mark on his psyche and finally, the funeral itself that took place amidst heavy rains that fell that day, beating staccatos on the mourners' black umbrellas.

Leslie remembered the crowd of people; relatives, friends, former patients, but could not recall a single face out of that crowd. All he saw was the very sad face of his son staring at Leslie with his large green eyes that seemed to be asking, "Papa, why did you let mom die?"

What in the world could he say to his grown son that would change the tragic situation? Could he say that he, Leslie didn't cause her death because he loved her much too much? He didn't break up their marriage either! It was he who took her back once her lover dropped her. How could he make Jeoffrey understand his own utter loneliness at this juncture of his life, his age and his Parkinson's disease?

He probably could not. The young never understand the old; the sated never understand the hungry. That is how it always was and would always be.

If he could only roll back time and freeze it to the time when he was a young G.I. posted to England. Not a single worry, 3 square meals a day, women and booze galore and a permanent smile on his face. If that was a war let it last for 1,000 years. Let the Brits complain that the trouble with Yankees was that they were overfed, oversexed and over here. No, that was centuries ago in another life. That is no longer the same Leslie.

This Leslie had changed into an old fart, and a sick one at that. What pained him more than anything else was the thought that Jeoffrey accused him of being responsible for Alice's suicide. Only God knows the truth: "Am I guilty, God?"

The answer from heaven was not forthcoming. He, Leslie, would have to find it himself.

In the meantime he had to live. He took care of all the routine matters of the household, or had someone else do the physical chores he was not capable of handling.

In a way he was glad that the Bidnyj's notified him about their arrival from Moscow to the States. Alice, were she alive, would be busy welcoming them to New York.

And now that she was no longer with them, he, Leslie, would continue in her footsteps. He glanced at the calendar hanging in the kitchen to make sure he didn't have another appointment the day they were to arrive.

My goodness! That day was today and he still had three hours ahead of him. From Forest Hills to J.F.K. Airport was hardly 15 minutes by cab. Would one cab be enough? There are so many taxis at the airport. If I need one more we can hail it down. It would be just great if I could muster a nap. He said to himself, "Alice honey, don't worry, I'll make it" . . . .

CHAPTER LIV

Yefim quickly realized that in capitalistic U.S.A. the dollar was king. He was very grateful to Leslie Schiff for all of his help, for prepaying rent on their apartment and for leaving them $300.00 to start their lives in Brooklyn. Very few, if any, Russian families received such help from a stranger.

The sum of $300.00 was a small fortune in Russia but in the States that amount did not seem to go very far. In the Soviet Union the rent was very cheap and medical care was free, but this was not the case in the States, where on the average, rent alone ate up to two weeks of ones salary, provided that one was lucky enough to hold a job. Without proper insurance medical care was very expensive and so were the prescription drugs as Yefim found out when Volodia ran a high fever and had to be seen by a physician.

Soon thereafter Liudmila broke a tooth while eating a piece of meat and had to see a local dentist who was recommended by the Razunskis. Leslie suggested the services of his son Jeoffrey, but Liudmila had no means of getting to Queens and not knowing the language, was afraid to use public transportation on her own. She preferred to be treated by a Russian-speaking dentist in her neighborhood.

Once her tooth was fixed she began to work part-time at the *"International"* store and earning her first salary in the United States. She offered the money she earned to Yefim and Elena but they refused to accept any of it, maintaining that Liudmila should keep her money for herself. They were satisfied with the food that she was bringing home from the store at the end of her working day.

Even Elena started to earn money by giving piano lessons to the children in the area. This left Yefim frustrated, as he could not get a job in his profession as a dental technician.

He approached an owner of a dental laboratory in the Mill Basin section of Brooklyn which was within easy reach by subway or bus from Brighton Beach but the owner, an immigrant like himself, told Yefim that he lacked the American experience needed to hold a job.

"Look, here in America we use different pre-polymers, catalysts, acrylics. Forget about the Soviet Union, they are at least 20 years behind America in this field. If you want me to teach you the American methods you will have to come up with $500.00. When you get the money, come back to see me."

"*Spasibo za vnimanie*," repeating in English, "Thank you for your attention."

In vain he tried other laboratories in Manhattan, but due to his limited English could not communicate with people on the subject. Still, he learned one more English sentence:

"We are not hiring anybody these days."

He realized that the first thing he had to do was to improve his English. He enrolled in a local high school where evening lessons for the foreign born were given.

By comparison, Elena was making rapid progress in this respect, most likely due to her ear for music and the sound of voices in any language.

Yefim, after a couple of months of living in the States still had at best a very limited vocabulary but could to some degree, communicate with other people.

During an initial meeting with his *viedushchaia,* Russian speaking social worker, Yefim explained his situation and the frustration of not being able to obtain a job in his field. She arranged for $87.50 in weekly financial aid so that he could concentrate on locating a job that would support his family.

"Remember, Mr. Bidnyj, this is a one time offer of help for a maximum of 3 months.

During this time you must find a job and start to support your family on your own.

After that, you might need to go on welfare and that wouldn't be good at all. Let me make a few telephone calls on your behalf. A number of people in New York City are familiar with our Organization."

On her fifth call she managed to secure an appointment for Yefim with one of the laboratories located on 57th Street between 8th and 9th avenues. The owner of "Hollywood Laboratory" agreed to interview him.

Mrs. Schochet, his social worker, wrote down the address of the Laboratory and how to get there by subway.

"Good luck! Maybe this is the beginning of a fine future for you and your family."

"Thank you very much. I will let you know how it went."

The proprietor of the "Hollywood Laboratory" Mr. Krygier, a Slovak Jew, who started the business just 10 years ago said to Yefim:

"I see that the Agency sent you to me, and I do want to help you. Watch how my men work. Notice the kind of materials and tools they use in different applications whether it's acrylic, porcelain, gold or plaster. We produce the best crowns, dentures, and partials, otherwise I don't ship them. They must be perfect. I pay close attention to the aesthetics of every finished piece, our reputation depends on it. One dentist recommends us to another but the bottom line is also the price. So, the first couple of days just watch what other people do and then I'll start you with simple pieces. I'll check on your progress and if you have any questions you can ask me. If I am busy you can ask my foreman, Abe. Come back tomorrow, we start at 8:30 A.M. sharp.

Yefim returned to Brighton with a big smile on his face. Everybody was happy for him. At least this was a beginning.

The next day he showed up at 8:15 in the morning. The shop was already open and Abe the foreman was dividing the work among the employees of the Laboratory. Yefim was astounded by the sheer variety of materials and the many products in pre-packaged form. He had to admit to himself that he had a lot to learn about dental technology.

He wasn't afraid of the work itself, but he needed time to absorb the new technology. Hopefully, Mr. Krygier would offer him that possibility.

Traveling in crowded subways was his only chance to read the Russian *Slovo,* and in order to improve his English, he read The New York Post with great difficulty. He would underline those words whose meaning he didn't understand and then look them up in the small version of the English-Russian dictionary that he carried with him at all times.

Often he would come home discouraged, and Elena, just by looking at him, was able to lift his sinking spirits.

"Durak! Did you expect to become an American millionaire overnight? Or can you wait a year or two for it?"

After that she would give him a smile and change the subject of the conversation.

"Yefim, go and play with your son, he missed you the whole day."

After washing his hands Yefim would pick up Volodia from his crib and put him down on the floor. Volodia would immediately start to crawl towards him. Yefim would change his position and Volodia would follow him no matter where he would go. It was obvious that both of them enjoyed this game.

"Sometimes I don't know who is the baby and who is the grown man," Liudmila would remark, watching the father and son at their games.

Friday evening Yefim brought home his first paycheck. It wasn't much but it was a beginning and that meant a lot to him and the family. He had started to earn a living.

The same evening Abrasha Razunski came in to see Yefim.

"Yefim, I need your help. Today my assistant suffered a burst appendix and was hospitalized. The way it looks he'll be out of commission for several weeks and I must finish a job I undertook. Since you're not working on Saturdays or Sundays how about giving me a hand? Of course I will pay you for your time."

"Abrasha, it's not the money. You need my help, you got it."

"That is very nice but I insist on paying you."

"Alright, alright, when do I start?"

Tomorrow at 6:00 A.M. We have to go all the way to Long Island. Don't worry,

I have a station wagon and all the necessary tools."

"Okay, I'll be ready, Abrasha."

"Thank you Yefim, see you in the morning. Good night."

Elena had been listening to their entire conversation but had not said a word.

"What do you think Elena?"

"What is there to think? Your friend needs help so give it to him. At the same time you will see if that kind of work is more suitable for you."

Basically it was heavy construction work but Yefim, being young and handy with tools caught on fast, especially under Abrasha's direction. He seemed to be quite happy with Yefim's performance.

Sunday night Abrasha came over and paid Yefim for his two days work.

"Isn't that too much Abrasha?" asked Yefim.

"No, not at all. Are you free next weekend?"

"Yes I am Abrasha." Yefim liked the money. He would have to work almost two weeks at the laboratory to earn that much.

The following week Mr. Krygier said to Yefim:

"We seem to have less work and I am putting the entire place on a 4-day work week.

You will get paid on Thursday and have Friday off until business picks up. I'm sorry but this happens from time to time."

That same evening Yefim informed Abrasha that he was also available on Fridays.

"Wonderful, if you could give me a whole week that would be even better."

"Sorry, Abrasha, but I have an opportunity to learn the dental technology I need, and I must see it through."

"I wish you good luck but I also wish that you would join me in business. We could make a good team, I can feel it. I'm telling you again, there is a lot of money to be made for a guy that is not lazy and has a little of *smekalka* in his head."

"Bear with me for a while if you can, Abrasha."

"Okay my friend, let it be."

Yefim needed the proper attire to work with Abrasha on home restorations; mainly heavy-duty blue jeans or overalls.

One evening Yefim returned home a bit earlier and the family decided to go shopping for those jeans. Yefim and Elena, pushing a smiling Volodia in his stroller went to the many stores lining Brighton Beach Avenue.

They located a men's store that had a large selection of men's suits, jackets, coats, trousers and blue jeans.

In one of the aisles Yefim noticed a vaguely familiar figure of a man loading a shopping cart full of blue jeans. The man turned around and faced Yefim. For a while they both looked at each other and suddenly they recognized each other.

"Mogamet?"

"Yefim, is that you?"

Mogamet was one of the boys that Yefim roomed with while they were both at Lysenko's Orphanage House.

It was Mogamet who found his tongue first.

"Yefim, what in the world are you doing in Brooklyn?"

"I was about to ask you the same question."

"I shouldn't even tell you but I always trusted you and know that you can keep your mouth shut. You see, after Lysenko, I was taken to the Air Force's Aviation Academy.

I graduated as a lieutenant and served for four years. After that, they needed pilots for the Aeroflot and here I am, a captain in the Aeroflot, flying among others, the Moscow- New York route. Each time I am in New York I come here to Brighton to buy a hundred or so blue jeans and I sell them near Dynamo Stadium to triple my money. What about you, Yefim? Is this your family?"

Yefim introduced his wife Elena and his son Volodia, and continued:

"We simply emigrated to the United States and we live here now."

"Oh, you lucky dog! How did you do it?"

"We're Jews and the *Vlasti* let us out."

"I think my mother was also Jewish."

"Can you prove it?"

"Not really. Listen to me Yefim. You can make money with me. Every 10 days buy me between 100 and 150 blue jeans and bring them to my hotel on Lexington Avenue. That is where we're supposed to rest before we fly back to Moscow, Leningrad or Kiev. For every pair you bring I will give you an extra two dollars above your cost. What do you say old friend?"

Elena, who had remained quiet until this moment, answered for Yefim:

"No, Mogamet, my husband is not interested. As it is he is working on two jobs already and is making a very good living. We thank you for your offer." Turning to Yefim she said:

"'Do you want to compare the Soviet jail with an American one? If so, don't bother coming home. I'm perfectly capable of making a living and providing for Volodia."

"Well, Mogamet, my wife spoke my words. Thanks buddy, but no. It was good to see you, take care of yourself."

"*Do svidania*, Yefim—too bad we couldn't do business together."

"You see dear Mogamet, experience is a wonderful thing, because it enabled Yefim to recognize a mistake before he made one for the second time."

She pushed the stroller with the sleeping Volodia and left the store with Yefim right behind her.

Yefim left his jeans on the same shelf and on the same aisle where he met Mogamet. His only conciliation was that he didn't pay for them. He would come back but would get those jeans at another store.

CHAPTER LV

The people working under his jurisdiction didn't exactly like Maksim's boss, Comrade Nikolai Voronov. To the contrary, he was actually despised and the more the employees of Ostankino disliked him, the more they liked Maksim. This is not to say that Voronov was a fool, far from it. It was obvious to Voronov the minute he saw how Maksim was greeted by the staff upon his return from Switzerland that Maksim's days at Ostankino were to be numbered.

The following week Maksim was called into Voronov's office where he was told without any preamble:

"Tretyakov Gallery needs a man for the research department and I recommended you for that position. By tomorrow afternoon have your desk cleared. I shall re-assign anything you have pending to someone else. Any questions Ziemtsov?"

"No, Dr. Voronov. Thank you for your recommendation. I was looking forward to working at such a prestigious institution. By tomorrow afternoon I will have my desk cleaned out and all my work completed. I won't leave any loose ends.

"*Do svidania.*"

Max was actually very happy with his new assignment. He had a million reasons for leaving Ostankino and that million was safely tucked away in a Swiss bank.

The famous Tretyakov Gallery had over 50,000 exhibits and its own library and research department. It was the Research Department that eventually gave him the freedom to travel, a rare luxury in the Soviet Union.

The next day Maksim was interviewed by the head of Tretyakov's Research Department, Dr. Mira Makarova, a middle-aged woman who knew her subject extremely well.

Maksim told her about himself, his educational background in Leningrad and his work under the tutelage of Professor Vasiliev who died at the Grand Opening of the exhibition in Switzerland.

Dr. Makarova listened intently to his every word.

"I didn't know that Vasiliev died. He and I were very close, too bad indeed. He was such a nice, cultured man, I will miss him. Coming back to you, Maksim, what are your interests?"

"I would like to concentrate on early Russian art, mainly icons."

"I'm so glad that you've asked for that because I had in mind to assign you to that branch. You will be required to travel to churches, former monasteries, possibly to regional towns where icons formed part of general historical exhibitions. Once you do locate any articles such as icons or paintings, the Party will request them for our gallery."

"Will I have the use of an automobile?"

"That is the big problem. We may not always be able to provide you with one. We have too many departments and not enough cars. When the need arises, you will have to use public transportation, I'm sorry to say."

"No problem, Dr. Makarova, I'll manage somehow."

"I want you to start your job by getting acquainted with our entire inventory of this department and the history behind each art piece. In addition you'll have to know how each icon was made and how it was preserved. In other words you will have to "eat and sleep" icons. Is that clearly understood?"

"*Tak tochno*, Comrade Makarova."

"Very well, Maksim, I'll introduce you around. By the way, I have seen your papers already, they were hand-delivered by a courier. You will be glad to know that your salary was raised by 20 rubles. You seem to have done a good job in Switzerland.

I wish you good luck young man, and now follow me."

They walked through so many offices and had seen so many people that Maksim hardly remembered their names, titles or positions held. No question about it, this job looked very promising.

"Well, Maksim, now that you've met everyone and it is already 3:00 P.M., it is too late to start you on the new job. You can go home and report to me tomorrowat 8:45 A.M."

"Thank you very much Dr. Makarova, I'll see you tomorrow morning."

Maksim decided to walk a bit just to collect his thoughts and plan future steps. He continued walking along the Kadoshevskaya Embankment, passing by the State Museum of Literature, the Church of Ivan the Warrier, Oktyabrskaya Square and the massive stone enclosure of the Architectural Museum. By this time, however, he was tired enough to take the Metro home.

Interestingly enough, after he returned from Switzerland, Galina and he had become even closer as a couple. He shared with her his impressions of Makarova and the Tretyakov Gallery. He felt strongly that his knowledge of icons would come in handy when dealing with collectors of Russian art.

From his days at Ostankino Museum and his personal research, Max knew that early Russian icons were not only adornments for churches, but also indispensable items of every Russian home. Icons belonging to prosperous churches or rich people were often covered with gold or silver trimmings.

Icons were painted on boards, mainly of basswood, as linden was not sensitive to humidity and was less likely to warp. Large icons were painted on several boards that were connected by pegs and braced by splints to avoid warping. The face of the icon was pasted over with *povoloka* canvas. The *povoloka* was covered with a smooth, solid coat of ivory colored *levka* priming. The icons were painted with tempera pigments mixed with egg yolk.

Older icons were sometimes hardly visible under oil varnish that blackened with time. Often the original painting was hidden under coats of paint made in subsequent years. A new technique of restoration made it possible to reveal the original layers of paint. Icons thus restored were sold to museums or private collectors for large sums of money.

Max introduced Galina to the restoration methods. Galina, as a woman and artist, had a "lighter" hand and had considerably more patience for that kind of job that Max. The few small icons that Maksim brought home for restoration and returned to Ostankino were done to perfection by Galina.

With much trepidation Max gave Galina the two icons be brought from the Zagorski Center.

"Can I watch you work Galina?"

"No, Max. I hate it when somebody hangs around while I work. I need quiet and nobody to disturb me. I hope you don't mind."

Galina worked on those icons for over two months. It was a very tedious and precise procedure. When she finished the job she called Max to see the finished product. Max's intuition had proven correct, by removing several layers of paint, Galina had restored the original paintings to all their glory.

Max had one look at the icons and almost fainted.

"*Bozhe moy!* This is Rubliov's work!"

He was referring to the legendary Andrei Rubliov, a monk of the St. Andronicus Monastery. The same one who painted the famous Old Testament Trinity and the main icon of the Sergius Monastery in Zagorsk. Other masterpieces attributed to him with a high degree of certainty were a series of icons of the Cathedral of Zvenigorod near Moscow.

Like all icons painted in his time, Rubliov never signed his works but his brushwork was unmistakable.

Max felt as though he had just discovered the painting of the Mona Lisa or an atomic bomb, because the issue of publication of his findings was just as explosive. The only solution left was to sell to a foreign collector, because if he was caught . . . . a cold shiver ran down his spine.

CHAPTER LVI

Coming back to Israel from Switzerland and France both Natalia and Marcel felt like they were floating on cloud nine. Not only did they visit countries, which up to this time they could only dream about, but also they were bringing back $250,000, which was much better than manna from heaven.

The first thing they decided upon was to return the money to their relatives and friends who were instrumental in buying them their present apartment. The second was to buy Israel's most popular car for themselves, a brand new Subaru. For the time being they jointly decided to remain in Ramat-Gan where their friends lived and shopped.

The skies never remain blue forever, and from time to time clouds appear on the horizon. That cloud in their lives was Marcel's complaint of being constantly tired.

"Marcel, I'm sure that the reason for it is all the excitement we experienced over the past few weeks. However, it might be a good idea for you to have a general check-up as a precaution. I'll make an appointment for you and will come along with you if you like."

"Thank you Natalia, that won't be necessary, I am not a baby."

"Okay, Marcel, I won't insist, but please make sure that they take a complete blood test."

"No problem, this won't be my first physical."

While waiting for that appointment they kept up their regular routine of bridge with friends and going to restaurants a bit more often then they had before. The only departure from Marcel's old routine was to take longer and more frequent siestas in the afternoon.

As instructed, Marcel didn't have breakfast prior to his check-up. His appointment was at 7:00 A.M. He got up early as not to wake up Natalia and drove to the Ichilov Hospital. He waited in the crowded waiting room over an hour before his name was called. The nurse took his temperature, blood pressure, drew blood for a complete C.B.C., weighed him, measured his height and brought him to another room where he undressed the upper part of his body in preparation for a chest X-Ray. Having done all this, the nurse brought him to the examining room and said:

"Wait here, the doctor will be with you shortly." The Hebrew "Rega Achat" or "waita minute" ended up being 45 minutes, during which time Marcel read every old magazine that he found laying on a small table.

Finally, the doctor barged in and said in Hebrew with a heavy Russian accent:

"Sorry, I had an emergency. Now, what is ailing you?"

"Lately I tire very easily. I seem to have lost all my energy. At night I get up several times to urinate. This upsets my sleep and I get up tired in the morning."

"Well, let's see what we can find out."

The doctor listened to his heartbeat, his breathing, told him to lie down and touched his stomach in several places.

"So far everything seems to be normal. Drop your trousers and make a position like you would like to shoot into the sky with your ass."

The doctor put on rubber gloves and smeared Vaseline on his middle finger.

It was far from pleasant but Marcel had gone through a similar procedure before.

"Your prostrate is enlarged but that is typical of men your age. I don't see anything abnormal in your case. Here are some tissues to wipe yourself with, and you can put your trousers back on. Mr. Kagan, your wife Natalia used to be my supervisor back in Leningrad. She is a fine woman and a fine doctor; please give her my best regards. In case you forgot, my name, its Rivkin, Evgeni Rivkin."

Someone knocked on the door. It was the nurse from the X-ray room holding Marcel's X-rays. Dr. Rivkin lifted the X-ray against the light and looked at it carefully.

"Well, Mr. Kagan, I don't see anything wrong here either. Your lungs are clear, your heart is normal and everything else seems to be okay too. For the final results of your examination I will have to wait for the results of your blood test. So far you are fine.

The nurse will give you a shot of vitamin B-12 and you should take about 200 mg of vitamin E daily. I believe you should be back to feeling like your normal self soon.

Give Natalia my love. I have to run I have many patients waiting for me.".

The nurse led Marcel to yet another room where she administered a vitamin B-12 shot and gave him a free bottle of vitamin E.

"See you next year Mr. Kagan."

"I hope so nurse. Thank you for the vitamins."

By the time he reached his home in Ramat-Gan it was lunchtime.

Natalia had been up for some time preparing Marcel's favorite dishes which included vanilla flavored leban-yogurt, tomatoes, hard boiled eggs and fresh rolls.

"How did your checkup go?"

"I was seen by Dr. Rivkin. He sends you his best regards. According to him I'm fine.

My heart, lungs, stomach and prostate are okay too. He has to wait for my blood results.

They also gave me a shot of B-12 and I'm energized and hungry as a wolf. Remember *moya golubka*, that I didn't have breakfast today."

During the next two days Marcel almost forgot about his visit to the doctor. The B-12 shot and the doctor's diagnosis that he was okay created some buoyancy in him. He actually felt much better.

That same day around 3:00 P.M. the telephone rang. It was Dr. Rivkin:

"Rivkin here. Mr. Kagan, we received the results of your blood test."

"Is everything okay doctor?"

"Not really. Your white blood cell count seems to be very high.

I want you to come to my office tomorrow at 11:00 o'clock and please bring your wife with you."

With these few words Dr. Rivkin hung up with no further explanation.

A few minutes later Natalia walked in carrying groceries from the local supermarket and Marcel told her about the strange phone call from Dr. Rivkin.

"Natalia, what is this all about? What does an unusual number of white blood cells mean?"

"Well, Marcel, don't jump to any premature conclusions. There are several medical reasons for a high count. For instance, it could be some type of infection, and so on.

Did he give you a number to call?"

"No, but we have to see him tomorrow at 11:00 A.M."

"Well then, we shall find out about it tomorrow. It could also be a mistake or a mix-up in the laboratory. These things do happen in a busy lab, so don't worry ahead of time."

The next morning they drove to Ichilov Hospital to see Dr. Rivkin. It was the very first time in Israel that Marcel was actually seen by a doctor at the appointed hour.

The receptionist brought them to Dr. Rivkin's office where the entire conversation was conducted in Russian.

"Come in, come in. How are you Natalia. Long time, no see."

"I'm just fine *Zhenia*, but how is my husband?"

"We seem to have some trouble here. His white blood cell count reached over 20,000.

We have diagnosed the reason for it as C.M.L. Chronic Meyalitic Leukemia."

"Doctor, you must be kidding! Only children suffer from that disease but not grown men," Marcel shouted.

"Mr. Kagan, you are free to get another opinion, as a matter of fact, I insist on it."

"What does this mean doctor, am I going to die?"

"Marcel, *moi mily*, will I let you die?" Of course not. Let's hear what the doctor has to say."

You see Mr. Kagan, the news is not altogether bad. One can

live with C.M.L. for 5 to 25 years. Golda Meir had a similar illness and she lived and worked to a ripe old age.

There are new tools to combat that disease. Chemotherapy and new promising medications can prolong the life of the patient considerably."

"Marcel, listen to Dr. Rivkin. We'll just take 20 years and after that we shall die together."

"Well, Natalia, I'll take the 20 years with you any time."

"That's the spirit. Let me write up all the prescriptions and the frequency of chemotherapy treatment for Mr. Kagan. By the way, there is also a very fine American trained oncologist working in Tel-Aviv. I can arrange for him to see Mr. Kagan. Would you like me to do that?"

"Please, *Zhenia* do it for me."

"I'll have my secretary call his office and arrange an appointment for you. Natalia, I need to ask you about your former patient Mrs. Rappaport. I understand you treated her before. Oh, Mr. Kagan, can you wait a minute outside while I confer with Natalia about that case?"

"Of course, Doctor. I'll wait outside for you Natalia."

Natalia never had a patient by the name of Mrs. Rappaport but understood that Dr. Rivkin wanted to talk to her alone without Marcel present during the conversation.

"Well, *Zhenia,* what is the *emes*?"

"I'm sorry to say that your husband doesn't have C.M.L. but the worst kind of Leukemia for which, as you very well know, there is practically no cure."

"What is your prognosis, *Zhenia*?"

'If he is lucky, six months at best."

"Thank you for being honest with me." Natalia left his office.

Two more tests including a marrow tap and a visit to that American trained oncologist confirmed Dr. Rivkin's original diagnosis.

Three months later Marcel Liebeskind-Kagan died in the middle of the night. He was buried in the Jewish tradition in the presence of his children, grandchildren and his wife Natalia, in the overcrowded Cemetery of the city of Cholon in the State of Israel.

CHAPTER LVII

Sometimes in life, very complex situations have a way of solving themselves. Such was the case with Maksim Ziemtsov who for weeks had been trying to approach Charles LeMay without raising the suspicion of the Soviet Secret Police. To use the telephone or surface mail would be to invite trouble. Surely, he had to find a better way.

Luckily, such an opportunity presented itself quite unexpectedly. A few weeks after starting his new job at the Tretyakov Gallery, Maksim was walking towards the main library when a large group of foreign woman all wearing caps marked "Canadian Wildlife Federation" blocked his way. Max stopped to let them through when one of the ladies approached Max and said: "Hello, Mr. Ziemtsov."

Max's face registered surprise because he could not recall who she was although he had a feeling that he had met her somewhere before.

"I can tell that you don't remember me but we met at the Swiss Embassy reception.

My name is Helen LeMay and I am the wife of Charles LeMay."

It came to him. Indeed they had been introduced but Maxim had spent more time speaking with Mr. LeMay as he had been impressed with his native-like fluency in Russian.

"Of course I do remember you now. How are you and how is your husband?"

"Just walk with me and I will tell you. We are all just fine. I understand that you were in Switzerland. How did you enjoy your stay?"

"It was very nice but too short. Tell me, please, are you both still interested in Russian art?"

"We definitely are. I sometimes think that Charles would sell his soul for some of those icons."

"What I am about to tell you must stay between us, otherwise I may lose my life."

"My goodness, this sounds pretty serious."

"I'm afraid it is. My wife and I would like to defect to the West, preferably to your Canada. Recently I discovered two of Rubliov's original icons. I would gladly give one to the person who could get us out of the Soviet Union. Do you think your husband would be able to help us?"

"I will ask him, but what are you planning to do with the second icon?"

"Most likely I will sell it. We'll need money to start a new life. How will Mr. LeMay let me know if he can or cannot help me?"

"In three days I will have an answer for you. I'll be walking along Old Arbat Street in front of the "Wine Cellar" coffee shop at 7:00 P.M. I will be wearing a blue jacket with a small crocodile brooch in my left lapel. If I should take it off it will mean that I want to talk to you about details. Is that clear to you?"

"Very clear Mrs. LeMay."

"In that case, I will rejoin my group. *Do svidania.*"

Maksim was a little taken aback when a Tetryakov Gallery guard asked him:

"Comrade, what did that foreign woman want from you?"

"Tourists! You know what tourists want; directions and information about the Gallery."

"Yeh, that is what they usually ask me about too."

That evening Max told Galina about his meeting with Mrs. LeMay, stating "this is our chance."

The next three days were interminably long, but on the third evening they got dressed and like any other couple and went for an evening stroll. As a prop, they took along one of Galina's many oil paintings, as Arbat Street had long been a meeting place for artists and writers.

The narrow 19th century pedestrian avenue was located to the west of Moscow's center between the Gates of Arbat and Kalinski

Bridge on one end and Smolenski Square on the other. The area was made even more popular by a poem by Okudzava entitled "My Arbat-My Homeland."

The kilometer long Old Arbat Street was lined with charming small stores and cafes and was known for its open-air flea market specializing in paintings and folklore art.

Holding hands like a couple on a date they passed the "Wine Cellar" café but it was still too early for their meeting. They were stopped a couple of times by people inquiring if the painting they were holding was for sale. Galina mentioned such a high price that she drew a comment from a potential customer: "What do you think, you have a Picasso for sale?" They ignored him and kept walking. On the opposite side of the street they noticed Helen LeMay walking towards them. She was wearing a blue jacket with a small crocodile brooch in her lapel.

When she noticed Max carrying the painting, she stopped him and asked:

"Is this painting for sale?"

"Yes, Madam."

"Can I see it in a better light?"

"Sure you can, here it is."

Helen took the painting from him and moved toward the streetlight. Anyone watching the scene would look upon it as a normal encounter between an artist and a potential buyer. Similar scenes had taken place many times.

"Charles told me that he will get you out of Russia but he wants to check the authenticity of Rubliov's work first. How will you get that icon to me?"

"How about tomorrow, same time, same place. I'll bring the icon wrapped in paper and another oil painting. I will pretend to sell you the painting just as I am doing now."

"Yes, that seems like a good approach. How much do I owe you for this painting? I really love it. Galina, you are very talented.

"It's a gift, but please give us some money in case we are being watched."

Mrs. LeMay reached into her pocketbook and took out 25 rubles. Max counted the money and put it into his pocket at the same time that Galina handed Helen the oil painting. She looked at the painting a little longer and went on her way, as did the Ziemtsovs, continuing their evening stroll along Arbat Street.

The next evening the repeat performance went without a glitch. The icon was wrapped in plain brown paper and Maksim held another oil painting on top of it, as both pieces were almost the same size. Again, a passerby asked them if the painting was for sale. This time they replied calmly, "We just bought it ourselves."

Helen showed up on time, wearing the same jacket. This second meeting went much better. After all, it had been rehearsed the night before. Helen again held the painting up against the light and gave the impression that she was haggling over the price. Again money changed hands and so did the merchandise.

"When will we hear from you Mrs. LeMay?"

"Make it in two weeks, same time, same place and the same blue jacket. Charles wants you to bring him your new passport photos, 4 of each. Will both of you please wear a white shirt or blouse with a black tie for the photos. Max, you need to get a haircut, preferably a crew cut. Or you can simply comb your hair in another direction. According to Charles, that will change your face."

"We will do that. Thank you so much for everything."

"There is nothing to thank me for yet. Have those photos with you at our next meeting."

She turned around and continued on her way carrying paintings purchased on Arbat Street under her arm.

"Max, I must say that Helen was right, you do need a haircut because you look like Pushkin with your long, wavy hair. I'll get a trim as well. There is a photo studio not far from our house and we can get our photos done there."

"No, Galina, it is not a good idea to get our pictures done in our neighborhood. I suggest that we do it far away from the area we live in.

"You are right as always, but why do you think the LeMays need two weeks before they can do anything?"

"Most likely he will airmail the icon to Europe so that art experts can verify the authenticity of Rubliov's work. If he is satisfied he will then start to make arrangements for us, and all this takes time my dear."

"Do you have any idea what kind of preparations he is making?"

"Not the slightest. I have no idea what he can or cannot do or who else might be involved. There is nothing else for us to do but wait. We'll get out photos done but not on the same day or place. Before we do that though, let's get our haircuts."

While waiting to hear from the LeMays they kept up the appearance of a normal life both at home and at work.

There was an enormous amount of work waiting for Max at the Tetryakov's Gallery Research Department. Dr. Makarova was a pleasant, friendly but demanding supervisor. She had an encyclopedic memory for the smallest historical detail and there was no way to contradict her knowledge of the art world.

One evening after a hard day at the office, Max's seemingly outer tranquility was shattered by a telephone call from his mother in Israel informing him about Marcel's death.

"What are you going to do now, Mother?"

"I'll remain in Israel for the time being. It is too soon to make any further decisions," and she hung up.

Max knew that his mother had been very happy with Marcel and would now be very lonely. She could not come back to Russia especially now when he was preparing to get out himself. Maybe in the future he would be able to do something for her. So much depended on Mr. LeMay.

Two weeks passed and Max and Galina went to Arbat Street to meet with Helen LeMay. They took the other icon with them wrapped in paper, inside which was an envelope with their photos. They also brought along another oil painting as they had done previously.

The familiar figure in the same blue jacket appeared on time.

They started with their well-practiced routine. While Max showed the oil painting, Helen gave him the update:

"To begin with, the Rubliov is authentic. Here is what Charles has in mind for you two.

This coming Sunday, that is exactly six days from now, he wants you to go to Sheremietivo International Airport's Lufthansa terminal. You must be there by 3:00 o'clock in the afternoon. You are to come carrying flowers as though you would be saying goodbye to friends or relatives. Do not, under any circumstances, carry any baggage with you. Go straight to the bathrooms in the main hall. You, Max, go into the men's room, and Galina, you go into the ladies room. In each bathroom there will be one cubicle marked "Out of Order." The door will be sealed with tape. Remove the tape and go inside. On the inside door will hang a clothing bag containing a uniform of a Lufthansa flight attendant. Change quickly into that uniform. Max, in the right pocket of your jacket there will be a German passport made out to Max Miller of Munich. Galina's passport will be in the black pocketbook laying on top of the toilet seat, made out to Greta Fleischer of Hanover. This bag will contain items that can be found in any woman's bag; cosmetic articles, comb, brush, lipstick and even sanitary napkins. Your wallets will contain money and various pictures. Both of you will have regulation size black valises on wheels, inside which are new articles of clothing. The clothing is new but has been washed or dry cleaned to give the appearance of being used. The same applies to your shoes. There are also magazines in German and English in addition to the book "Russian for Beginners." We have noticed that Russian custom officers are much nicer to foreigners who take the trouble to learn their language. You will have exactly five minutes to get dressed. Please leave all your things, I repeat, put all your belongings in the same clothing bag that held your airline attire. These items will be collected by the bathroom attendant and forwarded to your new residence, wherever that might be."

"It looks like you have done this before, Mrs. LeMay."

"Let me be perfectly blunt with you, Max. It is none of your business. The less you know the better it will be for everyone involved. Let me continue because time is of the essence. As soon as you are dressed you are to come out with your airline valise and bag. Again, do not take anything with you of Soviet origin, is that understood? Outside of the bathrooms there will be a team of four flight attendants, two men and two women, waiting for you. You are to join them as if you were a part of the same crew. Greet them with "Gruess Gott" and follow them. One attendant will pay close attention to you,

Max, and one will be stay close to Galina. Walk unhurriedly, smile often, and repeat the word "Ya" from time to time. When you reach the passport control watch your colleagues and do the same as they do. If asked to open your luggage, comply. There are also American cigarettes in your valise. Sometimes, depending upon circumstances, you can leave a pack or two, but do it discreetly. You're flying to Frankfurt, Germany because Air Canada doesn't fly directly to or from Moscow.

Charles will be waiting for you at the Frankfurt Airport, and from there on you will be in his hands. This is all I can tell you at the present time. Do you have any questions?"

"We have thousands of questions and none. We made the decision to leave Russia so let's hope that everything will go according to plan. Any failure will mean our end."

"Don't worry, the two of you will be just fine, keep cool. I have to leave, so good luck."

That night Max and Galina just tossed and turned and did not sleep a wink.

"Galina, if you are worried we can remain in Moscow. We really don't have such a bad life here."

"We don't have a good one either. We made a joint decision and know what awaits us should we fail. I say, let's go for it!"

"Exactly my sentiments. After all, I am the son of a Hero of the Soviet Union, let's not forget that either."

"That's why I married you, Max."

As was the Russian custom, they put on their best Sunday outfits, bought two bouquets of flowers and went to the airport, giving them ample time to reach their destination by 3:00 o'clock.

A militiaman at the entrance to the Lufthansa terminal stopped them.

"What is the nature of your business in here?"

"We are seeing our friends from the Diplomatic Corps off to Germany."

"Your papers, please."

Max showed him his C.P. Identification card, which completely satisfied the guard.

"Please proceed, comrades."

They walked around the terminal, observing the human traffic. There were long lines in front of each counter and gate. Most of the passengers as far as Max could tell, were foreign tourists and businessmen.

Two minutes before 3:00 o'clock Galina and Max went into their respective restrooms. Sure enough, the last cubicle in each room bore the sign "Out of Order." Nobody was watching them as everyone was occupied attending to their own needs. Even the orderlies seemed to be busy cleaning a sink at the far end of the bathrooms.

Max quickly removed the tape from the door and walked in, locking the door behind him. There on the door hung a black clothing travel bag. Max unzipped the bag finding a Lufthansa flight attendant's uniform, in his size. Everything was there as Helen LeMay had promised it would be. Max shed his own clothing, stuffed it back into the zippered bag and put on the provided articles of clothing. Everything seemed to fit properly until he came to the shoes. No way would his feet fit into those shoes. Max happened to have wide feet. He broke out into a cold sweat until he realizedthat the black shoes he was wearing, purchased in Switzerland, should be fine. All he had to do now was put on the black socks that were provided for him. It took him a full six minutes to get dressed. He then grabbed the two pieces of luggage and emerged as a full-fledged member of the Lufthansa Airline. Galina was already there standing by the four other Lufthansa flight attendants. He walked over to them wearing his very best smile and said, "Gruess Gott."

In response he heard, "Gruess Gott Max, kom schon Mench." Surely he didn't need any prodding.

A good looking flight attendant began talking to him and Max, as instructed, shook his head as if he fully understood what she was saying and muttered "Ya," from time to time.

They walked towards the Passport Control gate and encountered a fairly long line that was moving at a steady pace. His companion reminded him: "Max, Deine Papieren." He had forgotten to check for his passport. Yes, there it was in his left jacket pocket, the very precious passport to freedom. As far as he could tell everybody in his crew held his or her passports ready, including Galina who gave him a wink with her eye.

The border policemen just glanced at his passport comparing it to that of the man in front of him. Satisfied, he stamped it and handed it back to Max.

Slieduyoushchiy! The next person was another member of the Lufthansa crew. The entire team passed the Control without a problem. The next hurdle was Customs, which everyone passed without stopping with the exception of one person, Galina.

"Otkroite vash bagazh" said the officer pointing to her valise. She opened the valise for him to have a better look. He went through her articles of clothing and cosmetics, and soon the book *Russian for Beginners* caught his attention.

"Are you taking Russian lessons?" asked the officer politely.

"Da" she said smiling, flirting just a bit.

"So what do you know in Russian?"

"I can count to 10."

"Let's hear it please."

"Odin, dva, tri, chetyrie, piat, shest, vosiem, dieviat, desit."

"Oh, you skipped number seven, but you can go or you will miss your flight, your friends are waiting for you," he said smiling.

Galina smiled back, took out a pack of Marlboro cigarettes and collected her valise, leaving behind the unopened pack of cigarettes. She turned around to see his reaction, but the officer had quickly placed the pack into his pocket, his lips forming the words *"Spasibo."*

Galina blew him a kiss, but the kiss wasn't just for him, it was also meant for Mother Russia.

The Lufthansa flight crew including Max and Galina boarded the plane ahead of the waiting passengers, both first class and coach. Once they had boarded, they were directed towards the end of the plane where a curtain covered two small benches. Curiously, that curtain had a sign in German as well as in English, "Crew Resting, Do Not Disturb."

The Lufthansa plane, which had a reputation for on time departures, was delayed this time over an hour and a half due to a mechanical problem, adding to the discomfort and fear of the passengers and crew. The Captain, sensing the atmosphere in the plane, ordered the bar to be opened and drinks were served, free of charge.

Finally, the plane taxied on the runway and took off to the general relief of both passengers and crew, not mentioning the Ziemtsovs who were petrified, imagining the worst.

The plane cruised at 30,000 feet straight in westerly fashion, destination Frankfurt, West Germany. During the flight they were fed twice and served unlimited coffee and soft drinks. One of the attendants who had boarded with Max and Galina suggested a mild sedative so they might get a little bit of sleep. They gratefully accepted her offer, as sleep would shorten their travel time and give them some much-needed rest.

Finally, they heard the announcement:

"Please put your seats in the upward position and fasten your belts for landing."

Whoever piloted the plane was an expert, because the landing gear hardly touched the ground and the plane moved slowly towards its designated gate.

Max and Galina had to wait until every passenger including those in wheelchairs, deplaned, before they were allowed to leave with the rest of the crew. Prior to reaching the Passport Control office, they were met by a smiling Charles LeMay in the company of two sour looking individuals. He gave them a bear hug, and this Yale University alumna said in purest Russian slang, "*kak diela rebiata?*" How are things, guys? He also introduced the other two men. They were functionaries of the West Bund Police, who were along to make sure that Max and Galina did not remain in Germany but would proceed to Canada, the country that gave Ziemtsov the right of asylum.

Charles took the valise out of Galina's hand and said: "Please follow me."

It was a long and tiring walk but they reached the First Class Lounge of Air Canada Airline. Charles went to the door marked "Private" and opened it with his own key. In the room was a closet full of men's and ladies apparel.

"Please change again into civilian clothes, and take your time, there is no hurry and no danger. You are no longer employees of the Lufthansa Airline; you are practically in Canada on the threshold of a new life. Welcome."

CHAPTER LVIII

In comparison to the last couple of days, the trip from Frankfurt to Toronto's Pearson Airport was a cinch for the Ziemtsovs.

Most of the legal obstacles up this point were taken care of by Charles LeMay. The rest, if any, were to be covered by Helen LeMay, who was to accompany the Ziemtsovs.

"Charles has to return to Moscow, but I will be with you until you get settled in Toronto where I have a number of errands to do; but you are my priority."

"We do appreciate that very much, Mrs. LeMay."

"When I speak with you I am reminded of my grandfather, Robert. He died when I was eight years old. He was a remarkable man and like you, came to Canada at the age of 14 from a small Russian town called Oshmiany. His original name was Rueven Sadovitzky that he changed to Robert Sanders. He started his career by collecting scrap metal. One day he was given an old bridge to take apart for scrap and it turned out to be a lucrative operation that he repeated on other occasions. Thus, he learned to assemble bridges by taking them apart first. After that he founded his own company that built bridges. Believe it or not, this semi-literate person build the Highland Creek Bridge, and the French River and Burlington Bay bridges in Ontario. During that time he also married my grandmother, Maureen Flanagan, an Irish-Catholic. Eventually he moved from building bridges to land development and became a real estate magnate. His ingenuity and basic "chutzpah" enabled him time and time again to undertake projects and succeed where others had failed. Still, he found the time to sire six sons. My father was the youngest. Interestingly, what grandpa Robert was able to build and amass, his sons were able to piss away. Like most Irish, the boys were heavy drinkers, gambled and carried on with questionable women. At the end, my grandpa died in an old age home, almost penniless. The only thing of value that my own father brought with him was his education, and that helped him to become a full Professor of Linguistics at the local university. I had a good life as a child but we never became rich and that is what I intend to rectify. I must have inherited my business genes from my Jewish grandfather. I dabble a bit in the ever-growing real estate market. My reason for going to Toronto right now is to secure a bank loan to pay off my partner. We jointly own a six-story apartment building on Finch Street. Harry, my partner, married a girl from Caracas, Venezuela, and is moving there and liquidating all his Canadian assets."

"How much money is needed Mrs. LeMay?"

"About $750,000 to $800,000 Canadian dollars."

"Does the building bring in a good income?"

"Very good indeed."

"Could two families live on that income?"

"Yes, of course, but why would that interest me? I want that money to invest in other deals. Why do you ask, Maksim?"

"Count me in, Mrs. LeMay. I will put up the money for half of that building, sight unseen Your word is good enough for me."

"Are you serious, Maksim? Where would you get that kind of money?"

"I have it in Switzerland. I also dabble in art occasionally, mostly on the selling end."

"Very well, Maksim, we have a deal, and please call me Helen."

"Thank you Helen. Do you think there is a vacant apartment in that building for us?"

"As far as I know, everything is rented, but I keep a small apartment there for us when we are in Toronto. It is a fully furnished, one-bedroom apartment with a fireplace, and one and a half baths with underfoot heaters that keep the tiles warm in winter."

"It sounds ideal."

"You can keep that apartment for the next six months. I'm sure that during that time you will find something a bit larger to suit your own taste. Toronto is a lovely city and its long winters will remind you of Moscow or Leningrad. If you still need more winter weather, there are places as cold as Siberia, but there are also other beautiful places. All you need to do is take a ride to Montreal and from there go to the Laurentian Mountains and do some skiing at Mont Tremblant. You do ski, don't you?"

"Of course, skiing was part of the school curriculum. In due time we hope to visit that area but coming back to the building on Finch Street, who takes care of it when you are away?"

"I have a very reliable man, a retired member of the Royal Mounted Police, Mr. Richard Potter. We have known him for years and actually, he is also Charles' godfather. There is no question as to his honesty."

"That is great. We would like to meet him one of these days."

"All in due time, but first we have to get you registered with the Canadian Authorities, get you located in the apartment, and take you to the bank where you will be able to arrange the transfer of your funds and open savings and checking accounts. You need to learn how to use your checkbook to pay bills. We will also get you credit cards that you will find very convenient. You are both young and you will soon adapt to the life in Canada. Oh, my goodness, I forgot to ask you if either one of you know how to drive a car?'

"Maksim knows, but I have to learn. I understand that all Canadian women drive cars."

"You are right, most of them do. Canada is a big country and having a car is almost a must. Max, do you have a driver's license?"

"Yes, I do. Before I left for Switzerland I took out an International Driver's License." "Will it be honored in Canada?"

"Most likely. I will look into it."

"All of this sounds very exciting. How in the world will we be able to repay you for all your trouble?"

"As I said before, don't worry about that right now. Obviously, we can't accomplish everything in one day. First things first, as I always say. We shall start with you going to the apartment for a good night's sleep. Sometimes it takes days to get over the jet lag. Unfortunately, I can't stay in Toronto that long. Tomorrow I will take you to the bank and help you there too. You will also have to engage the services of an attorney to make sure that your interests are fully protected. I can't recommend my own lawyer because it would be unethical. Don't worry; there are many lawyers in Canada. Perhaps the bank officials can recommend someone suited to your needs. Am I putting too much weight on you?"

"Not at all, we are fully aware that we'll have to face of these things. Your help will reduce what you call a "weight.""

Surprisingly there was little if any "red tape" at the airport. They traveled light with a limited amount of luggage, mainly items provided by Charles LeMay at the Frankfurt Airport.

Helen brought them by taxi to the apartment building on Finch Street. The apartment was a bit dusty and stale, but otherwise perfect for their immediate needs.

"While you're unpacking and making yourselves at home I'll go around the corner to the grocery store and bring you some food to get you started."

"Helen, I'll go with you, Galina can manage on her own, but where will you stay?

We can all squeeze in here without a problem."

"Thank you Maksim, but Charles'sister lives just two blocks from here and they havea large house. Besides, I also want to see my niece and nephew."

"Very well, let's go to the grocery store. Helen, lead the way."

"Keep in mind that next to the grocery store there are other stores where you can buy whatever you wish, all you need is money. Talking about money, do you see that tall, modern building on your left? That is the Toronto-Dominion Bank, and diagonally across from it is the Royal Bank of Canada, where I'll bring you tomorrow to settle our deal. The Royal Bank is one of the largest and enjoys a good reputation. They also have the most successful money managers who can provide you with a stream of income by investing in tax-free bonds. Max, you will have a lot to learn about our society, customs, insurance and so forth. Remember the Russian proverb "Moscow wasn't built in a day?," and neither was Toronto. Okay, here is the grocery store owned by Armenians, I think."

At the entrance of the store Helen took a shopping cart and started to load it with bread, butter, milk, cold cuts and orange juice. Maksim paid for these items with the Canadian currency he found in his Lufthansa uniform.

"Can you carry all this Maksim? Will you find your way back? If so, I have to leave.

Tomorrow morning at 10:30 I'll pick you both up and we will go to the bank, as both of your signatures will be needed. Good night, *spokoinoi nochi*."

"Good night Mrs. LeMay and thank you again."

"Max, I told you, it's Helen."

"I need to get used to it Mrs. LeMay, I mean, Helen."

"That's much better, so long."

Max carried two large brown bags full of groceries to the apartment. In the meantime, Galina changed the bed linen and dusted off most of the furniture.

"Max, let's have something to eat, I'm starving. As soon as I eat I'll take a fast shower and go to bed, I'm falling off my feet. It's been a very long day."

"Same here *moia golubka*, take what you need and I will put the rest away."

Hastily they ate ham and cheese sandwiches, washed down with glasses of orange juice. Max left the dirty dishes in the sink while Galina went to the bathroom. When she came out, she found Max fast asleep. She joined him in bed without disturbing him.

The telephone rang at 10:00 A.M. waking them from a deep sleep. It was Helen.

"I was sure that you would still be sleeping but I need you to be ready at the latest by 11:00 o'clock. Remember, I'm flying back today and still have a ton of things to do.

Please hurry, I will see you in an hour."

After quick showers, and a cup of instant coffee for breakfast, the Ziemtsovs were ready for Helen who was waiting for them in the lobby of the building.

"Good morning everybody. Let's go. The Royal Bank is an easy walk from here."

Helen introduced Max and Galina to Mrs. Marian Parks, the vice-president of the bank, who also handled Helen's account. Helen briefed Mrs. Parks about the commercial deal between Helen and the Ziemtsovs as well as their future banking needs as customers of the bank.

"We shall start with the transfer of your funds from Switzerland. In the adjacent room there is a phone linked directly to your bank. You will have complete privacy over a secured line. You will have to divulge your secret code and the amount of money you wish to have transferred electronically to our bank. Upon completion of the transfer you will be able to settle your obligation to Mrs. LeMay. I will also open a checking account and provide you with a few blank checks with your account number until printed checks with your name and address are delivered to you in 2-3 days. I will also open a savings account for you and get both of you credit cards. I would strongly suggest that proper papers be drawn up by a real estate attorney."

"We don't know anyone in Toronto."

"In that case may I recommend the offices of Otto Littmann and Son, located in this same building on the 12th floor. If you wish I can contact his office for you.

In the meantime, kindly call Switzerland." She pointed to the other room.

Maksim lifted the handset of the phone:

"Hello, hello, Fischer here, who am I speaking with"?

"Herr Fischer, Maksim Ziemtsov on the line."

"I had the pleasure of dealing with your mother. How is she?"

"Thank you for asking. She is fine but her husband Marcel died of cancer recently."

"I'm sorry to hear it. He was such a nice gentleman. Now, Her Ziemtsov, what is your code?"

"Mickiewicza Street #18, Herr Fischer."

"That is correct. How much do you wish to transfer?"

"A sum that would be equal to $900,000 Canadian dollars."

"It's all done, and thank you for using our bank."

"And I thank you, Herr Fischer, Auf Wiedersehen."

Maksim noticed that Mrs. Parks was a very experienced and efficient person. Still, there seemed to be no end to the documents requiring both their signatures.

"I made the call to Mr. Littmann's office, the attorney I mentioned. Luckily, he is free to see you. Mrs. LeMay will accompany us as she has all the paperwork. Your payment for half of the building on Finch Street is $777.000 Canadian dollars. You should have your credit cards delivered to you within 7-10 days. If you have any questions, please do not hesitate to call me. Here is my card and my private telephone number."

"Thank you Madam. We will need some cash until our checks and credit cards arrive."

"Here are a few withdrawal slips. Just fill in the amount, sign it, and give it to my teller on the floor."

"Thank you again Mrs. Parks."

"You're welcome."

On the way to Mr. Littmann's office, Helen mentioned to Maksim that she had received a telephone call from Charles. He told her that he gave the second icon to an antique dealer and it was sold for $118,000 plus commission. Charles wanted to know where to send the money?"

"Now that we have an account at the Royal Bank he can send the money there, but only $100,000 because we are sure that he had all kinds of expenses connected with that sale. Our account number is 635-9470-09B."

They entered the office of Mr. Littmann located on the 12th floor.

"You can go right in, he is expecting you," said the receptionist and she directed them to the third office on their right.

Mr. Littmann, a tall man in his forties, impeccably dressed in his Seville Row suit and matching silk tie, greeted them politely and asked them to sit around the conference table. He listened attentively while Helen presented him with the facts related to the purchase and partnership of the apartment building on Finch Street #1818.

From time to time Mr. Littman asked pertinent questions regarding the building.

"Mr. Littman, my problem is that I must fly back to Moscow where by husband is posted and I won't be back here for some time."

"If that is the case, I'll put several of my best people on this and we can wrap up the deal by the time you come back from your lunch. I will need an hour at the most.

I highly recommend our own cafeteria located in the basement of our building. Ask them to charge your lunch to our account. The head waiter's name is Eduardo and he will take good care of you."

"That is very kind of you Mr. Littmann. By the way, Mr. Ziemtsov and I will pay your fee jointly."

"Clients recommended by Mrs. Parks of the Royal Bank do receive special consideration from us."

They took the elevator all the way down to the basement. It was Eduardo who greeted them at the entrance to the cafeteria.

"You're Mr. Littmann's guests, please follow me."

They all opted for hamburgers and well-done French fries and steins of cold beer.

"Well, Maksim, everything seems to be working out okay. I'm sure that you will be able to manage on your own from now on."

"Helen, I have a question that I meant to ask you some time ago. When will I be able to visit my sister living in New York?" asked Galina.

"All the preliminary papers that are required for traveling to the United States should be in your possession within 2-3 weeks. The flight from Toronto to New York is hardly an hour.

"That would be just perfect. My sister is making a birthday party for her son, Volodia,and of course we are invited."

"I'm sure you will be able to make it."

"This gives me an idea. Maybe I should call my mother in Israel and see if she can meet us in New York City."

"I hope she makes it to that party. An hour is up, let's go upstairs."

Helen checked out the papers carefully. It seemed that Mr. Littmann had seen to it that everything was done in a timely and correct manner.

"Yes, the papers are in order, where do you want us to sign?"

The papers were then properly signed and witnessed. The Ziemtsovs and Helen were each given an elegant folder containing all the pertinent documents.

"We do appreciate your fast service and are sure we will be doing business again with your firm."

"It will be our pleasure and privilege."

Helen embraced and kissed the Ziemtsovs goodbye. There was a taxi standing idly by in front of the building which Helen took, saying:

"I have to pick up my luggage from my sister-in-law's house and rush to the airport.

Do svidania."

The Ziemtsovs were finally on their own. They walked along Finch, Butherst and Young streets, trying to absorb the peculiarities of their new neighborhood, occasionally stepping into the stores and making purchases of household items. In no time at all they were loaded with packages and the only sensible thing to do was head back to their apartment.

While walking they also noticed a variety of restaurants that they planned to visit one day. In the lobby of their building they met Mr. Richard Potter, who helped them with their packages.

"Mrs. LeMay asked me to look after you. If you have any problems, please call me at this number and I will be more than happy to be of assistance to you."

"Thank you, we will do that, Mr. Potter."

They were very busy over the next few days, and accomplished a lot towards getting settled.

On their third day in Canada they received their first piece of mail. It was a letter of welcome from the Royal Bank along with two boxes of freshly printed checks with both their names and address. Three days later they received credit cards, one for Maksim and one for Galina.

On that same day, a package arrived from Germany containing the clothing that they left at Moscow's Airport. In the pocket of his jacket Maksim found his Communist Party identification card.

"Galina, look what I found!"

"Keep it as a souvenir, because you will never have any other use for it."

"Yes, my dear, that period of our lives is over for us. Good riddance, I say."

CHAPTER LIX

"Look, *Golubka*, we have a letter from France," said Max to Galina.

"From France? But we don't know a living soul in France. Are you sure it is from there?"

"It says here: Journal "Le Monde" 21 bis, rue Claude Bernard 75242 Paris,"

"Open it and let's see what this is all about."

Max opened the envelope inside which they found a letter from Helen LeMay and a newspaper clipping from "Le Monde." The letter was written in Russian.

"Max, read it, I want to know what Helen has to say."

"Dear Galina and Max:

The enclosed newspaper clipping is about the tragic death of Mr. and Mrs. Pierre Dupuis of Toronto Canada, who came to Paris to celebrate their 25th wedding anniversary, only to die in an automobile accident on Ave. Marceau. The Canadian couple were owners of an art gallery in Yorkville, an area full of artists and art galleries. According to the press, they left a 22-year-old daughter, their only child. There is a possibility that the daughter may want to sell or liquidate that gallery quickly. It dawned on me that such a gallery might be an ideal place of business for the two of you, considering your own academic background. It would also provide Galina a ready place to paint and display her work, which, by the way, is outstanding. Yorkville is the right place for this kind of business. Other locations such as Dundas Street near University Avenue are surround by a Chinese neighborhood, which is not conducive for prospective art buyers. Also the area of McMichael Collection of the Group of Severn is actually outside Toronto proper, it is in Klineberg, Ont. This is also not a recommended area for you. A good area is Harbour Front, an exclusive area of the rich, but you are not ready for that. I strongly suggest you contact Mr. Richard Potter and ask him to take you to Yorkville. If the place is for sale, and the price is attractive enough, get in touch with Mr. Littmann's office and have him prepare a sales contract. Give it a try; you have nothing to lose by going there. My husband wrote this letter because I write in Russian even worse than the way I speak it, if you can imagine that. By the way, he is very much impressed with the way you handled the sale of Rubliov's icon. Best wishes to you both. Fondly, Helen."

"I do admire Helen, she is a businesswoman, all the way."

"She makes a lot of sense, so why don't we ask Mr. Potter if he can take us there?"

Mr. Potter expressed his willingness to take them to Yorkville, an area that reminded the Ziemtsovs of Arbat Street in Moscow, only with more life to it. Just walking the streets of Yorkville made the Ziemtsovs feel almost at home.

Without any difficulty they located the "Dupuis Art Gallery" just as a young woman was about to hang a "For Sale" sign on the front door.

"Young lady, hold off putting up that sign for a while. We would like to talk to you about it."

"Please, do come in. My name is Loretta Dupuis, and you are . . . ?"

"We are the Ziemtsovs, Galina and Maksim, and this is our friend, Mr. Richard Potter.

We are very sorry about the loss of your parents."

"Thank you. It's such a pity to fly to Paris to celebrate a 25th wedding anniversary only to meet your own death." It's almost like a short story by O'Hara. If you people are interested in the gallery, please look around. I will be happy to answer any questions you might have.

The three of them looked at the tastefully arranged and well-illuminated art gallery. The panels, easels and paintings had been placed with a great deal of thought and enabled visitors to see them at their best advantage.

The paintings were well grouped as well. The styles of Poussin to Matisse, spanning almost three centuries, took up almost half of the gallery. The remaining half showcased a remarkable collection of impressionist styles of paintings reminding the viewer of Russian avant-garde artists, similar to Malevich or Kandinsky. The pleasant strain of classical music was wafting throughout from a hidden radio, adding to the atmosphere of well being in the gallery.

In the far corner of the gallery Max noticed a door marked "Private," and asked Loretta what it meant.

"Come, I will show you. My father kept his tools there and would often change or fix frames for customers. Most of the time a new frame would insure a sale."

Max, followed by Galina and Mr. Potter walked into the room. On a pegboard above a flat fabric covered table, hung an assortment of saws, screwdrivers, hammers, pliers and stapling guns. On the table were two unframed paintings. Max picked up one of the paintings to have a closer look at it. No, he was not mistaken, his experienced eye told him he was holding a painting that came from the famous Shchukin and Morozov collection that had been expropriated by the Bolsheviks after the 1917 revolution and divided between the Pushkin Museum and the Hermitage. Max was 100% sure of this, but wondered how in the word the painting ended up in the Dupuis Art Gallery in Toronto, Canada? This was a mystery he wanted to solve.

"Where do these paintings come from?" Max asked, nonchalantly.

"All I know about them is that my father bought them for cash from some old Russian gentleman."

"Do you have any idea what he paid for them?"

"No idea, whatsoever. My father always kept a certain amount of cash on hand because very often some young and hungry but promising artist would sell his work."

"That makes a lot of sense. How much are you asking for your place, Miss Loretta?"

"I spoke with my lawyer and he suggested a price of $125,000 dollars which includes everything in the gallery; the inventory, furniture, good will, and a10 year lease covering our store, as I said, everything."

"May I ask what you are planning to do once the gallery is sold?"

"I'm getting my degree in journalism in a couple of months and then I plan on traveling a bit and after that I will look for a job."

"Miss Loretta, my wife and I studied art. After graduation I landed a job as an assistant curator in one of Moscow's museums I'm telling you this so that you understand our interest in your gallery. This is what I intend to do: To begin with, I will give you a binder of $5,000 and ask you or your lawyer to get in touch with our attorney. I understand this is how business is conducted here in Canada. Here is his name and telephone number. Upon signing the papers, we will pay you $100,000 in cash and the balance of $25,000 later, under the proviso that you will stay with us for six months.

During that time if you decide to stay with us and work out well, as I think you will, we will make you a 10% partner in our business. So what do you think of our offer?"

"It seems to be very fair. Let me discuss it with my attorney and I will let you know by tomorrow afternoon. May I have your telephone number?"

Max wrote down his address and telephone number and gave her a check for $5,000 as a binder toward the purchase of the gallery.

"Miss Loretta, if you need my credit references please contact Mrs. Parks, the vice- president of the bank, at the branch office address printed on my check."

"Very well Mr. Ziemtsov, I will do just that. Until tomorrow then, goodbye."

Elated, they left the gallery just as the radio was playing Ballet Parisienne by Offenbach.

Mr. Potter, who stood in silence during the entire business transaction, could not hold out any longer:

"Is it that easy for you to spend $125,000? I am amazed!"

"You see, Mr. Potter, I read somewhere that in America or Canada it takes money to make money. I have a good feeling about that gallery. I also listened to Helen LeMay who has a good head for business, and it was she who suggested that I take a look at this gallery."

"I am much more conservative by nature."

"I can fully understand that, but you see, I have Russian blood in my veins, and very often we had to put everything on one card. There is a Russian proverb from the Second World War that goes like this: "Either a chest full of medals or a head in the bushes." Mr. Potter, I am aiming for medals."

Mr. Potter remained silent as he politely dropped them in front of their building on Finch Street.

"Max, I also kept quiet. I didn't want to interrupt you, but do you know what you are doing by spending our last *kopeck*?"

"Don't worry, my darling, just those two paintings in the tool shed are worth over $150,000."

CHAPTER LX

With every passing day he missed Alice more and more. Only now he realized how truly happy he had been while she was alive. Every household item reminded him of her.

A couple of weeks ago a fire broke out in the basement of his building. As a precaution the firemen decided to evacuate the entire building. All the tenants left the building carrying with them their most valuable possessions—their children and pets. Leslie, however, did not budge from his apartment. He could not have cared less whether he lived or died. It was Jeoffrey who banged at his door, yelling: "Dad, come out, I know you are in there! Open the door or I will break it down!" Only then did Leslie come out.

And there was another matter. Leslie felt that an invisible wall had arisen between him and his son after he returned from Florida with Alice's coffin. His warm and caring relationship with Jeff had changed into a respectful and dignified one, but certainly was not what it used to be. Leslie spent countless hours reflecting about it but could not find an explanation or a solution to it.

He was aware of Jeoffrey's strong attachment to the dental hygienist who worked with him in the office. Carla Genoa was a fine young woman, whose Italian father and Jewish mother had been patients of his some years ago. It was an open secret that Jeoffrey was going to marry Carla as soon as the mourning period was over. Jeff was her entire world.

No, Leslie wasn't about to interfere in Jeff's life. The sooner they married the better for everyone concerned, including Leslie. The idea of having grandchildren had started to appeal to him lately. Who knows, maybe he would live long enough to take his grandson fishing. Leslie was totally convinced that his first grandchild would be a boy.

In the meantime, Leslie remembered that today was Volodia Bidnyj's birthday party and he promised the parents that he would attend. He even bought him the latest Fisher-Price toy and attached a nice check to the birthday card.

All he had to do now was to get dressed and call the car service. He also had to shut off the television set in the other room, as he was becoming forgetful lately, and did not want to leave the T.V. blaring for hours. He had been watching the NBC weatherman, the "unpredictable" Dr. Fields, who was now predicting strong winds and heavy rains in the area for the afternoon. Leslie looked out the window only to see cloudless blue skies. "This man doesn't know what he is talking about," thought Leslie.

The service car took him to Brooklyn. While passing Coney Island, he thought, and not for the first time, that this was not the same Coney Island of yesteryear. Gone were the Steeplechase, Luna Park, and the 14" frankfurter for a nickel, and nobody was drinking celery tonics or "2 cents plains." The word "knish" had become a foreign one and Lundy's restaurant a distant memory.

The present Russian Jews ate *kielbasy* and drank *kvas*. No one played stickball anymore.

The Cyrillic alphabet replaced the former Yiddish signs. Times surely had changed!

The Belt Parkway was competing, sometimes successfully, with the Long Island Expressway for the title of the world's largest parking lot. The domineering edifice was the Verazzano Bridge, connecting Brooklyn to Staten Island.

The service car dropped Leslie off in front of 3101 Brighton #2 where the Bidnyj's resided. The walls of the creaky elevator in the lobby were heavily marked with black magic markers. Whoever had done the graffiti was certainly no artist.

The elevator stopped with a jerk on the 5th floor. Leslie went straight to apartment #5-A where he had visited once before. He heard the sounds of a party even before he entered.

Since the door was slightly ajar, he walked in without bothering to ring the bell. There were many people there that Leslie did not know.

Yefim noticed Leslie standing and hesitating to join the party. He walked over to him and embraced him warmly:

"Attention everybody! This is our benefactor, Dr. Leslie Schiff that I told you so much about. Do come in, you are our guest of honor and I want to introduce you to everyone."

Yefim took Leslie's arm and walked him over to Maksim's mother, Dr. Natalia Isaakovna, who arrived two days ago from Israel for the occasion. While making the introduction he said:

"I am sure the two of you will find a common language, but let me also introduce you to the rest of our guests:

"This is Galina, Elena's sister and her husband Maksim Ziemtsov. He is the son of Dr. Natalia, who you just met. They live in Canada."

Leslie could not help but notice that the young couple were extremely well dressed. Galina's designer pantsuit could only bring credit to the front page of Vogue magazine. No wonder that everybody's attention was focused on her and Maksim who was talking about his life in Toronto:

"After I became a partner in a real estate firm I also purchased an art gallery. There I discovered a valuable painting that I framed appropriately and promptly displayed in the window, removing all the other paintings. I placed a large price tag of $100,000 next to the painting. The sign caught the eye of a young reporter living in the area.

His article about the $100,000 painting appeared in "Globe and Mail" and soon after other reporters from the "Star" and "Mirror" came to the shop to interview me. With all that free publicity, I sold that picture at full price."

Elena, who just came in from the kitchen, heard Max's last words and said aloud:

"Max, now that you are rich, how about lending us $50,000 so that Yefim can become a full partner in Abrasha Razunski's building company?"

"What kind of company? What is your involvement in it?"

"The company refurbishes and rebuilds old apartment buildings and houses."

"What is Abrasha's profession?"

"He is an architect with many years of experience."

"That sounds good to me. You can have the $50,000. However, I would like to retain 10% of the business. I will only be a silent partner, and my money stays in the business.

Do we have a deal?"

At this point, Abrasha Razunski took the floor.

"I have no objection as long as I keep my 50%. The 10% must come from Yefim's half of the business. It's all up to him now."

Yefim looked at Elena and seeing approval in her eyes, agreed to the deal. That was when Elena noticed Leslie.

"Oh my God! Dr. Schiff is here." She walked over and kissed him on both cheeks.

"Thank you so much for coming. Did you meet everyone?"

"Not yet, I didn't have a chance. Where is your mother?"

"She is in the kitchen preparing stuffed cabbage, she will be right out."

"Who is that tall man?" asked Leslie pointing discreetly to a man in an ill-fitting suit.

"That is Mogamet, a captain in Aeroflot, a childhood friend of Yefim's. Would you like to meet him?"

"Not yet, maybe a little later." Leslie wasn't sure if Elena said Mogamet or Mohamet,

, as he knew there was no letter "h" in the Russian alphabet.

"Where is the young man of the hour, where is Volodia?" I brought him a gift."

"You are too kind. He must be with his *babushka* somewhere. He will be here any minute. Please come to the table."

By now Leslie was familiar with the fact that when it came to entertaining, the Russians did not do anything in half measures. There were so many dishes piled with food on that table that it was impossible to find a place to put down a plate. The choice of food seemed endless: herrings, cheeses, salads, hot and cold meat dishes, bowls of boiled potatoes with dill, breads, rolls, butter, sour cream, and a variety of *kielbasy,* marinated fish and fresh fruit.

Puzzled, Leslie did not know where to begin. Someone handed him a glass of vodka, which he promptly spilled. He hands were shaking more than usual.

Dr. Natalia noticed this and came over to him and asked:

"May I fix you a plate? Please sit down and I will bring it to you. Is there anything in particular that you like?"

"I'll leave it up to you."

"In that case I'll prepare two plates and you can choose which one you prefer."

"You are very kind."

She came back with two larges plates full of delicacies and two glasses of vodka. They hardly had a chance to say *na zdrovie* when lightening struck, followed by loud claps of thunder. Soon a heavy rain pounded the windowpanes.

"Aren't you glad that you are inside, Dr. Schiff?"

"Yes I am, but please call me Leslie."

"In that case, call me Natalia."

They conversed in English that Natalia learned in Israel while working in the hospital. Occasionally she mixed in Yiddish words, which Leslie understood but could not speak very well.

"As you know, I am a physician and I can tell that you are suffering from Parkinson's.

How are you feeling?"

"I manage as well as can be expected. Some days are better than others."

"Are you experiencing any difficulty in walking or swallowing?"

"To some degree. I also feel that my muscles are getting weaker and occasionally, I lose my balance. It is very embarrassing at times, because people think that I'm drunk."

"In Russia, because of the high consumption of alcohol, you would be appear to be absolutely normal. Yes, unfortunately, those are typical symptoms of the disease."

"You don't suggest I move to Russia just to appear normal?"

"God forbid."

"Enough about me. Tell me a little bit about yourself."

"What is there to tell? I lost my first husband in Russia during the World War and my second husband in Israel due to cancer. I have been through some very tough times.

There, you have it in a nutshell. Now I am all alone living in Israel while my only son is in Canada."

"Do you intend to move to Canada to be near your son? It is a nice country, you know."

"I don't know, as yet. Maybe I'll just come to visit from time to time." Young people do not need a third party. Perhaps when they have children I will consider it."

Another clap of thunder hit the area and the lights went out briefly.

"This storm reminds me of a Russian poem. Loosely translated it goes like this . . . .

"I love a storm in the beginning of May . . . . "

"We also have a song about rain: "Rain, rain, go away, come again another day."

Any further conversation was interrupted by a now four year old Volodia.:

"Mr. Schiff, thank you so much for the toy."

"You are most welcome, young fellow. I've something else for you which I almost forgot to give you, but you better give it to your mommy for safekeeping."

It was the birthday card with the enclosed check that he had in his side pocket.

"Ladies and gentlemen! It's time to light the candles and cut the cake. Volodia and his grandmother will do the honors."

Once the candles were lit everybody started to sing Happy Birthday in English and Russian. Coffee and tea were then served.

An old *samovar* made in Tula was standing on the corner of the table; strictly there for ceremonial purposes. The tea came from an electric teakettle. In addition to the large chocolate cake there was an assortment of cookies and jelly donuts.

Natalia brought Leslie a plate with a slice of the birthday cake.

"Thank you so much but I can't eat anymore Natalia."

"What? For refusing to eat a birthday cake in Russia you would be punished with a 10 year jail sentence."

"Thank God I do not live in Russia, but I'll eat the cake, alright?"

"Drink more tea, it's good for you."

"My wife Alice used to say the same thing. What is the use of anything?"

"Don't give up, Leslie. Life is too interesting to miss a single day."

"Natalia, your son Maksim shows promise of being a good businessman. I understand that he was an assistant curator in one of Moscow's museums. What made him switch to business?"

"I really don't know the answer to your question. Why don't we ask Maksim?"

Max, can we see you for a minute? The good Dr. Schiff wants to know what made you want to be a businessman rather than a curator of a museum?"

"Hm, I actually gave it a lot of thought because I really love art. There is a great difference between liking a subject and being good at it. God only knows how hard I've worked at it. My professors used to tell me "Maksim, you're not bad." At my very best I was just a notch better than an average painter. While working in the museum I was surrounded by paintings, all of them masterpieces. Each painting seemed to say to me that I would never be able to paint like that. Somehow I knew that if I stayed in that field I would be a starving artist for the rest of my life. On the other hand, I can clearly see business opportunities connected with the world of art. My knowledge of art and artists give me a big advantage over my competitors. I believe that I can make a lot of money which will give us a chance to live well, travel the world over, and live in a country where a knock on your door means a neighbor asking to borrow a cup of milk and not the Secret Police coming to arrest you."

"Yes, Dr. Schiff, I want to live as a free man in a free country and believe me, only people deprived of liberty know the true meaning of being free. I will be a good Canadian just as my relatives will be good Americans or good Israelis. I will work hard and who knows, maybe I'll discover a future Rubens or Picasso."

"Well said Maksim, good luck to you. Look outside, it has finally stopped raining. I think I will call for my cab to drive me home. Natalia, see that beautiful rainbow?" It probably reaches from Brighton Beach in Brooklyn all the way to the Golden Gate Bridge in San Francisco."

"That is a good omen for Volodia and Maksim."

"I must admit that I have enjoyed talking to you, Natalia. Maybe we'll get together for dinner one of these days when you are in New York."

"Perhaps, one can never tell. Take good care of yourself Leslie."

"And you too, Natalia."

Leslie said his goodbyes to the host and hostess, kissing the little Volodia and shaking hands with the rest of the guests including Mogamet.

Yefim took Leslie down the elevator to the street level where the car service was already waiting for him. It was the same driver who brought him to the party originally.

The rain was gone. The sky, clear of any clouds, was blue again and was reflected on the west asphalt streets.

"Yes," Leslie said to the driver. "Take me home. If you like rainbows, you must also like the rain, my friend."

"Dr. Schiff, if you don't mind my saying so, you look a bit sad."

"No, my friend, to the contrary. I just got a new lease on life. Did you ever hear of John Burroughs?"

"I'm afraid not."

"Well, he said what I want to say now: "I still find each day too short for all the thoughts I want to think, all the walks I want to take, all the books I want to read, and all the friends I want to see.""